SILENT RUNNING

GEORGE WALLACE
DON KEITH

SEVERN RIVER
PUBLISHING

SILENT RUNNING

Severn River Publishing
www.SevernRiverBooks.com

ISBN: 978-1-64875-433-3 (Paperback)

ALSO BY THE AUTHORS

The Hunter Killer Series

Final Bearing

Dangerous Grounds

Cuban Deep

Fast Attack

Arabian Storm

Warshot

Silent Running

Snapshot

Southern Cross

Also by George Wallace

Operation Golden Dawn

PROLOGUE

George Washington Jackson—"Zipper" to his friends and rather sizeable family—sat back and enjoyed the smooth ride as the Yellow Line train he piloted burst out of the underground darkness and into the brilliant, late-afternoon sunshine. He was tired, but there was still another three hours on his extended shift, then an hour commute before he could fire up his new Big Green Egg smoker grill and relax with the grandkids.

In the capital city of the USA, the Fourth of July holiday was by far the busiest day of the year. And by this time on the holiday, the National Mall was teeming with humanity. Shuttling hundreds of thousands of tourists to and from the Mall kept the Metro at capacity, even with every train running on a rush-hour schedule since before dawn. Hordes of tourists and plenty of locals hurried to claim the best spot to watch the massive evening fireworks and to take in the huge annual concert. Finally, with pandemic restrictions completely lifted, everyone wanted to be there live and in person.

Zipper merely smiled and enjoyed the view. After more than twenty years operating Metro trains, most of them driving the Yellow Line between Huntington and Greenbelt, he still appreciated these particular few seconds of the ride between the Pentagon and L'Enfant Plaza. The train sat high up on the bridge while the Potomac River's greenish-brown water flowed sluggishly beneath the rails. Washington, DC's iconic monuments popped into view in his broad windshield. Thomas Jefferson, almost dead ahead, peered at him from between those tall columns. The Washington Monument pointed to heaven from its base to Zipper's left. And his favorite, the calm face of Dr. Martin Luther King, looked at him through the trees, assuring him things were peaceful. Not perfect but hopefully getting better.

Much too quickly, though, the tracks plunged back down into the tunnel, aiming for the next stop on the line. A stop that would doubtless be even more chaotic than typical on this special day.

L'Enfant Plaza Station was less than a mile ahead. Out of long-developed habit, Zipper reached over to begin throttling back for entry into the station. But he pulled his hand away. That was no longer part of his job. In fact, his supervisor had reprimanded him at the end of his previous shift for overriding Metro's brand-new and cutting-edge computer-controlled Automatic Train Operating System. It was especially difficult for Zipper to overcome the urge to slow the train himself, to rely on some computer chip somewhere to do his job for him. He had been a young train operator, just starting out, on that tragic day in June 2009 when a Red Line train, using the old ATO system, slammed into the rear of a stopped train up at the Ft. Totten Station. Eight people died that day. Everyone lost faith in the automatic system. For a long time, nobody fussed when Zipper and the other operators insisted on driving manually.

Now, though, all these years later, the Metro Board of Supervisors had again decided that computers were smarter, better, and more reliable train operators than people would ever be. Zipper knew better. He also knew the ATO would soon spell an end to human operators entirely. No problem. He would finally retire and spend more time with his grandkids, watching the Nationals play ball while enjoying the big grill to which he had treated himself. Meanwhile, he would just do what his super told him to do. The in-cabin video camera above his left shoulder did not allow him any leeway anyhow. His every move was on record.

Get by two more months, three days, and two hours. Then the only computer he would have to worry about was the one where he followed every bit of news about the Nationals and posted pictures of those grandkids on Facebook.

The underground Y where the Green Line tracks merged with those of the Yellow Line shot past. That was when Zipper realized something did not feel right. The train should be starting its smooth deceleration before entering L'Enfant Plaza. Instinctively, his hand shot to the throttle control even as the S sign, indicating a thousand feet to the station, flashed past. That meant L'Enfant's crowded platform was coming up quickly. The train should be automatically slowing to a crawl by now.

But no. He could feel it accelerating instead. Definitely accelerating. Felt like full throttle.

Zipper yanked back hard on the throttle lever. The train ignored him. If anything, it picked up even more speed.

By now, the ATP—the Automatic Train Protection System—should have kicked in. Barreling into a station crowded with several thousand holiday revelers could be a worst-case disaster. And if the northbound Green Line train was still there, delayed by off-loading so many people, it would be massive carnage. Far worse than the Ft. Totten incident.

Zipper had no choice. He slammed the emergency stop button, knowing the sudden screeching halt would send his passengers flying. But better a few bruises and broken bones than a massive pileup. At the same time, he screamed a warning into the microphone for the system's spanking new "Astro Voice" comms system.

Then, straight ahead, he saw the flashing red lights at the back of the other train. The platform packed with people. The red-and-white bunting strung across the gallery above the tracks in celebration of democracy and Independence Day.

That was the last thing George Washington Jackson ever saw.

Zooming ahead at full throttle, his train plunged into the stopped Green Line train. The force of the collision caused the cars of both trains to derail and go whipping up and across the teeming platform. No one even had a chance to run. And they were so closely packed together, working toward the escalators, that escape was not possible. Swirling steel cars scythed through the crowds, spraying metal, bodies, and debris across the platform. Fire belched past the turnstiles and up escalators to the outside.

Just then, a southbound Yellow Line train packed with riders, running on the adjacent track and also racing out of control at full throttle, bolted into the station. Without slowing, it charged into the smoke, fire, and hurtling wreckage, adding to the chaos of flying rail cars.

Two blocks away, people emerging from the Air and Space Museum at the Smithsonian were knocked off their feet by the concussion. Beyond, on the Mall, those gathering for the best view of the concert wondered if the fireworks had started early for some reason.

Many of them clapped and cheered. Others, waving flags, began toasting the noisy salute with smuggled glasses of wine, singing "God Bless the USA."

Ψ

Mie Ping stretched mightily before closing her laptop. She allowed herself the barest of satisfied smiles as she called out to her supervisor, three cubicles away. He did not respond.

She stood, walked over, and stuck her head into his tiny workstation. As usual, he was already deeply lost in some spreadsheet or another, the bane of any mid-level government employee, even in the deepest recesses of the Middle Kingdom's most top-secret cyber warfare unit.

"What? Sorry? Budget time, you know," he finally responded.

"The operation. It all worked just as we predicted," she told him.

"Oh, excellent. The minister will be well pleased with your work, Mie."

"Our work. We have an excellent team. Breaking through that new Cloud Access Security system they are so proud of was child's play. Particularly with the back doors we had in place already. And we made very sure to erase every trace that we had been there."

"Very good. Very good."

Mie Ping pointedly yawned and stretched again. She tried not to notice that her supervisor had suddenly turned his attention from the spreadsheet to her breasts.

"Now, if it is all right, I need to get some sleep," she said as she backed away from the cubicle.

"Certainly. Your success...it may even help me here," he said, waving at the spreadsheet on his display. His attention was already directed back there. "Budget time, you know."

As Mie Ping stepped out the doorway of the huge but nondescript office building, she was surprised to see the sun was already up. That the busy Hangzhou traffic indicated a workday was beginning. She had lost track of time as she watched her digital worms do their work, the bits and bytes falling into place to accomplish her long-term mission half a planet away.

She needed a shower, a nap. She had lunch scheduled with her sister. They would celebrate her sister's newly-confirmed pregnancy, now that having a third child had been approved by the Chinese government. Then Mie would enjoy a night on the town with the handsome new social media specialist six cubicles down and two to the right from her own.

The sun was warm on her face as she waited for the traffic signal to allow her to cross the busy street. The fact that the work she and her cyber-attack team had done had just resulted in the deaths of hundreds of Americans was of little concern to her. She had done as she had been told for the good of her country. To protect its sovereignty and allow it to once again assume its rightful place in the order of world powers. Something she had prepared for since, as a child, she sang the song "I Compare the Communist Party to My Mother" each morning six days a week to begin the school day. And since the day a teacher noticed her exceptional aptitude with numbers and computer algorithms.

Today, she had done her part. Now she needed a nap and a shower. No doubt her supervisor would have a new assignment for her tomorrow.

1

The night was tar-black dark. Chet Allison, the skipper of the submarine USS *Boise* (SSN-764), spun the periscope around to complete a full circle. They seemed to be all alone in this patch of the Pacific Ocean, but it was difficult to confirm visually. Thick clouds obscured even the stars. The only way he had to make sure that he was actually staring at the night sky, and not the equally black sea water, was the occasional reassuring wave slap on the periscope.

Meanwhile, the normal control room hum of quiet communications barely registered with Allison as he continued to comb the skies above them. Nothing. Nothing but darkness.

"Radio, Captain." Allison spoke into the open mike above his head, working to keep the irritation from his voice. "We in comms yet by any chance?"

"Captain, Radio." It was ETR-1(SS) Luke Hanson, *Boise*'s leading radioman, who answered. "Nothing, sir. He isn't up on the circuit yet. We'll keep trying."

"Damn flyboys," Allison muttered under his breath. "Probably still sitting in the O Club." Then he raised his voice enough for the mike to pick it up. "Radio, Captain. Keep trying. Is the XO in Radio?"

"Yes, sir, I'm here." Commander Henrietta Foster's voice came over the 21MC speaker.

Allison pulled away from the periscope eyepiece. *Boise*'s control room was rigged for black, so other than a few dim red lights, the area looked very much like what he had been seeing outside. Pretty much nothing.

"XO, draft a message to CTF 74. Tell them no joy on rendezvousing with their P-8. Intend to go deep and proceed with our mission. Will attempt comms again in six hours."

As he stepped back from the periscope, Allison felt a drizzle of ice-cold water down the back of his neck. Damn scope packing was leaking again!

The skipper looked hard at Chief Jeanette Walters, the diving officer. She was also the auxiliary division leading chief.

"Chief, get your guys up here and see if they can fix this damn leak. I'm tired of getting a cold shower every time I want to use the 'scope."

Walters frowned, then reached out and smacked the back of the helmsman's head. "Damn it, Kowblowski! Mind your planes. You're a foot off ordered depth." Then, without a pause, she responded to her captain. "Yes, sir. We've tightened the packing as much as we can. We're at max torque on the gland nuts now. The best we can do is try greasing it again. That might slow the leakage some."

"Well, at least rig some poly," Allison grumbled. "Maybe you can direct some of that water to the bilge drains instead of down the back of my neck." He well knew that the poly sheeting was, at best, a temporary and jury-rigged fix. They would have to live with the leaking packing gland until they could get back into port and properly repair the periscope. He also knew he was allowing the annoyance with the tardy aircraft to magnify his irritation with the pesky water leak.

"Captain," the XO's voice blasted from the 21MC speaker. "CTF 74 acknowledges. They say that the P-8 had to RTB with a mechanical. They just sent us new tasking. Suggest we go deep and digest what they want us to do now."

Allison nodded, though his second-in-command could not see him, and called out, "Officer of the Deck, you heard the lady. Let's go deep. Make your depth three hundred feet, come around to course two-six-five to conform to the navigator's track. And speaking of the navigator, send your messenger to get him out of his nice warm bunky. Tell him to drop his teddy bear and come help us figure out what the boss wants us to do now."

Allison reached up into the overhead and spun the big red ring to the left. The Type 18 periscope smoothly descended into the 'scope well.

Lieutenant Bob Bland, the on-watch OOD, answered crisply, "Yes, sir." In a slightly louder voice, he ordered, "Diving Officer, make your depth three hundred feet. Helm, left five degrees rudder. Steer course two-six-five. Chief of the Watch, rig control for white, send your messenger to find Lieutenant Commander Chastain and inform him that the captain wants to see him in Control."

As the lights blinked on in the compartment, Commander Allison stepped off the low periscope stand and headed forward. "Officer of the Deck, I'll be in my stateroom changing to a dry poopie suit. And Chief, kindly make sure A gang gets that poly rigged."

Ten minutes later, Commander Chet Allison—now in a clean, dry uniform—along with Commander Henrietta Foster and Lieutenant Commander Jeremy Chastain gathered around the electronic navigation display table, not-so-cleverly named by some obscure government engineer as the ECDIS, or Electronic Chart Display and Information System. Chastain had already entered the newly received operation order into the ECDIS. The projected ship's track displayed as a bright green line arrowing down to the southwest.

"Well, XO," Allison noted. "Looks like CTF 74 hasn't forgiven us for denting the *Boise*-fish. I'm not suggesting that Admiral Jorgensson carries a grudge, but we've been playing nuclear rabbit for airedales ever since we got back from repairs in Pearl. And now this."

The *Boise* had been badly damaged by a submarine attack and then an air assault, both by the People's Liberation Army Navy near Taiwan the previous year. The story was squelched by both the US and Chinese militaries. It was an incident that never made the newscasts on CNN or the pages of *The New York Times*. Rear Admiral Dan Jorgensson, Commander Submarine Group Seven and Commander Task Force Seventy-Four, had been particularly upset when Allison risked the submarine to rescue a pair of downed pilots. The damage had required Allison and his crew to bring the sub home while steaming all the way back to Pearl Harbor at three knots.

Since then, he and his boat had mostly been conducting anti-submarine drills with Navy P-8 aircraft. An "airedale" was a derisive submariner term for naval-gazing pilots, Navy or not.

Henrietta Foster squinted hard as she studied the chart.

"Skipper," she finally offered, "don't look at it that way. We just need to do what the boss tells us to do in the best way we can."

Foster was not only one of the first female submarine officers but also one of a very few African American women qualified to command a nuclear submarine. She also was one of the few who could be so direct with her captain and get away with it. "Look, I figure if he wants us to be a target for the airedales, we'll be the best damn target he has. No reason to feel picked on, I don't reckon."

"You're right, as usual, XO," Allison answered. "Nav, how long until we're in the exercise box?"

Chastain played with the ECDIS touch controls for a couple of seconds. A text box popped up on the screen. He whistled softly before answering.

"Skipper, COMEX for the first event is at zero eight hundred local tomorrow, twenty-three hundred zulu tonight. It's a little under six hundred nautical miles to the edge of the box. It's on the East China Sea side of Amami Island. That's at the north end of the Ryukyu Archipelago."

Allison whistled, too.

"XO, tell me again that the admiral ain't toying with us. We'll have to run at flank all day. We should just skid into the box with our tongue hanging out in time for the first run." He turned to Bob Bland and ordered, "Officer of the Deck, make your depth six hundred feet and come to ahead flank."

Ψ

Tan Yong, the First Secretary of the Chinese Communist Party and President of China, was at this moment feeling more like a schoolboy. He was probably the most powerful man in the world, capable of deciding life or death for thousands with a mere wave of his hand, but he was completely cowed by this little individual with the thick-lensed spectacles who sat across the desk from him. In his many years doing financial prognostication for China's most powerful leaders, Qián Dài had built an unassailable reputation for uniquely accurate insights and always speaking the unvarnished truth, regardless to whom it was directed. Even the president, who rarely was willing to listen to anything negative or in opposition to his own beliefs.

"Tan Zǒng," Qián Dài said, using the common honorific, as if Tan Yong were some mid-level manager rather than the near dictatorial leader of the world's most populous country. "You tasked me with looking into the future and to honestly report what I see. Remember that there is an ancient proverb attributed to Master Confucius that directed, 'Do not make predictions, especially about the future.' The best that I can do is to tell you what I see dimly through the veil and how I interpret it."

"Honorable brother Qián," Tan Yong responded, but with an honorific typically reserved for equals. "Please allow us a vision based on your wisdom and experience."

Qián Dài nodded and began with a strong pronouncement. "I fear for the future of our Mother China. I believe we are greatly extended beyond our intrinsic strength. Our most worthy desire to right the wrongs from the Century of Humiliation has led us to reach out across oceans and continents using vast sums from the treasury. But this has now made us dependent on that reach. We are now required to take more from the treasury in order to purchase resources to feed our economy. Those purchases strengthen our enemies with the sweat from the brows of our people. Those enemies are now able to exert leverage over us because of our need for resources and our dread of any hasty economic sanctions should those enemies need to score points with their electorate."

"Honored teacher," Tan Yong murmured, deeply considering but not quite comprehending Qián Dài's words. "Surely we must have all the resources we need. Raw materials to sustain our economy, to best our enemies. To feed our vast number of people."

"It is true that we have the resources we need. But there are costs involved in reaping them. Paying for them is a different matter. And, to offer a real possibility, if the Americans once again come with their tariffs and sanctions, we do not have the cash available to weather the storm. With our investments to curry favor, and with little hope of capital return anytime soon from them, our ledger is dangerously out of balance to the debt side. We have access to what we need but not the currency to pay for retrieving it. I believe we must find another way to take it."

Tan Yong's brow wrinkled. "Teacher, you are counseling war."

Qián Dài smiled. "Remember what Sun Tzu said. The art of war is of vital importance to the State. It is a matter of life and death, a road either to safety or to ruin. Hence it is a subject of inquiry which can on no account be neglected." Qián paused. The smile disappeared. "Unless we find a way to acquire all the things we need for less capital, we will be greatly diminished. China's future existence and your ability to remain its chief depend on how you lead in this vital matter."

Ψ

Tranh Bien finally had the opportunity to sit on the stern transom of his fishing boat and enjoy a welcome smoke. The long, hard night of laying out and then pulling in his squid nets was now almost over. His bright-blue boat was stacked with bins, each of them filled with live squid, a bounty ready for offer at Bach Long Vi's morning market. With a fine catch secured, it was time to relax, to watch the orange sun rise from the steel-gray waters of the Gulf of Tonkin.

He never tired of that familiar sight. Tranh had been fishing these rich waters all his life. He knew no other existence. His father, his grandfathers, and generations before them had netted their livelihood from the teeming life that inhabited the sea surrounding what was now their tiny home island. His own sons, now six and eight years old, would certainly follow him one day soon.

Bach Long Vi was little more than a speck of dirt and rock poking up from the waves precisely in the center of the Gulf of Tonkin. The Tranhs had been among the first families to move from the mainland to the island early in the twentieth century. That came when a permanent source of fresh water was discovered, making life possible and placing them much nearer to their quarry, the bounty of the sea. Depending on which way the fickle winds of diplomacy blew, Tranh's family had been citizens of French Indochina, China, and, for the last half century or more, Vietnam. It did not really matter to Tranh what flag flew over the Harbor Control Building so long as he could, peacefully and without interference, reap the sea's harvest. The squid, octopi, and abalone did not care the nationality of their captor either. And in all those swaps of claimed sovereignty, there had yet to be a shot fired or a life taken over ownership of the little island.

Tranh had also mostly ignored the expanding Vietnamese military base that now claimed a large part of the skimpy bit of real estate that made up Bach Long Vi. The base had been built in the sixties as an early warning platform to track American fighter planes. Weeds had all but taken over the small facility, at least until recently. Then, with concern over China's bellicose stance and expanding territorial claims, the Vietnamese military had rebuilt and expanded the base. Now several hundred soldiers called Bach Long Vi home.

Other than more of the land being fenced off and more traffic on the few narrow dirt roads, not much really changed. The travel restrictions and special security requirements that had come with the base did not affect Tranh's catch at all. And, of course, the soldiers stationed there were reliable customers for his fish.

Tranh's reverie was suddenly broken by a pair of very large explosions. Thunder? No, the sky was clear, the winds calm. But as he turned to look in the direction of the distant blasts, he saw huge crimson-orange fireballs erupting from the island's spiny ridge. They appeared up where the new military radars had been built only the year before. Then a flight of four fighter bombers roared by, just over his head, barely missing his boat's stubby mast. The fisherman could easily see the red stars painted on the underside of their wings. Chinese. Then four more planes zoomed in from farther east. Then another four flashed by from the north. All headed toward the island.

Tranh was no expert on fighter jets. He certainly could never identify the types of Chinese warplanes. But with all the bombs hanging beneath their wings, it did not require an expert's eye to deduce their intent. Seconds after blowing past the little fishing boat, the jets climbed to make their own attack runs on Bach Long Vi. Too stunned to move, Tranh watched open-mouthed as the new arrivals made their long, shallow dives. Then their bombs fell away, hurtling downward toward the base, buildings, and homes below. Bach Long Vi, peacefully bathed in the early-morning sunlight, suddenly erupted in a series of orange-red flashes, smoke, and flying debris. The thunderous explosions rolled out over the water and reached Tranh a few seconds later.

Then, his shock abated, he had a terrible realization. His wife and sons were beneath those explosions! He must hurry ashore, back to the island, and protect them. Tranh punched the start button to bring the boat's creaky old diesel engine to life. After a maddening few seconds, the engine finally coughed to a start with a burst of black smoke. He jammed the engine into gear and then opened the throttle wide.

The old boat was built for fishing, for trolling, and not for speed. Deep inside, Tranh knew that there was really nothing he could do for his family. This unimaginable attack would be over by the time he could get back. But he had to try!

The fisherman pointed the bow toward the harbor mouth and then watched the blue-gray warbirds dash and dart above the island like so many seagulls diving on crusts of bread. Each swooping dive brought more explosions. The tiny landmass already seemed to be totally engulfed in flames. Billowing black smoke was rising high into the deep-blue early-morning sky. Yet the attack continued, the planes relentless in inflicting their mayhem.

It took a half hour for Tranh to reach the mouth of the manmade harbor on Bach Long Vi's south end. The war birds had finally tired of their destructive play—or had more likely expended all the ordnance they carried—and disappeared back to the east, roaring off just above the wavetops.

Tranh had to proceed cautiously. The usually busy, broad anchorage was now strewn with floating wreckage. Smoke and flames hid most of the buildings lining the harborside frontage road. The whole island appeared to be ablaze.

He jammed the fishing boat hard up alongside a pier and quickly threw a line around a bollard. Then he dashed down the road through the smoke and cinders and up the hill toward his house, less than a kilometer from the fence that surrounded the military base. He hardly recognized the street. Nothing but wreckage and bodies strewn about. It took several moments before he realized that he had arrived in front of where his own house had stood.

Tranh squatted in the dust and cried in the wake of all the destruction. He dreaded having to dig into the rubble, learning the fate of his family.

In his grief and shock, he did not notice the warships appearing on the eastern horizon. Numerous ships, steaming inexorably toward what little remained of the island of Bach Long Vi, dead center of the Gulf of Tonkin.

2

Tan Yong sat back and looked around the small but ornately furnished conference room. He had long since learned that remaining silent, his face impassive, and allowing a few minutes to pass before formally opening a meeting had a powerful effect on its attendees. Those men seated around the table, unsure of their boss's disposition, were just beginning to look furtively at each other, wondering if the pause this time was a good or bad sign.

In the complicated and extremely nuanced Chinese power structure, Tan Yong held many titles. Some were merely ceremonial. Others were awesomely official. All were vested with real control, whether dictated by the Party Constitution, earned through political maneuvering, or simply achieved by raw power grabs. However, most of the world best knew Tan Yong as the General Secretary of the Chinese Communist Party and President of China.

Finally, Tan sat up straight, placed his hands on the tabletop, and opened the meeting.

Seated around the deep-burgundy zitan wood table were four of the most powerful men in China, thus also making them among the most powerful in the world. Meeting as the Central National Security Commission, these four men conferred with and advised the chairman on matters of strategic and tactical importance. And more immediately, they discreetly passed down the decisions emanating from these meetings to the agencies that would ultimately be charged with making them happen.

For men who wielded such formidable power at the highest levels, these four were all but unknown outside of the General Secretary's Office in Qinzheng Hall. Or within the inner halls of the intelligence agencies of the world's major powers.

Lei Miayang had risen from his position as a minor functionary in the Central Committee for Discipline Inspection. From there, he quite literally knew where all the bodies were buried. He was utterly ruthless in employing that knowledge for the good of the party. General Shao Jing was no less ruthless but had worked his way up through the Central Military Commission of the CCP. His tentacles reached deeply into the People's Liberation Army. Sun Yang had made his bones working in the Guoanbu, the much-feared Ministry of State Security. Deng Jiang represented the Ministry of Foreign Affairs. However, his real talent lay in cyber warfare. All four had been snatched from relative obscurity by Tan Yong when he recognized their specific talents and their absolute loyalty. Loyalty to him and to their leader's vision for the future of their country.

Tan's first nod was to Deng, with a request for details of the Commission's latest cyber-attack within the United States. As Deng gave details, a full-wall video screen at the far end of the conference room played a CNN report of the devastation inside L'Enfant Plaza in the US capital. Then, an assembled group of news commentators began confident speculation—their words translated into subtitles on the screen—declaring that while the Independence Day tragedy could have been a blatant cyber-attack by some foreign government or terrorist group, they were, to a man, convinced that there was no evidence to support such a determination. And, according to the network's sources, neither the National Security Agency nor the cyber experts at CISA, the US government's Cybersecurity and Infrastructure Security Agency, had yet found any signs of a hack. The image cut quickly to another "expert" who went to great lengths expounding on how the administration's new "Zero Trust" system was virtually impossible to hack into. And besides, three Senate committees and two from the House of Representatives had already announced that hearings on the incident would begin within the month to determine what might have gone wrong with the system software.

Deng was actually chuckling, a rare occurrence indeed, as he muted the television discussion. All the other men were nodding and smiling, primarily because their leader now seemed pleased.

"As you are aware, sir," Deng proudly continued, "the American Zero Trust system had additional code that was built in by Chinese experts carefully operating in key positions for many years within the employ of certain contractors. And the code they were able to place totally disappears without any trace once it has served its purpose."

Tan Yong steepled his fingers under his chin. The room fell silent once more as he thought for a few seconds.

"And are you absolutely certain that this penetration cannot be traced?"

"Yes, the code is designed to be assembled for a one-time use and then to self-destruct," Deng answered confidently. "The assembly sequence is built at the chip level and is very, very specific in its purpose. There is no way to access and activate it except by our very sophisticated signaling method."

The Chinese leader nodded, seemingly still satisfied. So far. "But as I understand it, others outside this room know the technical details and ultimate outcome of the operation."

Deng fully expected and was prepared for this challenge from his boss. But the other men in the room sat up a little straighter, listening just a bit more intensely to hear and internally evaluate Deng's response and gauge how it might impact them.

"*Lingxiu*—revered leader—we have operated with full awareness of the rigid security that you have required for these operations. It has been considered vital that no one would ever be able to trace them back to Qinzheng Hall. I am pleased to report that it is as you commanded. Only the smallest number of required team members at the Cyber Warfare Center in Guangzhou were involved, and even they were compartmentalized and unaware of the full scope."

Deng stopped and pursed his lips, attempting a mock expression of sadness. "However, unfortunately, a terrible bus accident occurred there yesterday as we transferred the team from one facility to another. I regret to inform that, despite the valor of those who attempted a rescue, none of the team involved in this project survived the tragic...accident."

"Most unfortunate," Tan Yong answered solemnly. "We, as do the Americans, really must improve the safety on our mass transit systems." Then he smiled. "Let's wait a reasonable amount of time before the next...ah...incident. We will consider its status and timing and I will give the final approval for its execution. Now, General Shao, please report on our Vietnam liberation activities. I trust your news is equally interesting."

Ψ

ST1 (SS) Joshua Hannon made a well-practiced swipe across the display on his computer screen. He hummed a little tune as he scrolled down the menu and selected an option. Then he sat back and watched as the data built up and a familiar pattern developed on the monitor. Hannon nodded. Pretty much what he expected. A few more minutes and he would be sure. Or at least certain enough to commit to a report.

The control room on the submarine USS *George Mason* was quietly active with the normal midwatch routine. Chief Jason Schmidt sat in the pilot's seat, watching the ship control display as the *George Mason*'s autopilot effortlessly kept the big submarine on the ordered depth, course, and speed as they drove through the waters of the Philippine Sea. Meanwhile, Schmidt was in the midst of a heated discussion with MM1 (SS) Stanley Dewlap, the co-pilot, about the best muscle car to emerge from the 1960s. Schmidt maintained that the Pontiac GTO was the epitome of muscle cars, easily the best. His dad had a '69 that had never been beaten off the line. Dewlap, on the other hand, remembered his granddad's Mustang Mach 1. With its distinctive styling and Cobra Jet engine, the car easily had the primary criterion necessary to win the muscle car sweepstakes. Even better, it was a sure bet to get women.

Lieutenant Bill Wilson, the officer of the deck for this watch, stood behind the command console, trying to ignore the banter coming from the ship's control team. He was working on his studies for his upcoming engineer officer qualification exam. He was already dreading leaving the ship for the trip to DC and the two-day-long grilling that he would face at "Naval

Reactors." That was the common name used for the Naval Nuclear Propulsion Program Office, the people responsible for the operation of the Navy's nuclear propulsion effort. The engineers back at NR would test the depth of Wilson's knowledge in every aspect of the complex nuclear reactor and engine room that constituted what her crew had dubbed "The *George Mason* Power and Light Company."

Passing the exam was a necessary hurdle that every nuclear trained submarine officer faced. It was the step to move up to the next rung in the ladder of their professional development. It was more than just pass/fail, too. How well the young officer did on this all-important test was a key for future selection to choice billets.

"Officer of the Deck," Josh Hannon suddenly called out. "Suggest you punch up the ship's self-noise function."

Bill Wilson looked up from his tablet. "We have a problem?" he asked, even as he punched up the display that would show just how quiet—or dangerously noisy—the submarine was operating.

"Look at hydrophone eight," Hannon said. "See that one-twenty-one-point-two line? Look at the historic trace. It's up two dB."

Sure enough, the offending red line had climbed a couple of decibels above the green historic average line. Not much. But enough that someone in the vicinity of *George Mason* with a very sophisticated sonar might be able to detect it. Someone like another submarine, and it could belong to a wide variety of other navies in the region.

The young lieutenant paged through the display to take a look at the rest of the hydrophones. Phone eight was the only abnormal one.

"Number two TG lube oil pump again, I'd bet," Wilson speculated.

"My guess, too," Hannon confirmed. "Frequency equates to a bearing race problem, just like last time. But last time the problem went away before E-div could isolate it to which bearing was the problem."

Wilson nodded as he picked up the phone handset. "Maneuvering, Officer of the Deck. We're getting high self-noise on number two TG lube oil pump again. Shift to number four pump and let electrical division know about the problem."

Wilson put down the phone and turned back to Hannon. "Maybe they can fix it before every Chinese submarine in the Pacific knows we're here. ST1, you got any more excitement to enliven this midwatch?"

"Mr. Wilson, how many times do I have to tell you?" Hannon shot back. "You don't dare say things like that. We sailors are a superstitious lot and you be jinxing us for sure."

Wilson grinned as he flipped open the Captain's Night Orders, read an entry, and checked the time. "Well, we'll see how prophetic you are, ST1. Next evolution tonight is to copy the seventeen-hundred-zulu comms broadcast. We've got fifteen minutes to clear baffles and come up. Clearing baffles to the right."

"Aye, sir," Hannon answered. The good-natured jousting was over for the time being. "No contacts. Ready to clear baffles."

Wilson turned to the ship control party—the crewmembers at their positions in the submarine's control room—and sharply ordered, "Co-pilot, send the messenger to wake the captain for the seventeen-hundred-zulu comms pass. Pilot, make your depth one-five-zero feet. Right standard rudder, steady course one-nine-zero to clear baffles. Slow to ahead two-thirds."

"Make my depth one-five-zero feet, right standard rudder, steady course one-nine-zero, ahead two-thirds, Pilot, aye," Chief Schmidt acknowledged as he reached forward to dial the new parameters into the autopilot.

The big submarine smoothly came shallow and circled around as Hannon and his sonar searched the surrounding waters for any sign of another ship, on the surface or below it. The waters in this part of the southern Philippine Sea were very quiet and very empty, but the baffle-clearing procedure was required to confirm it.

Josh Hannon was just reporting that they had the sea all to themselves when Commander Brian Edwards, the boat's skipper, walked into the control room, still wiping the sleep from his eyes as he nursed a mug of steaming black coffee. He stepped over to the command console and leafed through the sonar displays as Bill Wilson, without a prompt, brought him up to date.

"Captain, we've made a careful baffle clear to the right. We hold no sonar contacts. Request permission to come to periscope depth to copy communications."

Satisfied that what he was hearing from his OOD was also what he was seeing on the screen, Edwards ordered, "Come to periscope depth to copy the broadcast. And let's ventilate the ship for half an hour. We could use a little fresh air. Some compartments on this boat smell like a locker room."

The skipper then stood back to watch his team in action. Two minutes later, they were at periscope depth. Another minute and the digital packet comms broadcast was onboard and receipted for. Then, there was pleasant confirmation that they were ventilating.

Edwards nodded and allowed himself the slightest of smiles. No matter how many times he saw this evolution on *George Mason*, he admired the efficiency and skill of the men and women who designed and built this warship. He now stood in a brightly lit control room, feeling the fresh, cool sea air on the back of his neck while he watched everything happening on the surface not through a periscope but on a large flat-panel display.

It certainly was a lot different from how he had done it on the old *Toledo*, back when he was second in command, the XO, on that submarine. On that ship and those that came before, the control room would necessarily be pitch black so the OOD could raise the periscope from its well and peer into the eyepieces. The crew would have to be feeling around in the dark to manually move ventilation flappers and dampers in order to ventilate the vessel with fresh air. But now, aboard the *George Mason,* everything was only a couple of button pushes. All he had to do was watch and enjoy his coffee. And the sweet-smelling sea air that flowed in from the surface.

"Captain, Radio," the 21MC box squawked. "New orders onboard. Patching them through to your display on the command console."

So there had been traffic worth catching on the comms operation. Edwards punched in his password and read the new messages.

"Officer of the Deck, send the messenger to wake the Nav. We need to plot a course to some place called Semporna on Borneo."

Edwards rubbed his chin as he pondered the orders, wondering what was going on. This cruise primarily was to be running up and down between the southern coast of Japan, past Taiwan, down into the Philippine Sea, then out to near Guam and back north, all the time listening and observing. Mostly looking for any unusual or interesting activity on the part of PLAN, the Chinese navy, submarine and surface. None of that involved a stop in Borneo.

"I got to admit I'm curious. Why Borneo?"

"It's like you always say, Skipper," Bill Wilson said.

"What is it I always say?" Edwards shot back as he took a sip of his now-cold coffee.

"They tell us to steam to Denver, we set the course and figure out how we'll maintain depth past Las Vegas."

3

Tranh Vu climbed up the ladder to the bridge of his submarine, the *Bà Rịa-Vũng Tàu* (HQ-187). Even though he knew what to expect when he emerged into the open, he was still surprised by the ferocity of the wind-driven rain. The remnants of a dying typhoon now felt just as powerful as the original storm at its most angry. Between the pitch-black night and the torrential downpour, the Vietnamese Navy commander could hardly see the pier just meters off the sub's starboard side. The assembled line handlers standing over there were mere wraiths in the night. If they had not had glowing ChemLights clipped to their life jackets, they would have been invisible. The large, modern Cam Ranh Bay Naval Base was little more than a bare glimmer of dock lights in the pounding rainstorm.

Tranh checked his wristwatch yet again. Finally, it was time. He yelled to be heard over the wind, ordering his officer of the deck to have lines cast off and to back the Vietnamese *Kilo*-class submarine away from the pier. Due to frustrating delays, in addition to the storm, they now had a very limited window to get out of port and into deep water, to a spot at which they could dive. Until they would be able to do that, the only things obscuring their submarine's departure from the distantly prying eyes of the Chinese were the dark of night and the raging storm.

The pair of frigates that were on-station, guarding the entrance channel, now reported that all was clear. No Chinese ships were visible on their radar screens. Tranh had zero confidence in those reports. The Chinese were far too clever and possessed the required technology to assure that a pair of rusted-out Russian-hand-me-down frigates would never be able to detect their presence. The Vietnamese submarine skipper was placing his trust in God's hands. The Catholic God. After almost five hundred years, Tranh was one of the few in his country who continued to follow the Catholic faith. But he also knew the storm offered far better protection than prayers or barely serviceable warships. Still, the storm would blow through quickly and daylight was not that far away.

All the other piers around them were now empty. The *Bà Rịa-Vũng Tàu* would be the last boat in the squadron to deploy. Not by plan but by happenstance. Tranh still cursed under his breath about the weapons-loading crane and its incompetent operator who somehow managed to jam its gears. That delayed his torpedo load. The incompetent fool had stretched the captain's patience to the very limit. Tranh had spent several frustrating hours pacing up and down the pier, railing at the crew that was struggling without success to repair the recalcitrant crane. Then the storm front hit. That chased him belowdecks and further stalled the workmen. Finally, he called the squadron commodore to tell him that the *Bà Rịa-Vũng Tàu* was getting underway immediately, even if she had loaded only twelve of the eighteen torpedoes she was supposed to be taking. There was simply no time to wait for the crane to be repaired and the last half dozen torpedoes to be loaded. Any more delay would mean having to steam out of Cam Ranh Bay in broad daylight, in full view of all the Chinese spy systems. Better to slip out during tonight's storm with at least a chance to accomplish a part of the mission.

"Captain," the officer of the deck called out, interrupting Tranh's thoughts. "The navigator requests to raise the radar mast and employ it in order to better navigate out in the weather. He reports that visibility through the periscope is zero."

Tranh snorted, then pounded the bridge railing with the heel of his hand.

"Does the fool have water buffalo dung for brains? If we light off that radar, the Chinese will detect it and have us targeted before the system completes its first scan. And tell that idiot not to trust the GPS, either. You can be sure that they are spoofing it. It would have us steering a course for Cambodia!" He paused and allowed the rain and wind to cool his temper. Then Tranh pointed at a faint blue light, barely visible a few meters in front of the submarine. "Just follow the pilot boat out. He will keep us in safe water."

The tiny pilot boat's stern light was little more than a dim glow through the driving rain even though it was only a few yards ahead of the submarine. The OOD passed down a stream of orders to the control room below. The submarine coasted blindly away from the pier and then slowly followed the pilot boat down the channel.

Cam Ranh Bay afforded the largest sheltered anchorage in all of Southeast Asia. It was well used by merchant ships, fishing vessels, and sundry other shipping. Regardless of the hour, the bay's navigation channels were normally clogged with ships going in every direction, either coming into the various port facilities to off-load cargo or heading back out into the South China Sea, bound for their next destination. Driving a tiny submarine out of this busy harbor on a dark night with all the running lights extinguished, with no radar operating, and with the AIS transponder secured —the ship's automatic information system inactive—would normally amount to an open invitation to get run over by some massive container ship. A vessel that probably would not even feel the bump.

But these were not normal times. The Chinese People's Liberation Army Navy (PLAN) had boldly and viciously attacked and invaded Bach Long Vi Island. Vietnamese territory. Open hostilities had broken out between the two former allies. Prudent merchant sailors were giving the South China Sea a wide berth if they could. Even though Cam Ranh Bay was almost a thousand kilometers south of where the attack had taken place, no one was taking any chances. Tranh was banking on no merchant captain being foolish enough to have his vessel out here, given the Chinese threat and the night's dangerous weather.

Tranh glanced down at the compass repeater and then at his watch. They were on a heading of due west, away from the piers. They had less than a kilometer of room before they would become entangled in one of the myriad floating lobster farms that dotted the bay. The wide array of buoyed pens would be all but invisible tonight, but they could quickly ensnare the submarine if they wandered into the wrong area. That would be an inglorious way to bring to an end such an important mission for his submarine and her crew.

Tranh estimated that they had ten minutes before they would need to turn. He kept checking his watch and finally ordered, "Officer of the Deck, put your rudder left full and come to course south."

Just as he uttered the command, Tranh saw the light from the pilot boat suddenly begin to move left. Whoever was out there, guiding them into the night sea, was thinking the same thing he was.

The black submarine now headed south, threading through the Cua Hep Passage. Separating the Mui Sop and Mui Hon Long headlands, and only a little over a kilometer wide, the "Narrow Door" was aptly named, particularly when trying to navigate the passage on a stormy, pitch-black night. Tranh could make out nothing of either shore even though they were close enough to hear the storm surf breaking against the nearby beaches with an ominous roar.

Tranh waited another ten minutes after he calculated that they had safely made their way through the needle eye of the passage. It was time to become a submarine once again.

"Officer of the Deck," he ordered. "Come to course one-six-zero. Dive the boat to periscope depth."

"What do we tell the pilot boat, Captain?" the OOD asked. "How do we signal them to go home."

"We simply disappear," Tranh replied with a snort. "They will go a few more miles and then realize no one is following anymore. Now, get us dived."

The captain dropped down the long ladder from the bridge to the control room. Coming from the wild weather topside into the red-lit congestion of the cramped control room was mildly disconcerting. But, for the longtime skipper, quite comforting. This was his element.

Tranh threw his rain slicker and hat into a corner. He ignored the hustle and bustle of getting the boat dived and made his way to the chart table. After taking a quick few seconds to look at the chart, he pointed to a spot and said, “Navigator, steer us to here, halfway between Dao Binh Ba Island and Hon Mui Island.”

The submarine slipped beneath the storm-raked sea and neatly bisected the Cua Lon, or “Large Door,” passage. The rocking and rolling of the submarine had ceased. They were out in the South China Sea, submerged, and free to accomplish their mission. And most likely without having been detected.

Of course, there was no way for anyone aboard the submarine to see the silvery cannister sitting on the bottom of the passage. Or to be aware of the network of sensors connected to it.

Twenty minutes after the *Bà Rịa-Vũng Tàu* passed overhead, the Chinese South Sea Fleet Command Duty Officer, who sat in his expansive underground command post in Zhanjiang, had already been briefed on the sixth Vietnamese submarine that had headed out to sea. Within an hour, anti-submarine warfare forces were being vectored to intercept the vessel.

Ψ

President of the United States Stanley Smitherman sat behind the Resolute desk and leaned back, a finger to his lips, apparently lost in thought. The windows of the Oval Office backlit him to the point that he appeared to have a golden halo. Secretary of Defense Harold Osterman had to shake his head to clear the effect. But he remained quiet. The president would speak when he was good and ready.

The two men had just watched the latest television news footage from the L’Enfant Metro disaster, which had happened only blocks from the White House. The mangled wreckage and torn bodies had dominated the news cycle for the past several weeks. The death toll continued its inexorable climb as more wreckage was slowly and meticulously cleared from what remained of the underground station.

“Harold, what the hell are we finding out?” Smitherman’s commanding baritone voice resonated across the room. That voice was probably the single most recognized feature of this president. That and his trademark armadillo-skin cowboy boots.

“Our geeks over at the Defense Information Services Agency have definitively determined that this was caused by a series of software malfunctions, each stair-stepping on the others, until we ended up with all this," Osterman answered, waving toward the large flat-panel TV on the far wall. "The NTSB people are saying that they are not seeing any signs of human error, but the information is really sparse. Most of the sensors and recorders got destroyed in the collisions and fire."

"Software malfunction," Smitherman parroted, considering the fuzziness of that description.

"Yes, but DISA is ninety percent positive that it was a Chinese cyber-attack, but they have not been able to find any evidence to back that up. Certainly not enough for us to make a public stink about it. Their fingerprints were wiped completely clean."

Smitherman slumped down in his chair, again lost in thought for a few seconds. Then he slammed his fist on the desk. Hard.

"Damn! Damn! Damn!" he roared. "We can't afford a major dust-up with the Chinese right now. Not when we've been nailing the other party as being wild-eyed anti-Asian racists, big time. The media has been kind enough to gobble it up and run with it. Our friends over there have kept it front and center. And we've been piling on with all our 'Cooperation in Asia' initiatives."

The president pondered the empty whiskey shot glass on his desk. Osterman remained quiet, knowing the next shoe was about to drop. And he knew precisely the direction the president would take.

"Hal, you know damn well elections are only three months away. We don't come up with some easy answer to all this, it'll be a disaster for the party."

Osterman held up his hand.

"We're on it, Mr. President. The DISA team is very small and they have been working under a security blanket a whole lot higher than 'Top Secret.' Their suppositions will die in the closet. We just leak to the press that the 'glitch' was an error in the programming and let the software developers be the scapegoats. They'll deny it but it won't matter. Couple of carefully placed leaks about corporate greed and taking advantage of the taxpayer...maybe a 'reliable source' story about kick-backs coming from members of the last administration. That will be the narrative and it will make all this a negative for the other party, not us."

Smitherman broke into a broad smile.

"I like it. It gives us cover through the elections. But I suppose we do need to let the damn Chinese know that we know who did this. Let's play a little hardball. Let's get Tan Yong on the phone and tell him what we know. Convince them we know even more. And hint that we expect some help with the elections in return for keeping this on the down-low. They know the other guys will be a hell of a lot less willing to play ball with their asses if they win. Tell him we expect his cyber people to help us out for a change. With the election, you know."

Osterman abruptly stood.

"Done, sir. Consider it done. And I'll make sure the Secretary of State knows just enough to catch the right drift on this mess."

"And, Hal, do we have something else we could hold over Tan Yong's head if we really needed to?" Smitherman pondered. "You know, something with some real teeth that we can use to bite him in the balls."

Osterman hesitated for a few seconds. Then he brightened. "I think I have just the ticket, Mr. President. I just got a brief a few days ago on a new special program. I'll not bore you with the details. Let's just say that it would allow us to really squeeze his gonads when and if we needed to."

"Well damn, Hal. Cut the crap and tell me all about it."

"No, sir. No details. I won't brief you on it." When Smitherman's eyebrows shot up, it always matched his anger. Osterman waved his hand back and forth. "Plausible deniability, boss. Just leave it up to me. And trust me, this is the perfect ball-buster."

Smitherman pursed his lips and picked up the shot glass. Noticing there was no whiskey in it, he promptly reached for the half-full bottle on his desk to rectify that situation.

4

His noise-canceling headset only helped to reduce the engine noise to a constant, annoying roar. No opportunity for a catnap on this particular excursion. Commodore Joe Glass concentrated instead on the extraordinary view of the South China Sea out the side window of the military aircraft as it climbed toward cruising altitude. As many times as he had traversed these waters during his US Navy submarine career, Glass had seen this vista—especially from this angle—on only a few occasions. And the main thing he noted was just how congested it was on the surface down there. The seascape was dotted with what appeared to be hundreds of ships randomly steaming off toward every point of the compass.

The MV-22 Osprey in which he rode as the only passenger—or "PAX" in Navy jargon—had departed Changi Naval Base in Singapore just as the sun was taking its first peek at the new day from beyond the eastern horizon. Up front, the pilots kept the emerging sun on the right side of the canopy as they took an east-northeast course across the southern end of the South China Sea.

Glass unbuckled his four-point harness, then awkwardly pulled himself up and out of the uncomfortable troop seat. He had been ensnared there for less than fifteen minutes but he already felt the need to stretch his aching back and get the blood circulating in his legs again. These particular aircraft were uniquely capable and extraordinarily versatile. But the accommodations for passengers were definitely designed for a twenty-year-old Marine or SEAL, not an old former submarine skipper who was now serving his country as a sub squadron commodore.

The co-pilot looked back over his shoulder and noticed Glass's discomfort. Their high-value VIP PAX was up and about, no longer safely strapped into the troop seat. Not the first and not the last to disapprove of the seating on his bird. But at least this one had not given him an earful about it, as if the aviator had designed the apparatus himself.

"Commodore, how about a front row seat up here and maybe even a little stick time in this bird?" he inquired through the AN/AIC-30 intercommunications system. At least that would get the passenger safely strapped into a seat again. These airplanes had enough acceleration to toss an untethered passenger or crew member right out the back.

Glass grinned, thankful the young Marine co-pilot understood how he felt. The co-pilot was already nimbly climbing out of the right-hand seat, motioning for Glass to sit down and get buckled up.

The first thing the senior submariner noticed was the wide view from the cockpit through a surprisingly broad expanse of glass.

"Man, you guys get a real picture-window view on the world," Glass said. "A whole lot better than looking through a periscope."

The pilot chuckled at Glass's reaction to the awesome view. "Something you bubbleheads don't get to see very often, I imagine," he joked. "For us, just another day at the office. And some of the places we have to set this machine down in require a nice view of our surroundings so we don't ding a fender."

Glass nodded. "Yep, it's a pretty nice view out the office window. But I'll stick with the boats as a normal mode of transport. As we sub sailors say, there are a lot more planes in the ocean than there are submarines in the sky."

The pilot, a Marine captain, smiled and nodded.

"Hey, you want to fly this bird for a bit, Commodore?"

"Sure," Glass replied.

"We are in horizontal flight mode right now obviously. We call it airplane mode, but, as you know, we can go vertical...helicopter mode...if we need to put her down on a postage stamp or some such," the pilot explained. "In this mode, the control stick handles just like any airplane stick. Pull back to go up, push forward to nose down. The rudder pedals push the nose around to where you want to go and hopefully the rest of the aircraft follows along."

Glass nodded. "Believe it or not, that sounds a lot like driving a submarine."

He pulled back on the stick a little and watched as the plane's nose came up. Then he pushed forward to return to level flight. The pilot pointed to the digital altitude display on the glass panel in front of him. The altitude had gone from five thousand feet to fifty-one hundred and was now edging back down to the original reading.

"Now this will be a little different from your boats," the pilot said as he pointed toward a control lever below Glass's left hand. "That's the thrust control lever. In horizontal mode, it determines our air speed by controlling the nacelle angle."

The submarine commodore had already become engrossed in the complexities of flying this remarkable craft and the similarities and differences between it and his usual mode of transportation. Watching the instrument display, he had not yet noticed the approaching green line on the horizon directly in front of them. The pilot certainly had. It slowly grew into the shoreline of Borneo, the world's third largest island and the biggest in Asia. Joe Glass's time playing "airedale" would necessarily have to come to an end. Flying over that rugged, mountainous territory would require that the first team man the controls.

"We are going feet dry just north of Bintulu," the copilot said as he maneuvered around Glass and dropped back into his seat.

The pilot reached back and pulled down the folding jump seat. "Commodore, you are certainly welcome to have a seat here and keep an eye on us. It gets a good bit more exciting for the rest of the flight. When we start climbing up over Borneo's central mountains, there will be some stretches of territory below us where Western man has never set foot. I've heard stories that there are still some isolated tribes of headhunters running around. Maybe even a Japanese soldier or two who doesn't know World War II is over."

Glass shook his head. "If it's all the same to you fellows, I'd prefer we not go down there for a guided tour."

"Me, too," the pilot answered. He patted the instrument panel. "But don't worry. This gal is real reliable. Good old American workmanship, delivered by the lowest bidder. We'll have you back aboard the good ship *Chesty Puller* in a couple of hours. But first, we're going to need to fly down in the mud for a bit. Make sure your boots are laced up tight."

Glass shot a questioning look at the Marine captain.

"Over water, we operated as a normal peace-time flight. Squawked on IFF Mode 3 so that we showed up as a normal aircraft on the air traffic controllers' screens. Now that we're over Borneo, we don't exactly want our Chinese friends to know where we are going or why, so we shifted to Mode 5. We won't be identified on any ATC screens, and at the altitude we'll be taking, radars won't see us anyway."

The pilot reached over to the center panel and dialed a new altitude into the autopilot. Then he shifted the radar to terrain-following mode. "The central mountains in this little paradise reach up to almost eight thousand feet and are almost always covered by clouds. Perfect cover for us to hide in, compliments of Mother Nature."

"And for us to collide with?"

"Us and all these electronics will do what we can to try to avoid that."

The Osprey nosed down before finally leveling off, in the clear, just above the treetops. Joe Glass realized he had held his breath for the entire descent, watching the gauges. Especially the altitude.

The ride became a whole lot bumpier as the two pilots delicately threaded their way up the narrow, jungle-shrouded canyons. Within minutes, they had climbed up into the clouds as the ground, still only a few feet below their aircraft but shrouded from view, rose up toward the peaks. It was as if everything outside the aircraft was now hidden by swirling white cotton. Glass could barely make out the treetops as they whizzed by beneath them, seemingly only a few feet away from their belly. However, the pilots seemed unconcerned. Their concentration was locked onto their screens and not the unforgiving jungle below.

Visibility only got worse as they climbed up and over the island's central mountains. At times rain lashed the windscreen and winds buffeted the aircraft as they bored a hole through a tropical thunderstorm. Even then, the Marine pilots kept the bird "down in the mud," with no more concern than if they were merely driving a bus full of tourists to their next stop.

It took over an hour of intense low-level flying before they cleared Borneo's mountainous spine and dropped below the clouds on the island's northeastern quadrant. The view out of the aircraft was still little more than a rolling, solid green landscape, miles and miles of dense jungle canopy, with an occasional opening where some logger had clear-cut and hauled away swaths of the thick vegetation.

"Charlie Papa, this is Mike Hotel One." Glass could hear the pilot calling ahead to the *Chesty Puller*, the ship he would be using as his temporary headquarters while tensions ran high in this troubled part of the world. She was actually and officially the USS *Lewis B. Puller* (EBS-3), a specially built expeditionary mobile vessel named after World War II and Korean War Marine hero, Lieutenant General Lewis "Chesty" Puller. "We are one hundred klicks out. ETA one-five minutes. Carrying one PAX and eight thousand pounds cargo. How copy? Over."

The headset crackled a bit before the three men heard a clear, welcoming voice. "Mike Hotel One, this is Charlie Papa. Copy all. We are ready to receive. You are cleared straight in to spot three. To Commodore Glass, welcome back to the *Chesty Puller,* sir."

The Osprey's pilot and co-pilot exchanged winks. Straight in. No circling. No waiting.

Carrying important passengers did have its benefits.

Ψ

"Man, am I bored!" Lieutenant Bob Bland muttered. His complaint was intended for no one in particular.

The young submarine officer had his eye to the Type 18 periscope eyepiece as he slowly traipsed a continual circle, rotating the periscope so that he could get a three-hundred-sixty-degree view of the ocean surface forty feet above where he stood in the control room of the USS *Boise*. "Dancing with the fat lady" was the common submarine term for these periscope searches. The "dance" was intended to make sure that no one snuck up on them while viewing the world through a soda straw.

"Nothing out there but sea and sky," he grumbled. "And I still got four more hours on this watch. My eyeball is going to be a permanent part of this damned eyepiece by then."

Fire Control Technician Second Class Jim Bosserman glanced over his shoulder from his seat at the AN/BYG-1 fire control panel, where he had been tracking contacts.

"Mr. Bland, I'll be glad to take a turn on the scope," he called out good-naturedly. "That is if it'll stop your bitchin' for a bit."

Bland scowled at him, then stepped back from the periscope.

"She's all yours, Bosserman. Lower power, on the horizon. Just completed an aerial search."

Jim Bosserman, tall and lanky, stepped up onto the periscope stand. He had to bend over to look through the eyepiece. "Low power, on the horizon, aye," he said as he started the same slow dance that Bland had been performing.

Bland stretched his aching back as he accepted a cup of steaming black coffee, offered up by the messenger of the watch. Taking a healthy swig, he plopped down at the bench seat that Bosserman had just vacated. The screen showed the positions of all the sonar contacts that *Boise* was currently tracking.

As he studied the display, Bland scratched his head and took another slug of the coffee. Something just did not add up, and now it was bothering him even more than his aching back.

They were patrolling a mere twelve miles off the city of Shantou, a key seaport with a population of more than five million souls located in the Guangdong Province of China. By all rights, the submarine should be busily dodging merchant ships steaming into and out of the busy harbor. The many toy factories in the area alone were enough to keep propellors churning in these waters, outbound for the US with prizes for millions of McDonald's Happy Meals.

But the sub should also be observing far more worrisome traffic here. The Chinese Navy ships home-ported at the People's Liberation Army Navy base just up the Rongjiang River should be plentiful. But since arriving, *Boise*'s powerful BQQ-10 sonar had only been tracking those half dozen merchant ships. And no warships. And so far, none of the merch ships had been visible through the periscope.

They had other ways to detect activity, too. The submarine had been stationed out here on China's front door on an Indications and Warning, or I&W mission, serving as a tripwire to give headquarters plenty of warning if the Chinese PLAN did anything especially interesting. The radio room was crowded with a full Direct Support Element team: cryptographic experts, intel weenies, Chinese linguists, the whole toolbox. Despite all the heightened anxiety and elevated tensions, there had been no indication so far that anyone from PLAN wanted to come out and play.

Bland grabbed the 21MC microphone and punched up the radio room. "Radio, Conn. The 'crippies' getting anything on the BLQ-10?"

ET1 Josh Hannon's voice crackled in response over the speaker. "Conn, Radio, so far the only thing they've intercepted is a cell conversation from some cabbie downtown trying to get lucky tonight."

Bland was still pondering the situation when the ship's XO stepped into the control room. As usual, she was cradling a full cup of coffee in her custom Thermos mug, one that seemed to hold at least a quart of joe. She claimed that she never wanted to run dry. Some in the crew maintained that was the reason Henrietta Foster never seemed to require sleep.

"Mr. Bland, I have relieved the captain as the command duty officer," the exec reported. "So, what is the contact situation by now?"

"XO, still no visual contacts. Sonar is tracking six contacts now. All merchants and all with CPAs beyond twenty thousand yards. And the DSE team still has nothing interesting to report."

CPA was "closest point of approach." Nobody was close by. And the guys in sonar who could detect a gnat fart at twenty miles were still hearing nothing.

"Yeah," Henrietta Foster replied, frustration heavy in her voice. "I caught that part. Pretty sparse report to call back to Group Seven. But we all know it's too quiet over there. Something's up." She took a sip of coffee, clearly not enjoying it. "Anyway, it's time for us to move out to sea. We need to be a hundred miles off-shore by midnight so we can make our nightly report."

Foster, with Bland in tow, stepped back to the ECDIS display at the aft end of the control room. She set the cup down and pointed to an area of the South China Sea about halfway between Pratas Island and Taiwan.

"You get us right there by midnight while I draft up the daily report. I'll be in radio with the DSE team if you need me."

"Yes, ma'am." Bland nodded and rubbed the stubble on his chin. "But I still can't figure it out. It's like the Chinese know we are here and are going out of their way to avoid us."

Foster picked up the coffee mug and stepped toward the radio room.

"Enough to make us feel jilted, right?" she called back over her shoulder. "But I'd bet they're giving the world the cold shoulder for the moment. Then they'll come on strong with a lot more attention than we really want."

Ψ

Admiral Jon Ward pushed his office chair back and tiredly surveyed his overflowing desk. He removed his reading glasses, closed his eyes tightly, and massaged his throbbing temples. The glasses were something new, a reluctant admission of a fact he had stubbornly denied as long as he could manage. His wife, Ellen, had been the one who ultimately convinced him to make the purchase. She tried to convince him they made him look distinguished. Even sexy. And, combined with the sprinkling of gray hair at the temples, caused him to appear downright "professorial." Considering the Chief of Naval Intelligence's general opinion of academia (not including his wife, who happened to be a botany professor), Ward was not at all certain that was a good thing. Besides, along with his aching back—the result of many years stooped over peering through submarine periscopes during a long career in "the boats"—the eyewear and inevitable gray hair in the mirror mostly just made him feel old.

Ward spun his office chair around and gazed out the window behind him. The view from his E-ring office in the Pentagon included Virginia Route 110, a stretch of four-lane better known as the Richmond Highway. As usual, it was still clogged with the evening commuter traffic, the last rays of the setting sun glimmering off thousands of windshields even at this late hour as a phalanx of office drones inched their way homeward to the suburbs, most of them laboring on behalf of the federal government and the US taxpayers.

Ward shook his head as he turned back and grabbed another file from one of the unstable stacks. It would be many hours before he would be able to wade through enough of this flotsam so he would not feel guilty about finally heading home to Ellen and dinner. As he opened the next folder, Jon Ward reminded himself yet again that he had welcomed the appointment to this high but demanding position. Not only did it give him the opportunity to continue to serve his country in an essential role, one in which he could make a difference every day, but he had also replaced Admiral Tom Donnegan in the job. Donnegan was a man under whom Ward had served in submarines and then again as Donnegan groomed him as his replacement. A close and dear friend, a surrogate father, and also godfather to the Wards' son, Jim. But that relationship only increased the pressure Ward felt to perform up to the high bar "Papa Tom" had set for the job.

Just then, Lieutenant Jimmy Wilson stuck his head through the office door, fracturing Ward's reverie.

"Boss, we're ordering some pizzas from that new place down in the food court. You want the usual on your pie?"

Ward looked up and grimaced. "Damn it, Jimmy! It's way past time you were home with the wife and kids. How many times do I have to tell you that this is shore duty? You're supposed to take advantage of it when you're lucky enough to get it." Ward glanced at the old-fashioned key-wind ship's clock on his office wall as it rang seven bells. 1930 already. "Besides, I don't need to be babysat twenty-four-seven. Now, get the hell out of here. And say hi to Suzy for me."

The young flag aide smiled as he shook his head. He had heard this speech before.

"Boss, if I take off now, who's going to be here for you to yell at? And who's going to make the coffee? Your recipe tastes more like diesel fuel."

Ward leaned back in his chair. "Why do I tolerate such insubordination?"

One of the civilian analysts appeared in the doorway behind Wilson, tapped him on the shoulder, made the universal thumb-and-finger-to-the-ear telephone sign, and nodded toward the aide's desk.

"Because we are indispensable," Wilson said with a grin. "Excuse me, sir. Duty calls."

Ward pulled the glasses back on and resumed studying the file as his aide backed out the door and eased it shut. Wilson stepped to his desk and grabbed his phone.

"Office of Naval Intelligence, Lieutenant Wilson," he barked. Then, immediately, he added, "This is not a secure line."

A distinctly female and familiar voice replied, "Jimmy, you know who this is." It was a statement of fact, not a question. "I need to speak to Admiral Ward."

"Yes, ma'am. I'll put you right through." Lt. Wilson knew better than to identify this caller on an open line, even one inside the Pentagon. He put the call on hold and rushed back to Ward's door.

"Admiral, Li Minh Zhou is on the outside line for you."

Ward dropped the folder and grabbed the phone without the slightest hesitation. Li was worthy of such attention. As enigmatic as she was beautiful, she was also a spymaster, with a network embedded very deeply—and effectively—in the highest echelons of the Chinese government and military. Less than a year before, she had been a key player in the resolution of a bold coup attempt inside the Chinese leadership by the Won brothers. A potentially disastrous flare-up that had threatened to spark a shooting war that could have engulfed not just the region but the entire planet. She continued to be America's best source of intelligence into that mystery-shrouded government.

But Li would only communicate with fewer than a half dozen people within the US military. One of those people was Admiral Jon Ward. His son, Jim Ward, a Navy SEAL, was another.

Wilson backed out of the room and quietly shut the door.

"Admiral, I need to talk with you privately. Face-to-face." The sultry voice sounded more like an actress than a hard-boiled, experienced intelligence agent. "I'll arrive in San Francisco tonight. Please meet me at Sam Wo's tomorrow. It's on Clay Street in Chinatown. Say six tomorrow evening. I know you're busy but it's important. And, if at all possible, ask your son to join us."

As was typical with Li Minh Zhou, the conversation was succinct and one-way. Even though he was one of the most powerful people in US military intelligence, Admiral Jon Ward found that he was now holding a phone with nobody left on the other end of the line. But he expected nothing else. It was not a discourteous slight. It was Li Minh Zhou minimizing the chances of getting herself exposed, tortured, and killed. And further confirmed that the purpose of this hastily arranged meeting was far too critical to rely on any other means of communication. Face-to-face it would be, then.

Ward jumped up and barked at the closed door.

Jimmy Wilson was already standing there, knowing the summons would come. He rushed in to find his boss already busily stuffing his laptop and a sizeable collection of file folders into his battered leather briefcase.

"Jimmy, get me a seat on the first flight out of Reagan or Dulles to SFO in the morning. And make a reservation at the Marines' Memorial Club for a couple of nights." Ward had another thought. "Oh, and call my son. Have him meet me there. I'll give you a time later."

The flag aide nodded. These mad dashes following a call from the mysterious Chinese spy were becoming almost routine. And Jon Ward's son —Tom Donnegan's godson—SEAL Commander Jim Ward, was usually involved somehow.

"Yes, sir. Anything else?"

"No, I don't think so," Ward answered as he grabbed the briefcase and headed toward the door. He took a quick glance at the ship's clock. "If I hurry and the traffic's thinned out, I can take Ellen out for a late dinner. Maybe a little of Fratelli's trout almondine and a bottle of Prosecco will make up for me skipping town for a few days."

"Sure ought to, boss. I'll cancel your anchovy and onion pizza then."

"Yep. Unless you want it, Jimbo," Ward called back over his shoulder.

The aide frowned and faked a gag, but Ward was already galloping out the door.

"No. No, thanks."

Then Wilson stepped back into Ward's office and began trying to arrange the stacks of files into some logical order. But the usually efficient aide could not concentrate on the task. The phone call and Ward's reaction to it were worrisome.

Something was up. Something big.

He was so lost in his thoughts that he uncharacteristically forgot to cancel the pizza order. Wilson was only reminded when he caught the aroma of it, still in its box, resting on his desk on the other side of the heavy office door.

The whole thing smelled to high heaven.

Ψ

The rotating presidency of the United Nations Security Council belonged to Chad this month. That nation's ambassador to the UN, Dr. Antoine Bongor, a French-schooled and evangelistic socialist, sat in the seat of power, a broad grin on his face. He had treated himself for the occasion to a new business suit from one of Fifth Avenue's finer purveyors of men's fashion. He paused before picking up the gavel to adjust the blue, red, and gold handkerchief—the colors of Chad's flag—that was tucked into the breast pocket of his new suit jacket. Bongor was quite proud that his poor nation had been raised to such an exalted honor. He had grown weary of Chad being declared by so many organizations to be the poorest yet most corrupt country on the planet. This day, though, the landlocked African nation was up front, on equal footing with some of the most powerful countries in the world.

The fifteen members, permanent and non-permanent, were just getting settled into their seats as Bongor called them to order. This would certainly be little more than a perfunctory meeting, the usual biweekly gathering with its typical quick, mundane agenda, with an adjournment early enough to allow its attendees to get a better table for lunch at their preferred eateries around the city's East Side.

The broad grin still on his face, Ambassador Bongor requested as a first order of business a motion for the Council to adopt the benign agenda that had been passed down from the Secretary General. This was a diplomatic organization, after all. They could not possibly conduct any business, no matter how pressing, that was not already well vetted and on the agenda. But before he could acknowledge the member from Ireland, who was ready to make the motion, someone else stood and loudly requested permission to speak.

It was the People's Republic of China's Ambassador to the United Nations, Tiaowen Ku. This was highly unusual and improper. Dr. Bongor was not sure what the proper protocol was in this case, so he simply nodded toward the officious diplomat. Maybe he wanted to make the requested motion. But that was typically done by one of the non-permanent members.

The Chinese ambassador, once acknowledged, pounded the desk with a closed fist, pulled the microphone closer to his lips, and began to speak. Loudly and forcefully.

"Mr. President, members of the Security Council, under Article Thirty-Five Dash One of the Charter of the United Nations, the People's Republic of China comes before the Security Council of the United Nations in order to make all members of this body aware of a matter of serious import and to plead for assistance. The Republic of Vietnam, aided and abetted by the United States of America, has commenced hostile and murderous activities against the People's Republic of China."

The Irish ambassador, who still had his hand in the air to make the requested motion about the agenda, slowly lowered it. Eyes wide, he and the others assembled in the big room listened as the Chinese ambassador continued his shocking accusations.

"These two renegade states first treacherously and without provocation attacked peaceful Chinese naval militia ships that were routinely operating in Chinese sovereign waters near our territory of Bach Long Vi Island. I repeat, sovereign Chinese waters. Then they compounded their belligerent aggression by conducting a massive and damaging offensive cyber-attack on Chinese infrastructure. The People's Republic of China calls upon the Security Council under Article Thirty-Nine to determine that an act of aggression has been perpetuated by the Republic of Vietnam and the United States of America and calls upon the members under Article Forty-

Nine to come to our assistance. Until that time, the People's Republic of China will, under the provisions of Article Fifty-One, exercise our own inherent right to self-defense."

Ambassador Bongor sat in shocked silence. The proud smile had disappeared from his face, replaced by a look of confusion. Nothing like this had ever happened. At least not in his memory. He had no idea how to properly handle such a thing.

The US ambassador suddenly jumped to his feet, yelling his objections to Tiaowen Ku's tirade. At the same time, the British ambassador tried to call a point of order for the Chinese ambassador's egregious breach of protocol. White handkerchief in hand, the French ambassador was waving it, seeking the floor to make a motion of his own.

Meanwhile, the Russian ambassador sat back, smiling, watching in satisfaction as the routine biweekly meeting of the United Nations Security Council devolved into utter chaos.

Ψ

"Honored teacher," Tan Yong said, standing as Qián Dài walked into his office. "It is good to see you. I understand that you have seen that our plan is coming together."

Qián Dài gave Tan Yong a quick bow. "It is good to see you, too. Yes, I have looked over the plan you have put together. I remind you again that you must remember the words of Sun Tzu. 'The whole secret lies in confusing the enemy, so that he cannot fathom your real intent.'"

Tan Yong chuckled. Hearing the aged, bespectacled little man speak of war was somehow incongruous. "Teacher, how is it that you quote Sun Tzu? Your area of expertise is said to be financial strategy."

"What is business on a world scale if not warfare? To master a craft, one must first study the masters," Qián Dài answered. "And one should also study the masters of one's enemy. The Americans have a warrior philosopher named Boyd who has taught them to sow confusion with their enemy by getting inside of his decision process. We must move their eyes to where they see what we want them to see. Then, when that happens, they will react in the ways that we want them to."

Tan Yong nodded. "I see the wisdom. Misdirection and deception to keep our American friends busy but ineffective."

"Yes. Busy but ineffective. All the way to the point that they have already lost the war just as they believe the initial thrusts and parries have only begun."

5

The twin columns of armor from the People's Liberation Army paid no attention whatsoever to the gates, flashing lights, and warning signs as they stormed right on through the China-Vietnam border crossings at Lao Cai and Dong Dang. They charged through without even slowing, scattering guards and shoving aside all obstacles in their way. The onslaught at the two crossings occurred almost simultaneously and against practically no resistance. A few squads of lightly armed Vietnamese Border Defense Force troops at each crossing were quickly overrun and pummeled by two hundred Type 99A main battle tanks and a division of mechanized infantry. The two waves of tanks hardly slowed as they motored down their respective highways, both leading to Hanoi. The Vietnamese border guards that survived scattered, running for their lives toward the hills.

Even as the tanks were smashing through the border checkpoints, swarms of PLAF fighter aircraft scoured the skies and air bases across Vietnam of any military aircraft. The suddenness of the surprise attack meant most of them were caught on the ground and left burning. The few warplanes that did manage to claw their way into the air were summarily dispatched before they could fire a shot. They were soon burning funeral pyres, sending mournful smoke skyward from the dense, jungle-covered mountains that had seen so much similar scarring more than half a century before.

After decades of bluster, threats, and occasional innocuous skirmishes, China's long-feared aggression against their former ally had abruptly become a reality. And now, the race toward Hanoi was on.

Chinese General Zuoyi Jundui's Fourteenth Army Group's tanks were at full throttle, rumbling out of the rugged highlands and down the CT05 expressway, always keeping the Red River on their right shoulder. The capital city was only two hundred and fifty kilometers away. Very little stood between their cannon and their objective. Zuoyi knew precisely where some minor speed bumps might pop up—the border crossing being the first—and how he would deal with them when they did occur. His troops would be at their destination before anyone in Vietnam could rally enough of a defense to try to stop them. And before the rest of the world even knew what was happening.

PLA General Kuijia Siji's Forty-Second Army Group did not have as far to travel, only a hundred and forty kilometers to Hanoi. They expected stiffer opposition. General Kuijia's tanks zoomed through the tiny village of Dong Dang and then the ancient city of Lang Son.

Lang Son was where the People's Army of Vietnam militia made a valiant attempt to stop—or at least slow—the invasion forces. The local militia rallied to try to stop the Chinese tanks in the city streets. It was an uneven fight. Barely trained militia and loosely organized troops fighting with small arms and Molotov cocktails were challenging one of China's best armor divisions. The militia did succeed in slowing the invasion a little, but at terrible cost. Barricades made from city buses and guarded by taxi drivers proved less effective and far more dangerous to the defenders than simply tearing down street signs to confuse the Chinese.

The nearest regular Vietnamese combat troops were the Second Corps, based in Lang Giang, some sixty kilometers distant. There was no way to get any of the country's three infantry divisions to Lang Son in time to make any difference. But Lieutenant General Dong Dinh Bhong did have a tank brigade under his command there. And he bravely vowed that he would personally lead them into battle against the Chinese. His brigade was, in reality, only a few dozen well-used and obsolete Soviet T-55 and T-72 tanks, all purchased more than two decades before—and in less than mint condition even then—from former Warsaw Pact countries.

The resulting fight outside Lang Son was little more than a twenty-first-century version of the Charge of the Light Brigade. Dong and his old tanks charged up the AH-1 highway, two lanes of macadam hemmed in by rice paddies on one side and jungle-shrouded hills on the other. The front line of Vietnamese tanks was almost to Lang Son's outskirts when a flight of Chinese WZ-10 attack helicopters broke into the clear above the horizon and unleashed a deadly swarm of HJ-10 anti-tank missiles. At the same time, the first wave of Chinese tanks emerged from several of the town's narrow, twisting streets.

Within seconds, the main highway was blocked by scattered, immobile, and burning hulks of destroyed tanks. The few Vietnamese tanks that survived the first missile salvo intact promptly slammed into reverse and, at maximum throttle, tried to escape and find some kind of cover to hide behind.

But they had no hope of outrunning the next salvo thrown their way. It consisted of depleted-uranium, long-dart penetrator rounds, fired from the Chinese battle tanks' 125mm guns. The meter-long penetrators punched through the Vietnamese tanks' armor as if it were butter. Then the depleted uranium ignited inside the tanks, brutally completing the death and destruction.

The first couple of Chinese tanks to arrive simply bulldozed what remained of their burning, wrecked Vietnamese counterparts off the highway and into the rice paddies. Then they resumed their determined journey toward Hanoi.

Ψ

"Nav, you need a fix?" Brian Edwards asked. "Looks like we're going to be in restricted waters for the next twelve hours or so."

Jim Shupert, *George Mason*'s navigator, glanced up from the ECDIS navigation display. He had been busily building the submarine's planned track from the Philippine Sea into the Celebes Sea and then over to Semporna, their destination on the northeast coast of Borneo. Most of the journey would be routine, passing through wide-open ocean, except for the relatively short stretch directly ahead of them. The route required that they thread a needle between Maru Island, which belonged to Indonesia, and Balut Island, a volcanic rock at the southern end of the Philippines. Through that passage, the waterway bottle-necked down to only about forty miles wide. However, getting through would require them to do more than two hundred miles of steaming in restricted waters.

"Should be okay, Skipper," Shupert answered. "We got a good GPS fix last time we were up. SINS has been tracking within spec."

SINS was the Ship's Inertial Navigation System, a highly accurate means for determining a submarine's geographic position by inputting the vessel's known past fixes, like GPS, and then using accelerometers to measure how far the ship traveled over time in all three axes. The result should, at least theoretically, be where the ship was now.

"Okay, but better check to make sure. Those forty miles are really only about sixteen miles of water we can actually use," Edwards explained. "Both the Philippines and Indonesia claim twelve-mile territorial limits. We can't be submerged in either. If we had to surface around here for some reason, you can bet those Chinese satellites would have us detected and targeted before we could get the bridge manned."

Shupert nodded to his skipper and called up the nav accuracy display from the ship's inertial navigation system. Then, with a quizzical expression on his face, he grunted. An ugly error message sullied the screen.

"I don't like that sound you just made," Edwards said.

"Skipper, we got a problem," the nav reported. "Says here that the dithering motor has failed."

"The what?" Edwards shot back. Now the quizzical expression was on the captain's face. "The dithering what? That sounds like what my wife does when I ask what restaurant she wants to go to."

Shupert folded his arms and went into lecture mode. It was rare when he could teach Edwards something new.

"Boss, it's really very simple. Our SINS depends on the ring laser gyro for the absolute reference plane. That's the plane the accelerometers sit on to tell us how far we've traveled in all three axes. The ring laser gyro uses the Sagnac effect to measure the difference in rotation of two separate light paths around the gyro. At low rotation rates, the light paths can get locked in synchronous by backscatter. The dithering motor induces a rapid vibration on the ring's input axis to prevent this locking. Got it?"

Edwards squinted, then nodded. "Got it, Nav. Failed dithering thingy equals bad."

"Yep, that's it," Shupert confirmed with a shrug. "Basically."

"Okay, but can we fix it?" Edwards asked.

"We can, but it's touchy and tedious," the navigator responded. "We've actually got a couple of guys aboard that have been to the school. And the maintenance kit contains a spare motor. The real problem will be in the alignment process afterwards. I figure it'll take at least forty hours by the time the Schuller oscillations are damped."

"Schuller whats? Never mind. You're just showing off now." Edwards frowned and did some quick calculations in his head. "That's just about the time we're scheduled to pull into Semporna." He took a long draw of coffee. "I guess we'll just have to do this the old-fashioned way."

The Chief of the Boat and Master Chief Electronics Technician (Navigation), Dennis Oshley, had been listening to the conversation. He now joined the two men standing at the ECDIS display.

"Old fashioned? Now you're calling my name," he said. "This is looking like a problem we had a lot when I was a minnow. SINS back then seemed to spend all its time on its butt. We were always having to go back to plotting nav accuracy circles and dead reckoning between GPS fixes. It ain't really all that hard. You just need to figure out what all the inaccuracies are and how fast they propagate. You know, things like how close we stay on course and speed, what set and drift are doing to us. Stuff like that. We just need to get a new fix before the error circles get into any water where we're not supposed to be swimming."

For a moment, the three men considered what the master chief was saying. Then Oshley raised a finger. "One more thing. We gotta remember Murphy's law, navigation supplement. You can be anywhere in the error circle. If there is one little rock anywhere inside that circle, you will hit it. So, the corollary is, 'keep the rocks outside the circle.'"

The men laughed but without much humor.

"Okay, I'll get us up to get a GPS fix," Edwards said. "Nav, you and the

COB set up the nav system for dead reckoning. And Jim, get your team working on drawing parts and putting the procedure together to fix and test the...uh...the whatchamacallit."

"The dithering motor," Shupert answered. "We're on it."

Ten minutes later the *George Mason*'s number one photonics mast broke the placid surface of the southern Philippine Sea. The sensitive antennas under the radome at the top of the mast were already scanning the heavens for the GPS satellite signal, even before the video cameras broke the surface to give a view of a sun-splashed but unpopulated seascape.

Edwards could not miss the look of consternation on his navigator's face.

"Captain, we're not receiving any GPS signal at all," Shupert called out. "I don't get it. We're inside the M-code spot beam for the satellite. It should be wall-to-wall and treetop-tall."

"Did you check your gear lineup?" Edwards asked.

The Nav looked hurt that his skipper would even question such a basic move. "Yes, sir. Everything checks on this end."

"That leaves three possibilities," Edwards shot back. "None good. Either the GPS system is down for some reason, which I've never seen happen, though I know it can. Or our Chinese friends are jamming the signal, which is a reasonable possibility. Or they have taken out the satellite, which amounts to an act of war. Bottom line is, though, none of that really matters to us right now."

Edwards stepped over to the ECDIS table while the *George Mason*'s deck tilted as they dropped back into the depths. There was no reason to stay at periscope depth any longer.

"Nav, make sure the latest high-accuracy charts are loaded into ECDIS. Looks like we're down to bottom contour navigation and dead reckoning now. The DMHAC charts are the best we have."

Jackson Biddle, the XO, walked into the control room. He had clearly not been awake very long. But he quickly read the frustration on his captain's face. "Morning, Skipper. What's going on?"

Edwards took a couple of minutes to explain the situation. Biddle listened, visibly growing more concerned as the story unfolded.

"Skipper, navigation isn't going to be the only problem," the executive officer interjected. "We're going to lose comms here pretty quick, you know. Remember, the crypto uses the GPS timing signal to maintain synch. No synch, no crypto, no comms. And all our over-the horizon weapons, like Tomahawk, depend on GPS for both targeting and synchronous timing."

Edwards merely shook his head. "Well, this morning is going to hell in a handbasket. One problem at a time. Nav, you and the COB get the Nav team set up for continuous bottom contour navigation all the way through the straits. Keep us in the middle of the channel, in international waters. Meantime, break out your copies of Bowditch and Dutton's. Read up on deep-water dead reckoning. If we're where we think we are, we've still got four hundred miles of the Celebes Sea to cross. And our goal is to not end up on somebody's beach somewhere this side of Borneo."

"There is a bright side, Skipper," Biddle chimed in.

"Please tell me what the hell it is, XO."

"This presents a wonderful training opportunity."

Edwards offered half a grin.

"Yeah, for all of us."

Ψ

Chinese General Kuijia Siji's Forty-Second Army Group stormed purposefully down Vietnam's AH-1 highway, encountering no resistance whatsoever. The lead elements were in the center of Bac Ninh, where they finally slowed. There, as previously planned, they halted altogether at the centrally located Vincom Plaza, a landmark left over from the town's French heritage. The circular park was the perfect place to stop and refuel their tanks, have the men enjoy lunch, and give the main body an opportunity to catch up with the forward elements of the Forty-Second.

The ancient city's narrow streets were clogged with traffic as most of its half-million residents tried desperately to flee ahead of the Chinese tanks and whatever else might be coming behind them. The invaders watched with some amusement the gridlock and panic all around them as they leisurely ate and relaxed. Aerial reconnaissance reports confirmed that every road, trail, or footpath leading away from the city was jammed to the point of being impassable. The helpless, panicked civilians were making no effort at all to defend their city or themselves. They were merely intent on escaping with their lives and what few meager possessions they had managed to cram into and onto their vehicles.

They had been hearing about and dreading this very action by the Chinese for decades. Still, it was a surprise to most when it finally came. They knew that when the Chinese tanks that had stopped in the plaza were rolling once more, they would not slow or take alternate routes to avoid the fleeing refugees. Those Vietnamese who could not get off the roads and out of their way in time would be shoved aside or ground up under churning steel treads.

After the stop, and as the other elements of Kuijia's forces rolled into and around Bac Ninh, the mass of tanks made a distinct left turn and headed eastward, toward the coast. The large port city of Haiphong lay in that direction, only seventy kilometers away. The general's orders were simple. Take the port. And then hold it. Within hours, Haiphong would once again become a vital military resupply hub, just as it had been a half-century before when the Americans were meddling in the region.

Though the PLA units could not see them yet, they knew that a convoy consisting of dozens of Chinese freighters, troop ships, and escorts were assembled and waiting in the waters just over the horizon from Haiphong. Many of them would be tying up at the city's piers and disgorging their cargo of war machines, ammunition, and fighting men before tomorrow's sun cast its first rays on the bustling scene.

The Vietnamese High Command chose the city of Vinh Yen as the place to stop the northern invasion. All the readily available troops of the People's Army were rushed there for a last stand to stop General Zuoyi Jundui's Fourteenth Army Group tanks roaring down the Red River valley. There was precedence for choosing this battleground. They would rely on the hilly topography to replicate the historic French victory at the first Battle of Vinh Yen, a fight in which the French Expeditionary Corps stopped the Viet Minh—ironically, communist "freedom fighters" trained and supported by China—from storming down the Red River and attempting to take Hanoi.

As had the French defenders, the commander of the Vietnamese forces, Major General Nguyen Dung Duc, placed his two regiments of tanks into hastily-dug emplacements up on the hills north of the city. Then he positioned his infantry battalions along the highway to attempt to fill in the gaps and protect his flanks. He arrayed his artillery brigade—over a hundred tubes strong—on the Heron Lake golf course, two miles south of the city, ready to rain hell on anyone approaching from the north. It was a defense plan that had been honed and practiced continually for years. Dung Duc had a significant advantage over the hapless Vietnamese tanks that had fallen earlier in the day at the debacle at Lang Son. Most of his forces were made up of much newer and far more capable Russian-made T-90 main battle tanks.

The last Vietnamese tank rattled down into its earthen revetment just as the first units of Chinese armor became visible through the humid mist, quickly making their way along roadways that ran through rice paddies flanking the little Pho Day River. At five thousand meters, they were just now approaching within range of Dung Duc's T-90s. He sent down the order to commence firing.

The tank guns roared almost as one. Three seconds later, the tanks' first salvo struck home. Almost simultaneously, the initial shells from the howitzer batteries on the golf course arched up into the midday sky and plunged back down to explode mightily amid the muddy rice paddies.

A dozen of the Chinese Type 99A tanks fell victim to that first barrage. Their burning carcasses promptly sent columns of black smoke into the still and sticky air. But the carnage seemed to have no effect on the rest of the invaders. They continued to race forward, firing back as they charged. The Type 99s' reactive armor protected most of them from the Vietnamese fire. And the Vietnamese howitzers only sent mud and shredded rice stalks mushrooming into the air with no effect on the charging Chinese tanks.

Meanwhile, though, Dung Duc's insistence on digging his tanks in was paying dividends in the battle. At least so far. Most of the brutal Chinese armor-piercing shells punched harmlessly into the black-dirt revetments. The Chinese gunners quickly shifted, though, to gun-launched anti-tank missiles, designed to fall from a far higher angle on top of their targets. This proved marginally more effective as several of the Vietnamese tanks were taken out and fell silent.

Then, as they raced closer, the Chinese tanks came within range of the

Vietnamese infantry's own anti-tank missiles. The Russian-made Konkurs were highly effective wire-guided missiles designed for this very type of skirmish. With an ominous roar, they arced across the valley, each of them impressively exploding as they plunged into fast-approaching Chinese tanks. Some resulted in instant, spectacular kills. Most, though, did not. Again, the PLA tanks were protected by their own explosive reactive armor. Only an unlucky few were turned into burning, smoking hulks. And there was no effect on the rest of the advancing machines.

Major General Nguyen Dung Duc and his hard-fighting troops had real hope that his force could achieve a victory here and stop the invaders, just like the French did in 1951. Maybe deter them long enough that they would slow, or pull back long enough for the rest of the world to react to such a brazen invasion. Long enough for the world's diplomats to somehow stymie the Chinese before more lives were lost.

But it was not to be. The general and his superiors had not read their history carefully enough. The primary advantage—and the primary reason for the French victory at Vinh Yen—had been overwhelming air support. This time, most of the Vietnamese Air Force lay in shambles, burning on tarmacs, runways, rice paddies, and jungles. For this showdown, the PLAF owned the skies and there would be no air support. At least for the Vietnamese.

Even as the Chinese tanks continued to move toward the defenders and their artillery and tank fire, flight after flight of brand-new L-15B ground attack jets suddenly dotted the skies at the horizon. They zoomed in and unleashed their HJ-10 anti-tank missiles and laser-guided bombs onto the Vietnamese positions. At the same time, swarms of WZ-10 attack helicopters came in from the north and added their anti-tank missiles to the lethal mix, raking the unprotected infantry with the choppers' thirty-millimeter cannons.

What had appeared to be a Vietnamese victory early on quickly segued into a rout and then a massacre as the Chinese boldly pushed forward, unleashing withering fire as they plowed ahead. There was no more shelling from the tank emplacements or the artillery on the golf course. Vinh Yen and the surrounding villages were leveled, as if bulldozed by giant earthmovers. The sky hung heavy with the pall of thick, black smoke.

Despite how the battle had so abruptly turned, People's Army Major General Nguyen Dung Duc had achieved one of his initial objectives. He had bought the Vietnamese government and High Command enough time to hastily abandon their offices in Hanoi and flee south.

However, those few hours' head start had come at a very high price indeed.

6

Admiral Jon Ward stepped out of the elevator and into a small lobby. This was his kind of place. He had always enjoyed his stays at the Marines' Memorial Club. Located right in the heart of downtown San Francisco, the club was equal parts museum, boutique hotel, and quiet respite within one of the country's most hectic cities. Although it was operated as both a club and a memorial for Marines, membership was open to all active-duty military as well as veterans. Jon Ward had been a member for many years and took advantage of that every time business or pleasure brought him to San Francisco.

As usual, and with a few minutes to kill, he made a slow circle of the lobby, stopping at each display to read the explanations accompanying the Marine Corps memorabilia laid out there. There was often something new to see and much history to be reminded of. The Marines were certainly active in various parts of a very dangerous world. There would never be a lack of items with a story behind them for him to see and consider.

He quickly checked his watch. His son, Jim, was due to arrive any minute. There should be ample time for a leisurely hike up Nob Hill while they took advantage of the opportunity to catch up in person with each other's busy lives. Maybe even a few minutes for drinks at the Top of the Mark—the iconic cocktail bar on the top floor of the Mark Hopkins Hotel—before they headed down to Chinatown for the meeting with Li Minh Zhou. The view from Top of the Mark would be stunning, fog allowing. There was an oft-told Ward family anecdote about the night Jon and his wife, Ellen, were enjoying their tightly-budgeted honeymoon in San Francisco. They had tipped the greeter at the entrance to the Top of the Mark twenty bucks to allow them to simply enter the lounge and walk over to the big windows for the vista. Once there, though, they found that the pea soup was so thick they could see nothing at all. Just gray and a few dim streetlights far below. As the disappointed newly-weds walked back past the greeter, the man simply shrugged as he pocketed the twenty and wished them a good evening. The only view the young couple had that night was from the Jack in the Box at Geary and Mason.

Now, Ward thought, he was just as foggy on why this in-person confab with the beautiful but dangerous Chinese spy had been called. Mystified about why she had insisted on meeting him in San Francisco and not DC. She was well aware of the demands on his time and attention these days. And why had she insisted that Jim also be present? There were about 2,500 active-duty Navy SEALs at any given time, but it seemed Li only trusted one of them. The one that just happened to be the son of the head of naval intelligence.

But Ward had already learned in previous dealings with her that there was no point in questioning the lady's highly unusual modus operandi. Few people—and quite possibly none—had her unique perspective on or placement within the highest reaches of the labyrinthian Chinese government. It was obvious her network had many tentacles. Even though Ward still wondered how much he could trust her, she had already proven her value in spades. That was why he had been willing to hop on the quick flight west, even if he did have to stop and change planes in Cincinnati, Dallas, and Denver. And why he had gone ahead and pulled rank to free Jim from an important "training exercise" in El Salvador.

Something still bothered him, though. How did Li know one of the most powerful men in the nation's military would cancel appointments, pack a travel bag, and take a full day from his duties to meet with her? She was so confident he would respond to her summons that she had not even bothered to confirm that he would make the trip. Or did she have ways of tracking his movements and knew he was en route? If she did have such capabilities, who else did? Ward was so preoccupied in his self-questioning that he did not notice the club manager approaching.

"Excuse me, Admiral," the man interrupted. "Your son just called. His flight had been delayed but he has just landed at SFO. He asked that we tell you that he should be here by seventeen hundred, traffic allowing."

Jon Ward glanced at his watch. It was not quite four o'clock yet. That meant he had over an hour to kill.

"Thanks, Eric," he responded. "When my son arrives, would you please tell him that I'll be up in the library?"

The facility's eleventh-floor library was precisely what someone would expect from a unique club like the Marines' Memorial. There were abundant comfortable leather chairs to sink into, bookshelves lining three walls stocked with volumes on all things military, and a bank of huge windows that provided plentiful light. Ward quickly found an interesting text and settled in for a read. He was deep into a detailed study of the Vietnamese-French battle of Dien Bien Phu when Jim Ward strode into the room, a broad smile on his face.

"Don't get up too fast, old man!" Jim told him. "You old folks tend to hurt yourselves when you..."

But the elder Ward had already jumped to his feet and enveloped his son in a long and emotional bear hug. Finally, he pushed the young SEAL away and growled, "Mr. Ward, when a senior officer tells you to be somewhere at a specific time, he expects you to be there. Not to leave him stuck cooling his jets while you show up at your convenience. If you are ten minutes early you are twenty minutes late."

Jim Ward snapped to attention. "Sir! Yes, sir! No excuse, sir!" he rattled off. Then he latched onto his father again in another bear hug. "But blame it on the ground crew at San Salvador who couldn't figure out how to remove the chock from under the front gear. That's what I get for flying commercial, you know."

Only then did the two step apart. "Dad, it's great to see you. How's Mom?"

"She's fine, if a little miffed that she's home grading midterms while I'm out here enjoying life with you. She did give me explicit instructions to order you not to miss Sunday's family Zoom call."

Jim suddenly looked worried.

"You sure you were supposed to tell her about this trip?"

"Don't worry. Flying out to meet you for a short visit makes a pretty good cover for whatever this little trip is all about in the first place. She's been around the block enough times to know not to press the point. And I'm not breaking secrecy when I tell you I haven't the foggiest what this is all about."

"Dad, speaking of which, is there anything about our meeting with Li that would raise any outside interest?"

Jon Ward shook his head. "'Outside interest?' No. Not that I know of. But as you know better than most, you can never be certain with that particular lady. Why do you ask?"

"Nothing I can really put my finger on, but my old Spidey senses have been setting off some alarms. I could've sworn that I was being followed at SFO. Then a Toyota panel van tailed my cab all the way up the 101 to here." Jim stepped to the window and peered through the gap in the curtains. "Yep. You see that pair hanging out by the UPS Store across Sutter? That's the same pair of dudes from the airport."

Jon Ward took his son's place at the window and glanced out. A couple of guys, pretty much nondescript in every way, leaned against the front bumper of a van double-parked on the busy street. They appeared to only be smoking, joking around, just killing time. But never losing sight of the club's front entrance.

"Got 'em," Jon Ward confirmed. "Go change clothes and make sure you have a ballcap to cover that blond mop of yours. Meet me in the lobby in five minutes."

Once downstairs, the manager obligingly led them out the back way, down to the health club that occupied much of the building's bottom floor. From there, the pair emerged onto Mason Street, around the corner and a half block down from the club's main entrance. They casually walked a couple of blocks down the steep hill. At Geary, they turned left and strolled leisurely over to Union Square where they hopped onto a cable car that was heading back up the hill on Powell. Anyone watching who might have seen the pair leave the club and followed them as they walked down the hill would now be left behind as the father-son team made use of one of the "City by the Bay's" oldest means of transportation.

As usual, the cable car was crowded with a mix of tourists and locals. The Wards stood on the runners and clung to handholds as the car climbed back up the steep side of Nob Hill. Then, as the vehicle swung around the curve onto Washington, they hopped off and headed down toward Chinatown. From there, they played tourist, wandering in and out of shops, taking in the sights, sounds, and smells, but always keeping an eye out for anyone taking even a modicum of interest in them. The mass of jostling humanity filled the sidewalks and spilled out into the streets, making it near impossible for anyone to maintain a tail on the two Navy men.

After an hour of aimless wandering, there was still no sign of followers, nor did anyone seem to take any special notice of the Wards. They walked a block down Kearny and right into Sam Wo's Restaurant.

They were immediately greeted by the maître d', a very officious-looking Chinese gentleman dressed in an elaborately embroidered rose-colored mandarin jacket.

"Esteemed sirs, welcome. Honorable Madam Li awaits you in the private dining room."

As he turned to lead them up the broad stairs to the second floor, the two shot each other a questioning look. Neither of them had said a word upon entering the crowded first floor, teeming with tourists and San Franciscans lining up for a meal or takeout at the landmark restaurant. Yet the maître d' had recognized them and was now guiding them past patrons and full tables of diners to their meeting with Li Minh Zhou.

The second floor was almost as crowded as the first, but was much more richly decorated, in keeping with its reputation as one of the very few five-star Chinese restaurants in America. The maître d' led them past all these seated guests as well to a shadowy alcove in the back of the large room. There, hidden in the heavy teak paneling, was an entrance to a small elevator. The man motioned the Wards inside, then hit the up button, bowed, and stepped back out of the elevator as the door slid shut.

As they were silently lifted upward, Jon Ward noticed his son tense and assume a defensive position, ready for whatever might greet them when the door opened. The SEAL had been trained to always be prepared to take on anything when in a situation where he had little control. And this had suddenly become just that.

But when they stopped and the door opened, no attackers waited for them. Instead, they were looking out on a small, sumptuously decorated covered terrace. Beyond, the Hilton and the Transamerica Pyramid loomed over them to the east while Chinatown stretched out to the north. The terrace was delicately lit with lanterns that swayed gently in a breeze off the bay and gave the scene a warm, welcoming glow.

Li Minh Zhou gave them a sincere, welcoming smile as she rose from her seat in an overstuffed banquette and glided over to greet the Wards.

"I am so glad that you could come to my little unassuming establishment," she told them, waving her hand toward the restaurant below them. Then, in turn, she warmly hugged the admiral and the SEAL and bussed each on his cheek. Jon Ward noticed she may have lingered just a bit longer in her embrace of his son. And the two of them did exchange a quick glance as they parted that was not necessarily all business.

One thing was for certain. Jim Ward was mesmerized by the woman's beauty. He was uncharacteristically quiet, still searching for an opening line, as she guided them back to the banquette.

Then, without notice, two men stepped from the darkness and stood on either side of the low table. Jim Ward again froze in a defensive position as his dad simply stared in disbelief. It was the pair from the white van on Sutter Street.

"Relax, Jim. I think you may already have seen the Chin brothers, even if you haven't been properly introduced." Her lilting voice and slight smile were just a bit sardonic. "John and his brother Don are in my employ. They were supposed to covertly watch over you while you are here, but you seemed to have given them the slip. I would request that you allow them to do their jobs and protect you for the rest of your stay." The smile faded. "You must understand that there are forces at play now that are very dangerous and very deadly."

As Li and the Wards slid into their seats at the table, the Chin brothers slipped out the back and were replaced by the sommelier. He poured glasses all around. Li swirled the pale flaxen-colored liquid, sniffed it, and took a small sip.

"Chalk Hill Chardonnay 2018. A truly great appellation," she almost sighed. "I just love the Sonoma Valley wines. Long on the fruit notes and almost no oakiness. So much more character than the Napa ones, don't you think?"

"I'm afraid I haven't had a chance to become a wine snob just yet," Jim Ward, having found his voice, noted. He took a sip of the wine. "Sailor bars don't typically have a well-stocked wine cellar. But this is some good stuff."

"For once I agree with this roughneck," Jon Ward added, tipping his glass toward Li. "I'm usually a Cab guy, but this is very nice."

Li took another taste of the wine, savored it, and was quiet for a moment.

"I took the liberty of arranging dinner for us all. I hope you like duck." Both men nodded. "Now, I fear that we must speak of business. Please do not have any concerns for security here. This restaurant is mine and the security systems are better than yours at Naval Intelligence, Admiral Ward. Now, the information that I must share with you is going to cause some serious problems on several levels. There are a couple of major areas. First off, the Chinese thrust into Vietnam is only a ploy. A diversion. They will drive down to the vicinity of Vinh and then they will stop. The country is only about sixty kilometers wide there, so they can easily set up a defense perimeter. But the intention is to draw all the world's attention to Vietnam. Then they will produce evidence—totally concocted and supported by faked corroboration—of Vietnamese provocation as the Chinese plead self-defense. Meanwhile, the real thrust will be across the straits directly at Taiwan. PLAN is already secretly gathering their amphibious troop strength even as we speak. And as the world postures and makes speeches in the United Nations, they will strike the real intended blow, the one we have so long dreaded."

Jon Ward listened, considered her dire words, then took a drink of the wine without really tasting it. "Li, does the Chinese High Command really believe that they can pull off a surprise invasion? Even with the distraction of this incursion into Vietnam? Don't they think somebody might notice?"

Li nodded. "Yes, but that brings us to the most dangerous part of this discussion. At least for you, Admiral. It seems the Chinese have people in their employ—or in their debt, it really doesn't matter which—and they present a serious threat. These people are in place at a very high level within your government. And they are in positions in which they would have the ability to prevent, or at least stall, any US intervention once the assault on Taiwan begins." She paused, as if choosing her words very carefully. "I must emphasize that these are very dangerous people. They will stop at nothing if they even have a hint that they or the success of their mission should become threatened. You need to be very, very careful in how you handle this threat."

Jon Ward was now sitting up straight, listening to her every word. Jim looked at her with his head slightly cocked, already trying to connect what she was sharing with what he might possibly become involved with in trying to prevent it.

The admiral finally spoke. "I assume you will tell us more. A hell of a lot more. The more we know, the better we will be able to deal with the internal threat. And somehow prevent the intentions against..."

Then there was movement in the shadows, in the direction of the elevator. Li Minh Zhou remained relaxed while the two Wards tensed. But it was only a waiter, pushing a cart carrying dishes and mounds of steaming food.

Ψ

Jim Shupert carefully checked the submarine's dead reckoning position against their bottom sounding. He mentally corrected himself. He was actually confirming *George Mason*'s estimated position. They had been doing their best to compensate for set and drift, so it really was an EP rather than a DR position. The sounding checked with the chart, but since the floor of the Celebes Sea was pretty much pan-flat around here, that really did not mean much.

"Nav, we about at the twelve-mile limit?" Jackson Biddle asked from his position at the command console. "Skipper wants us on the roof with our flag flying before we cross into Malaysian waters."

"Si Amil Island should be at fifteen miles, bearing two-seven-zero, XO," Shupert answered. "Give or take five miles," he added, but under his breath.

The voyage across the Celebes Sea had been a real test of the young navigator's nerves and resourcefulness. Trained in the techniques and technology of modern electronic navigation, he was most comfortable when he knew where his boat was all the time, plus or minus a couple of meters. Now, denied all of that technology, he felt like he was no better off than Ferdinand Magellan's pilots had been when they first crossed this water while circumnavigating the globe more than five hundred years before. Shupert had even tried to do some celestial navigation the previous night, but storm clouds totally obscured any useful heavenly bodies.

"I don't see anything that bearing," Jackson called out. "How confident are you?"

"*Sailing Guide* says it's uninhabited," Shupert answered. "Wouldn't expect it to be visible. It only has a low hill. So, at fifteen miles, our little island would still be below the horizon."

"Mr. Wilson, come around to course north." Biddle directed his command to Bill Wilson, the officer of the deck. "And prepare to surface."

"Course north, prepare to surface, aye, sir," the young watch officer repeated.

Biddle turned his attention back to Jim Shupert and the navigation problem while Bill Wilson led his team through the process of changing course and getting everything ready to surface the submarine.

"Nav, you have the piloting party ready for navigating in restricted waters?" he asked as he glanced down at the ECDIS display.

"XO, we've pretty much had it manned for the last two days," Shupert answered. "All we need to do is to set up for radar nav and for visual inputs from the photonics mast. It'll sure be nice when we're able to see where we're going for a change."

"Yeah. Pray we don't find out that we're surfacing off Fort Lauderdale. Let's take a look at the track into our anchorage," Biddle said. "You have the Move Ord?"

The pair then became so occupied checking the Movement Order against the planned track that they barely heard the 1MC announcement: "Surface! Surface! Surface!" Or noticed the deck incline as the boat turned toward the wavetops.

The boat's commanding officer, Brian Edwards, smelling strongly of sunscreen and uncharacteristically wearing a ball cap and dark shades, had been standing back, watching his crew work. Now he leaned over to study the nav chart. "Looks reasonably straightforward. Pretty much a straight shot. Dog leg to port after we clear the Palau Salakan reefs. Nav, keep us off the coral heads and in the center of the channel if you don't mind. We don't want to scratch up the *GM*."

Shupert nodded. "Will do, Skipper."

Edwards turned to Biddle. "XO, we still anchoring out? I would feel a lot more welcome snugged up alongside *Chesty Puller* than swinging on the anchor."

Biddle held up his laptop. "I've been texting with squadron ops about that. The *Puller* parking lot is full, I'm afraid. They got a couple of LCSs tied up on her portside and the *Carson City* on her starboard." Biddle noted his skipper's questioning look. "*Carson City*'s one of those fast transport catamarans. Faster'n a rocket on skids. The thing can haul a whole bunch of crap, but she still has a shallow draft. That kind of canoe is right handy to have out here for haulin' Marines and their gear."

Edwards shook his head. "Guess it's the price we pay when we use the Marines' travel lodge as a sub tender. Did the 'Pork Chop' get the LOG REQ message out?"

"Skipper, you take care of getting us into port safely. I'll handle the admin," Biddle chided Edwards. "Pork Chop" was Navy slang for the ship's supply officer and a LOG REQ was a logistics request message, much like a detailed shopping list for the submarine's supply needs, everything from fresh veggies to spare parts. "Chop's message went out, along with the engineer's voyage repair request, both as soon as we surfaced."

Edwards laughed. "As long as there's real salad for dinner tonight. I've had all the three-bean salad that I can handle for a bit." He turned to Shupert. "Nav, relieve Bill of the deck long enough for him to get up to the bridge. I'll be on the bridge working on my tan."

Edwards climbed the long vertical ladder up to the bridge, emerging into a brilliant tropical afternoon. The turquoise sky merged with the deeper azure sea off at the horizon. The earthy smell of tropical rainforests wafted along on the slight breeze that rippled the otherwise flat surface.

He could barely make out the faint green smudge of an island far off on the starboard bow. That would be Palau Bohayen. The little islet marked the eastern entrance to the deep channel leading up to Palau Maiga and the beginning of the shallow coral reefs that would tear the bottom out of any ship foolish enough to venture in that direction. The Palau Bum Bum, still over the horizon to the northwest, formed a large part of the western barrier.

The waters were dotted with lepa-lepas, the unique half dugout and half plank-constructed boats indigenous to Borneo and the southern Philippines. To Edwards they seemed awfully rickety to be venturing out into open waters, but the Sama Dilaut people had been living on these vessels for centuries. They appeared to take no notice whatsoever of the big, black visitor as they continued to fish.

As the *George Mason* headed into the narrow channel between the Selaken and Bodgayan Reefs, Edwards could see the high gray sides of the *Chesty Puller* anchored just to the west of Palau Maiga. The submarine's anchorage would be half a mile south.

"Mr. Wilson, you all set for an anchoring?" he asked his young officer of the deck.

"Yes, sir. I think so," came the tremulous reply. "Never anchored before."

"Don't feel all alone." Edwards laughed. "None of the rest of us have either. Not something we do all that often. But there's a first time for everything, right? Anchor ready for letting go?"

"Yes, sir. Water depth in the anchorage is forty-seven feet, so I ordered a snubbing scope of fifty fathoms." The anchor may dig into the bottom, but it was really the weight of the anchor chain that kept the ship in place. A sailor's rule of thumb was to use six feet, or one fathom, of chain for every foot of water under the keel.

"Good," Edwards approved. "That much chain on the bottom should keep us in one place. Just remember to be backing down when you let go the anchor." The anchor on *George Mason*, as on most US submarines, was stowed in an after ballast tank. Backing down stopped the ship and also prevented the anchor chain from inadvertently hitting the lower rudder. It also set the anchor into the sandy bottom.

"Bridge, Nav," the 7MC blared. "Recommend turn to course two-six-zero. This is our approach track. Letting go bearing is on Selakan Dive Lodge pier, bearing one-five-seven. Recommend coming to all stop."

Wilson grabbed the 7MC mike and ordered, "Left full rudder, steady course two-six-zero. All stop."

Edwards nodded. So far, so good. Then the captain watched as the *George Mason* slowly swung around until it was aimed at a wall of coral reefs a mile directly in front of them. Even with an "All Stop" bell rung up, the boat still had enough momentum that it could glide forward onto the reef if things went wrong.

"Pier bears one-seven-eight," the Nav called over the 1MC.

The boat glided forward.

"Pier bears one-seven-one."

"Better get the COB and line handlers topside," Edwards suggested to Wilson. "We can expect the commodore and a slew of workers as soon as we get anchored."

Bill Wilson passed the order down to the control room. Jackson Biddle replied, "Officer of the Deck, Skipper, it'll be a couple of minutes for the COB. He spilt a cup of coffee and is changing into a clean uniform for our visitors. Line handlers standing by to lay topside. Opening the upper hatch."

Edwards laughed. "Wouldn't want to get cross-wired with the COB the rest of the afternoon. I suspect he is not going to be in a good mood."

"Pier bears one-six-five."

"Bridge, Co-pilot, lockout hatch indicates open."

"Pier bears one-six-one."

Edwards glanced back to the main deck. The lockout hatch had indeed swung open and personnel were climbing topside.

"Pier bears one-five-seven."

"Back one-third," Bill Wilson ordered. "Let go the anchor."

"Answering back one-third," the pilot answered.

"The anchor is let go. Snubbing scope is fifty fathoms," the anchor watch reported from the engine room.

"All stop."

The *George Mason* came to a halt, rolling easily in a gentle swell.

"Request to secure the main engines," Bill Wilson asked.

Edwards shook his head. "Let's keep the mains online and warmed until we're sure that the anchor is holding. Make sure the nav is plotting our position every three minutes, too. And good job."

The sub's anchor had hardly settled on the bottom when Edwards spied the commodore's launch churning away from the *Puller* and then heading arrow straight for the *George Mason*. Joe Glass was standing in the stern, watching the whole anchoring evolution through binoculars. No doubt Glass, the former submarine skipper for whom Brian Edwards had once served as executive officer, would have a critique ready with pertinent comments highlighted by the time Edwards climbed down from the bridge to greet him.

"Welcome to Borneo!" Glass yelled through cupped hands. "Permission to come aboard?"

"Glad to be here," Edwards called back. "Permission granted. I'll meet you in my stateroom as soon as we're sure the anchor is holding."

"Not a bad idea, Skipper! Don't need this sewer pipe drifting around our nice, safe harbor."

Master Chief Oshley and a couple of his line handlers snugged the commodore's launch alongside the big submarine. Oshley grabbed Joe Glass's hand and helped him up onto the *George Mason*'s smooth, round deck.

"Welcome aboard, Commodore," Oshley offered. "It's really good to see you again, sir." It was clear the chief's greeting was sincere.

"Great to see you again, too, COB," Glass responded with equal sincerity, smiling. The two sub sailors had spent some harrowing times together in previous service. "Hope you're keeping this bunch straight. And sorry about having you anchor out."

"No worries, Commodore. I reckon the skeeters will find us just as easy over here."

"Most likely. Something tells me you and your guys won't even notice. The next few days are going to get real damn busy."

7

Vietnamese Navy Captain Tranh Vu frowned as he peered through the *Bà Rịa-Vũng Tàu*'s periscope. He had spent almost a week deliberately maneuvering his *Kilo*-class submarine up through the South China Sea and into his assigned position two miles off Hainan Island. And then another tense week circling China's southernmost provincial island trying to see what was there. At times, he dared to slip close to each of the dozens of small harbors that dotted the island's shores. That painstaking observation had gradually painted a very disturbing—and somewhat puzzling—picture.

Hundreds—probably thousands—of blue-painted and armed fishing vessels filled every available space along the piers in most of the harbors.

Tranh was very familiar with the Chinese People's Armed Forces militia ships. The distinctive blue armada had been rudely shoving his people off their historic fishing grounds for years now, ignoring diplomatic objections and international censure, and dealing brutally with those who dared resist such blatant trespass. But why were they all now in port, tied up alongside the piers? Why were they not out somewhere in the South China Sea, doing what they usually did, forcefully staking claim to a bit of sea that had been harvested by the Vietnamese for centuries?

Tranh decided that the answers to his questions required that he slip in a little closer to one of those ports. That would be the only way he could figure out what was going on. But it also raised the risk that his submarine might be detected. Remaining hidden as he observed the situation was his top priority, and his number two directive from his commanders for this mission. Number one was finding a Chinese warship worthy of sinking and proceeding to do just that.

Finally, he decided drawing closer was worth the risk.

Tranh lowered the periscope and stepped over to the chart table. Yubao Harbor, on the backside of Hainan Island from open sea, looked to be the perfect place to investigate. The small harbor was located on the Chengmai Peninsula, a skinny finger of land jutting out from the main island. That made it easier for them to get close with less chance of detection. And since the peninsula was located on the Qiongzhou Strait, it was unlikely the Chinese had the sophisticated monitoring or defense systems that a port facing the open South China Sea or the Tonkin Gulf would have.

By midnight, Tranh had maneuvered the *Bà Rịa-Vũng Tàu* to a position only a little over a kilometer from the small coastal town. Only then did he dare raise the periscope and shift its optics to high power. Sure enough, a pair of the militia ships was tied up on either side of the lone, brightly-lighted pier. He could easily see troops pulling their gear from transport vehicles queued up along the coastal road. Each soldier was bringing what looked like full loads down to the piers to be placed aboard the ships while other trucks were having canvas-covered cargo unloaded. Cargo that could almost certainly be the requirements for an invasion force.

Tranh scratched his chin, more perplexed than ever. If the troops were bound for the fighting already taking place in his home country, would not the Chinese simply truck them in by the fastest and most direct route, down the highway where they had already cleared a path across the breach at the border, and deeper into Vietnam? Using the militia ships as transports would be slower and subject to interdiction. None of this made sense.

Then the captain had a sudden realization. Perhaps they were not reinforcements heading for Vietnam at all. But if that were the case, then where were they headed?

Tranh was at a loss. Fortunately, however, understanding Chinese military strategy or intent was not his job. He would report what he had observed. Let the generals in Ho Chi Minh City figure out its meaning.

But first, he would need to steam far enough away from Hainan to radio home. Then he could begin looking for that worthy target.

Ψ

"Conn, Sonar, new contact bearing three-one-six on the sphere. Designate Sierra Four-Two." ST 1 (SS) Paul Warsky, the on-watch sonar supervisor on the submarine *Boise*, studied his screen intently as he spoke into the 21MC microphone. The contact trace slowly developed on the BQQ-10 screen, but it was still a very weak signal, right at the edge of even being detectable. The dot track looked like a zero-bearing rate, so it was either distant or coming right at them. Right now, he could not tell which.

It was really unusual that the initial detection had popped up on the sphere and not on the towed array. The sphere was a large ball of over one thousand hydrophones at the very front of the submarine. It was a very accurate fire control sonar. But since it operated in the mid-frequencies, its detection range was limited to a few thousand yards unless the contact was very noisy. On the other hand, the towed array, a long line of hydrophones towed far behind the submarine, should have been much more likely to make an initial detection on a ship or submarine because it operated in the very low frequency range, a bit of the spectrum that carried for great distances in water. Somehow, the target Warsky had named Sierra Four-Two had managed to avoid detection on the towed array but popped up instead on the sphere. The sonarman scratched his head as he tried to not only figure out what this mysterious contact could be but also why it had been detected bassackwards.

"Sonar, Conn, aye." Lieutenant Bob Bland, the officer of the deck, acknowledged the target report over the 21MC. "Classification?"

Warsky shook his head. He knew the question would be coming. He also knew that the young lieutenant, who was standing on the conn, could not see his headshaking.

"No idea. I have never heard anything like it before."

"Sonar, coming right to open track and getting a leg on this guy," Bland countered. Simple truth was, they needed to find out what this guy was and where he was, but without being detected or run over in the process. Bland turned to the helmsman and ordered, "Right full rudder, steady course zero-two-zero."

The helmsman swung the rudder over and answered, "Rudder is right full, steady course zero-two-zero, aye," as the gyro repeater swung around to steady up on a northeasterly course.

"Got something interesting, Mr. Bland?" The boat's captain, Chet Allison, asked the obvious question as he stepped over to the sonar display. "Think you might want to tell me about it?"

"Just getting ready to call you, Skipper," the young lieutenant quickly responded. "We have a new contact, Sierra Four-Two, on the sphere." Bland glanced at the sonar screen. "Currently bears three-three-one. Sonar is unable to classify so far. Petty Officer Warsky is stumped and you know that never happens. I'm coming right to open track and starting TMA on this guy."

The *Boise* CO said nothing, but he watched the track on the sonar display develop as the boat swung over to the new course. The waterfall display was very weak. There was no doubt now, though, that it was a legit contact.

Allison did a little quick mental math. The way the bearing was changing, this contact—whatever the hell it was—had to be close. Certainly inside three thousand yards. The thing also had to be very, very quiet if it had managed to sneak in that close to *Boise* before the submarine's sonar had detected its presence.

Allison stuck his head through the nearby sonar room door, bypassing the microphone to ask a very pointed question. "Warsky, any chance this guy could be a submerged contact?"

Warsky screwed up his face and smacked his forehead. Hard.

"That's what I was missing! Yes, sir! He does sound an awful lot like our *Orca* UUV. Real quiet like."

The *Orca* was one of the Navy's large unmanned underwater vehicles, a drone submarine used for reconnaissance and other clandestine missions.

The passive broadband operator suddenly called out, "Contact zig. He's coming around to point us." Just as he finished the report, the WLR-9 acoustic intercept receiver began loudly alarming. "Damn! He's going active on us. Twenty-five kilo-hertz, plus forty SPL. He has us cold."

The mystery contact had just locked its own active sonar on *Boise*. Whoever or whatever it was, it knew exactly where the submarine was in the ocean and could attack if it was so inclined. Then it became terrifyingly clear it was so inclined.

"Torpedo in the water!" Warsky yelled. He clutched his headphones to his ears, as if that might help him track the warshot better. He stared in disbelief at his screen. "Jesus! The son of a bitch just shot at us!"

"Ahead flank!" Allison called out, working to keep his voice calm. As if this were only another drill. "Left full rudder, steady course south. Make your depth eight hundred feet."

The big boat heeled over hard as it accelerated and turned. It was swinging around sharply to the new course. Allison could clearly hear the reactor coolant pumps shift to fast speed.

"Man battle stations, torpedo!"

Immediately the general alarm klaxon pealed throughout the submarine, calling the crew to battle stations. If the sudden sharp maneuvering had not let those men know that something serious was happening, that raucous sound certainly did. Drill or real, it did not matter. Men were going to where they were supposed to be in one hell of a hurry.

"Launch two evasion devices. Launch the CRAW from each dihedral!"

Both the evasion devices and the CRAWs were stored in watertight launchers in a pair of dihedral fins just below the stern planes on the boat's exterior hull, ready to be launched in seconds.

The evasion devices were designed to try to deflect any torpedo rushing toward them by filling the water with noise. Noise that would confuse the weapon's guidance mechanisms and, hopefully, send the torpedo on a wild goose chase off in left field until it ran out of fuel and sank to the bottom, harmless.

The Compact Rapid Attack Weapon—or CRAW—was a small, short-range torpedo. It had been specifically developed and implemented for just this situation, an up-close and personal dogfight. The CRAW was needle-like, only about six inches in diameter and seven feet long. Its lithium hydroxide-powered steam turbine could drive it at better than sixty knots and its control systems could turn the little dart on a dime. But it also had short legs, limited range. And its small, shape-charged warhead really had no hope of taking out a full-sized submarine. It could, however, give one a very bad headache.

It did have enough of a fist to take out a torpedo. They could only hope they could punch squarely in the nose the one that was rapidly spinning toward them. So far as Chet Allison knew, the CRAW had never been employed in a live situation, only drills. That was about to change.

Bland slapped the buttons on the evasion launcher panel and called out, “Evasion devices launched. Both CRAWS launched.”

“Incoming torpedo lost in the baffles,” Warsky called out. The deadly weapon was now in *Boise*’s sonar blind spot, behind the boat. “Evasion devices and CRAWs lost in the baffles. No good bearing on any contact.” Their own recently launched weapons were invisible to them, too. “Active sonar on WLR-9 bears three-five-five, SPL plus forty.” That confirmed the shooter was still out there, tracking them on active sonar. No way to know, though, if he was going to throw a follow-up punch.

All of a sudden, lots of things were dancing around out there in the sea near the submarine, in places that their sonar could not keep up with it.

“Come left to course one-two-zero,” Allison ordered sharply. “That should at least put him on the edge of the baffles. Make tubes one and two ready in all respects, set submerged tactics.”

It was time to cock their own gun, even as they ducked and dodged. Now they only needed to get a bead on something to shoot at if they could. If they had time. If the incoming weapon did not find them first.

The klaxon had barely quit bonging when the battle stations fire control party rushed into control and manned their stations. The boat’s exec, Henrietta Foster, looked as if she had just been awakened from a deep sleep as she joined the others in the control room. She slipped on a set of headphones and began studying the tactical picture all around her.

“Regain incoming torpedo, bearing three-five-five. Drawing aft!” Warsky shouted, the tension now heavy in his voice. “Regain one CRAW merging on the same bearing. Regain second CRAW bearing three-five-nine. Losing all contacts back into the baffles.”

The two little weapons were chasing the torpedo. Could they possibly intercept it? The *Boise* crew could not tell. The drama was once again playing out in their own shadow.

"Launch two more evasion devices. Steer course one-zero-zero," Allison ordered, again speaking precisely, fighting the urge to shout. He had to be in control. And he had to be understood. Turning to Foster, the captain said, "XO, I'm going to spiral around, keeping that incoming weapon just on the edge of the baffles until we have come around enough to find the bastard that shot at us. I intend to light him up with active and then stick an ADCAP up his ass."

"Sounds like a good plan to me," Foster said as she stepped back to the ECDIS table. "I'll steer you around so you are four thousand yards out from where he launched. Weps reports tubes one and two are ready in all respects, submerged tactics verified."

In the middle of her speech, the messenger handed Foster her thermos mug of coffee. "Here, ma'am. You'll fight better with this."

What the messenger said was true. The XO nodded and took a big swig, but she never took her eyes off the ECDIS display.

"Incoming torpedo bears three-zero-zero, drawing into the baffles," Warsky called out. "Torpedo has shifted modes. Looks like he is range gating." His voice, bearing bad news, shifted up an octave. The torpedo was close enough to *Boise* that it had just gone into final attack mode. They needed to do something fast to avoid this ambush. But it could well be too late already. The next update was even more dire. "He's blown past the last evasion devices, Captain. First CRAW on the same bearing."

Without hesitation, Allison ordered, "Launch two more evasion devices. Steer course zero-eight-zero. And grab something solid in case—"

The stunning explosion shook the boat mercilessly. It was difficult to imagine such a big chunk of metal could be jolted so radically sideways and downward. A fine dust and bits of insulation immediately floated in the air. Anyone not clinging to something solid was tossed about the compartment where he was working, thrown hard against a bulkhead or to the deck.

Chet Allison managed to stay upright. He shook his head and looked around the control room, bracing for a wall of water that was almost certainly about to hammer into him.

There was nothing.

"The CRAW got him!" Warsky whooped. "Damn! The CRAW got him!"

Allison blinked and nodded. His ears were still ringing from the explosion. He shook his head to try to clear the sudden fog, then ordered, "Ahead one-third, come to course north. XO, find out what kind of damage we have."

They had to move. As soon as their attacker figured out that he had missed, he would surely shoot again. The next bullet might already be in the water. It was past time to go on the offensive.

"Now let's get that SOB! Sonar, line up to go active."

He watched as his team picked themselves up off the deck and got back into the game. Then he glanced over at Foster.

As usual, she was one step ahead of him. Also as usual, she had the correct take on the situation.

"Best bearing to the shooter two-nine-zero," she called out before the skipper could even ask. "Recommend come around to point him."

Allison nodded. "Sector search around bearing two-nine-zero," he said, completing the order to sonar. "Mr. Bland, come to course two-nine-zero."

Meanwhile, Foster read from a list that she had been hastily scribbling in grease pencil on the plotting table as reports came in from different parts of the submarine.

"Captain, maneuvering reports number one turbine generator tripped off mechanically during the explosion. Reset and back up online. One and two reactor coolant pumps restarted in fast speed. Number three air conditioning plant tripped off. Reset and back online. Chief Butler has a broken arm. He's being evacuated to the wardroom. Sonar reports loss of the TB-34 towed array. Zero continuity. Getting reports of various cuts, scrapes, and bruises but nothing else serious. *Boise* is ready to fight."

Allison was about to thank her when the speaker crackled.

"Captain, Sonar. Ready to go active. Sector search around two-nine-zero, max power."

"Sonar, go active," Allison ordered as he shifted the control room sonar display to the active display. If the aggressor thought the American submarine was gone, he had just gotten a big surprise. The captain watched the screen as the trace developed. At first, there was only a lot of junky backscatter from close to the boat. Then only black as the trace developed. Finally, a tiny dot appeared, almost too small to even be considered a return. The captain slewed the cursor over and read out the range and bearing. The dot was at bearing three-one-two and at a range of forty-five hundred yards.

"Conn, Sonar, solid active return on Sierra Four-Two. Captain, this guy is tiny. He can't be more than sixty feet long. Classified as a UUV."

"A UUV with a nasty stinger," Allison replied. No human on the attacking vessel to detect *Boise*'s sonar and realize its target ship still floated. But a computer chip on the unmanned vessel was now aware and likely executing lines of code to duck and cover. "Firing point procedures on Sierra Four-Two, tube one. Tube two will be the backup tube."

Lieutenant Bland called out, "Ship ready!"

Henrietta Foster checked the fire control panels and added, "Solution ready!"

FT2 Jim Bosserman made a final check on the weapons systems and reported, "Weapon ready!"

"Match sonar bearings and shoot," Allison ordered.

With a whoosh of high-pressure air, the ADCAP torpedo was shoved out of tube one, on its way toward the small but deadly target. Bosserman checked the signal sent back from the wire-guided torpedo.

"Normal launch. Weapon running normally."

Paul Warsky listened intently to the ADCAP as it dutifully started up its motor and headed off toward the target. Only then did he call out, "Normal launch from sonar."

Henrietta Foster stepped over to where Allison was watching the sonar display. "Too bad we couldn't capture that UUV and haul it back. Whoever it belongs to, it would have been a real intel treasure."

Allison chuckled drily. "You mean like trying to capture a cobra without getting bit? I'll just be glad when that 'intel treasure' is a pile of scrap iron on the bottom of the South China Sea. I think we all know whose it is, too."

"Agreed, Captain. Still, I can't help but think..."

"XO, I'm thinking that our Chinese friends have crossed a real line here, sending out UUVs programmed to shoot to kill. Can't know if it was going to try to take out any submarine it saw in these waters or if it was specifically looking at a US boat. Let's get a message ready to Seventh Fleet to tell them about this and see what they want us to do. Assuming we hit the..."

As if on cue, Bosserman yelled, "Detect! Detect!" Three seconds later came, "Acquisition! Weapon shifted to high speed." Then, immediately, he reported, "Loss of wire continuity."

A few seconds later, Sonarman Warsky joined the chorus with, "Loud explosion on the bearing to Sierra Four-Two. No longer hold Sierra Four-Two on sonar."

He need not have bothered. The blast rattled the fillings of every man and woman on *Boise*.

Ψ

The president of the People's Republic of China, Tan Yong, sat back and listened with a noncommittal expression. The others gathered in the room knew that to mean that he was pleased with what he had heard so far. And that the impassive look was about the only sign of approval any of them were going to get for the bold and complicated plan now playing out in multiple locations around the globe.

At the moment, General Shao Jing was quietly explaining in detail exactly what was taking place with elements of the Chinese army inside Vietnam. His placid tone belied the brutality of what was happening as well as the general's notorious ruthlessness. So far, he reported, the invasion plan was sticking almost exactly to the established timetable. Such precision was vital if the other elements were going to work out as planned. Shao told them that the Fourteenth Army Group had successfully joined up with General Kuijia Siji's Forty-Second Army Group. At that point, they had stopped their relentless southward march, as intended, just below the city of Dong Hai. There, Vietnam's waist narrowed to only a twenty-five-mile-wide stretch of rugged territory between the sea and the Laotian border. Most of those twenty-five miles consisted of mountainous jungle, all but impassible except for a couple of poorly maintained north-south highways. For any tactician studying the invasion from afar, General Shao noted, this would be the obvious location and time for the CCP Army to stop, regroup, and resupply before resuming its brisk charge further south.

Tan Yong showed a rare smile at the general's statement. That was precisely what he wanted the Americans and their allies to think. Now it was time to initiate the next phase.

"Very good, General Shao," he said, instantly bringing the general's brief to a halt, whether he was finished or not. The others in the room, all members of the Central National Security Commission, had worked for—and remained within the good graces of—the president long enough to know when to speak and when to quietly bow off the podium.

"Thank you, President Tan," the general said, gathering his papers and meekly returning to his seat at the big table.

No one cheered. There were no outward signs of excitement or anticipation. But the atmosphere in the room was powerfully and dramatically kinetic.

8

Joe Glass sat in a small chair directly across a tiny table from Brian Edwards, sipping coffee from a mug that was inscribed with the name *George Mason,* as the two submariners casually caught up. The commodore had a fleeting realization. Even with all the great new technologies and capabilities he had observed in his years in the submarine service, a commanding officer's stateroom was still just as cramped as ever. Certainly not what the typical non-submariner would think of when the word "stateroom" was used. Even though *George Mason* was the most modern boat in the fleet, the CO's accommodations were every bit as spartan as those on the *Sturgeon*-class boats he had ridden in the early days of his career.

Glass shook his head and took another sip of coffee. And the coffee was just as black and strong, too. Despite how far submarines had come technologically, some things would never change.

He smiled as he voiced his observations to Edwards, *George Mason*'s CO. "I must be getting old, Brian, reliving old times like that."

"I'd say you're just missing all that glamor and glory, Commodore. Mostly skippering a desk nowadays, right?"

"Maybe so. Maybe so. Okay, back to the problems at hand. We've got too much going on for me to get all nostalgic and teary-eyed." Glass's mood shifted noticeably. "Brian, intel informs me that things around here are getting very interesting. And not in a good way. I understand you've been briefed about Chet Allison, over on *Boise*, right?"

"Yes."

"Then you know he was attacked by some kind of UUV. Chinese, we suspect. And we're damn lucky he and his men are still with us. He's on his way here for repairs and some re-arming. I understand that he needs a new towed array. Oh, and about a hundred and forty pairs of clean undershorts."

The two submariners chuckled as Glass picked up a manila envelope from the little table. He broke the seal and pulled out a plastic shell, popped it open, and then extracted a compact disc. The shell was noticeably marked with red and white diagonal stripes around its edges, meaning its contents were strictly classified. And large red letters on the cover verified it, proclaiming that whatever information was on the disc was "Top Secret – Special Compartmented Information – OP PLAN 2475."

Neither man was chuckling now.

"Brian, things are heating up enough that Seventh Fleet has ordered the preliminaries for OP PLAN 2475 to be implemented. I know you know what that means." He solemnly handed the disc to Edwards. "Even so, brush up on it. Bring your team up to speed. You know who needs to know and who doesn't. Make sure they understand the 'Rules of Engagement' part. And the surveillance implementation plan. We've never gotten this close to engaging 2475 before. It's big boy stuff, as you know, and you and your boat are front line. Let's hope it doesn't come to it this time. But we will be ready."

"We certainly will, Skipper," Edwards confirmed. Neither man noticed he had called Glass "Skipper." Old habits die hard.

"I know. Now, we'll bring you alongside the *Puller* this afternoon to load your mission equipment. I expect that you'll get your OP ORD within twenty-four hours. We need to be ready to go to sea as soon as the mission gear is onboard and checked out. You got any questions?"

Brian Edwards shook his head. "Not right now. Maybe when we get the op orders." He held up the disc. "Might have some when we've digested this, too. You know we won't be bashful about asking. But *George Mason* will be ready to go."

Joe Glass stood awkwardly in the crowded space.

"I knew you would be. Now, if I can remember how to find my way to a hatch and get off this sewer pipe, I gotta get back to the *Puller*. Stan Readly wants to brief me on his plan to do ASW."

Edwards followed Glass out the stateroom door.

"Readly and ASW still don't go together in my mind," Edwards said.

"I know. I'm still trying to wrap my head around Marines doing anti-submarine warfare. But I have to admit that his plan makes a lot of sense and should make coverage of the South China Sea a whole lot better. We just need to work out how to do the coordination and how to get weapons on target. And hopefully before we really need to."

The two stopped at the ladder leading up to the sub's topside deck.

"What does the good colonel have up his sleeve?" Edwards questioned.

Glass glanced around to be sure no sailor was within earshot.

"It seems that the Marines have been working with the underwater weapons folks up at Newport," Glass explained. "They've come up with a deployable fixed sensor system designed specifically for small, advanced bases. The kinds of places where the Marines are typically going into anyhow. And the gear is something the jarheads can set up and tear down quickly." He continued speaking as the two climbed up to the deck. "You remember our old friend, Sam Smithski, from our little adventure down in Exuma Sound a while back?"

"Sure, I do. Got me a head full of gray hair from that episode. Is he supplying us some more of his 'whammo-dyne' gadgets and geeky software?"

Smithski was an acoustic engineer from the Naval Undersea Warfare Center, commonly called NUWC, located in Newport, Rhode Island. His work more resembled the stuff of science fiction. But his help in a tense showdown between the US Navy and the Russian naval fleet had saved the day a few years before. And possibly saved the planet.

"Well, we'll soon know. He's on his way out here, coming in on this afternoon's COD flight from Singapore, and we'll see if he has Buck Rogers and Mr. Spock with him." They were on the deck now, the tropical sun beating down on them, and a humid breeze doing little to help. "We're heading up to Balambangan Island right after we get your berth shift done.

That's where we are setting up the shore terminal for the Marines. Would you like to come along for a little sightseeing? Might be helpful for you to see how the sausage is made."

Edwards grinned. "They serving any of those fruity umbrella drinks up there? I bet I could find my swim trunks and flip-flops somewhere around here."

"Maybe some SPF-85, too. Good chance to work on that submariner's tan."

"I'd love to."

The mood had shifted yet again. Whistling past the graveyard? Glass was still grinning as he headed over to his waiting launch.

Ψ

The big CH-53K King Stallion helicopter's cargo bay was filled with pallets of gear and a platoon of Marines, ready to go. Joe Glass, Brian Edwards, and Marine Colonel Stanton Readly ran across the *Chesty Puller*'s expansive flight deck, clambered aboard, and the chopper's doors quickly slid shut behind them.

As the men found seats and their eyes adjusted to the dark interior, they spotted Sam Smithski, already settled in, studiously cleaning his spectacles and grinning from ear to ear. It was not every day that a NUWC engineer was allowed to escape the confines of the high-tech research and development facility in Newport. Especially all the way to the South Pacific. Smithski was enjoying every second of his grand adventure.

By the time Joe Glass had gotten strapped into his seat, the pilot was spooling up the helicopter's three massive T408 turbines. The giant gray bird promptly lifted off, spun around briskly, and headed northwestward, climbing only high enough to cruise a couple of hundred feet above the wavetops. The pilot kept Borneo's densely forested coast on his left shoulder as he threaded his way just above dozens of small outlying islands. Most were little more than a volcanic rock with a necklace of encircling coral. They could easily see people standing and waving on the few islands large enough to be populated.

At a cruising speed of one hundred and seventy knots, the flight took a little less than two hours. Then the King Stallion flared out and settled down on a broad, sandy beach. The deep-blue South China Sea stretched out toward the setting sun to the west. Balabac Island, at the southwest corner of the Philippines, was just visible across the Balabac Straits to the north. The USNS *Carson City,* a relatively new type of fast expeditionary ship, rode easily at anchor a mile or so offshore. Her boxy catamaran shape caused her to look more like a barge than a ship in the last rays of the setting sun, but she was impressive, nonetheless.

The Marines went right to work unloading the King Stallion. Commodore Glass and the others had had no opportunity to talk on the flight, what with all the noise of the chopper's motors. Glass motioned for Smithski to join him in stretching his legs with a walk along the island's deserted sandy beach.

"Beats Newport in the wintertime, doesn't it, Doc?" Glass asked.

The engineer, as typical, seemed mostly oblivious to his surroundings, even the tropical paradise around them. And anything else besides his sophisticated equipment and the computers that attached to it all.

"What? Oh. Guess so," he answered. "Commodore, all I know is that this is the optimum site to establish our first Marine Expeditionary Forward ASW Sensor Site. Perfect!" He pointed out to the west. "We'll be using a line of our new Lightweight Advanced Deployable System out that way to look into the South China Sea. Good sound channel out that way. Calculations show that we should be able to detect anything running between here and the Spratly Islands with a ninety-five percent confidence interval for detection. That is, assuming a standard Gaussian distribution for noise sources."

Ignoring Glass's quizzical look, the scientist next pointed to the north as he continued his description of his new system.

"And another LADS line up that way. That one works as a tripwire for anything going between the South China Sea and the Sulu Sea. Don't have the same theoretical range on that one, but anyone going through there will have to go right over the top of it. The *Carson City* was easily able to lay both arrays in less than a day. Nice vessel, that one. We should have shore termination done in a couple more hours. Amazingly nimble! And we have every assurance it will be sensitive and highly accurate."

A pair of eleven-meter RHIBs (rigid hulled inflatable boats) were heading in their direction from out at sea, making their way toward the beach, each unrolling a cable over the side. Glass and Smithski watched as the boats ran up on the shore and the Marines pulled the cables up toward where another group of Leathernecks were busily erecting a collection of tents—some of the cargo the CH-53K had brought—placing them just back amidst the tree line. The canvas structures all but disappeared within the vegetation.

"The Sensor Correlation System is the real heart of the MEF-ASS," Smithski went on. "It allows us to analyze data right here at the deployment site. But it also sends that data out over a high-speed digital link. They can see it back at the ASW Center we set up on the *Chesty Puller.* And it will also be available instantaneously at the Theatre ASW Command in Yokosuka. That gives us the capability to make detections at any of these sites. And more importantly, we can vector attacks directly from any one of them as well."

"As usual, I'm impressed as hell, Doc," Glass said. "But won't all this activity out here on a mostly deserted island raise some suspicion with our friends up north?"

Smithski smiled slyly.

"Commodore, in what little spare time the US Navy allows me, I enjoy the hobby of amateur radio. For months now, we've been advertising in the ham radio magazines and websites that we will be conducting what we call a 'DX-pedition' to this island. We do this kind of operation all the time, set up a station here and hams all over the world attempt to contact what we consider a rare new country or island or mountain peak. That tent over there by itself? We really do have a ham radio station operating there, handing out contacts to hobbyists worldwide via the shortwaves. And that operation covers beautifully everything else going on here. If you still remember some of your Morse code..."

"Doubt I'll have time, but looks as if you have, as usual, thought of..."

"Commodore!" On cue, Stan Readly was calling to him from near what Glass had just learned were the SCS tents. "The helo's about ready to lift off. You don't want to miss your ride home. Otherwise, you'll be enjoying MREs for breakfast with the rest of us sandfleas."

After a quick tour and a good look at all the gizmos inside the tents, as well as more dense explanations from Dr. Smithski, Colonel Readly finally escorted Glass and Edwards back to the King Stallion.

"Stan, thanks for the tour. And for saving me," Glass said with a laugh as they double-timed toward the waiting helicopter. "I had forgotten how deep into the technology Sam is and how much he likes to talk about it."

"How could you ever forget that, Commodore?" the Marine responded. "But his stuff could save our bacon one day. Good flight home, men."

Edwards and Glass climbed aboard as Readly walked back toward the tents, shielding his face as the climbing helo raised a cloud of blowing sand.

The full moon had just shown its rim, peeking above the distant watery horizon. Before long, its brightness would erase the canopy of stars over Balambangan Island.

9

The weapons-handling crane lifted a fat yellow cylinder from its shipping cradle on *Chesty Puller*'s main deck and swung it out over the *George Mason*. The crane operator, sitting in his cab fifty feet above the submarine, skillfully guided the Snakehead II Large Diameter UUV onto a complicated-looking cradle that had been carefully bolted to the submarine. The LDUUV was no more than settled onto its cradle when three members of the *George Mason*'s weapons handling party swarmed all over it, firmly securing it to the resting platform. Then the crane again lifted the unmanned submersible along with its attached cradle until it sat vertically, directly above the submarine's tube number ten, the aftermost of the boat's four payload modules.

Chief Jason Schmidt, *George Mason*'s weapons department leading chief, scurried around like a worried mother hen, watching each movement, checking every detail. Getting these LDUUVs safely stowed in the submarine's payload modules without dinging them up, denting the submarine, or getting anyone hurt was his mission this day. Fortunately, this would be the last one they would have to load. The other three were already safely aboard, checked out, and put to bed.

His shirt was sweat-soaked and his rimless glasses were fogged by the dense humidity as Chief Schmidt squatted down to check the alignment of the UUV cradle with the tube's launch rails. He muttered a few colorful sailor phrases in annoyance. He really could not see anything. The rails were obscured. His only option was to reach down with both hands to try to feel if everything was lining up properly. Satisfied that all was ready, he signaled for his team to lower the LDUUV. And held his breath.

"How much longer, Chief?" The weapons officer, LCDR Aston Jennings, had walked up behind Schmidt unnoticed. And his question came just as the final yellow cylinder began slowly descending into the submarine's launch tube.

"Ten minutes to get her down and seated, sir," Schmidt answered. He almost added, "If we don't break this last one," but then thought better of it. No point in jinxing the operation. "Then a couple of hours to hook up the umbilicals and run a complete diagnostic on the system. Assuming everything checks out..." Schmidt looked at his watch and did some quick math. "...twenty hundred tonight."

The LDUUV continued its slow, deliberate descent into the dark tube without incident.

Ψ

It was late on a hot tropical afternoon when the *Boise* was finally safely snugged up against the starboard side of the US Navy's first purposely built expeditionary mobile base vessel, the *Chesty Puller*. The brow was barely down between the ships when Joe Glass charged across to the submarine. He came to a halt at the foot of the brow and, in a tradition as old as the Navy, snapped a salute at the US ensign flying from the jackstaff. Despite his rank, he then requested permission to come aboard.

Henrietta Foster had just climbed out of the nearby hatch and greeted Glass.

"Welcome aboard, Commodore. The captain is wrapping up things on the bridge. He said to invite you down to the wardroom. He'll meet you there in a minute."

Glass smiled but shook his head. "Love to, XO, but I'm afraid I don't have time for sea stories right now. Just pass to him that as soon as he gets things wrapped up here on *Boise*, I would like for him, you, the Nav, and the

Weps to meet me up in my cabin. It's quite the party room, up on the O-2 level, port side, all the way aft."

Foster nodded, her face noncommittal, then turned and headed in the direction of the boat's sail, while Joe Glass charged back across the brow and onto the *Chesty Puller*, the urgency as obvious in his step as it was in his voice.

Ψ

Chet Allison knocked on the door, noticed it was cracked open already, and then entered Joe Glass's expansive stateroom on the *Chesty Puller*, followed closely by the requested members of the *Boise* crew. The impressive compartment was less personal living quarters and actually more of an office/conference room with a small bunkroom and head arranged along the starboard bulkhead. Glass's cluttered old monster of a desk filled most of the port bulkhead, while a large conference table with ten chairs occupied the midships space. A coffee maker sat on a small side table, along with a tray of cups and all the fixings.

"Grab a cup and a seat," Glass said from his position behind his ancient desk. Since he had been promoted off submarines and to shore duty, he had unintentionally begun to emulate many of the habits and quirks of one of his Navy idols, former Chief of Naval Intelligence Admiral Tom Donnegan. Taking his favorite desk with him wherever he was billeted was one of those quirks. If the Navy ever sent him back to subs, he would have a problem. The thing certainly was not regulation for a skipper's stateroom, even if they could get it through the hatch and passageway.

Glass waved Allison and his team toward the conference table as he made a final note on the papers in front of him. Brian Edwards, Jackson Biddle, Aston Jennings, and Jim Shupert—the *George Mason* invitees—already occupied four of the seats. Allison, Henrietta Foster, Jeremy Chastain, and Bob Bland each grabbed a cup, Allison poured each of them a cupful of deeply black joe, and they took seats opposite the *George Mason* group.

"Chet, looks like you've lost some weight," Glass commented. "You dieting or something?"

"Nah," Allison responded. "Just one of the hazards of the job. Getting shot at turns you into a slim, trim, sexy machine."

Foster just shook her head. Glass let the comment drop. Time to end the small talk and get down to business.

Nobody said anything for a moment but the atmosphere in the room was electric. The situation was ratcheting up and they were surely about to find out what their role was in how things were to play out.

Joe Glass got up from behind his desk, grabbed his pile of papers, and stepped over to the head of the conference table.

"Glad you could all get up here this evening on short notice. I know that you all have important work to get done, so let's keep this short and to the point. Brian, from what I understand, *George Mason* should be about ready for underway."

Edwards nodded. "Yes, sir. All four of our new little toys are onboard, checked out, and put to bed. That new celestial nav system is up and checked out, too." He shook his head and pursed his lips. "I admit I still don't understand how that whiz-bang gadget can get a star sighting in broad daylight. As my Nav here tells me, it's 'PFM,' pure frigging magic."

Glass chuckled. Some of the tension was broken. "You and me need to admit it's the twenty-first century, Brian. And the taxpayers have been very generous when it comes to gizmos that help us continue to be a deterrent to the bad guys. Okay, so with final stores load in the morning, you should be good to go. Let's plan on a twenty-two hundred underway tomorrow night. That give you enough time to load beans and weenies?"

Edwards looked at his team. Each gave him a thumbs-up.

"We can make that work, Commodore."

Glass next turned to Chet Allison. "The new TB-34 came in this morning. I was really surprised that damn thing would fit in an Osprey, but it does. We'll be ready to install it as soon as you have divers' tags hung."

"Tags were being hung when we left," Allison answered. "We should be ready for the divers by the time we finish here. Since we had that little set-to out there the other day, we'll need the dihedrals reloaded with CRAWS and evasion devices. And replace the one ADCAP we shot. Then we'll be good to go."

"About that," Glass interjected. "I'm afraid we're going to need to offload all the weapons from your torpedo room except for a couple of self-defense weapons." Glass noticed Allison's frown. "Look, let's move this discussion over to the OP PLAN and your individual OP ORDs and you'll see where we're headed."

With that, he extracted a pair of file folders from the sheaf of papers stacked on the table before him. He passed one file to Edwards and slid the other one over to Allison. Both skippers broke open the seals and quickly scanned the contents. As they finished each page, they passed them to their respective XOs. Glass sat back, sipped coffee, and waited patiently until every person had read each sheet.

"Basically, it lays out like this," Glass explained. "When you get underway, I want you both to dive as soon as you are in deep water. Then make certain that you run over Sam Smithski's hydrophone arrays. Two reasons. That will give us a chance to check them out. And we can delouse both of you at the same time."

The sensitive listening equipment would have a good profile of both submarines and would not confuse them with any other submerged vessels that might appear. Even more importantly, they would also know if either boat was making any noise sufficient enough to give away their presence should they find themselves to be somewhere they were not necessarily supposed to be, doing something they were not necessarily supposed to be doing.

"Brian, since you have a two-day head start on Chet and *Boise*, I want you to do an ASW sweep up between Palawan and the Spratlys. Then your Op Ord has you running over to the Spratlys and launching your pretty yellow toys to implant monitor systems on Fiery Cross, Subi, and Mischief Reefs. All three of these reefs have been greatly enlarged and built up over the last six months and now they have some serious Chinese naval and air installations in place. We've seen sat images but activity in the area has dramatically picked up lately. We need to know exactly what's going on there, preferably before our Chinese friends can pull any surprises out of their hat."

"Boss, that's three fish. I have four LDUUVs aboard," Brian Edwards interrupted. "What's the plan for number four."

Glass took another sip of his coffee before he answered. "That one is a backup. If the first three check out fine, and they're doing what they're supposed to do, then take *George Mason* up to Scarborough Shoals and plant your last plaything there. Don't worry. We won't waste it. We may wish we had a couple dozen more. Anyway, by that time, we should have further tasking for you."

Turning to the *Boise* team, Glass continued the briefing. "Chet, we are loading you up something new. You remember the old Submarine Launched Mobile Mines?"

"You mean those old codgers from the '80s?" Allison asked. "A reused Mark thirty-seven torpedo? It was useless as a torpedo and only moderately more useful as a mine."

"Well, this is a greatly improved SLMM, called, of course, the SLMM-I. New guidance system, command activated, better range," Glass explained. "Best of all, it has an entirely new warhead. The eggheads at NUWC have figured out how to stick an electromagnetic pulse generator on it. You might remember reading about the threat of a high-altitude nuclear explosion creating an EMP—an electromagnetic pulse—that has the potential of frying all our electronics without really damaging anything else. Well, this one uses something called a 'conventional explosively-pumped electromagnetic flux compression generator.' A whole lot smaller boom, but it will absolutely fry any close-by electronics."

Foster raised her hand and questioned, "Commodore, why would they stick that on a mine? The whole idea is to blow the bottom out of a ship, not toast the entertainment system and every microwave within range."

"Good question," Glass responded. "You need to remember that our ships nowadays are almost completely electronically controlled. You zap all the circuits, you take out the whole ship. Nothing left but some worthless floating iron and very few casualties, if any."

Foster nodded. "Okay, that makes sense. I'd say we wouldn't want to be too close when we throw that switch, though."

Glass continued his explanation. "Exactly. That's where the ORCA comes in. The SLMM-I is designed to be launched by an ORCA Extremely Large UUV, but we need a whole bunch of them laid real quick. You have the only torpedo room in the whole Western Pacific that can still handle the SLMM, so you won the lottery."

"Great!" Allison said, not even trying to dim his disgust. "So here we are, going on a war footing, and I get stuck with a load of frigging mines? Ancient technology. No navy in the world uses submarines to—"

"Skipper," Henrietta Foster interrupted. "I'd say they gave us this mission because they figured nobody else could do it. We both know we can. Let's prove *Boise* can do the job."

Allison chewed on his lower lip a moment, then nodded. But he was only partly mollified. "Okay, we'll show them. Commodore, what are the targets?"

Glass smiled. He could identify. Back when he captained a submarine, he, too, may well have bucked up at such a seemingly unglamorous and outdated mission when he was sure he and his boat could do more good—and damage—elsewhere.

"Chet, you may feel better when you find out where you are headed. You are going into Hainan. Your job will be to plug up the PLAN sub base there. It would be like the Chinese coming up the Thames out of Long Island Sound and planting a crop of mines at the end of the piers in New London."

Allison noticeably brightened.

"Besides, these boys are hardly ancient technology," Glass continued. "They tell me that these new SLMM-Is are accurate enough that you can send them right into that tunnel entrance they got there. And then we can command activate them whenever we want to. If we need to. Our Chinese submarine counterparts think they are safe inside that granite mountain of theirs. We'll see. With the help of *Boise*, you and your crew, we'll see."

The room was quiet for a bit. Every man and woman there understood why Chet Allison was initially disappointed in his assigned mission. And appreciated the bit of logic Joe Glass had just employed.

"Or not," Henrietta Foster said, quietly breaking the silence. "Let's hope we never have to find out how much damage we are capable of up there. That just the realization that we could do it will be enough to stop in their tracks whatever those bastards are planning on doing. That they'll finally decide grabbing power does not justify the needless loss of life. Or at least not worth the risk if they know we can and will make them pay the price."

"Amen," Joe Glass said. "Amen."

Ψ

The southbound Taiwan High Speed Rail train pulled out of Wuri Station at precisely 9:30 PM local time. On schedule, as always. The Automatic Train Control system, a complicated swirl of computer code on a server deep in a typhoon-safe structure in a mountainside somewhere outside Taipei, smoothly accelerated the twelve-car bullet train up to speed. Smooth enough so its five hundred weary passengers could settle back comfortably into their seats for the evening ride down the island's flat western coast. Everyone was in a celebratory mood. Tomorrow would be the start of the Moon Festival, not only in Taiwan but throughout most of East Asia. It was considered equal to the fervor associated with the Chinese New Year, a time for family reunions, the fifteenth day of the eighth month on the Chinese calendar. It would be a festive couple of days of feasting, celebrating, and, of course, admiring the bright, full moon. But first, these passengers had to transit the almost eight kilometers of the Baguashan Tunnel, which ran beneath the Wu River and its surrounding marshes.

Once the train was up to cruising speed, stewards began wending their way through the crowded cars, pushing their carts, serving hot meals and cold drinks to the paying customers. Parents quieted excited children and tried to convince babies to nap. Babies who had no idea of the import of the upcoming holiday but nonetheless sensed the excitement of their fellow passengers and were reluctant to sleep. Business travelers had their own method for dealing with the anticipation. They had already started quaffing their pre-dinner drinks as they studied spreadsheets on their tablets or reviewed emails on their phones before they lost signals for a few minutes in the depths of the tunnel.

The crowded train was exactly at the tunnel midpoint, fifty feet beneath the Wu, when all the lights onboard suddenly, without even a flicker or warning, went dark. The only illumination was the screens of the tablets and phones. At the same instant, the emergency braking system slammed the train to an immediate stop. Not the quick but smooth stop it was designed to implement in the unlikely event it should ever be necessary, but a hard, crashing, screeching stop.

The passengers, brutally thrown about the cars by the abrupt halt, and stunned by the plunge into utter blackness, screamed in pain and terror.

After a few seconds, cell phone flashlights began to wink on. The meager luminescence revealed battered people—some not moving—luggage, blood, wreckage, and much confusion. Outside the train cars' broad windows, the tunnel's cement walls reflected back blankly from only a meter away. There was no lighting out there, either.

Slowly, it dawned on the stunned passengers that there was no way to escape the train should that become necessary. No way to get help for those injured by the hard stop. No one to tell the frightened passengers what had gone wrong, what to do. Even the doors at each end of the cars appeared to remain locked.

They were stuck here until someone restored power and got them moving again. That realization caused some to simply sit back, try to stay calm, and wait. The power company, the railway, the military, someone would fix it. But that same realization of their plight caused others to panic and scream even louder for help.

In the confusion and blackness, no one noticed that the massive pumps, used to keep the tunnel dry of the constant seepage of water from the river, had stopped working and, lacking power, were now silent. Without them, water had already begun to slowly fill the sump below the tracks, to rise up to and then above the wheels of the motionless train. The passengers would notice it soon enough, when it started to creep beneath the locked doors at each end of the car, spilling into the aisles and beneath their seats, soaking those injured passengers still lying there.

They had no way of knowing, either, that the sudden loss of power was not limited only to them. Above ground, with the nearly full moon hidden by a heavy cloud layer, it was equally dark. Normally, the brilliant lights around Taichung City could be seen for almost a hundred miles on a clear evening. Now, the entire metropolitan area was shrouded in darkness. The wall of gloom spread northward toward Taipei and south toward Kaohsiung City, too. One after another, every single one of Taiwan's generating plants tripped offline, as if some giant unseen hand was throwing switches in succession. At the same time, backup generators, programmed to immediately come to life and fill much of the void, simply refused to respond to the command. Distribution breakers designed to isolate system faults failed to trip.

The sluice gates guarding the penstocks on Taiwan's dozen massive hydroelectric powerplants slammed shut, starving the hydroelectric turbines of water. That caused the turbines to slow and then stop spinning. But then the floodgates lifted, sending walls of floodwater plunging down normally dry spillways and onto unsuspecting villages below.

The skies above the island quickly devolved into a congested mess of confused airplanes. Every pilot, after the initial expletive shouted in a dozen different languages, vainly asked what to do. Air traffic control had simply disappeared, the frequencies quiet except for frenzied and desperate pleas from flight crews caught in the cluttered approach pattern without instruction. The pilots were forced into a game of high-speed, three-dimensional bumper cars as they used their onboard radars to try as best they could to avoid slamming into the ground or each other.

The two-dozen inbound flights heading for the island's four international terminals simply declared air emergencies, ignored previous routing, and pointed their aircraft toward the closest airports. A couple had fuel enough to aim for the Philippines or Okinawa. Others had no choice but to make for airports on the Chinese mainland.

The forty or so domestic flights that had the misfortune to be in the air faced a similar dilemma. Suddenly, they could see nothing below them but darkness, broken only by the occasional light hooked to some kind of emergency power source. No way to find an airfield since every one of their emergency systems appeared to have failed, improbable as such a thing might be. That meant all the air traffic control radars were sightless, too, so even if the radios were working, the controllers could not guide them to a runway in any kind of safe, orderly sequence.

Most domestic pilots opted for the same solution as did their larger international brethren. They declared air emergencies, reluctantly seeking permission and then diverting to airfields on the mainland. Well before they got close, they picked up unrequested escorts. Fully armed fighter jets from the PLAAF, the Chinese Air Force, ominously shadowed them the whole way. Then, once they touched down and taxied to a designated spot on the airport tarmac, they were immediately arrested, as were the passengers and remainder of the flight crew. No one questioned how the PLAAF managed to scramble that many fighters on such short notice.

A few pilots in their own small planes or corporate craft, low on fuel or reluctant to go to the mainland, opted for emergency water landings. Success varied.

One resourceful director at Chiayi Airport grabbed a handheld radio, used it to direct all the emergency vehicles and every car he could commandeer, and got them into position to illuminate one runway with their headlights. Then he safely guided six planes down with his walkie-talkie before the batteries expired and he was unable to locate replacements.

Of course, the engineers at Taipower, Taiwan's integrated electrical power generation and distribution company, were on the job at once. But they were stymied, and not just by having to operate in darkness until they could manually start backups by flashlight. Once rebooted, the complex, computer-controlled power grid control system refused to respond as the manuals and emergency re-start guides said they should. Or offer any clue as to why it had suddenly rebelled, acting as if it had a mind of its own. The system ignored any commands from its human controllers, including built-in overrides. As frantically as they tried, the engineers could find no way to restore the generators or reconnect the system.

The sun, peeking over the central Chung-yang Mountain Range, finally provided enough illumination to reveal a shadowy scene of devastation and despair spread across the entire island. A few hospitals and several military bases were operating with limited electrical power from emergency diesels. Some radio stations blessed with backup power were returning to the air, but they had few sources of news or information to relay. The police and military, unprepared for such a widespread and seemingly impossible failure, were just getting back up to speed, sending troops and officers out into the larger cities to determine what the priorities were.

Meanwhile, the remainder of Taiwan had reverted to the eighteenth century.

10

Jim Ward was just thinking how proud he was of himself for having made his way up the steep climb through the thick jungle growth and still be barely breathing hard. Then he slipped, and had he not grabbed hold of a thick bush and hung on, he would have been back at the bottom of the hill on his butt and forced to start the climb all over again. Assuming he did not break something vital on the way down. Bad form for the guy who was supposed to be leading this parade.

The steep, mountainous terrain and the wet, rotting vegetation made footing treacherous. It seemed that for every step forward, he was sliding back at least two. A thick, misty rain damped out all sound and hid whatever moonlight that might have filtered down on them. Terrible conditions, but perfect for the operation he was leading.

Once he was sure he was not on a slip-and-slide back down the mountainside, Ward turned and looked behind him. He could barely make out the dozen dim shapes slowly moving up the mountain toward where he still clung to the bush, hoping they had not seen his near catastrophe. Even with his night vision googles and knowing where to expect the team to be, the soldiers were almost invisible.

Jim Ward had spent the last month living out of a crude bivouac high up in the remote mountains of Wutai Township in southern Taiwan. The team that he was now watching consisted of a squad from the Liang Shan Special Operations Company, the Taiwan Army's elite special operations unit. Mixed in were a couple of members of his own SEAL team. His assignment was to develop common operational tactics so that the Taiwanese unit could operate smoothly with the American SEALs should the need ever arise. Rough territory on a moonless and wet night were exactly the conditions to test how successful the training of the Taiwanese soldiers and his SEALs had been so far.

Two nights before, the team had been driven to the road's end somewhere fifty kilometers or so south of where they now trekked near vertically. The assignment was to find and covertly "take out" a high-value communications station located somewhere on a mountaintop at the very head of this watershed. The rest of the Special Operations Company and the remainder of the SEALs were deployed to locate and interdict Ward's team before they got there and did the deed.

Finally, someone caught up with Ward. Master Chief Rex Johnston used a vine to pull himself up to where Ward waited.

"Boss, these guys are good. I'm having a tough time keeping up with them," he whispered so the others would not hear his positive review. And him trying to catch his breath. "How much further to the target?"

"Master Chief, you're just getting long in the tooth," Ward said with a quiet chuckle. "I've seen you climb bigger anthills than this and not break a sweat."

"Maybe so," was Johnston's curt reply.

"The way I've got it figured, we crest this ridgeline, then follow along it up a klick to Maxibaxiu Mountain," Ward explained. "It's the highest piece of real estate around these parts. It's where I'd stick a comms station if I needed to reach out a ways." He checked the time. "We've got two hours to cover that last klick, infiltrate, and take out the station. We need to finish this up before first light so the other team doesn't catch us. Then call for our taxi back home and breakfast."

With that, the young SEAL team commander finally released his grip on the bush and headed on up the muddy mountainside. When he looked up and ahead, he could just make out the dark black ridgeline against the faintly lighter but cloud-covered night sky above him.

It took an additional half hour to traverse the last kilometer to where the ridge joined a broad shoulder of Maxibaxiu Mountain. Then Master Chief Johnston and Tony Martinelli each led a half dozen Taiwanese Special Operators along different trails toward the summit. Surprisingly, they met no opposition along either route.

When Ward walked into the tiny encampment, Jason Hall, the SEAL communications specialist, was waiting. No mock challenge. No attempt to interdict. Something had changed the plan for the drill.

"Skipper, we need to get down off of this molehill," Hall reported. "The whole country of Taiwan has been hit with a major cyber-attack. The bastards took out the entire power grid and that has made a real mess of things."

"Okay. And I suspect another shoe might be about to drop," Ward added.

"Suspect you're right. That Chinese lady friend of yours is at battle stations. She's saying that this is probably the first shot before the ChiComs come charging across the straits with fire in their eyes. She wants us, meaning you, back at the National Security Bureau's command center. A chopper is on the way."

Ward barely had time to collect his thoughts about the beautiful Li Minh Zhou and the intelligence operation she led before the UH-60 Blackhawk popped up over the ridge and quickly settled down on a tiny level space a few hundred meters down the trail from where the SEALs waited. Five minutes later they were airborne and heading northwest toward a mostly dark Taipei.

Ψ

Deng Jiang swiped through the screens on his display as the reports continued to flood in. The Tiān Dēng Caozuo—the Heavenly Lights Operation—was already a resounding success even though it continued to play out as the sun began to rise over Taiwan. As he read and re-read each update, Deng, the Central National Security Commission's cyber warfare expert, allowed himself one of his very rare smiles. The Tiān Dēng Caozuo had been in the works for years. Planning, staging, and deploying the operation had taken untold man-hours of excruciatingly detailed and complicated labor. It had cost billions of yuan, but, of course, with all expenditures carefully hidden, off the books, and buried so deeply that no one would ever dig it up.

And Deng had led it from the start. Now that it had been such a resounding success, he would finally be rewarded. It was a major coup in his quest for more power and a greater voice in the Commission. This operation was only the next step in what he could accomplish against those who would deny his country its rightful leadership role among the nations of the world. Fiddling with national elections and putting small municipal utility services out of whack were merely the beginning.

Deng took special pride in the next screen. Satellite imagery showed the offshore island as nothing more than a darkened mass between the Formosa Strait and the Pacific Ocean. Very few lights illuminated Taiwan's normal gaudily vibrant landscape. Deng had always considered all that luminescence to be little more than bragging on the part of the illegal breakaway nation's leaders. Where was all that capitalistic swagger now?

Other reports were slowly filtering back from Taiwan—or the "Rebellious State," as Tan Yong, the General Secretary, preferred to call it—and widespread devastation was now confirmed. Casualties were still being counted but the dead would certainly number in the thousands. The toll would rise. It would be many days before power was fully restored. Then years before life on the island returned to normal. Some of Deng's code remained deeply entwined in certain algorithms in the island's electrical system to ensure that.

The strike had been so successful that General Shao Jing, the Commission's military expert, had lobbied for an immediate cross-straits invasion. Deng Jiang had supported the general's arguments before the Commission. Their proposal made much sense. Taiwan's electronic defenses and its command-and-control capability were all but absent. Communication was nonexistent or chaotic. The Chinese could claim they had intercepted rumblings that the island-wide outage was merely a smoke screen by Taiwan, an effort to attract naval and air units from China that they knew would rush to aid their brethren in a time of such severe need. But then, when the Taiwanese military and their allies observed ships and aircraft approaching, the Taiwan forces would open fire on them, later claiming that what they were seeing was the long-anticipated invasion. The one they had been paranoid about for so long. And, in the resulting confusion, PLAN's necessary self-defense would be the basis for the massive and final attack. The one that would finally bring the breakaway province back to where it rightfully belonged. And none of the so-called allies of the Rebellious State would dare come to their aid under such circumstances.

Tan Yong had politely listened to the complicated plan, a noncommittal look on his face. Then he tacitly vetoed the idea with a slight wave of his hand.

"The time is not yet ripe," he said quietly. "Nor can we rely on such multiple coincidences and hoped-for reactions to drive what we have so long sought. We will allow this to be a foretaste of things to come. And we will give the other nations of the world no reason to believe we had anything to do with this unfortunate foundering of the inept government over there. Their utter failure to adequately build out their electrical system as they put on a hollow show of prosperity for the world to see. In the meantime, let us extend a very public offer of humanitarian and technical aid to our wayward brothers in the wake of this unfortunate cataclysm."

Tan Yong abruptly rose and strode out of the conference room. Qián Dài, his mentor, was seated comfortably in the president's inner office.

"The Heavenly Lights Operation is successful. This will draw the American eyes north to Taiwan while we work south," Tan Yong gloated.

Qián Dài wagged a finger. "There is much still to do and much danger still lies ahead. Best not to boast of killing the tiger until your foot is firmly on its neck."

Ψ

Commander Louise Gadliano settled back into her position on the USS *Canberra*'s spacious bridge. The heavily padded seat, complete with seatbelt and shock absorbers, was situated on a low platform that gave her an unobstructed view of everything happening in her ship's control center. Gadliano smiled every time the image of a throne came to mind. From here, on high, she could survey her kingdom and issue edicts to her "subjects." But being skipper of an LCS (littoral combat ship) was hardly the same as divine rule. Maybe that was because she wore a ball cap instead of a jeweled crown. And a leather flight jacket rather than an ermine robe. But it was an interesting resemblance to contemplate as she oversaw her crew, efficiently running the ship and doing their duty.

Immediately in front of her, the officer of the deck and the junior officer of the deck sat at their stations and worked to steer the *Canberra* through the maze of reefs that made up the territory dubbed for centuries by sailors as the Dangerous Grounds. The low-lying reefs and barely submerged shoals that littered these tropical waters were keeping the two young officers very busy. The bones of many shipwrecks—and those of sailors who had not survived such calamities—littered the area. They were harsh testimony to the hazards of allowing even a moment's inattention. The *Canberra*'s watch team was determined that their ship would safely navigate through the treacherous waters without even so much as scraping her bottom. At least they had advantages not available to most of those who had felt the bite of the reefs and rocks. *Canberra* was using every electronic gizmo that technology could deliver to keep them whole.

Only a couple of thousand yards to the east lay Ardasier Reef, a large area of calm turquoise waters and sandy shoals. Station Uniform, the tiny Malaysia Navy offshore station, was barely visible across the breakers on the reef's south side. The base was little more than a helicopter landing pad and a couple of ramshackle metal huts thrown up on less than an acre of bare sand. The land had been built up a foot or so above the high tide line. In truth, no boat that drew more than a couple of feet could even think about floating in and tying up at the station's tiny pier. The *Canberra* would have no chance of getting within a couple of miles should she need to.

There was another landmark not quite visible to the LCS in the other direction but showing up on her radar screens. Dallas Reef, even smaller than Ardasier Reef, lay just over the horizon to the west. The *Canberra*'s mission this run was to skirt the Dallas Reef to its north and then steam over to Amboyna Cay and scout out what might be happening with the Vietnamese Navy installation that had been constructed there. Nations in this part of the world all seemed determined to put guns, radar, and an air strip on every chunk of coral there was, whether it was rightfully in their territorial waters or not.

Gadliano planned to lie low near their present position between the two reefs until nightfall. Then they would dash across the more easily navigable sixty miles to Amboyna Cay under the cover of darkness. In the meantime, she would launch their MQ-8C Fire Scout to search out the seas ahead of them. The unmanned helicopter, based on a Bell 407 utility bird, served as Gadliano's eyes-in-the-sky for searching well beyond the *Canberra*.

The sun was just setting, dipping into the sea on the western horizon, when the ship's general announcing system blared commands that set everyone aboard into motion.

"Now flight quarters. All designated personnel, man your flight quarters stations. Stand clear of all weather decks. Now flight quarters."

The officer of the deck turned the ship until she faced into what little wind blew across the placid South China Sea. Then he cranked the speed up to twelve knots. On *Canberra*'s expansive flight deck, a crew quickly wheeled the pale gray Fire Scout out of the hangar, parked it precisely in the center of the landing circle, and unfolded the rotor blades. Then they stepped back and watched.

The pilot of the small chopper was sitting comfortably down in the ship's Mission Control Center. He used a joystick to spool up the Rolls-Royce 250-C47B turbine on the helicopter up on the flight deck. The Fire Scout—nicknamed "Cathy"—obeyed the command and lifted off the deck. Then it hovered for a second, awaiting word on what to do next.

Everyone with a view watched the Fire Scout abruptly charge away, disappearing into the growing darkness. But their attention was rudely diverted when *Canberra*'s AN/SPS 77 air search radar suddenly began pealing an alarm. The Integrated Combat Management System immediately showed a dozen bogeys coming in their direction from the north. Coming very low and very fast and likely with ill intentions.

Louise Gadliano glanced at the radar display for only a second before she declared the bogeys as hostile. She had undergone enough training to know that they fit the attack profile for a Chinese air strike. The bogeys had become bandits.

The tactical action officer switched the SeaRAM close-range air defense system to AUTO. Simultaneously, the fifty-seven-millimeter Mark-110 gun spun around to home in on and track the incoming threat.

"Ahead flank. Conduct evasive maneuvers," Gadliano ordered the officer of the deck. Instinctively, she reached down to make sure her seatbelt was secure even before she heard the two big GE 2500 gas turbines belowdecks whine up to full throttle. The ship leapt forward, increasing speed from twelve knots to better than forty in only a few seconds. The officer of the deck slowly moved the combinator controls randomly back and forth, causing the racing LCS to zigzag while still heading more or less northwest.

"Captain, receiving multiple Chinese electronically scanned radars," the electronic warfare operator yelled out. "Equates to Shenyang J-15 carrier-based fighter jets. And they're in attack mode. I have initiated jamming."

Before Gadliano could respond, the radar operator called out, "Two bandits peeled off. They look inbound." He paused for the briefest second. Then, voice rising a full octave, he yelled, "Vampire! Vampire! Missiles inbound!"

These approaching bees were not only in a foul mood. They had just unleashed their deadly stingers at *Canberra*.

Before the echo of the radar operator's report had died out on the bridge, a whooshing roar enveloped the space. The ship's SeaRAM launcher had just sent out four rolling-airframe missiles to impolitely greet the incoming threats. The Mk 57 Bofors gun barked a half dozen times, adding six Mark 332 guided projectiles to the airborne traffic jam out there above the Dangerous Grounds.

"Launch the chaff! Launch a decoy!" Gadliano commanded, shouting to be heard over the din created by the SeaRAM and the Bofors gun. Within seconds, they felt and heard the solid thud of the SRBOC launcher as the chaff dispenser headed off into the evening sky. That was quickly followed by a similar thump as the NULKA decoy hurtled skyward. Hopefully, all the metallic confetti and junk would attract and confuse any of the inbound missiles that might survive and get past all that outbound ordnance.

"Splash one Vampire!" This time the radar operator's voice was high-pitched with excitement. The home team had scored the go-ahead touchdown. One of the Chinese missiles had just joined all the other far less state-of-the-art wreckage on the bottom. "SeaRAM got it!"

There were a few not-quite-suppressed cheers on the bridge.

But the radar op had barely had time to draw a breath when he followed with, "Splash one bandit!" One of the warplanes responsible for shooting the missiles was now history, too.

The Bofors gun bucked and spat four more rounds.

"Second Vampire in the chaff cloud," the operator said, keeping up his narrative of the battle happening in the sky. "It's gone for the decoy."

As if to confirm the radar operator's play-by-play, the deadly missile detonated with a loud explosion and a blinding flash, all a mere hundred yards astern of the *Canberra*. They had been just that close to being part of a spectacular conflagration.

"Second bandit has broken off. Looks like he's also aiming to give Station Uniform a pasting while they're in the neighborhood." A long moment of silence, then, "He's shot his wad. Climbing and heading back the way they came from. The others are blasting the island."

Commander Louise Gadliano took a deep breath and allowed herself a quick look around the bridge. The digital clock on the far bulkhead told her that the entire attack had taken less than two minutes. It felt like hours.

Then, with a slight shiver, she realized that she was wet with sweat. But her team had done a great job. All that drilling had paid off. They had successfully defended the *Canberra*. But even so, they still had to carry on with their mission.

"Officer of the Deck, slow to twenty knots and steer for Amboyna Cay," she ordered, surprised that her voice was so calm and matter-of-fact. "Have mission control steer Cathy to do a full sensor search of the Cay and surrounding water, as intended. Oh, and have the SeaRAM, SRBOC, and NULKA launchers made ready, just in case."

"Already in progress, ma'am," the OOD confirmed.

Gadliano nodded at him as she stepped down from her command chair and walked back into the Interior Communications Center. Time to call back home to DESRON SEVEN in Singapore and report this little dust-up.

It should be an interesting call. She figured that it would take about an hour from the time she reported the Chinese attack until the shit really hit the fan. Then she would be called upon to explain to some very high-ranking people every possible nuance of every action *Canberra* had taken in those wild and wooly two minutes.

Many similar events had occurred over the years. Nobody outside the military and the diplomatic corps of the countries involved ever heard about them. Families of people lost and the news media were told there had been a mechanical malfunction. Bad weather. A flock of birds. An unavoidable crash. A tragic sinking of a ship due to undetermined causes. No opportunity to recover bodies. A memorial service, time and place to be determined at a later date.

However, this had been a first for Commander Louise Gadliano. For all she knew at the moment, she had just been involved in the first skirmish of World War III. She hoped an hour would give her enough time to shower, change into a fresh uniform, and prepare notes on whatever the hell had just happened to her and her crew out there in the Dangerous Grounds.

Ψ

Captain Tranh Vu raised the periscope carefully but slowly so that it just barely broke the sea surface. He had been deliberately maneuvering his Vietnamese submarine, the *Bà Rịa-Vũng Tàu*, to conduct a close-in covert surveillance of the Chinese base on Cuarteron Reef, a speck of land made up of only about thirty hectares of dry coral and sand surrounded by eight square kilometers of shallow reef set amid the Spratly Islands in the South China Sea. It would not be a good thing for his periscope to be seen by the Chinese, who were certainly intently watching from over there on the tiny island. Not when he was only a thousand meters from them and in water far too shallow for him to go deep and run should he be spotted.

The island was located on the southwest side of the Spratlys. Despite its diminutive size and lack of obvious value, the reef was, in fact, very strategically located. For that reason, it was claimed by the Philippines, Taiwan, and Vietnam. And China, who had taken it over sometime in 2015. Since then, the People's Liberation Army Navy had built up a sprawling, heavily armed base on what was by now a much-enlarged and mostly man-made island.

The Vietnamese Navy had recently received intelligence reports that something new had been happening around Cuarteron. That was why they had vectored the *Bà Rịa-Vũng Tàu*, to try to learn what might be going on and if it presented a threat. Tranh Vu had muttered several choice epithets under his breath, questioning the command staff members' intelligence and family heritage, when he initially received orders for this mission. The *Bà Rịa-Vũng Tàu* was Vietnam's only surviving submarine, and as far as Tranh was concerned, he should be using those weapons down in the torpedo room to put large holes in the bottoms of the PLAN warships that were already attacking his country, not out here taking pictures of a godforsaken pile of sand, coral, and cement.

His mood changed when he found the island to be humming with activity. Once the 'scope was up, Tranh could clearly see the masts of several warships inside the harbor. He could make out a destroyer and at least a couple of frigates. Probably more. It appeared that a dredge had been working on the west side of the harbor, almost certainly enlarging and deepening the protected anchorage and using the spoil to enlarge the island. But in daylight, the machinery was covered by massive canvas tarps, likely to shield it from the view of satellites.

However, it was the work being done on the east side of the island that really attracted Tranh's attention. A large airfield was nearing completion there, stretching across the island from surf zone to surf zone. One big enough to handle just about any military aircraft the Chinese might want to sortie from here. From Cuarteron and such a large airfield, all of Vietnam would be only six hundred kilometers away. Easily within range of planes based here and circumventing Vietnam's air defenses now pointed toward the north.

The discovery was literally breathtaking. But Tranh needed pictorial evidence to show his superiors just how real the threat was to his country.

The submarine captain worked his boat in close to the airfield construction to get some good photos. But seconds after again raising the periscope, the sub's EW alarm shrilly sounded. Someone had just lit them up with a gigahertz radar. Such a system was certainly accurate enough to detect the periscope if it was close enough. The high signal strength indicated that it was.

Tranh frantically reached up and grabbed the periscope controls. They had overstayed their welcome. It was time to get out of here. Maybe even past time.

"Make your depth thirty meters, ahead flank," Tranh ordered as he stepped away from the lowering periscope and looked at the fathometer display. They needed to get to deep water and fast. Right now, they were swimming in about thirty-five meters of water, meaning there was less than five meters under the keel. The submarine jumped ahead as the battery-powered electric motors screamed at full tilt.

"Come to course south," Tranh ordered. The closest deep water was due south.

Tranh did some quick mental math. From where they had been detected out to water deep enough to get them off the reef was roughly four kilometers. At flank speed, that would take them about six minutes. Assuming the radar had seen them, and the operator knew what had been painted by his powerful beam, and if the Chinese were intent on taking out such an interloper, did the Vietnamese submarine have six minutes before a weapon could be launched?

Probably not, Tranh decided. They needed a diversion. They were too shallow for an evasion device. There was not enough depth available for them to hide beneath an inversion caused by different water temperature layers. Maybe a "knuckle" would work.

"Right full rudder," Tranh ordered. As the boat leaned into the sharp turn at full speed, and as the compass rose began to swing wildly, he gave another command. "Left full rudder, steady course one-five-zero."

Now their very existence likely depended on anyone tracking them with sonar being fooled by such heavy water turbulence—the knuckle—all caused by the sub's rudder swinging the boat through those violent turns.

"Captain," the sonar operator called out. "Bottom is dropping. We are off the reef. Depth one hundred meters."

"Make your depth ninety meters," Thanh ordered without hesitation.

The *Bà Rịa-Vũng Tàu* had just begun to angle downward when the sonar operator reported, "Loud splash, bearing zero-seven-zero, high-speed screws in the water." There was a moment of awful silence. Everyone in the submarine's control room knew what report would likely follow. And it did. "Captain, torpedo in the water!"

Tranh knew precisely what had happened but could do nothing about it. The Chinese had tracked his escape, and as soon as they were in deep enough water, one of their destroyers in the vicinity had launched an ASW —anti-submarine warfare—missile to chase them down. Most probably one of their new YU-8 missiles that he had recently heard about.

The veteran submariner stared at the various gauges in front of him. If the missile had been accurately fired, there was no way for his vessel to escape the ASW torpedo it carried.

If there had been some slight miscalculation or error, then they would live. Either way, they would know in a very few seconds.

He braced himself, thought of his late wife, his children, his grandchildren. No commands were necessary. No prayers either. The ending of this scenario had already been written.

The YU-8 lightweight torpedo had by now homed in on *Bà Rịa-Vũng Tàu*'s wildly spinning screw. The weapon raced ahead, ready to take a bite.

The explosion instantly blew the screw off its shaft, ramming the shaft brutally into the submarine's engine room. That tore a hole a full meter wide in the hull around the engine room. Sea water flooded through the gouge, quickly drowning the seven watch standers on duty there.

Fortunately for everyone else aboard the *Bà Rịa-Vũng Tàu*, the submarine had six water-tight compartments. They were all sealed.

Unfortunately, though, the sheer weight of the water that rushed into the flooded engine room was far too much for the vessel's buoyancy to overcome. The submarine was unable to float. And she never would again.

Instead, the boat and her crew quickly slipped downward until slamming hard into the bottom of the South China Sea.

In the cold darkness two hundred and fifty meters below the sparkling, starlit surface.

Ψ

Party Secretary Tan Yong sat back and stroked his chin. Those in the room with him knew their leader was doing all he could to control his legendary temper. Meanwhile, the admiral who occupied most of the big-screen monitor on the far wall, his chest covered with medals, shards of light glinting from them, droned on and on. He swung his pointer like a sword to highlight the talking points projected onto the wall behind him. There was also a large-scale chart of the South China Sea. It was colorfully decorated with bright red stars, expansive arrows, and miniature orange explosions, each representing the brilliantly conducted operations overseen by the presenting admiral.

"Honorable elder brother," Admiral Fukua continued, standing very straight and looking directly into the camera. "I am pleased to report that our PLAN forces have once again proven themselves indomitable." He waved his free hand toward the expansive bright-yellow arrows that slashed across the map. "Our Naval Air Forces have swept the Nánshā Qúndǎo—what the Americans and others insist on calling the Spratly Islands—of all foreign military establishments. The coordinated airstrikes wiped out twenty-one illegal facilities operated by the Vietnamese. Another nine held by the Philippine regime are now under our control. And five more that were previously occupied by the Malaysian military have now been liberated." The admiral puffed up his chest even more as he strutted across the stage, dutifully followed by the camera operator keeping him in frame. "We accomplished total surprise. Returning pilots are reporting that there was little, if any, attempt at defense. All of the illegal facilities were obliterated. And the crowning touch, an American ship, one of their newer LCS vessels, was foolish enough to try to interfere with our mission. It was necessarily destroyed in order to protect our own units and the lives of their crewmembers."

The admiral motioned to the camera operator to zoom in to one spot on the chart, a location in the central Spratlys, and linger there for a moment. Then the screen shifted to a satellite image of Cuarteron Reef and its surrounding waters.

"Our naval forces also brilliantly and efficiently destroyed a submarine that was detected by our skillful technicians reconnoitering in our waters around Huáyáng Jiāo. They engaged the hostile vessel by employing our latest anti-submarine missiles. We could not classify it before we destroyed the submarine, but in all probability, it was also American."

Tan Yong steepled his hands under his chin and looked directly at the admiral's image on the screen. The hot glow in the president's eyes was telling.

"Admiral Fukua, you say that all the military facilities in the Nánshā Qúndǎo are destroyed?"

"Yes, Mr. President, I am pleased to confirm..."

"And our naval units are moving forward to occupy our possessions?"

The admiral smiled. "More precisely, Mr. President, units of the naval militia are moving to the possessions. Utilizing the blue hulls of the militia was felt to be more benign than sending PLAN warships to take possession."

"So, tell me this, Admiral. Was this decision made by the same blithering idiot who decided not to inform me immediately that we had attacked and sunk two American warships?" Tan Yong growled. Then, for emphasis, he slammed his fist down hard on the table. The other men in the room flinched. The admiral on the screen stood there, mouth agape.

Tan visibly worked to calm himself. After a couple of deep breaths, he went on. "Admiral Fukua, do you realize that this incompetence has given the Americans time to react, to retaliate, for these actions? I will have the xìngxiàn (the testicles) of the fool who ordered these actions. I will place them in a little glass jar. And they will be on rotating display at every location in which the PLA and PLAN train future military officers as a reminder of the consequences of freelancing without prior approval from the president and Central National Security Commission."

Tan Yong suddenly punched a button on a remote control near his right hand, killing the large-screen display. He turned to face General Shao Jing, who controlled the People's Liberation Army, including his country's navy.

"Please, at your greatest speed, find that popinjay a suitable position far from anything important. Officer in charge of an internal border station in the Gobi Desert should be appropriate enough."

General Shao smiled. Or an expression that could only tangentially be categorized as a smile. His evil smirk had been known to cause combat troops to cower in fear and even the highest-ranking underlings to soil their uniform pants.

"Honorable leader, he is clearly not fit to command any PLAN fighting ships. Maybe a ship of the desert is better suited for Admiral Fukua's leadership."

Tan, his face still flushed, nodded and then visibly shifted gears. "As some of you know, we have heard through diplomatic channels about the attack on the LCS vessel. As with so much else, Admiral Fukua managed to botch this. The LCS was not sunk, merely sent scurrying. We have responded in the usual manner, that the American warship was in Chinese waters illegally and when warned, the encroaching vessel opened fire. We, of course, protected our assets and personnel by firing back. We have heard nothing of any loss of an American submarine, though we do have confirmation of the admiral's claim that a submersible was fired upon near Huáyáng Jiāo Island. We speculate it may not have been American at all."

Tan paused to take a long drink of ice water from the glass in front of him. Then he looked from one face to the other. "What this means is that the incompetent fool has managed to place at risk our nation's most ambitious plan to finally realize several of our key goals. He has diverted the attention of the Americans and their allies to precisely where we do not want it to be. Their efforts, instead, must be directed to protecting what they believe to be our 'imminent' assault on Taiwan, not on the South China Sea and the nations that surround our sovereign waters there. Attacking one, or possibly two, of their warships down there has, I am afraid, put our entire mission in most severe jeopardy."

General Shao again smiled. The other four men at the table could not suppress shivers. Once again, each man silently gave thanks that the general was loyal to the People's Republic of China, the Communist Party, and its leader, Tan Yong. They could only hope he would remain so.

"We already have something ready to initiate that will once again have their attention on that rogue island, as you require," the general reported.

Tan Yong looked sharply at him. "It must be executed quickly. We have little time before we must deviate from the preferred current schedule."

General Shao bobbed his head in acknowledgement.

"I am certain we have just the thing. And contrary to our most recent presenter..." He glanced tellingly at the dead monitor screen. "...I am now going to share it with you and seek your permission to proceed."

With the slightest of nods from President Tan, General Shao reached for the remote control, reactivated the monitor, and unhinged the laptop computer that had been waiting on the table in front of him.

Ψ

Lieutenant Jimmy Wilson, Admiral Jon Ward's flag aide, rushed into his boss's office, carefully navigating the piles of reports stacked on the floor and every other horizontal surface. The young naval officer shook his head. This was the office of the man commanding what was probably the most high-tech military agency in the world yet Ward still relied on masses of paper. It was not that the admiral was afraid of technology. He had, after all, not so long ago been an engineer on and then later commanded a nuclear submarine. But somehow, this old-school approach of his when it came to keeping up with all that was going on in a dangerous world seemed to fit perfectly with Admiral Ward's character. He claimed it allowed him to consider each bit of data much more effectively on a piece of paper than watching it flit across a computer monitor.

"Jimmy, since you just double-timed into my office without knocking, I must assume you have something important to tell me," Ward said, without even looking up from the file he was perusing.

"Admiral, we just got a call from DISA," Wilson reported. "They need you over at Fort Meade, like, a half hour ago." The Defense Information Security Agency—as with most government agencies, usually referred to by its acronym, DISA—was charged with protecting all of the military's information systems from cyber-attack. That mission had become much more important and challenging over the last few years as the various governments of the world became infinitely more sophisticated in their use of such methods. The agency's headquarters were located in, and much of their activity was conducted from, an inauspicious cluster of windowless buildings hidden on the back side of the heavily guarded and highly secretive Ft. Meade complex twenty miles east of Washington, DC.

With that word from his aide, Jon Ward finally looked up from the thick report, removed his reading glasses, and rubbed his eyes. Then he carefully bookmarked the report and placed it and his glasses on the battered old oak desk that dominated his office.

"Any clue as to what all the excitement is about, Jimmy?" Wilson was remarkably wired into a network of aides and assistants around the Pentagon and the far-flung military installations around the world. His scuttlebutt was often more accurate and up-to-date than what Ward received through official channels.

"I'm in the dark on this one, boss. The general's office called. They request that you come over to DISA as soon as possible. They have a developing situation that you need to know about. The commanding general is requesting that you personally come."

Ward glanced at the antique ship's clock on his office wall and groaned. "We'll be at the ass end of rush hour traffic, Jimmy. It'll take at least a couple of hours to drive to Ft. Meade this time of day."

Wilson smiled and shook his head. "Boss, you have to get used to your status as a heavy-hitter around this town now. They have laid on a helo just for you. We got ten minutes to get down to the helo pad."

Ward acknowledged with a mock salute, grabbed his battered old briefcase, and stuffed a couple of reports into it to read on the flight over and back. He was just heading for the door when Jimmy Wilson blocked his way, nodding toward the side table next to Ward's desk. The admiral stepped back to grab his cell phone from its charger.

"Oh, yeah. My tether. Something else I didn't have to screw around with when I rode the boats."

The flight from the Pentagon helicopter pad to Ft. Meade actually took less than fifteen minutes. General Samuel Gray—call-sign "TBD," the commanding general of DISA—personally met Ward and Wilson at the helo pad. That further confirmed something big was brewing. After a quick handshake, he escorted them directly into the underground facility buried beneath the DISA building complex. The Air Force general did not say much along the way. Just a few pleasantries, speculation on the outcome of the Air Force and Navy football game, inquiries about Ward's wife and son, all as he flashed credentials or swiped a card as they passed through multiple locked and guarded doors.

At one point, as they walked down a long cement passageway, Ward asked, "How did you ever get a callsign like TBD? Most of the ones I hear are like Hotshot or One-wire."

Gray chuckled. "We don't get to choose our callsign. Usually someone finds something to hang over you and that's what we get. Not like Tom Cruise getting 'Maverick' in *Top Gun*. When I was in basic flight school and they were posting the list for check rides prior to soloing, I was a little behind and the first couple of postings had my check ride instructor pilot listed as TBD. Thereafter and forever more, I have been TBD."

Finally, they arrived in a large, dimly lit room filled wall-to-wall with desks and computer monitors. Most of the illumination came from the large flat-screens that hung in almost every available spot on the walls around the big room or the monitors at the many workstations. The place was certainly a kicked-over anthill of activity. Busy but purposeful, though. Men and women, some in uniform and some in civilian dress, were hunched over keyboards, staring at the screens, or scurrying about the room, consulting with their fellow geeks.

General Gray waved them toward the far corner of the room where a small team seemed to be especially excited as they huddled together in front of a large collection of screens. Figures, graphics, and text flew by on the monitors, all going much faster than Ward could decipher.

"Jon, this is what I wanted you to see for yourself," the Air Force officer told Ward as he waved toward the screens.

"TBD, I'm a little slow with all this computer stuff," Ward answered. "Since I'm well past twenty-five years old and never even owned a beanie with a propellor on it, you're going to have to spell it out for me."

General Gray grinned. Jon Ward's aversion to technology was well known throughout the military intelligence community. Not quite as much as Ward's predecessor and mentor, but close.

"As you know, we here at DISA are tasked with defending all our military data systems from cyber-attack. Or any kind of digital mischief. What a lot of people don't know is that we also have offensive capabilities. What I'm going to show you is an offensive defense at work. And I know you know this stuff is all about as hush-hush as it can get." Gray pointed to one of the screens. More bits and bytes that Ward did not understand flashed across. "We have been watching some Chinese efforts at hacking into our JWICS system. It started pretty primitive a few years ago but has gotten steadily more sophisticated. Then, a few weeks ago, we detected someone sniffing around the Seventh Fleet connection, probably trying to access the comms path between that facility in Yokosuka and the Indo-PACOM Headquarters in Pearl Harbor. They know that if they can tap into that little party line, they could access everything we have for fighting in the Pacific. All our deepest secrets would be laid bare. Even more effectively than we were able to accomplish when we had the Japanese naval code in World War II."

Jon nodded, concern painted on his face. JWICS—the Joint Worldwide Intelligence Communications System—carried the most highly classified data that the military handled. It was extensively protected, and commonly acknowledged to be impossible to hack. If someone did manage such a breach, it would be bad. Very bad.

But as Gray related the issue, he did not appear to be especially concerned. Ward waited for the next shoe to drop.

"When we first detected this intrusion attempt, we set up a little honey trap," Gray told him, pointing toward another screen. "Over here, we set up a loop that looks just like the JWICS node, but without several of the protection layers. We dangled this node out there in front of our Chinese friends and they snapped at it. Took the bait and swallowed it whole. They've convinced themselves that they happened upon a backdoor into the JWICS system. Almost certainly the most heavily shielded military comms system there is." Gray paused for a breath and for Ward to absorb his words.

"How do we know they took the bait?" he continued. "They started downloading a ton of data just before we called you. If they were onto us, they would have cut the cord and gone away, assuming we would quickly figure out who they were if they didn't. But they have not even slowed down. So far, in less than a day, they have happily downloaded maybe ten petabytes, and the meter is still ticking."

General Gray noticed Ward's quizzical expression.

"Sam, I know that's a lot of bits and bytes, but..."

"Indeed, it is. It confirms to us they are hungry for whatever data they've tapped into and they intend to grab it and go, but they will without a doubt leave an opening to come back for more later. Jon, what they have downloaded already is equivalent to the data for roughly twenty million full-length theatrical high-definition movies."

"And I am assuming you boys are not allowing them to suck up any valuable information."

"Depends on what you call 'valuable information,'" General Gray explained with an odd grin. "First off, we encrypted all of that data with a two-hundred-fifty-six-bit encryption key. We know they'll eventually be able to crack into the data, despite all that digital mumbo-jumbo, but it will take them weeks, even with ganging all of their best supercomputers together into a giant cluster computing network. And all that encryption will convince them they have some primo stuff they can access once they crack the code."

Then the general broke into a laugh, and the workers gathered around the workstation joined in. Had the general just made a very funny joke? "Oh, and just when they have splashed around flutes of the rice wine or whatever it is they use to celebrate their victory over us ignorant westerners, they will realize that they now have in their possession the world's largest collection of low-class pornography. Now you see what I mean by an offensive defense? They think they are seeing the American Pacific war plan. Instead, they're getting *Debbie Does Dallas* and *Deep Throat*. In digitally-enhanced 3-D."

11

Captain Tranh Vu struggled to get up off the deck of his stricken submarine and balance himself against a chart table. He felt a trickle of something warm and sticky running down the back of his neck. When he instinctively tried to wipe it away, the hand came back red, covered with blood. His blood. But he was alive and fairly clearheaded. There would be time later to see about the throbbing wound on the back of his head.

Tranh quickly took stock of the *Bà Rịa-Vũng Tàu*'s control room. Other than his submarine being tilted at an odd angle, everything appeared normal. The lights were on. The ventilation fans gently murmured. An alarm of some kind tweeted in the distance. At a quick glance, most of the boat's systems seemed to be working. The digital depth indicator at the ship control station read two-hundred-forty-seven meters. But ship speed was zero. Those two indicators revealed to him that they were truly stuck on the bottom of the sea.

The crew who had been on watch in the control room were now slowly rising from wherever they had been flung during the quick, crashing dive to the bottom. Those who were able were now returning to their watch stations. Some were assisting shipmates who appeared to be more seriously injured. Reports had already begun to filter in from the other spaces up and down the length of the boat. From all except the sixth compartment, the now flooded engine room. The *Bà Rịa-Vũng Tàu* seemed to be remarkably intact, considering she had been struck by a Chinese undersea weapon and slammed hard into the sea floor. Intact, but still she was stuck on the bottom of the South China Sea. And with the engine room full of water, she would never go anywhere under her own power.

Tranh sat on a stool and gathered his thoughts for a few moments as reports continued to come in and be distributed. The harsh truth was that there was likely no way in which they could escape this deep-sea tomb. If there was any chance at all, he would be the one to have to figure it out, explain it, and execute the plan. Time was not on their side, but still, they would need to carefully think through whatever they might attempt. They must not panic and do something foolish. That might erase any chance they had, assuring their demise.

From his first days in his country's Naval Academy at Nha Trang, he had been taught to always first, if time and circumstances permitted, assess the situation before deciding on a course of action. The picture had now become all too clear. Out of his crew of fifty men, he had lost seven in the heavily damaged and flooded after compartment. Three more had died as a result of the initial explosion from the Chinese weapon or in the brutal crash into the bottom. Eight more men had suffered serious injuries. Most of them were unlikely to survive more than a few hours if they could not get better medical treatment than what was available to them on the submarine. That left him with thirty-two able-bodied sailors to work with, should a plan be concocted. But at the moment, there was not much for them to do.

They were simply too deep to attempt an emergency free ascent, making use of the escape hatch, leaving the submarine, and floating up to the surface. That would require a journey of only a couple of minutes, but they would be transitioning from greater than twenty-five atmospheres pressure at the bottom to one atmosphere at the surface. The human body was not designed to undergo such torture. The physiological stress was more than most could tolerate. Tranh knew that there was a less than ten percent chance that even a healthy man could survive. And, of course, that was no option at all for any of the injured. Even if someone did manage to make it, he would pop to the surface and immediately be in the clutches of the People's Liberation Army Navy.

Fortunately, both batteries checked out fine. However, after their frantic attempt to escape from the reef and into deeper water, the batteries were now showing a less than thirty percent charge. Sitting there immobile, and if they conserved power usage to only the essentials, they should still have enough to last them for a few days. A quick glance at the atmosphere control panels confirmed for Tranh that they had enough air and air regeneration equipment to allow them to breathe for maybe eight days. His engineer confirmed the captain's estimates.

So that was the bottom line. They had about eight days—maybe four with light and power—to somehow get word of their plight back to headquarters. Just over a week for his commanders to figure a way to mount a rescue effort. And for them to conduct that extrication right on the doorstep of a major Chinese naval anchorage, within sight of the very ones who had dispatched the Vietnamese submarine to the depths. Should that prove to be an impossibility, Tranh and his crew would be doomed to suffer a truly horrible and slow death.

Tranh glumly shook his head. Perhaps it would have been better, after all, if they had been killed instantly. In all likelihood, there was very little chance that he and his crew would come out of this predicament alive. But it was not in his nature to give up. Nor would he allow any of his crew to do so, either. Surrendering to death would assure that death would win in the end.

The captain had just begun to fashion a list of potential things to try when he had an epiphany. They should have one of their communications buoys left. One that had failed a pre-launch check and the crew had stowed in the radio room to take back to base for repair. A malfunctioning piece of equipment now offered them a surprising amount of hope.

It took his two radiomen eight hours of tedious, exacting work to troubleshoot and finally repair the buoy. It turned out to be nothing more than a cold solder joint on a surface-mount component on a tiny printed circuit board. But they had been at the point of giving up when one of the men found the flaw and re-soldered it.

Then it required most of another hour while they prepared and encrypted a message back to headquarters. One that could not be mistaken for a trap sprung by the Chinese, with whom their country was at war.

Since they had necessarily broken through the buoy's watertight barrier to repair its inner workings, and since they had no way to test that they had successfully re-sealed it against leakage, Tranh was well aware that it might flood out when they launched it. They did use a bit of duct tape to protect it as best they could, but, although submariners told many tales of duct tape holding at test depth, in reality the tape was hardly rated for the water pressure it would be encountering at the depth from which it would begin its float to the surface.

But it was their only hope. He ordered the device launched and then, having been brought up in the Catholic faith, he made the sign of the cross as best he remembered how and uttered a quiet prayer as the buoy was ejected out of the launcher tube.

Ψ

The blood-red sun was just touching the wavetops on the western horizon when the buoy popped to the surface of the South China Sea, only a couple of miles south of the Cuarteron Reef. For a long moment nothing at all happened. It appeared that Captain Tranh Vu's fears had come to pass, his prayers unanswered. The briny sea water had likely found an opening in the buoy's cover and fouled its sensitive circuitry.

Then a small antenna suddenly sprang out of the bobbing device. A circling seagull overhead noticed the motion and flew closer, then decided it was not a fish at all and flapped away.

Not visible was the radio-frequency waves that energized the antenna. Nor the encrypted radio signal that hurried away at the speed of light, only to be bounced back to earth off an orbiting communications satellite.

Bounced back down to a monitoring station of the Vietnamese People's Navy 4th Regional Command Headquarters at Cam Ranh Bay.

Though they had no way of knowing it at the time, the fate of the surviving crew members aboard the *Bà Rịa-Vũng Tàu*, though still dire, had just become the slightest bit brighter.

Ψ

The International Submarine Escape and Rescue Liaison Office—usually referred to as ISMERLO in the ever-present military acronym lexicon—was located at the NATO Submarine Command Center in Northwood, England. It was usually a very quiet place, particularly on a Sunday afternoon. The ISMERLO office had been established in 2003 in response to the sinking of the huge Russian nuclear submarine *Kursk* and the loss of all 118 men aboard back in August of 2000. At the time, the Russians refused any aid in attempting to rescue possible survivors. The Russian president, Vladimir Putin, did not even bother to interrupt his seaside vacation. The outrage of the world governments led directly to the creation of ISMERLO.

Even now, in the rare instances when the center was called upon to assist in aiding a submarine in distress, it could be a complicated operation. The office had the unenviable task of coordinating the rescue operations for almost all the navies of the world that operated submarines. Most of the time, that involved making certain that all of the various rescue systems were interoperable with all of the different types of submarines. Sometimes it required resolving minor technical squabbles between the various submarine services. So far, though, there had been no operations that involved diplomacy or working in a war zone.

The mission, though, was always critical. When the red phone on the desk of the officer on station at ISMERLO rang, it meant there was a submarine down or missing somewhere in the world. At that moment, the quiet office turned to a mad, but well-planned and rehearsed, scramble.

This sleepy Sunday in Great Britain, when that phone rang, the watch officer, a Royal Navy sub-lieutenant, was deeply involved in watching the English cricket team take on the rival Aussies on the Oval in London. To a Brit, the television action was mesmerizing. He groaned when he heard the peal of the phone. But even so, he answered before the first ring was complete.

The message was succinct. The Vietnamese Navy had a sub stranded on the bottom. Unable to move or surface, but with survivors. And it had been no accident. The Chinese PLAN had fired on and sunk the stricken vessel.

The young officer on duty was perplexed. He quickly scanned the manuals on his desk. He could not find a checklist anywhere for dealing with a submarine that had been sunk as the result of hostile enemy action. Nor had he or anyone else on duty in the center ever drilled for such an eventuality. But he did know that the best course of action was to immediately call ISMERLO's commanding officer, Italian Navy Capitano di Vascello Guiseppe Fredo.

Capitano Fredo hesitated for only a moment. He knew that he was about to navigate uncharted waters. But he also knew that those sailors stuck in their damaged submarine did not have time for him to go through normal diplomatic channels or create policy before attempting to rescue them. A quick check of his database showed that the Singapore Navy had the closest submarine rescue system to where the *Bà Rịa-Vũng Tàu* was down. Fredo was immediately on the phone to his counterpart at the Singapore Navy Submarine Rescue Command. Colonel Wong Su answered on the second ring.

Colonel Wong Su confirmed that their system was operational. But critical in this situation, their Deep Search and Rescue (DSAR) 500 Class submarine extrication vehicle, called the DSAR 6, did not employ a tether to a surface support ship as most such platforms did. Theirs was really a miniature submarine that could travel some distance while remaining clandestinely submerged, then search out, find, and mate with a stricken submarine. Then it could rescue up to sixteen survivors per trip back to a mother ship. The original idea was to be capable of conducting rescue missions in the worst weather. But that ability was now essential to attempt to save men from beneath a hostile warship that might be circling on the surface.

It took Colonel Su only a couple of minutes to figure out that this rescue would be far more complicated and dangerous than the usual mission. A peacetime rescue was already complex and hazardous enough. But one under hostile circumstances raised it to a whole new level. It would take much planning and coordination between the Singapore Navy, their Vietnamese brothers, and, almost certainly, the Americans. He had some phone calls to make.

But in the meantime, the Motor Vessel *Swift Rescue* and her DSAR 6 hitchhiker needed to get moving, posthaste. No matter what the final plan turned out to be, the ship had almost five hundred miles to traverse. Her top speed was only twelve knots. That would eat up three days on an already ticking clock.

Each man up and down the chain did the same quick calculations in his head. The original distress message indicated enough power for only three or four days. Enough oxygen for perhaps seven days.

Without unseen delays, this was a rescue mission. But if something slowed them down, that spot at the bottom of the South China Sea would forever be the final resting place for the submarine and every person who made up her crew.

12

Brian Edwards made one last sweep around with the number one photonics mast. Both the normal optics and the infrared camera showed an empty ocean except for a couple of seagulls diving for a late-evening meal. He pushed the button to lower the mast and ordered, "Mr. Wilson, make your depth one-five-zero feet. Make preparations to launch the UUV in tube nine."

"Make my depth one-five-zero feet, make preparations to launch tube nine, aye, sir," the young lieutenant shot back for confirmation. This operation—launching the unmanned underwater submersible vehicles from the submarine's payload module, the VPM—was getting to be almost routine. The *George Mason* team had already successfully deployed UUVs with their intel packages off Mischief Reef and Subi Reef. The one designated for here at Fiery Cross Reef would be the last one destined for the Spratly Islands. Next, they would steam north to Scarborough Shoals, off of Luzon, the northernmost island in the Philippines. Then, finally, they would be allowed to play traditional anti-submarine warfare for a bit and try to figure out what was going on with the most recent belligerence on the part of China's navy. But first they needed to successfully get this fish in the water and on its way to where it would nest on the bottom and patiently gather information.

Edwards felt the *George Mason* angle down in response to his ordered maneuvers. He turned to LCDR Ashton Jennings, who was hunched over the launcher console. The boat's weapons officer was animatedly talking over a headset while frowning at what he was watching on the launch control panel screen. From the officer's body language, Edwards could see that Jennings was not having a good day.

"Problems, Weps?" Edwards asked.

"We're not getting a good datalink from the fish in tube nine at the moment," Jennings answered. "The umbilical in that tube has been giving us a fit. Sometimes it works fine. Sometimes the damn thing won't cooperate. We really do need to go into the tube and check it out. That would probably take a couple of hours if we find the glitch and get it fixed pretty quick."

Edwards shook his head. "Uh-uh. No time for that right now. Shift the mission to the fish in tube ten. We'll troubleshoot tube nine later, when we have time."

"Shift the mission to tube ten, aye," Jennings answered, already running the list on what that would require. "Let's see. It'll take about ten minutes to power up the fish, download the new mission package, and pre-launch the tube. Maybe another minute or two to final checks."

Edwards nodded and turned back to Bill Wilson, who was standing at the command console, listening to the exchange. "Officer of the Deck, secure tube nine. Tube ten will be the launch tube. Make preparations to launch tube ten when Weps tells us it's ready."

Ten minutes later, the *George Mason* was hovering at a depth of 150 feet and a position fifty miles north of Fiery Cross Reef and the Chinese air base that was located on what was almost entirely a man-made island.

Brian Edwards looked around the control room. Everything appeared ready. No sonar contacts. The ship was stable and hovering at zero speed and zero vertical velocity. The UUV was checking out perfectly this time. It was time to launch.

"Flood tube ten, open the upper hatch tube ten," the skipper ordered. Thirty seconds later, the launcher panel showed the tube fully flooded and the "hatch open" light flashed red.

“Firing point procedures, UUV, tube ten,” Edwards called out in a loud voice.

Bill Wilson double-checked that all the ship’s systems were prepared. He responded, “Ship ready.”

Ashton Jennings checked one more time that tube telemetry was operating as expected and that the mission was loaded in the UUV’s computer. Then he called out, “UUV ready.”

Edwards ordered, “Launch tube ten.”

There was not much indication that anything had happened. Nothing like the shove and whoosh when a torpedo was expelled from its tube. The umbilical cable-flooded alarm flashed on. The “UUV away” note appeared on the launcher panel. Then Josh Hannon, the sonar supervisor, called out, “Indication of normal UUV launch from sonar. Normal UUV start-up. Bearing three-two-two, down doppler.”

Edwards smiled. Despite the hiccup with the submersible in tube nine, they had launched on time. Now the only thing they needed to do was to pop up the comms mast, report home, tell the boss that they had done what they set out to do, and then saunter over to Scarborough Shoals.

“Officer of the Deck, shut the upper hatch, tube ten. Post launch tube ten. Secure hovering and come to periscope depth. Time to tell the boss that we are done here.”

The trip to periscope depth was uneventful as well. They apparently still had this piece of the South China Sea all to themselves. Edwards decided that this would be a good opportunity to ventilate the ship for a few minutes, to pump in some fresh air.

The action report was quickly sent and receipted for. Then the XO, Jackson Biddle, called on the 21MC from the radio room.

“Skipper, I think you should come to radio. We received revised patrol orders. You are definitely going to want to see these.”

But Edwards was already making the short trip to the submarine’s radio room, a puzzled look on his face.

Ψ

Commander Louise Gadliano briskly guided her team as the *Canberra* slowly circled Rifleman Bank on the western edge of the sprawling Spratlys. They had to navigate very carefully here. Rifleman Bank was a large, submerged reef. But only barely submerged. It would easily tear the bottom out of an unwary mariner's vessel. And it had done so many times throughout history. In the 1980s and 1990s, the Vietnam Navy had built a series of small platforms supported by steel pilings to serve as meteorological stations and aids to navigation on many of these lonely, desolate, and near-invisible reefs. They were typically manned by a few sailors, there only to maintain the facilities and equipment.

But the difficult and treacherous navigation problem was not the foremost thing on Commander Gadliano's mind at the moment. After witnessing the Malaysian Navy's Ardasier Reef facility getting annihilated, they had hurried on only to find Vietnam's Amboyna Cay station little more than a smoking pile of rubble. She could only assume all this damage was part of the same air attack that had come close to sinking the *Canberra.* They had seen no signs of any survivors at either station.

That also appeared to be the case on Rifleman Bank. What little of the rubble that remained above the waterline continued to smolder and smoke. Again, there appeared to be no one left alive. A few bodies floated in the water, already under attack from the aquatic life. Gadliano clenched her fists in anger and frustration. This was nothing more than cold-blooded murder. The sailors, serving long, boring duty on these rigs, had no means to defend themselves against such a vicious surprise air attack. Thank goodness she and her littoral combat ship had enough firepower to fend off the attackers, and even take one of them down, or else she and her crew of forty may well have suffered the same brutal fate.

The tactical action officer stuck his head out from behind the curtain that separated the bridge from combat center on the warship. "Captain, just received a message with new orders from DESRON SEVEN. They want us to mosey back over to the vicinity of Amboyna Cay. We are to rendezvous with that Sing sub rescue ship, *Swift Rescue,* and escort her. There is a sub down around there somewhere, and the Singapore Navy ship is the only one that can approach and conduct a rescue underwater. And it sure as hell sounds like the Chinese may not take kindly to any attempt to try to save those folks."

"Okay, plot us a course back to Amboyna Cay. And make sure all our weapons systems are up and ready."

A submarine down. A rescue vessel on the way. A submerged rescue vessel. And the Chinese sitting right there, set to blow out of the water anybody daring to even attempt a rescue.

Now, she and *Canberra* were steaming to a spot right in the middle of that shitstorm.

Ψ

"Boss, you're going to love this!" Colonel Stanton Readly said with great enthusiasm. He and Commodore Joe Glass were standing in the primary flight control room, looking out onto the expansive flight deck on the aft end of the USNS *Carson City*. The *Spearhead*-class expeditionary fast transport ship was riding easily at anchor just off Banggi Island, the northernmost populated island of Borneo. A monsoon rainstorm was sweeping across the ship's broad deck, soaking everything in a torrential downpour.

"They are finally giving us some teeth," Readly said proudly as the pair observed the deck crew connecting a sling harness to the CH-53K King Stallion helicopter. The other end of the harness was attached to an odd-looking vehicle that appeared to be a cross between a Humvee utility vehicle and a missile box launcher. What was really strange was that there was no place for a driver to sit. "This NMESIS thing is great. Completely unmanned and each vehicle is capable of shooting two Navy Strike Missiles. These babies can really reach out and touch someone."

On a signal from one of the deck crew, the big gray bird lifted off the flight deck, hauling the NMESIS into the air. Then the chopper turned and headed north, up and over the jungle-covered island, before soon disappearing into a wall of rain and haze.

"That's the last one," the Marine colonel noted. "Sergeant Major Ramirez has already set up the command module on Sibumong Point. And he has hooked into the Link-16 network while his team is hiding the other three launchers. When this last one gets there, he will have four NMESIS launchers hidden back in the jungle, ready to roll out, launch, and then scoot back under cover. Those puppies could be a real nasty surprise for any surface warship that might be trying to run the Balabac Straits or sneak down the west side of Borneo to do some mischief."

"That's all nice, Stan," Glass said. "And I am impressed. But we spent a lot of time and effort setting up a submarine array up there. You Marines have an answer for that?"

Readly laughed. "That's what I really want you to see." He turned and headed toward the passageway door. "Come on down to the mission bay. I've got an early Christmas present for you, Joe."

The two men climbed down ladders from deck to deck until they stepped out into the vast parking garage that constituted the ship's mission bay. In the middle of the bay sat eight large green trucks, their cargo hidden by tarpaulins.

"Joe, this is the answer to your question. We took our old High Mobility Rocket Artillery System and modified it so they could use some other missiles." Pointing at the four trucks closest to him, he went on, "These four are loaded with Evolved Sea Sparrow anti-air missiles. We packed in twelve birds per launcher. We have them hooked up through Link-16 for fire control and they'll work just like the NMESIS launchers. That gives us a real good medium-range anti-air capability."

"Okay, but that has no effect on submarines."

Readly pointed at the four trucks parked on the other side of the bay. "Those are the answer to that ASW question you keep asking. Those are HIMARS launchers, but they've been modified to fit your standard Navy RUM-139 ASROC missiles. We control them from Sam Smithski's tent up on Balambangan Island. They reach out and drop a Mark 54 torpedo on any unsuspecting sub that saunters by."

Glass stared at the trucks for a bit. HIMARS was High Mobility Artillery Rocket System, a multiple rocket launcher developed in the late 1990s by the United States Army, primarily for the battlefield. Relatively old technology, but quite effective in tactical situations. But if somebody had figured a way to use the HIMARS system to fire the RUM-139 anti-submarine missiles, it could have real value in the right situation.

"Mighty high tech for the Marine Corps, Stan."

"Well, I'll admit there is still some pretty low-tech stuff involved, too." Readly motioned for Glass to follow him. The two walked around the big green machines. “The fact is, these things are way too big for the 53s to haul. We’ll have to get them up there and in place the old-fashioned way. We’ll drive them up to Sibumong Point. With all this rain and given how rough the coast road is, we won’t be able to get up there until tomorrow sometime.”

Just then, the *Carson City*’s communicator rushed out into the mission bay, interrupting the conversation.

“Excuse me, Commodore. I think this is urgent.” He handed Glass a ThinkPad laptop computer. “It’s from COMSEVENTH FLEET.”

Glass grabbed the device and quickly read the message displayed on its screen. “Yep, it’s urgent all right. Please call back to the *Puller* and get an Osprey up here to pick me up ASAP.”

“One’s already on the way, sir. ETA in fifteen minutes.”

Glass turned to Readly, who was clearly bursting with curiosity.

“Stan, looks like I won’t be going with you on your little road trip through the jungle. Seems the Vietnamese have a sub down, right under the nose of the Chinese. We need to figure out the best way to cover the rescue attempt. And hopefully not ignite World War III in the process.”

13

The Taiwanese cable-laying ship *CS Myoung Song* lay at anchor a mile offshore on the eastern side of Gaodeng Island, a few miles off of China's eastern coast. The ship's precision dynamic positioning system was keeping the *Myoung Song* within a few centimeters of her plotted position despite the roiling five-foot seas that were amplifying the normally small-scale night swell in these waters. A compact workboat bobbed through the waves nearby, pulling a light steel messenger cable from the *Myoung Song* toward the island's rocky beach. It took her sea-soaked crew almost two hours to finally land the craft. On the shore, a work crew, along with a troop of Taiwanese army personnel, helped feed the cable around a quadrant pully before hooking it to a tow bar on a large, bright-yellow Komatsu bulldozer parked on the sand.

The bulldozer's diesel engine belched black smoke and roared to life as the operator slowly tugged ashore the messenger cable, followed by the much heavier winch cable. The sun was just rising far out on the eastern horizon when they lowered the sea plow from the *Myoung Song* and winched it across the open water, then up onto the beach.

The submarine fiber optic cable termination was just starting its journey from the big ship's cable drum to the shore when a man in military dress strolled down the beach, tea cup in hand, to observe this complicated operation. Colonel Dǎo Zhǐhuī Guān was the commander of this heavily fortified and often disputed bit of ground. And this was a very important day for him and his troops.

Gaodeng Island just happened to be Taiwan's closest observation point to the Chinese mainland. It was only a little less than ten kilometers from the island's shoreline to the Huangqi Peninsula, which was the People's Republic of China. A man equipped with a loud-hailer could and often did hurl verbal insults—frequently vile and profane—across the narrow expanse of water. The Chinese Communists did the same. There was real competition for creativity in the content of such exchanges, though there never had been any evidence that this bit of give-and-take convinced anyone from the other side to surrender his allegiance.

For many years, Colonel Dǎo and his troops had felt isolated from their Taiwanese brethren, perched as they were out there at the very tip of the spear pointed toward the behemoth of China and with one hundred and seventy-five kilometers of blue water between them and any aid from Taiwan. Today was a major step. They were finally receiving a real high-speed fiber optic data link with headquarters.

Though they hoped it would all go more quickly, that the bigger vessel would be well out from the island by daybreak, it took most of the day for the team to wrestle the unwieldy cable through the rollers on the plow, into the shore-side trench, and then up to the cement block termination building. Dǎo stood there most of the day watching, as if that might speed things up.

The commander had a very tight knot in the pit of his stomach. It was unlike his across-the-channel neighbors to allow something as consequential as the cable laying to go unnoticed and unanswered. Steps had been taken to make this appear to be a minor maintenance project. Nothing that would excite the Chinese. But once they realized that this was a major step up in Taiwan's monitoring capabilities, he expected their eventual response to be quick and violent. To be ready, he had ordered all the firing positions to be fully manned and supplied, ready to defend their island. In truth, his half-dozen ancient gun emplacements with their near-antique coastal defense cannons would be of very little value for mounting any real defense. Not against what the Chinese would likely employ once they decided to do more than simply claim sovereignty over Gaodeng.

Dǎo was more concerned about the new facilities that were just now coming online, the modern monitoring resources that Li Minh Zhou's shadowy organization had just completed. He was not at all sure what her science-fiction-worthy sensors were supposed to be monitoring. The mysterious woman had not offered to tell him, though they were like bait in a trap that might attract a Chinese attack against his command. Dǎo had only seen Li Minh Zhou in person twice. She looked completely different each time. He was not sure which was really her. Or if either was. Even in his lofty and important position, he knew very little about the woman. Only that she knew what the people in Beijing were thinking before they even had the idea. And she was on his side. Or at least he hoped she was.

Still, her monitoring stations were the real and only reason for the high-speed data link cabling. That was a capability Dǎo had long coveted. Whatever information her sensors gathered could be fed back to the intel center in Taipei, enabling Dǎo to be better prepared for what might be coming his way. Even so, if the nosy neighbors found out about this facility, they would be even more upset. Maybe enough to go right ahead and do something rash.

Finally, the huge winch on the *Myoung Song*'s stern pulled the thirty-ton deep-sea plow off the beach and into the water. As designed, the plow bit into the sea floor and began wedging open a three-meter-deep trench in the sandy bottom that the optical cable easily dropped into. It was now time for the cable ship to start the slow voyage back toward Taipei. The two-hundred-kilometer journey would take about four days as they slowly plowed the cable into the floor of the Taiwan Strait.

With the plow firmly embedded in the muddy bottom, set to follow them home, the *Myoung Song* crew started the process of raising the dynamic positioning anchor system so they could slowly steam away. And still no nudge from the PLAN. That was odd. Practically anything that happened off the usual schedule on Gaodeng Island would be enough to elicit at least a flyover or cursory visit by a distant patrol boat.

But then, before Dǎo could even twist around to take a look, two PLAN Type 56 corvettes roared around the southern point of the island at full speed, both throwing bow waves high up on their gray-green hulls. Three more of the vessels bellowed around the north side of the tiny island. They appeared to be making directly toward the cable ship. The AK-176 seventy-six-millimeter cannons on each of the corvettes slewed around, obviously tracking the *Myoung Song*.

To add to the threatening chaos, a pair of gray-black CAIC WZ-10 attack helicopters popped up over the ridge behind the Taiwanese commander, zooming in from the west. But the choppers did not waste time sighting and tracking. They wheeled around in unison and unleashed their HJ-10 anti-tank missiles, sending them shrieking into each of the island's gun emplacements. Within seconds, before any of the defenders could even fire a shot in self-defense, the emplacements exploded, sending debris and human bodies skyward.

Then the warships joined the fray. The gun on the lead northern corvette spat once. A plume of water erupted forward of the *Myoung Song* and splashed down onto the ship's forecastle. Four of the Chinese ships circled slowly a couple of thousand yards from the cable ship while the fifth glided to a stop five hundred yards off the *Myoung Song*'s port bow.

The cable layer's master was on the radio, busily trying to report the attack back to headquarters in Keelung and to plead for assistance. It was the marine band radio at his elbow that crackled and told him, "On the *Myoung Song*, you are the prisoners of the People's Liberation Army Navy. Stand by to be boarded. Any attempt to resist arrest and you will be destroyed at once."

Ψ

Li Minh Zhou slammed down the microphone in a rage. She could not believe what she was hearing. How had the Chinese found out about her carefully guarded cable laying plan? It had been well disguised as a simple dredging operation, not unlike scores of other dull and boring tasks that were so often done around the little island's anchorage. She had very purposely not taken any action or allowed any discussion outside of her few closest compatriots. No more than a half dozen people had any idea that they were laying a key optical cable to transmit data between their forward sensors on Gaodeng Island and Keelung. Only a half dozen more learned about the true nature of the work the previous morning. The whole idea was to get the cable laid and buried before the notoriously bureaucratic Chinese had the time to form any kind of reaction. Even then, it would typically have been all bluster, buzzing flyovers, quick runs at the big ship, and then back home for them. And that would have been it.

But they had attacked, claimed lives, and taken the cable ship and its crew into custody before it could even get underway. There was now no question of a leak somewhere in her inner group. She would have to ferret out the traitor and destroy him.

But first, there was a higher priority. The *Myoung Song* must be taken back. And the rest of the cable would need to be strung and buried and hooked up to the computers in the next trailer over from where she now sat.

Navy SEAL Jim Ward had never seen the beautiful Chinese spymaster so upset. But he knew her well enough by now to gather it was not yet the right moment to ask what was happening. The makeshift command center where he now rested was established in a couple of trailers alongside a pier inside the sprawling Keelung Naval Base. A big diesel generator chugged along just outside, feeding the trailers and much of the naval base with power. Most of Taiwan remained in the dark, still trying to recover from the massive power outage that had swept over the island a week before. Ward had been summoned to this place by Li for a briefing on what was known about the blackout and other worrisome activities around the region, most at the instigation of the Chinese State Security Committee, and at the behest of the Chinese president himself. That briefing had been about to begin when Li received word about the PRC's response to her data cable project.

Ward sensed she might tolerate his curiosity now.

"What has you so worked up, Zhou?" the SEAL commander asked. "You look like you're ready to take on the whole CCP in a single-handed knife fight."

"Oh, I would if I could," Li Minh Zhou responded, her voice shaking with anger and frustration. Then she shared the few details she had on the attack on the *Myoung Song*. She also told him that there was a leak in her operation. One she knew she could plug quickly and cleanly once she had the opportunity. But now, they would have to get the ship back and the island secured. It was a vital link in the chain of intelligence she had established, and now, of course, was a most crucial time. Not just in the Taiwan Strait but the entire region. Even worldwide.

"Well, if you can swing some air cover, those Liang Shan Special Operations boys that we trained with would be real helpful if my guys are going to do a takedown," Ward said. "A pair of UH-60s and a couple of Apaches would be real helpful, too."

Li Minh Zhou chuckled drily. "I assumed you would come up with that very plan, Commander Ward. We already have a flight of four Mirages scrambling out of Hsinchu. They were already on a 'ready sixty,' so we can have them orbiting the island by nightfall. The special operators are saddling up as we speak."

"You know I need authorization for us to participate," Ward told her. "But I know a guy. What's the timeline on the special ops team?"

"They are giving me a two-hour ETA. We'd better get our gear ready."

Ward cocked his head and gave her a long look. Lord, she was beautiful. And smart. And dangerous as hell. He was pretty sure he had fallen in love with her the first time he saw her. Sometimes he dared to think the feeling might be mutual.

"Whoa there. What's this 'we' that I just heard?" Ward shot in her direction. "Since when do you get to be a special operator?"

Li smiled, then slowly shook her head. "You have much to learn about me, young warrior. And if you think that you're going to fly out there and have all the fun while I sit here and worry, you need to think again."

Ψ

The sun was on the verge of setting when Ward and Li lugged their combat gear across the helo pad to the waiting UH-60 Black Hawk chopper. SEAL Master Chief Rex Johnston had already grabbed Jason Hall and Tony Martinelli and they had piled their gear into the bird. The latecomers had no more than harnessed in and hooked up to the intra-aircraft comms system when the bird lifted off, wasting no time in heading west.

Li Minh Zhou immediately took charge. "What is the airborne situation?" she demanded from the ground controller back at Keelung. He responded that the Mirages were on the scene, orbiting just outside the range of the HQ-10 anti-aircraft missiles the Chinese corvettes carried. Those warships were maintaining station around the *Myoung Song*. It appeared there was some problem in attempting to get the cable-laying vessel underway.

The Mirages were reporting they had about another hour on station, then they would be relieved by a flight of four F-CK-1 Ching Kuo fighters already primed and waiting on the tarmac. Or they could be airborne in seconds if things got out of hand in the meantime.

Li Minh Zhou directed the helicopter pilot to follow a circuitous route that would take them around Matsu Island to the south. Then they were to fly at wavetop height and max speed as they approached the west side of Gaodeng Island. That would allow the island's mass to hide them from the corvettes' air search radars, and they would also be below most radars on the Chinese coast. By the time they arrived, the night would be coal black and the eight attack jets would be rendezvousing ten miles to the southeast.

They apparently made it undetected. There was no greeting from the Chinese. It was go time.

On Li's order, the jets swung around and dove for the deck, then headed inbound on the Chinese vessels. As the warplanes started their high-speed firing passes at the corvettes, the Apache helicopters suddenly appeared just above the island's ridge line and set loose two pairs of Hellfire missiles, followed by two more. Their thirty-millimeter chain guns then added to the awful roar of hot ordnance being unleashed.

The Type 56 corvettes were surprised and overpowered by the ferocity of the airborne assault. By the time the UH-60 helicopters crossed the ridge line, three of the ships were nothing more than burning hulks and the other two were beating a hasty retreat toward China.

As the lead UH-60 pulled up in a hover, thirty feet above the *Myoung Song*'s broad work deck, ropes dropped out of both cargo doors. Jim Ward and Li Minh Zhou raced in, fast-rappelling down to the deck. So far, there was nobody shooting at them. They hit steel at the same instant, both in a combat crouch, their Mark 18 CQBR carbines constantly scanning back and forth, snapping around like cobras looking for prey. The two of them rolled for cover as if they were a choregraphed dance team.

Meanwhile, Master Chief Johnston and Tony Martinelli hit the deck right behind them, closely followed by Jason Hall and the Taiwanese special operators. By then, small arms fire spattered the deck around them. Johnston let out a pained yelp and fell, clutching his thigh. Martinelli immediately grabbed hold of him and yanked him behind the cable reel. He started first aid as Hall and Ward sprayed the upper deck with fire.

Li and the Taiwanese, having studied the ship's layout on the trip over, quickly worked around to the port side. Ward caught a quick glance of her as she raced up a ladder to the next deck, skipping two rungs each step, constantly firing as she ran.

He knew it now. He loved this woman.

But then, the darkness was ripped apart by bright light as there was a sharp, ear-numbing explosion. Someone had used a grenade on the upper deck.

Then it fell deathly quiet. No shooting. No shouting.

Clearly, that part of the fight was now over. And there was no way to tell who had won the round.

Ψ

As Qianting Laoda climbed up the long vertical ladder to the bridge of his brand-new *Improved Yuan*-class submarine, he contemplated a long-held complaint of his. The unimaginative Chinese People's Liberation Army Navy bureaucracy had, somewhere in the far distant past, determined that submarines should only have pennant numbers, not names. Therefore, his recently commissioned boat was officially known as Pennant 346. However, since no self-respecting submariner would ever be satisfied having his boat be named something that sounded like the address of someone's apartment, the crew had unofficially named her the *Shizi Yu*. The *Lionfish*, a showy marine species with distinctive banded coloration but nasty, venomous fins.

Now he was about to get the *Shizi Yu* underway for their first real-world mission. The orders were really quite simple, not very challenging at all. He was to steam down to the Spratly Islands to conduct a covert security patrol. After two weeks of very boring operations, he was to pull into Fiery Cross Reef to refuel, then head back to homeport. It was a great opportunity to take his inexperienced crew out to sea and shape them into a powerful fighting group, a real lionfish.

But still, he was hearing bits of news of far more interesting activities by PLAN, and much of it in the area in which he and his crew would mostly be doing little more than treading water. Qianting was just as certain he could prepare his men with real action on this very useful vessel. The captain was considering the possibilities of his boat being dragged into some of the action as he reached the top of the ladder and emerged from the gloomy bridge trunk into the bright morning sun on the bridge.

From this position, high above the boat's main deck, he had a good view of all the last-minute activities before they moved away from the pier. The boat's two big diesel engines were burbling quietly, thin traces of diesel smoke wafting up into the fresh morning breeze. The shore-power cables had all been disconnected and were now piled neatly on the pier. The brow had been lifted away and a tug was tied up to the two forward cleats, ready to pull the submarine's bow away from the pier. All the boat's crewmen who were assigned to be line handlers were now standing at rigid attention in formation just aft of the sail.

The captain nodded to his watch officer, who returned the gesture. All preparations were completed. Time to get the *Shizi Yu* underway. The watch officer barked a few orders. The line handlers scurried to cast off all lines. The tug belched a cloud of gray diesel smoke as its screw bit into the water. Open water appeared between the boat and the pier. The lines strained mightily as the tug pulled the *Shizi Yu* out into Yulin Harbor. It took only a few seconds to cast the tug off, separating the two ships, and then for all the line handlers to lay below.

Qianting felt the sea wind on his face for the first time as they cleared the breakwater at Shenjiao. As usual when he left homeport, he felt relief from the stilted rigors and regulations of the Sanya Naval Base and Hainan Island. He was leaving them behind. Now, he was in total control of vessel and crew. And it was time to face the adventures of the open sea, to finally discover what the *Shizi Yu* was really capable of.

14

Captain Tranh Vu awoke with a start. For a few very pleasant minutes, he had been back at home in Cam Phuc Nam with his family, enjoying a meal. But now he had been rudely returned to the reality of a truly bad situation. He had awakened from a pleasant dream and thrust into the midst of a terrifying nightmare.

He was lying on his bunk in his stateroom of the sunken submarine he commanded, the *Bà Rịa-Vũng Tàu.* Instead of being home, he was marooned, his boat resting on the bottom of the South China Sea. As his head cleared, Tranh realized that it was already day three of this ordeal. The clock was ticking and he still did not have a good answer for the question of how they might best survive.

Tranh slowly swung his legs off his bunk and rose. His stateroom was dark and only a single bulb dimly illuminated the passageway outside the door. He remembered that the previous evening he had ordered all unnecessary lights secured so they could conserve the dwindling electric power from the submarine's batteries. That was also when he had ordered all the heaters secured, too. It amazed him that they were located only eight degrees north of the equator—barely nine hundred kilometers—but the sea-bottom temperature was only three degrees Celsius above the freezing point. He clutched his jacket tighter around himself and stepped out into the passageway. Best to walk around the boat and make certain that the crewmembers were as safe and comfortable as possible, that their spirits had not dwindled, and that they were ready to do whatever they had to do to try to save the submarine when the time came. When they had some idea what those measures might be.

He only wished that his thumping headache would ease a bit. Each heartbeat was akin to a hammer blow to his temples.

Three of the injured men had succumbed during the night. The captain found most of the surviving crew huddled together on the mess decks, trying to maintain their morale. They were wrapped in blankets. Some attempted to nap. Others toyed with their food. Tranh smiled ruefully. At least food was not one of his problems.

He stopped at the air monitoring station. The atmosphere's oxygen level appeared all right, if a little low, at nineteen percent. The carbon dioxide level, however, had come up enough that it was something to be concerned about. Where it had been five hundred parts per million the previous day, it was now reading almost six thousand ppm. That certainly explained his headache. And the higher the CO2 level climbed, the more dangerous it would become. If it reached a reading of forty thousand parts per million, it became lethal. Before long, they would need to put down another layer of the CO2 absorbent chemical, calcium hydroxide crystals, to keep the concentration from rising any faster. They normally carried enough cannisters for two weeks' emergency use. But half the cannisters had been stored back in the engine room and, of course, were now lost. The rest were stored up in the torpedo room. But they had just discovered that several of those cannisters had been contaminated from leaking hydraulic oil and would be of no use to them.

Thanh calculated that they had enough cannisters for maybe six days if they were careful with how they used them. But his real problem was the atmospheric pressure inside his ship. They were already up more than two atmospheres and it would only climb. Little leaks from the high-pressure air system, bleeding oxygen from the storage bottles, or quite simple things like digesting food or expelling methane all added to the air pressure.

Thanh tried to remember all the complicated partial-pressure equations that governed how the human body reacted to the various gases as the pressure built up. But he was unable to calculate easily. This headache was not allowing him to think at his best. But there was one thing of which he was stone-cold certain. The combination of the rising pressure and increasing CO_2 levels were the real dangers they faced. Those two things would kill him and his crew well before they ran out of oxygen.

Thanh shivered and stepped back to his stateroom to grab a blanket. Then again, maybe the cold would get them first. He was not certain, though, which might offer the easiest and most comfortable route out of this life and into the next one.

After all, he had never before died in a stricken submarine at the bottom of the sea. And those who had could not tell their tale.

Ψ

President Stanley Smitherman sat back in the Jefferson wingback chair and swirled the ice in his bourbon glass. Secretary of Defense—and now vice-presidential candidate—Harold Osterman lounged tiredly on the red leather chesterfield sofa with his feet propped up on the pricey antique mahogany coffee table. The two were sitting in a room that was advertised in all the White House literature as being the presidential dining room. President Smitherman had redecorated it along the lines of an English gentlemen's club and mostly used it as a smoking room, a place to have a drink and enjoy a good cigar and commiserate with whoever was amenable to listening to him.

He and Osterman were enjoying a little down time at the end of a busy day of campaigning just across the Potomac in vote-rich Northern Virginia. They had a more far-flung agenda set for the next few days' campaigning, but some damn pesky international flare-ups necessitated they postpone and remain close to home. Certain members of the press had already given him grief for allowing politics to interfere with his duty to keep America safe.

The large-screen television that filled most of the room's far wall was tuned to CNN. A network reporter had just finished a recap of Osterman's most recent swing through the upper Midwest along with his quick run through the Commonwealth of Pennsylvania. The network used video footage that had been carefully framed and cropped to insinuate that the events had been heavily attended by enthusiastic supporters. That, of course, had not been the case at all.

Osterman puffed on his stogie, then reached over to the side table for his Manhattan glass. "They do manage to get some good camera angles," he commented. "Sure would be nice if we really did have the crowds like what they're reporting."

Smitherman snorted. "They damn well better get good camera angles. We sure as hell feed them enough exclusive stories and prime material ahead of anybody else." He took a good, stiff swallow of bourbon. "At least they did try to put a positive spin on the polls, God bless 'em."

The television news update shifted to international stories. The top news was about the dust-up between Taiwan and the People's Republic of China over some inconsequential little island over there. This one was, apparently, more serious than the decades of ranting and threats that hardly drew any news organization's attention anymore. This time, actual live rounds of ammunition were being exchanged. And there had apparently been loss of life among some of the Taiwanese troops on the island.

"A worrisome escalation," the grave-faced news anchor called it.

Secretary Osterman was about to say something more about the disappointing direction the campaign was going, but President Smitherman held up his hand as he leaned in to listen more intently to the TV report. He flipped the replay button on the remote control so he could go back to the beginning of the story.

"Hold up, Harold. You hearing this? You know what they always say. 'Don't ever let a good crisis go to waste.' I think we just got handed our 'good crisis.'"

The two puffed their cigars as the commentator rambled on about the death and destruction at the north end of the Taiwan Strait. Then President Smitherman sat back and smiled broadly.

"Harold, they briefed us on this on the trip back from Virginia, but I bet neither one of us realized what's being given to us on a silver plate here by that damn Tan Yong. Let's ramp this thing up and kill two birds with one stone. We'll get Tan to cool his damn jets by reminding him we can just slap a big enough tariff on his ass to put his economy in the shitter, even as our holiday shopping season approaches. And we can have Congress cancel that wheat, chicken, and hog trade agreement they need so damn desperately to feed all those billions of Chinese this winter. And if Congress is too worried about the votes that'd cost them, we'll do an executive order. But at the same time, you can get those admirals of yours to park a couple of their carriers just far enough off the coast to say, 'We ain't shootin' yet, but...' And that's what we feed to the media. Show 'em this administration is tough as a pine nut when it has to be. China or the Middle East oil cartels or those obstructionist senators on the other side of the aisle..."

Smitherman stopped. His Secretary of Defense was frowning.

"Mr. President, I don't know how hard we want to push back right now. We're hearing some dangerous rumblings from Tan and his bunch this time around. It could be a delicate..."

"Damn it, Harold. He's giving us just what we need just when we need it most. I'll make a back-channel call to make sure his guys know to stay in the box. A little bluster and sword rattling could help us both and I'll make sure the bastard understands that." The president excitedly grabbed up the phone. "I'll have Sally set us up a press conference tomorrow first thing so we can express our grave concern about the deterioration in the international situation—certainly due to the mismanagement and incompetence of the previous administration—and to explain how, as a seasoned, stabilizing force, the Smitherman team will maintain peace and world order."

Harold Osterman lost the frown. A big smile slowly claimed his flushed face.

"I love it. Just enough bullshit to be plausible. This just might work."

The president sat back and smoked for a moment. Then he leaned forward, a quizzical expression on his own flushed face.

"Harold, you and all your guys won't let this go too far, will you?" he asked. "I reckon we don't really need there to be a shootin' war over some little old island."

Osterman looked hard at his boss.

"Not unless it allows us to reclaim Ohio and Wisconsin and still keep Virginia!"

Both men hooted, clinked their glasses, and toasted, "To not quite a shootin' war."

Ψ

The orange hull of the M/V *Swift Rescue* shone brightly in the morning light. Samuel Leong, the Singapore rescue vessel's civilian master, braced himself against a chart table on the vessel's bridge and stretched his aching muscles. His wife kept telling him that he was too old to be driving a ship at sea. Lately, he had begun agreeing with her. It certainly would be nice to sit out in the garden with a cup of tea and play with the grandbabies. Maybe when this mission was done. But he knew there would always be another mission. Thankfully, they came few and far between. But when they did, they almost always involved saving human lives. And Samuel Leong was absolutely correct in his belief that he was among the best in the world at what he did.

Leong checked their navigation position on the charts. GPS had been acting very strange, giving random erroneous positions. However, GLONASS, the Russian GPS system, seemed to be working just fine. 112.92 East longitude and 7.708 North latitude. That was just about where he was supposed to rendezvous with his American escort, the LCS ship USS *Canberra*.

Leong really was not sure what the purpose of the escort ship was. If the Chinese wanted to prevent any rescue attempt, the little LCS would offer only very limited protection.

"Motor Vessel *Swift Rescue*, this is US Navy helicopter Three-two-six inbound to your position with three pax," the bridge-to-bridge radio blared. That was the other reason to have his ship at this coordinate. The "pax"—passengers—would have more information for Leong and his crew, and among them, they hoped to quickly formulate a plan. Time was short, if they were not too late already. "Request permission to land."

Leong grabbed the microphone and answered, "Three-two-six, permission granted. Welcome to *Swift Rescue*." He looked out the bridge window as the haze-gray MH-60S helicopter came in out of the sun and swung around the ship.

Five minutes later Colonel Wong Su, the Commander of the Singapore Navy Submarine Rescue Command—and ostensibly Leong's boss, or maybe his customer since the command relationship for the rescue service was really murky—stepped into the *Swift Rescue*'s bridge house. Two uniformed men accompanied him. Wong Su introduced the pair as Captain Huan Kuan, Commodore of the Vietnam Navy's 189th Submarine Brigade, and Captain Joe Glass, Commodore of the US Navy Submarine Squadron Seven.

The new arrivals accepted cold bottles of water and then the four huddled around the chart table at the back of the bridge house. Each man studied a large-scale chart of the area. Huan Kuan measured off a point on the chart about thirty-five kilometers south of Cuarteron Reef, then drew a one-kilometer circle around that point.

"Our best estimation on the *Bà Rịa-Vũng Tàu*'s location, based on the comms buoy information we received, is 8.875 degrees North and 112.811 East," the Vietnamese captain told them. "We estimate the accuracy as about one kilometer." He tapped the point on the chart with his index finger. "Our sub is right there, gentlemen. Water depth is about two hundred and fifty meters. If there are still survivors, they have only a short time remaining to live."

Leong stared at the chart for a few seconds, then shook his head. "That's too far for the DSAR-6—the submersible rescue vessel—to operate away from the *Swift Rescue*. Her max range is only about fifty kilometers." He used his fingers to step off the distance from where they were now located to the wreck site. "We're at ninety-five kilometers here. We need to get fifty kilometers closer."

"Problem with that," Joe Glass chimed in, "is up here at Cuarteron Reef. There are a whole bunch of Chinese warships that don't appear to be very hospitable right now. They sank your submarine and I suspect they are not going to want it un-sunk. I'm thinking that we need to stand off as far as we can and still make it work, preferably with some islands or reefs screening us a little."

The group stared at the chart for a long moment before Huan Kuan pointed at a reef off to the east a bit. "What about up here at Bãi Thuyền Chài. You Americans call it Barque Canada Reef. We had three communications towers there until the Chinese destroyed them all. Murdered twenty soldiers at the same time. According to my measurements, if we deploy in the deep water to the northwest of the reef, we would be slightly less than fifty kilometers from the wreck."

Leong nodded. "That would be marginal. But it appears to be our only choice. We are only three hours from there now. I'll get us underway immediately and get the DSAR-6 ready to launch."

Joe Glass spoke up. "If you gentlemen will excuse me, I need to fly over to the *Canberra* and bring them up to speed with the plan. My heart is with those bubbleheads down there, and much as I'd like to be there to shake their hands when you bring them up, I need to do what I can to give you the best chance of making it happen. I'm going to see about getting a couple of those Marine NMESIS systems flown over to that reef. It might be helpful to have a couple more anti-ship missile launchers handy."

Each man nodded somberly and shook hands again. All except Samuel Leong. He was already on the communicator putting things in motion.

Then Joe Glass was double-timing across the deck, headed for the MH-60S helicopter resting on the landing pad but now spinning up, raring to go.

Ψ

The aide quietly swung the heavy teak doors open just enough to slip inside the room. Entering the expansive office, he bowed from the waist and murmured, "A thousand pardons, honored elder brother, for interrupting."

Tan Yong, First Secretary of the Chinese Communist Party and President of China, glanced up from the report he was studying. "Yes, Min Toa, what is it?"

The aide referred to a piece of paper in his hand. "Honored elder brother, the video conference call with the Central National Security Commission. All are connected and ready for the meeting," Min Toa said, still whispering. "General Shao Jing is in the Navy Command Center at Fuzhou. Deng Jiang is at the Cyber Warfare Center in Hangzhou. Lei

Miayang and Sun Yang are at the Southern Theater Command Center. They have General Zuoyi Jundui with them."

Tan Yong nodded. "Please establish the link to my screen and check to make sure it is verified as secure before we proceed."

As the aide nodded and left the office, Tan rose and stepped over to look out the heavy bulletproof glass window that filled one full wall of the big room. He allowed happy thoughts as he gazed upon the view outside. The late fall sun cast a golden glow over the placid South Sea Lake and the peaceful Zhongnanhai gardens. Tan Yong loved this view. Especially the quiet orderliness. And it was more relaxing than ever on a beautiful autumn morning. Even if the ever-present pollution appeared to have dropped a thick curtain that prevented him from seeing anything any more distant.

"Honorable elder brother." Min Toa interrupted the president's rare minute of revery. "The links are established and verified secure."

Tan Yong turned back to his xiangzhi wood writing table and waved the aide out of the room as he plopped down in front of the screen. Before activating the system, he first checked his face in a small mirror he kept close at hand. He had to be certain there was not a hair out of place or a speck of food on his chin.

"Xiānshēngmen, gentlemen," he said when General Shao appeared on the big screen. He could not see the faces of the two others in squares at the bottom of the screen. "We have much to discuss concerning both the results of our current activities and the details of our upcoming plans. First on our agenda is General Shao's report on our northern diversion activity."

The Chinese general's face filled the center of the screen as he started his report. He was a veteran of many difficult and deadly situations, both in open combat as well as in this more subtle but just as hazardous type of political knife fight. He well knew that everything depended on appearances. Success was all that mattered, and the Gaodeng Island diversion had to be considered a success. Or at least, he would have to sell his commander on the notion that it was.

"Zūnjìng de dì yī shūjì, Honorable First Secretary, the northern diversion activity is well underway. We have made our first rather restrained moves. Our wayward brothers on Taiwan responded with great violence.

More than our intelligence had predicted. Even so, the timeline is proceeding as planned. The American media is reporting the heightened tensions widely. Using our normal assets in the West, we have planted stories in their media of major troop movements and possible invasion preparations. We have reliable reports that we can expect American ship movements very soon."

Tan Yong rubbed his chin for a few seconds. Then he spoke quietly, evenly. The general shivered noticeably on the screen.

"General Shao, a very concise report, indeed. However, I am not at all certain that we can correctly term the loss of three of our warships and the failure to capture the Taiwanese ship as a successful first step on our well-planned path."

"Honorable leader," the general responded, "remember that this is only the first step of a very sophisticated plan. Despite the minor difficulties, it was a step in the right direction. We have accomplished much of our aim of deflection. The cost was low, only three inconsequential ships and a few sailors. The strategic gains are significant."

The Chinese president nodded. Now was not the time to chastise the general. He was, after all, correct. The strategic goal was still well within their grasp, even if the tactical victory had eluded them this time. Tan Yong remembered Qián Dài's wise council. Taiwan was merely a diversion. The goal was still the resources surrounding the South China Sea. Those he must have for survival. Once they were in hand, he could pluck Taiwan like a ripe plum.

Tan Yong pursed his lips and told Shao, "Very well, General. Please continue to supervise this plan to its conclusion." Turning slightly, he clicked on the small box to the bottom left and continued, "Now, Deng Jiang, please bring us up to date on the activities at the Cyber Warfare Center."

The window on the screen enlarged to show a large, well-lit room filled with cubicles in the background. People sat in them, hunched over flickering computer screens, punching away diligently at their keyboards, obviously doing their best work for the People's Republic of China and the Communist Party. Deng Jiang, the Committee's cyber expert, sat in a chair in the foreground, centered on the screen.

"Zūnjìng de dì yī shūjì," Deng greeted the First Secretary. "Our operations here are going well. We are conducting the final tests on our next cyber-attack, which we have named 'Kill Shot.' It will bring America and her lackeys to their knees. We will be ready in time to coordinate with Lei Miayang and Sun Yang and their planned efforts in the south."

Tan Yong's face broke into a smile. The president rocked slightly back and forth, considering the import of what his cyber warfare specialist was telling him. This was a crucial element of the overall plan. And once it was enacted, there would be no recall.

"And how are you doing with the tap on the military communications circuit?" Tan asked.

Was there a tell-tale pause in the cyber expert's response? Tan chose to listen and not probe.

"Yes. We already have succeeded in capturing a massive amount of what we believe will be very useful data. The Americans have layered in very sophisticated protective algorithms, but we will soon penetrate and have access to a very exciting trove of information."

"That is good to hear. Now let us see if our brothers down at Southern Command have equally good news."

The screen shifted to what was obviously a military command center. Large-screen displays covered the walls in the background. Each was filled with maps festooned with hieroglyphics, symbols that the indoctrinated could easily translate into troop or ship movements. Uniformed men wearing headsets sat around desks on the periphery of the scene. Most were talking into their microphones, apparently passing orders or information out of the command center to those on the front lines. Lei Miayang and Sun Yang were in large leather chairs at the end of a small conference table. General Zuoyi Jundui sat to their left. Lei Miayang started the conversation.

"Honorable First Secretary, I am proud to say that, due to the diligent efforts of our loyal PLA troops and PLAN sailors, all is in readiness to commence Operation Southern Sweep. Upon your orders, our ships and planes will clear the South China Sea of all the unwanted vermin that now infest it. With those waters once again restored to their historic position as a Chinese lake, our forces will sweep across it in unprecedented numbers to protect our sovereign position at the southern end of the First Island Chain."

The room and the video conference circuit went quiet. The import of those words—"southern end of the First Island Chain"—was stunning when they were spoken out loud and in the context of the plan that was already unfolding. While typically including all the primary archipelagos off the east coast of China including Japan and all the way to the Aleutians, each leader knew they were now talking about the Philippines and the large island of Borneo, then on around the South China Sea to Vietnam. Eventually, too, Taiwan. But not just yet.

As each man considered the historic magnitude of the upcoming operation, Min Toa stepped quietly into the room, leaned down to Tan Yong, and whispered in his ear. The president nodded, then turned his attention back to the video monitor.

"Gentlemen, an excellent briefing. Our plans go forward. We will commence Operation Southern Sweep in two days. Launch Kill Shot in coordination. The time is near when the Middle Kingdom will once again stand in its rightful place atop the order of the world's nations. Now, please excuse me. The American president is seeking the opportunity to speak to me on the secure phone." The menacing glint in his eye was obvious even on the big-screen displays. "It will be most interesting to see what he has on his mind."

With that, and without waiting for any response from his top commanders, Tan pushed the button that cut power to the display.

The screen went blank.

15

LCDR Jeremy Chastain considered the location where the latest bottom contour fix placed their submarine. The inertial nav system had been working within tolerance, but it sure would be nice to have a good old GPS fix before they launched their fish. The USS *Boise* would need to be inside the launch box, fifteen nautical miles south of the Chinese PLAN's Yulin Naval base. That part was easy. The hard part was that each unmanned, mine-carrying submersible needed a precise position—best within ten yards—prior to launch if they were going to steer themselves into the harbor and settle down into their proper resting place on the bottom. Now, with the Chinese fiddling with the GPS signals, he simply was unable to get the required accuracy to give to the submersibles.

"Got a problem, Nav?" Henrietta Foster, the *Boise*'s XO, had noticed the young officer's concerned expression. "You look like somebody just flipped over your 500-piece picture puzzle."

"Damn close, XO. I ain't figured out how we're ever gonna meet launch specs for those SLMMs down there in the torpedo room," Chastain answered. His usual Philly accent became more pronounced when he was under stress. "Those mines need to know where they start from if they're s'posed to get to the place they're s'posed to be goin'."

Foster stared down at the electronic chart display for a moment. Even with the best bottom-contour navigation fix Chastain had just plotted, the error circle around where they believed the *Boise* now steamed was almost half a mile in diameter. They needed to get that error circle down to near a pinpoint to be sure the mines would be properly placed. Foster squinted at the chart for a bit as she tried to remember exactly how the position error inputs to the inertial nav system worked. It was new hardware and learning about it so far had been mostly OJT. On-the-job training.

Meanwhile, Chief Jimbo Dertmond, the navigation department leading chief, appeared to read the XO's mind. He leaned over the ECDIS table and opened his laptop, flipped through a bunch of screens, then stopped at one that explained the inner workings of their brand-new AN/WSN-9A Ring Laser Gyro Inertial Navigation System.

"XO, Nav," Chief Dertmond drawled, "I done read through all this stuff 'bout Baysian statistics, Gaussian distributions, and such like. Way I figure it, this here algorithm thing takes a whole buncha position inputs, does some kinda statistical analysis calculation thingy, and then pretty much says we're at the center of all them locations. Way we used to settle on a property line when we surveyed for a fence we was building back in Lubbock. Run a bunch of line-of-sights to all the wrong iron stakes that had popped up over the years and pick the average of the bunch."

Foster chuckled as she realized that she had just heard the most succinct description of inertial navigation error analysis ever to come out of West Texas. A "Navy brat" herself, she had heard plenty of dialects growing up near homeports all around the world, but she still wondered sometimes if she might need an interpreter where Chief Dertmond was concerned.

The bottom line was that if they assumed that all of the input errors had a normal distribution and if they could get enough position inputs, they could calculate out the wrong data. Even if none of them were as accurate as a true GPS fix. Now, all they needed was a bunch of valid fix sources to average. Then the XO looked down and realized the answer was right there on the ECDIS charts.

"Nav, Chief," she said. "Let's go talk to the skipper. We don't have a lot of time."

Chet Allison was sitting at his desk reviewing fitness reports when the trio arrived at his stateroom door.

"Skipper, we got a problem and a solution," Foster told him.

"Usually only get the former and not the latter," the captain said, idly rubbing his sternum and wincing.

"You okay?" Foster asked.

"Yeah, I don't think Cookie's turkey chili agrees with me. Making me sweat like a pig, too," he growled. "So, what you got?"

Foster shot him a questioning look. The cook's chili was bland to the point of tasteless. And she noted that Allison's skin color was not good, very pale. But he clearly did not care to discuss his health right now.

She nodded to the navigator to begin the explanation. It took him only a minute to explain the problem and outline their solution.

Allison listened quietly and then asked, "Will this work?"

All three nodded.

"Okay, what do we need to do?"

Chief Dertmond took over the discussion. "Skipper, easier to explain if you punch up the chart on your computer." When the chart of their current location appeared, the chief continued. "Way I got this figgered, we need as many nav fixes as we can grab to get a good read. Best way to do that is to do some in-shore piloting. We snuggle up close to the coast and take a bunch of range and bearing fixes off all those ritzy condos the 'Workers Paradise' has built above those beaches." Dertmond pointed to a spot on the chart. "We go to about here, real quiet, like we're sneakin' up on a polecat. Then we stick up number two scope, take a bearing, and use the laser range finder quick as we can. We got Sanya Point, Jinmu Point, and Baihu Point about sixty degrees apart from here. That's dang near perfect. We grab that statistically significant buncha fixes and then we hightail it back to deep water."

Allison looked over at Foster. "XO, you know that if we get caught, we are committing an act of war, right?"

"Skipper, we'll be committing an act of war whether they catch us or not," she responded. "And by the way, we're fixing to plant a bunch of mines in their harbor. I figure that's an even bigger act of war."

Allison smiled, still rubbing his breastbone with his thumb. "You've got a point there, XO." He stood. "Guess we had better get over to wherever

Chief Dertmond thinks works best." He waved the other three out of his stateroom and followed them into control.

Thirty seconds later, the damage control lights flashed to signal the crew to silently man battle stations. People scurried to their assigned positions, water-tight doors were carefully dogged shut, and damage control equipment was broken out and readied, all precisely as they had drilled scores of times before. This time it was for real. The *Boise* was ready to fight if it should come to it.

At ahead one-third, it took almost an hour to close the Chinese coast. But slow, stealthy, and careful would be the watchwords for the next little bit. The control room was eerily silent. Orders and reports were quietly passed in low voices. There was none of the usual watch-stander banter. The quiet only heightened the tension.

Jeremy Chastain had stationed himself beside Jimbo Dertmond at the ECDIS table, each watching the ship's position as they crawled north toward the small green circle that marked their goal. But well before they reached that green circle, they crossed over a much more worrisome line on the display, the red one that designated the beginning of China's internationally recognized territorial waters. If *Boise* were to be detected now, they could and almost certainly would be attacked without mercy. Nobody could argue they did not deserve it, either.

Finally, they reached the green circle. Chastain signaled the skipper with a thumbs-up.

Allison glanced around the control room. Time to go to work.

"Silence in control," he quietly ordered, although no one was speaking. "We're going up to periscope depth. I'll do a safety sweep first and then we'll grab range and bearings off the leftmost condo on each point on the first sweep. I'll drop the scope for a few seconds and then we'll repeat on the rightmost condos. We'll repeat this process two more times, then we'll get the hell out of Dodge and the good folks over there will never know they were on *Candid Camera*. Sonar, keep your ears open for any high-speed screws. In here, patrol craft are the biggest threat. ESM, report any periscope detection radars. Especially any low-power, SHF, FM-CW radars."

He looked around the control room one more time. Everything and everyone were seriously ready. Then he noticed Henrietta Foster looking at him oddly.

"You good, XO?"

"You look really pale, Skipper. You sure you're okay."

"I'm good. I'm good. Damn it, I'll get some Pepto or something from Doc Ballman when we're done. Raising number two scope. Dive, make your depth six-two feet."

The *Boise* slid up out of the depths. Allison watched as the scope broke on an ink-black sea. A quick sweep around showed a surprisingly empty patch of water with a dark, cloud-filled sky overhead. No moon or stars. Perfect.

"Left full rudder," Allison ordered. "We'll do a slow continuous circle here to help the fix accuracy and not close the beach." He spun the scope around toward the jut of land called Sanya Point. "Bearing Sanya, leftmost condo. Mark." He pushed the red button on the right scope handle. "Range, mark." He punched the laser range finder button on the periscope's left handle.

Chief Dertmond, reading the repeaters, gave the numbers in a stage whisper. "Bearing three-five-one, range nine-five-hundred yards."

"Bearing left, Jinmu. Mark. Range. Mark."

"Bearing, zero-five-seven. Range, seven-five-five-zero yards."

Then, an interruption to the series of quick exchanges.

"Conn, ESM, multiple surface search and air search radars, no threats."

Chastain continued to take the data as the chief was calling it out, inputting it into the WSN-9 system and awaiting the next bearing and range numbers.

Just then, Chet Allison let out a loud groan. Especially loud in the otherwise subdued control room. Then he grabbed his chest and slumped hard to the deck.

Without hesitation, Henrietta Foster reached up and lowered the scope with her right hand even as she grabbed the 1MC microphone with her left.

"Corpsman to control. The captain is down. Repeat. Captain is down." She turned to Lt. Bob Bland, the battle stations officer of the deck, and ordered, "Take care of the skipper." She then turned to the battle-stations team and said, "The captain is down. I'm assuming command. I have the conn. We'll continue with the operation."

Bland was already on his knees. He rolled the captain over onto his back, felt quickly for a pulse at Allison's throat, and then immediately began CPR. At the same time, he said loudly to the chief of the watch, "Get the doc up here now!" as he kept up the rhythmic chest compressions.

Foster had to lean over the two men sprawled on the deck at her feet as she reached up to raise the scope once again and put her eye to the eyepiece.

"Bearing left Baihu. Mark. Range. Mark." She lowered the scope for a moment as the submarine continued in its lazy circle, then again put it up just above the wavetops as she stepped over the captain, still prone on the deck, and as Chastain called out and entered the information.

"Bearing zero-six-seven. Range one-two-nine-four-zero yards."

None of them took time to notice as Doc Ballman, the boat's corpsman, rushed into control, carrying his automatic external defibrillator and first-aid bag. As Bland paused the CPR, Ballman knelt beside Allison and felt again for a pulse at the captain's jugular. Doc shook his head as he reached for the defibrillator. No heartbeat. He turned the little machine on and quickly positioned the pads on his skipper's chest. A recorded robotic voice —shockingly loud in the otherwise quiet compartment—called out, "Shock indicated. Stand clear of patient and push red shock button."

Thankfully, after only the lone shock, the AED's readout confirmed that Allison's heart had begun beating seemingly normally again. Doc gave a thumbs-up to Foster. Then he and Bland carried the unconscious skipper toward his stateroom.

Foster surveyed the control room as Allison was being carried out. The team was still doing their jobs but were clearly worried. The rest of the crew, up and down the length of the ship, probably felt the same. Everyone would have heard her summons of the corpsman and why. She grabbed the 1MC microphone and spoke just loudly enough to be heard on the announcing system throughout the *Boise*.

"Attention, crew. The skipper is alive but still unconscious. Doc is taking good care of him right now. Between God looking down and Doc's good hands, the skipper will be okay." She paused for a few seconds, then pointedly added, "For the rest of us, we still have a job to finish."

She put the mic back on its clip, reached up, and raised the periscope once more, as if there had been no disturbance at all.

"Bearing, Baihu rightmost condo. Mark. Range. Mark."

The team went right ahead with the process of gathering fixes, sweeping from right to left and then back as *Boise* steamed in a slow circle. It was nerve-wracking and tedious. Foster worked to make the fixes as accurate as possible while keeping the scope above the surface and exposed as little as absolutely necessary. She was just finishing the third round of fixes when the 21MC loudspeaker broke in on the process.

"Conn, ESM. Picking up a low-power FM-CW radar. Could be a periscope detection radar or could be just a fishing boat. If a periscope detection radar, this is a threat."

Threat indeed. Foster made a quick three-sixty sweep around and lowered the scope. She looked back at Chastain. "Nav, we have enough data?"

Chastain shook his head. "Still not within launch parameters. We need at least another sweep. Two would be best."

"Okay," she answered. "Raising number two scope."

It was already going up and near full height when she called out, "Bearing, Sanya leftmost condo. Mark. Range, mark."

"Conn, Sonar. New contact, Sierra Four-two. Bearing zero-one-two. High-speed screws. Classify patrol boat."

Not a fishing boat. Something with teeth. Foster swung the scope around a few degrees and calmly called out, "Bearing, left Baihu, mark. Range, mark."

"Conn, ESM. FM-CW contact, increase in power. Definite threat."

Not just teeth. Fangs, too.

Again, Foster swung the scope a few more degrees and clearly announced, enunciating perfectly so as to be easily understood the first time, "Bearing, left Baihu, mark. Range, mark."

"Conn, ESM, picking up a Z-20 surface search radar. ASW helicopter threat."

Another uninvited attendee, this one with fangs, claws, and talons. Foster slapped up the periscope's handles and lowered it.

"Folks, we may well have overstayed our welcome here," she said. "Dive, make your depth three hundred feet. Ahead full. Helm, steer course south. We need to be somewhere where we currently ain't."

16

The *Swift Rescue* rolled easily in the gentle swell. Barque Canada Reef and the North Tower wreckage were just visible on the southeast horizon. The *Canberra* circled protectively a few thousand yards away. It was a peaceful, quiet scene, except for the bustle of activity on the rescue ship's fantail. The glistening-white DSAR-6 rescue submarine dangled from the ship's stern-mounted A-frame crane. The deck crew swarmed around it making last-minute adjustments as they prepared to deploy the submersible into the waters of the South China Sea.

Major Jiang Tay, the DSAR-6's officer in charge, nestled down into the pilot's seat, donned his headset, and adjusted it for comfort. He looked out through the thick plexiglass bubble that made up the nose of the small submarine. He could watch the deck crew as they removed the power umbilical, effectively cutting the little submarine off from its mothership. For the next twelve hours or so, they would depend on the lithium-ion batteries housed under the deck plates beneath Tay's feet.

It was not lost on the major that most of the materials necessary for the manufacture of those vital batteries came from China. The same country who would most certainly be willing to shoot him and his little rescue submersible out of the water if they knew they were there and what they were trying to do.

The co-pilot, Military Expert-4 Sonny Tui, wormed his way through the hatch from the passenger compartment and plopped down into his own chair. He gave Tay a thumbs-up.

"Everything's ready in the back of the bus," Tui reported.

Jiang Tay smiled. "Okay, Sonny, let's get this show on the road and go rescue some guys." He made one final check of his control panel and keyed his microphone. "Mama, Little Boy. All systems are go. Ready to deploy."

"Little Boy, Mama," came Samuel Leong's voice in the two men's headsets. "Roger. Beginning deployment sequence."

Tay felt the DSAR-6 being lifted and swung out over the *Swift Rescue*'s stern and then lowered toward the water. The view through the bubble abruptly shifted from light-blue sky to deep-blue water. As the submarine settled into the sea, they felt the jolt as the crane released them. Tay flipped the toggles that energized the motors, eased forward on the joystick, and the vessel smoothly slipped down into the depths. After setting a course of three-one-two into the autopilot, he sat back in his seat, settling in for the next six hours. At a top speed of five knots, it was going to take them that long to get to the wreck site.

For the next six hours, he and his co-pilot had very little to do. Except, of course, contemplate what they would find when they ultimately reached the sea floor and, hopefully, the stricken submarine that awaited them down there.

Ψ

Henrietta Foster stepped down from the low periscope stand in *Boise*'s control room. The submarine had been running south for almost an hour after the near-encounter with Chinese submarine hunters. Even so, sonar could still hear the distant pings from somebody's active sonar somewhere behind them. Time to slow down and quietly slink away. No sense in letting those angry hornets back near Hainan get another hint of their presence. No, best plan was to clear datum and then sneak back in later to complete the mission and get those mines in place.

With things a little calmer in control, Foster stepped forward to find out how Chet Allison was doing. She saw that the CO's stateroom now looked more like a hospital ICU unit. Allison was lying, still unconscious, on his bunk. Electrical leads stretched from Allison over to a small portable EKG monitor that rested on his desk. Several lines danced across the machine's tiny screen. A bag of saline hung from an IV stand at the foot of the bunk. The tube ran across Allison's body to where a needle fed the solution into his left wrist.

Doc Ballman was taking the patient's blood pressure when Foster stepped in.

She waited until he looked up before she asked, "How is he, Doc?"

Ballman shook his head, frowning. "Not really sure. He had a definite atrial fibrillation incident and the heart stopped. The shock from the AED kicked the heart back to a rhythm, thank goodness. But the EKG is showing continuing abnormalities. He is showing high ventricular rates. I have him on an IV of amiodarone. That's supposed to stabilize the heart rhythm. My books call for a 150-milligram bolus over a ten-minute period."

Foster was in over her head but not afraid to admit it. "Bolus?"

"Sorry for the jargon," Doc said with a weak smile. "Bolus is just a one-shot dose of a medication. We'll see if that stabilizes the rhythm. I'm worried that he hasn't regained consciousness yet, though. We really do need to get him somewhere that we can medivac him. Or at least where I can talk to a cardio specialist and get some ideas. In the meantime, I'm going to start him on propranolol as a beta blocker and diltiazem as a calcium blocker as soon as I get the IVAC pump rigged up."

Foster was well aware that she was facing a quandary that required a tough decision. She told the corpsman she would have an answer for him shortly. She walked forward the few paces to her own stateroom. There, she first grabbed a couple of ibuprofen tablets from her medicine cabinet. Once she had washed them down with a glass of water, she sat down on her bunk to think.

On the one hand, Chet Allison needed medical attention. Certainly more than Doc Ballman and the *Boise*'s limited medical facilities could provide for him. His life could be hanging in the balance. But to get him help, they would have to run many miles out into the South China Sea before they could even pop up the comms antenna and tell SUBGROUP SEVEN about the problem. To safely do a medivac, they would need to run all the way across to the Philippines. That was a full-day transit in each direction.

On the other hand, the *Boise* was on a critical mission. One that could very well prevent a shooting war. They had already worked their way—at considerable risk to the ship and crew—into a position where they were close to successfully completing the job. There was no way to know if they would ever be able to get close enough again without even more risk of the Chinese finding them. From here, it would take them the rest of this day to work their way back up into the launch box. Then all night to load and launch the mines.

Would Chet Allison survive the extra day's delay?

Foster wrestled with the decision for several minutes. There was no one aboard the *Boise* she could turn to for advice. So, she did what she always did when facing a knotty problem. What would her dad have told her? He had been chief of the boat on four different submarines over almost thirty years in the Silent Service. She would never forget the look of pride on his face the day she graduated from sub school in Groton. He had only lived a few more months after that happy day.

But there was that time she had asked him about making tough decisions. He had surely made his share over the years. And he quoted Teddy Roosevelt for an answer. "In any moment of decision, the best thing you can do is the right thing, the next best thing is the wrong thing, and the worst thing you can do is nothing."

Doing nothing was not an option here. But what was the right thing?

The sound-powered phone buzzed noisily. Foster picked up the handset. "XO."

"XO, Officer of the Deck, request you come to control. We're at the south end of our operating box. We need to know what to do now."

Foster slapped her thighs and stood up. She had made her decision.

Hang in there, Skipper. Duty called. Time to head back north and finish their job.

"Appreciate it, Pop," she said, not quite aloud, as she stepped toward control. But she had no doubt he had heard her.

Ψ

Tranh Vu shivered involuntarily. The cold had become almost unendurable. But he endured. His head still pounded and he was often dizzy, but he endured that, too. At least, so far.

He checked his wristwatch, a gift from his late wife and children many years before. For Christmas, a holiday hardly celebrated in Vietnam. Just by the small number of remaining Catholics and a very few Protestants. Sometimes, if he lay very still and put the watch to his ear, he could hear its faint ticking. He thought of it as his wife's heartbeat and it gave him some small manner of comfort.

They were now well into day five of their ordeal. Five days resting here on the bottom of the South China Sea, wondering if anyone even knew they were here, let alone if somebody might be coming to attempt to rescue them. Tranh would never admit it to his crew but he was on the very edge of giving up all hope and surrendering to the inevitable. It would be so much easier to place the wristwatch next to his ear, listening to his wife's heartbeat as he slipped into peaceful sleep, not to awaken until he had transitioned into the next life and could be with her once again.

Then Tranh Vu shook himself. Such thoughts were dangerous. Unbecoming to a leader of men. He had a crew that depended on him. If he gave up—or if he even offered a hint to any of them that he was giving up—then all hope would be lost for them, too. He had to keep up the appearance that he remained certain everything would be all right, even if he no longer believed it at all.

He walked to the mess decks. His entire surviving crew huddled there in a mass of blankets, all in an effort to preserve a little warmth. The men had long since stopped feeling uncomfortable about hugging each other beneath those blankets. Whatever it took to stop the shivering. The two remaining injured men were near the center of the huddle. The rest occasionally rotated positions to give everyone equal chance for warmth, much like the penguins that Tranh had read about somewhere. Two people had remained on duty at all times—starting out standing four-hour watches—up in the control room. They were there to listen on the underwater telephone for any sign of rescuers. If they heard anything—anything at all—they were to begin banging on the hull every five minutes with a big wrench. It had become so unbearably cold in the last day that those two were now being rotated every half hour.

Tranh pulled the blanket even more tightly around his shivering body. He needed to check the remainder of the boat. Maybe the movement would raise his body temperature a bit. But there were other practical reasons as well.

First stop was the atmosphere control panel. It appeared that the carbon dioxide had more or less stabilized at about ten thousand parts per million. Remaining immobile may have helped. But the truth was that to keep the deadly gas at that level, they had been forced to use their calcium hydroxide at an alarming rate. Now, they had only two unopened cannisters left. Maybe enough for two more days.

The pressure in the boat was even more worrisome. It had built up to four atmospheres. That was akin to scuba diving down to forty meters and then living there for a week. Any potential rescuer would have to have the capability to decompress the entire crew for several days or they would all die of the bends. That, he knew, would be a very painful way to go.

The Vietnamese skipper next wandered back into the fifth compartment. The space housing the big diesel engines and electrical controls normally hummed with activity. It was now deserted, deathly quiet. He checked the battery status. Both showed about twenty percent capacity. Maybe now they could afford to energize the mess deck heaters, if only for a couple of hours.

Tranh allowed himself a very thin smile. He had even stopped shivering for a moment at the very thought of it.

A bit warmer for a couple of hours. Then, at least, they would be more comfortable when they all ultimately slipped into the sleep from which they would never awaken.

It would ultimately justify the wastefulness of draining the precious energy from the batteries. He turned and began stiffly making his way back to give the order.

Ψ

Major Jiang Tay now had the DSAR-6's forward lights illuminated at full power. Down two hundred and fifty meters under the South China Sea, the water was eternally pitch black. Not even a stray photon ever penetrated this deep. The pilot's eyes constantly scanned the depths as he searched for the downed *Bà Rịa-Vũng Tàu* Vietnamese submarine. But the pilot also made sure to keep one eye on the battery power meter. That was, in effect, DSAR-6's fuel gauge. When it got down into the forty-percent charge, they would have to head home, whether they found the sub or not. There was no marine version of AAA to come out and give them a tow. Especially considering they were only a few miles from some very hostile Chinese PLAN warships.

The co-pilot, Sonny Tui, was locked in on the tiny submarine's side-scan sonar display. They had a far better chance of locating the lost submarine using the side-scan than they did visually by just looking out the bubble and seeing the limited distance the light could show them. The high-frequency sonar system swept a band five-hundred meters out on either side of the DSAR-6. But the side-scan sonar had a blind spot immediately underneath the unit. The gap was only about fifty meters wide, but anything lying in that blind zone would be missed. The visual search was the best option they had to act as a "gap-filler" to cover the blind zone.

Tui also listened on a passive sonar system for any noises in the water. Submariners the world over were taught that the quickest, surest way to be found if they were stuck in a stricken sub was to bang on the hull with some tool. Low-tech as such a thing was, the loud clanging noise could carry for several miles in the water.

For about two hours now, they had been "mowing the lawn," searching in an expanding spiral around the original ground zero point. Sonny had seen all manner of trash and old, rusted wreckage and discarded scrap that appeared as blips on his screen. So far, though, nothing that looked like a sunken submarine.

"Seeing anything, Sonny?"

"Nothing but beer cans and the occasional stray fish. You?" Tui responded.

"Nope, just lots and lots of mud and silt," Tay answered. Then, for the hundredth time, he glanced over at the battery power meter. "Uh-oh.

Sonny, we're at forty-percent capacity. Much as I hate it, it is time to head back to the barn. Pray those guys can last at least one more day."

"And that we can get charged up and back down here before the PLAN chases us off their so-called property," Tui offered.

Reluctantly, Tay made careful notes of their precise coordinates, the point at which they would resume the search, then nudged the controls around to point southeast and engaged the autopilot. It would take them six hours to motor back to the *Swift Rescue*—maybe a bit longer since they would be stretching their power capacity to the max—and then another eight hours to re-charge the batteries before they could once again start the long return to resume the deep searching.

A thousand yards away, the *Bà Rịa-Vũng Tàu* rested amid the mud and darkness on the bottom.

Ψ

The DSAR-6 popped to the surface one hundred yards astern of its mothership, the *Swift Rescue*. It took twenty minutes for the little rescue sub to come alongside and be wrestled into the lifting harness. Then the sub was lifted up onto the deck and crewmembers quickly hooked up to the electrical umbilical even before helping its two occupants out. Fully recharging the batteries would require the next eight hours. Meantime, Jiang Tay and Sonny Tui could grab a quick, hot meal before heading to their staterooms for some much needed shut-eye.

After the quickest of debriefings with Tay and Tui, Samuel Leong gathered with Wong Su and Huan Kuan on the rescue ship's bridge wing. A gentle tropical breeze barely ruffled the Singapore Navy flag that flew from the mast. A Technicolor tropical sunset painted the western horizon. But the three men paid no attention to nature's brilliant day-end display. They were far too concerned now about the possibilities for finding and rescuing the crew of the lost submarine.

"The turnaround time is the killer," Leong grumbled. "Twelve hours of transit and eight hours to re-charge yielding only two hours of search time. I'm going ahead and moving the *Swift Rescue* closer to ground zero. Every mile we close is an extra half hour devoted to actually searching."

"But that is not safe," Wong Su protested. "The closer we get to ground zero, the more likely the Chinese are to see us. And you can bet that they will try everything they can to stop us."

"It's international water according to the Law of the Sea," Leong countered forcefully. "Captain Kuan, your nation has claimed that island for generations. We are free to steam anywhere we want here. Right up to that reef and thumb our noses at them if we want. I do not give a damn about the Chinese. What I care about is rescuing those submariners."

Captain Huan Kuan listened to the pair and sensed the rising tensions.

"Gentlemen, I really appreciate your concern for my countrymen, but I can't ask you to sacrifice your ship or yourselves," he interjected. "I propose a compromise. Why could we not head toward ground zero during the night so that we get at least halfway there by daybreak. We launch the DSAR-6 at first light and then scurry back here. We wait here until sunset and then make best time back to meet and pick up the sub. According to my arithmetic, that will give us about six more hours of valuable search time with less risk of being challenged by the Chinese."

Su and Leong looked at each other for a few seconds, doing their own mental calculations. Su was the first to agree to the suggestion.

"That works for me. It still presents great risk. Even a bit more than remaining here, hiding behind the reef. But it gives us more opportunity to find live survivors to rescue. We are at day six now for those poor bastards. If any remain alive, they do not have much time left. This could be our last shot."

Leong was already in the process of swinging the boat around and opening the throttles.

"One of you two call Joe Glass," he called back over his shoulder. "Make certain he knows what we are doing and that he has our protection ready to go."

17

Henrietta Foster stood at the back of the control room and watched the position bug as it traveled across the ECDIS navigation display. She had steered the *Boise* back north to where they were only about fifteen miles off Hainan Island. The little indicator showed them to be almost dead center in their launch box. They had loaded SLMM-I mines in three of the sub's four torpedo tubes. The fourth tube had a warshot ADCAP torpedo, ready and loaded, just in case they suddenly needed a self-defense weapon. All the tubes were flooded down and ready to launch their contents. The crew was at battle stations. It was show time.

"Officer of the Deck, come to ahead one-third, steer course north," she ordered.

The big boat slowed and swung around to the launch course and new speed.

"Open the outer doors, tubes one and two. Firing point procedures, SLMM mines, tubes one and two."

"Ship ready," Bob Bland, the OOD, reported.

"Missions downloaded and verified. Weapons ready," the weapons officer sang out.

"Shoot tubes one and two," Foster ordered. "Shoot" was the command but not really very descriptive of what happened. Because the SLMM mine was a "swim out" weapon, its electric motor started turning its screw and pushed it out of the torpedo tube rather than being flushed out by an impulse of high-pressure water, like an ADCAP torpedo. That meant there was no confirming "bang and whoosh" sound. Only a light on the weapons control panel verifying that something in the tube had been launched.

The first two mines emerged and began their slow approach toward Yulin Harbor, one of the most secure and heavily monitored anchorages in the world. It would take the mobile mines over an hour to swim into the harbor, find their exact target location, and then sink to the bottom. There they would sit and wait to be command-activated remotely. On their long swim in, about a mile from their final destination, each mine would drop off a small comms device and then continue on while reeling out behind it a thin, nearly invisible fiber optic line. The remote acoustically activated communications module would eventually relay to the mine its signal to go live.

These first two mines maneuvered into the harbor and then into the massive cave that had been dug through a solid granite mountain to allow submerged access. As programmed, they dropped to the bottom, right alongside the submarine piers that were assumed to be protected from any intruders by the caves. The next three mines followed those two into the submarine pens.

All through the night, the crew on the *Boise* loaded SLMM-I mines into the boat's torpedo tubes and then sent them off on their journey. It was almost dawn on the surface when they finally "shot" the last mines. The mission completed, *Boise* turned and headed south. Thankfully, they had so far not needed to use the torpedo waiting in its tube.

Henrietta Foster gave the crew a strong attaboy, then walked out of the control room and stuck her head into Chet Allison's stateroom ICU. Doc Ballman was dozing in a chair beside the captain's bunk. He quickly awoke and rose when he sensed the executive officer standing there.

"No real change," he told her. "The drugs seem to be doing what they're supposed to. I've cut the amiodarone to half a milligram per minute. But dang it, I sure wish he would come around."

"So do I, Doc," Foster replied. "So do I. Look, we've finished the mine plant. As soon as we've cleared the coast by twenty miles, we'll come up to flank. In a couple of hours, we'll be far enough off the coast to come up and call home. I need for you to draft up a message asking for whatever you need or need to know." She stifled a yawn with her hand. "I think I'm going to go hit the skid for that couple of hours. Driving a submarine all night is exhausting." She flashed him a grin. "Thanks, Doc. Take care of that guy there. Okay?"

Ψ

The ORCA UUV carefully steered its precisely programmed course through the narrow Guangzhouwen Passage, which separated Nansen Island to the north from Donghai Island to the south. The channel was narrow, less than a thousand yards wide at its tightest point, and shallow, continuously dredged to a depth of forty feet. And, worst of all, the passage, which formed the main channel leading to the port of Zhanjiang, was very busy, choked with all manner of shipping, fishing, and ferry traffic. Most importantly, it was the primary channel to China's PLAN South Fleet's main naval base, the homeport of most of the fleet's surface ships. That was the reason the ORCA, designated Mission Victor Seven, was inching its way along the channel bottom at a deliberate crawl.

Victor Seven passed under an outbound container ship as it crossed Zhanjiang Gang, the broad outer harbor for the port. Then it made an abrupt turn north to skirt Techeng Island. Precisely two-point-one miles north of Techeng Island, in the narrow channel that separated Maxie Point from the Jiefang District, Victor Seven got busy dispensing its cargo of Clandestine Delivered Mines. Each CDM, looking most like a small trash can, sank to the bottom at a precise location, settled into the mud, and then sat there, patiently waiting to be command activated.

This small minefield could effectively bottle up the Chinese surface fleet in their homeport. Such an interdiction without far more risk of detection would have been impossible only a few years earlier. So far, the Chinese—or any of the world's other navies—had no idea such a thing was possible. Now, with the last of the ten CDMs dropped into position and its mission completed, Victor Seven turned around and retraced its steps back to the open waters of the South China Sea.

At the same time, its sister ORCA UUV, Mission Victor Six, dropped its CDMs across the Guangzhouwen Passage. Mission Victor Eight did the same job in the Nansen Hekou, the back channel into Zhanjiang. The latter two's work went just as flawlessly as the first one's had.

The three ORCAs next headed east for the long transit back to Guam, even as similar missions were being completed at Shanghai, Xiangshan, Fujian, and Zhoushan Naval Bases. In all, a fleet of fifteen ORCAs had just laid a series of deadly traps for the Chinese Fleet. And PLAN had no idea they were there, and certainly not how potentially crippling those devices could be.

Ψ

Daylight was little more than a promise on the eastern horizon when the DSAR-6 once more slipped beneath the waves. The *Swift Rescue* quickly turned one-hundred-eighty degrees and headed back toward the little safety offered by Barque Canada Reef.

Once underwater, the submersible again pointed toward the best coordinates they had for the sunken Vietnamese sub. Meanwhile, the US Navy littoral combat ship *Canberra* floated just over the horizon, extending its protective umbrella out to cover the rescue ship, continually searching for any threatening intruders that might venture into the neighborhood.

By midmorning, Jiang Tay and Sonny Tui had reached the spot where they had broken off the search the previous day. There they resumed their hunt with hopes still high. Tay kept his eyes on what lighted area he could see through the bubble window. Tui watched the side-scan sonar and listened intently for any noises. The tension inside the command module was palpable. Both men knew that if they were not successful in the next few hours that their battery power allowed them to look, any chance for a rescue would become infinitesimal.

Then, only a half-hour into the tense search, Sonny Tui heard something. A loud metallic clanging.

Seconds later, the side-scan radar began painting a beautiful picture.

The unmistakable portrait of a bottomed submarine. They had found the *Bà Rịa-Vũng Tàu*!

Now they needed to determine if anyone had survived besides the man wielding whatever tool was making the clanging noise.

"Yesterday," Jiang Tay said. "Yesterday, we were so close." But both men had the same thought. Had submariners died because they had been forced to end the search when they were so near to success?

Tay spun the DSAR-6 around and headed directly toward the sunken sub as fast as she would go. He descended until they were only a few meters off the muddy bottom, deep enough to see it when they drew near but hopefully not so near the sea floor that they would raise too much blinding silt.

Mere minutes later, the battered hull of the *Bà Rịa-Vũng Tàu* filled the submersible's bubble. Tay carefully maneuvered the DSAR-6 for a three-hundred-and-sixty-degree look at the sub. They had to look for potential dangers, the possibility of the big sub shifting or tipping, or other hazards. Everything forward of the engine room looked fine. But the screw and shaft were missing completely. The rudder and stern planes were smashed. The after-ballast tanks had all been torn open. This hulk was never going anywhere again.

But most importantly, she was resting upright. The forward escape hatch had apparently not been fouled. The DSAR-6 was designed to mate with a sunken submarine that listed up to sixty degrees, clinging like a leech to its hull, and she had a heavy duty articulated arm to clear debris. But one that was clean and sitting level on the sea floor made the effort much simpler. And, more importantly, quicker.

Tay looked over at Sonny Tui with a broad grin.

"Okay, Sonny, call them up on the underwater telephone and see if anyone is home."

Ψ

Tranh Vu had accepted the fact that the end was near. He could only concentrate on making his men as comfortable as possible until they all drew their last breath.

They had spread the last cannister of calcium hydroxide the previous day. The carbon dioxide levels were already rising again, well into the dangerous range. Levels were now at twenty thousand parts per million. At forty thousand, they would all be dead, but at least the splitting, pounding headache would stop.

He figured that the crew could don their emergency air breathing masks and survive on the limited air available out of the ship's compressed air system. That would perhaps give them another day. However, it would raise the pressure inside the boat dramatically. It was already reading six atmospheres. That was the equivalent to over sixty meters of sea water. But it was one more day of life.

One more day to hope the little buoy had survived to relay their plight and position. To hope someone was out there now, looking for them. They had long since passed their scheduled check-in, so their commanders knew they were missing. But if the buoy had failed, or if, for some reason, no one heard it, they would have no idea where to concentrate a search.

Still, it was not folly to hope, Vu told himself. As long as there was life, there was hope. Small as it may be.

The submarine captain had involuntarily dozed off just after hearing the latest clanging of the big wrench against the hull. The clanging he could only pray would be heard by someone equipped to help. But then he was startled, rudely awakened by the ship's announcing system. At first, he thought he might still be dreaming. He had not heard the speakers since the boat had come to rest on the bottom.

"Captain, come to control!"

Tranh Vu shook his head to try to clear the fog of sleep as he rushed up to the control room. He found his two watch standers jumping for joy and pointing at the underwater telephone.

"We are saved! We are saved!" they cried.

The telephone speaker crackled and hissed and the voice was almost lost in the noise. Though it was barely understandable, Tranh Vu could tell it was a human voice, and it was speaking a language he understood. He tried to contain his emotions. After a few seconds, he was finally able to discern what was being said.

"On the submarine, this is rescue submarine. Please respond." The message was being repeated every thirty seconds.

Tears poured down Tranh Vu's face as he grabbed the microphone. He tried to speak very slowly and distinctly but it was difficult as elation welled up within him.

"Rescue submarine, this is *Bà Rịa-Vũng Tàu*. We are so glad to hear your voice!"

"*Bà Rịa-Vũng Tàu*, we will dock on your forward escape hatch. How many are you and what injuries?"

"We are thirty-four. We have two with internal injuries and several with broken bones."

"How is your atmosphere?" Thank God, the rescuers knew the proper questions to ask.

"Rescue sub, pressure is at six atmospheres and carbon dioxide is twenty thousand parts per million."

There was a pause as the rescuer considered that answer.

"*Bà Rịa-Vũng Tàu*, roger. We will transfer you under pressure. We can take seventeen at a time. Please have the first seventeen standing by under the forward escape trunk and have someone ready to open the hatch under my command."

Tranh Vu closed his eyes and said a very short prayer of thanks. Then he hurried to get his crew up and into motion. It took only a few minutes to get half of the crew, including those with the worst injuries, up into the torpedo room beneath the trunk that would lead to the escape hatch. Meanwhile, all of them could easily hear the rescue submarine as it maneuvered around and sat down with a metallic reverberation on the main deck of the *Bà Rịa-Vũng Tàu*. Then there was forceful hammering on the escape hatch. The most beautiful, painful racket any of them had ever heard. Someone was actually up there, ready to rescue them.

Tranh Vu signaled to open the hatch. As it swung open, the men closest to the vertical shaft stared up into impossibly bright white lights and a masked man signaling for them to climb up the ladder. Tranh watched as his crew first lifted the injured men up and then climbed after them. Though several of his crew encouraged the captain to be among the first to be rescued—several even volunteering to remain behind to allow him to do so—he declined. He would be the last to abandon his vessel.

Still, it was almost impossibly difficult to watch the escape trunk hatch swing shut above him while he stood watching from his beleaguered submarine.

Ψ

Sonny Tui stared down into the black hole of hell. Like wind from a centuries-old crypt, the cold, foul air blowing up out of the downed submarine chilled him to his very soul. He swore he could smell the foul stench, even with his air mask tightly cinched. But the thankful faces that stared up at him through the open hatch told a different story, one of hope.

He reached down and helped the first injured victim up into the DSAR-6's passenger compartment. Tui stuck an air mask on him and helped him to a seat along the sub's bulkhead.

It only took ten minutes to get all seventeen survivors onboard, including several on stretchers. As the last injured man, strapped to a backboard, was lifted up, Tui looked down through the hatch and into the eyes of the *Bà Rịa-Vũng Tàu*'s commander.

"That is all we can take this trip, sir," Tui yelled. "We will return for you in about eight hours. Be strong."

The captain nodded solemnly, then smiled.

Tui swung the submarine's hatch shut and watched as the handwheel turned and it was dogged from inside. He knew that he would never be able to fathom the bravery of the man who now stood at the bottom of that ladder. The man who had just watched as his own means of escaping that hellhole leaving with half his crew onboard. From the readings the captain had given them, there was no guarantee he and the remainder of his crew could survive until the rescue vessel returned.

And especially if their mothership had encountered trouble from PLAN up there on the surface. She may not even be there when they got to her. He tried not to think about such a contingency as he helped the men settle in.

Tui hurried to secure the DSAR-6's lower hatch and did a quick survey of the survivors. Most were sucking greedily on their air masks, forcing the foul air out of their lungs. Unless something went wrong with the submersible—and *Swift Rescue* was there waiting—the worst of this ordeal was hopefully over for these men.

Next, he stepped forward, into the airlock that separated the passenger compartment from the pilot's compartment, and shut the after hatch. Now came the really boring but absolutely essential part of the rescue for him. He would be required to sit here in this tiny closet of an airlock and decompress. Since the survivors had spent several days at high pressure, they would remain at pressure until they were back on the *Swift Rescue*. There they would need to undergo a long and involved decompression regime that would hopefully leave them with few or no long-term issues.

Tui had been at pressure for only a few minutes while he helped the survivors get aboard. Even so, he required decompression, and that would take a while. He checked the pressure tables posted in the air lock, then glanced at his wristwatch. He had been at sixty-two meters depth for fourteen minutes. That meant he needed three decompression stops: nine meters for three minutes, six meters for seven minutes, and, finally, three meters for twenty-seven minutes. Fortunately for him, the whole operation was entirely automated, computer controlled. The computer set the pressure and the duration for each stop. Then it controlled the rate of pressure change between each stop. He had no choice in the matter, even if he wanted to try to cut it short. Only when all the steps had been completed correctly would the computer allow the forward hatch to be opened. He could do nothing but sit back and wait.

Sonny Tui keyed the bulkhead mounted intercom.

"Jiang, I'm in the air lock and the decompression is underway. Our passengers are all safely bedded down. Let's head for home."

Jiang Tay's voice boomed back on the intercom.

"Roger that. Heading back now. It certainly would be nice for our passengers, and especially those guys we just left behind, if we were not facing a six-hour trip back home. I'm going to go up on the roof and call back. I want to see if we can meet up a little closer than planned."

"Excellent idea," Tui replied. "But could you slip me a margarita and the latest issue of *Playboy* for the ride?"

"Only for first class. See you in a half hour or so."

Tay had already pointed the bow of the DSAR-6 up toward the surface. Once there, he called back to the *Swift Rescue*. Thankfully, she responded immediately. The ship had just arrived back at Barque Canada Reef, but everyone was thrilled to learn the Vietnamese sub had been located and half her surviving crew was now on the surface.

Within ten minutes, the rescue ship had turned around and was heading at full speed back toward a determined rendezvous spot.

Even with a combined speed of seventeen knots, it took almost two hours before they could rendezvous. Once they were reunited, the stern crane hurried to lift the DSAR-6 out of the water and then lower it onto the docking cradle with the rescue submarine's stern facing forward. Next, the cradle was winched forward until the passenger compartment's after hatch was mated to the Transfer Under Pressure chamber housed on the *Swift Rescue*'s deck. The TUP chamber was already pressurized to match the same six atmospheres as inside the DSAR-6's passenger compartment.

Medical personnel waiting inside the TUP scurried to assist the survivors in moving into the chamber. This would be their home for the next couple of weeks while they decompressed. It took almost three hours to complete the transfer and then get the DSAR-6 back in the water and on its way for the rest of the men left down there in hell.

The electrical charging hookup had been rejuvenating the submersible's batteries for the entire time it was resting on *Swift Rescue*'s deck. Maintaining pressure in the passenger compartment stole precious power. They should now have enough juice to complete the rescue unless they ran into problems somewhere along the way.

Still, Jiang Tay glanced at the battery meter and crossed his fingers as he steered the rescue sub back toward where the *Bà Rịa-Vũng Tàu* lay on the bottom of the sea. And with her captain and sixteen more men hopefully still alive, well, and awaiting their return.

It took another three hours to drive back to the *Bà Rịa-Vũng Tàu* and mate to the forward escape trunk again. This time Sonny Tui was emotionally ready when the sub's hatch swung open. The seventeen remaining crewmen climbed up into the DSAR-6, with Tranh Vu being the last man up the ladder. He took a final look down into the dark hole that led to the compartments that had very nearly been their graves. Only then did he move on up into the rescue vessel and take the last seat.

Sonny Tui was already in the airlock, starting his decompression, when Jiang Tay lifted off from the sunken sub.

18

"Skipper, we got company!" The tactical action officer yelled through the curtain to Louise Gadliano. "Slow bogey coming from the north. No IFF."

Gadliano, the skipper of USS *Canberra,* jumped down from her seat and stuck her head into the littoral combat ship's tiny combat control center. What in hell did the Chinese have against her and her ship? Why were they constantly running in her direction?

"What you got?" she asked the young lieutenant who was staring intently at the flickering screen in front of him.

"Inbound helo. Radar signature equates to the surface search on a Chinese Z-20 ASW helicopter," the TAO reported. "Range twenty miles, closure speed two hundred knots. He ain't out for a Sunday drive. Bastard's looking for us."

"Lock him up with the SPS-77 radar in fire control mode," Gadliano ordered. "Track him with both the gun and the SeaRAM."

The SeaRAM ship defense system was specifically designed for just such attackers, defending against supersonic and subsonic threats including cruise missiles, drones, and helicopters. Gadliano grabbed the radio microphone.

"Inbound Chinese Navy helicopter, this is the USS *Canberra*. State your intentions."

The reply came almost instantaneously. "*Canberra,* you have violated Chinese sovereign waters. You will leave the area immediately or we will engage."

It certainly sounded as if the PLAN guy meant what he was saying.

"Chinese helicopter, we are in international waters. Stand clear or we will exercise our right of self-defense." Gadliano knew that the Chinese pilot was almost certainly detecting the SPS-77 radar signal. Hell, it was probably causing their dental work to tingle. A single helicopter would want no part of what that promised.

Ten seconds later, the TAO updated his report.

"Captain, the helo has turned tail and is running way."

"Keep your eyes open to the north," Gadliano responded. "I wouldn't expect them to run away so quick next time." She reached over and shifted channels on the radio to the bridge-to-bridge frequency.

"*Swift Rescue,* this is *Canberra*. Suggest you get a move on. We just had some curious Chinese visitors. I expect there will be more in a very few minutes."

Samuel Leong's voice crackled over the speaker. "Roger *Canberra*. But we don't expect DSAR-6 back with the rest of the survivors for at least another hour. Could you cover us until then?"

"Samuel, we'll do our very best," she promised. "We just need to see what the Chinese are going to do."

Next, she flipped over to the military encrypted channel and called Joe Glass. She really did need to tell him what was going on. He was not surprised by the news and promised to get whatever help he could out to them. However, they both knew there was not a whole lot he could do if the Chinese did get all trigger happy. International waters or not, they were still in China's backyard.

Gadliano turned back to the TAO. They simply had to be ready for anything.

"Bring the ship to battle stations. Shift both the gun and the SeaRAMs to auto mode. There's a good chance we may be busy in a few minutes. May as well let all that tax-payer-funded technology do what it does."

She had just sat back down in her chair and sent the messenger for a cup of coffee when the TAO was once again bringing bad news.

"Skipper, detecting multiple Dragon Eye radars to the north. That stuff's carried on Chinese Type Fifty-Two Alpha and Type Fifty-Five destroyers. Best bearings between zero-two-zero and three-four-zero. Toward Cuarteron Reef. Definite missile threat."

"Sure as hell is," Gadliano confirmed. "Are they on the Link?"

After a slight pause, the TAO responded, "Yes, they correlate to four tracks on the Link, tracking away from Cuarteron Reef. And toward us."

"Spin up the Naval Strike Missiles. Assign two missiles to each track number." The Chinese were apparently sending the big hardware. She grabbed the radio to inform Joe Glass. He and his team were ahead of *Canberra*. Glass said that he already had the tracks on his Link-16 and now had his own missiles assigned.

Lord, she thought. Our guys have big ears lately!

"Good luck, Captain," Glass told her.

She had just taken a sip from her fresh cup of coffee. But before she could swallow it, the TAO was calling out another disturbing update.

"Detecting Z-20 radar, bearing three-five-seven. Designating track Bandit Four-Two. Bandit Four-Two range ten miles."

Gadliano swallowed the coffee and responded, "If they're just putting on a show, they're doing a good—"

"Detecting fast-moving inbound tracks! Vampires! Vampires inbound! At least six missiles inbound!" the TAO shouted.

The LCS skipper knew at once that unless they did everything right and all systems performed perfectly, they likely had less than a minute to live.

She realized immediately what had happened. The PLAN Z-20 helicopter was acting as eyes for the Chinese ships that were already just over the horizon. Those destroyers could all shoot YJ-18 anti-ship cruise missiles. They would fly in at eighty percent the speed of sound. Then they would enter a deadly sprint the last twenty miles, ramping up to 2.5 mach.

The SeaRAM would simply have to handle them.

"Splash the helo with the gun," she ordered without hesitation. "Launch the strike missiles on all tracks." Gadliano had barely finished giving those orders when the fifty-seven-millimeter Bofors gun spat three times. Anti-aircraft cannons were normally considered older equipment, dating back to World War II. But with its automatic handling and tracking systems, plus the new Mark 332 guided projectiles, this gun still worked well against the right targets. Like helicopters. "Ahead flank! Circle the *Swift Rescue* at two thousand yards."

The LCS leapt ahead as the two massive LM-2500 gas turbines came online, quickly shoving the little ship up to forty knots. The vessel heeled over as it began to circle the stationary rescue ship.

Then eight anti-ship cruise missiles roared out of their box launchers in quick succession and arrowed away from *Canberra*, headed out to the north. The Bofors anti-aircraft gun barked again and again, now sending specialized ordnance out in an attempt to stop the incoming missiles. The Mark 332 guided projectiles would twist and turn as the shells tried to home in on them.

Gadliano shouted to be heard over all the noise. "Launch a decoy! Launch chaff! Reload and launch again! I want a wall of chaff and decoys all around the *Swift Rescue*."

Just then, the SeaRAM began firing out its rolling air-frame missiles as the CIWS radar and optical sensors tracked the incoming anti-ship missiles.

"Splash the helo!" the TAO shouted. "Splash one Vampire." The Chinese Navy's helicopter was no more and one incoming missile was gone.

The team's eyes did not deviate from the radar screen now. Whether they lived or died this day depended on how well their sophisticated defense systems worked. It was all about to play out on that radar screen, like an unbelievably high-stakes video game.

"Splash two more Vampires!" A couple of the 332s had done their jobs well. "Vampire into the decoys! Splash another Vampire!"

"Yes!" someone on the bridge shouted. But there was one more hurtling their direction.

That last YJ-18 missile evaded its killers and tore through the *Canberra*'s thin aluminum skin just forward of where the Bofors gun was still doing its job. The YJ-18 was designed to penetrate through several inches of hardened steel that formed the hulls of most warships, then explode and do maximum damage belowdecks. But with the LCS's thin aluminum skin, the missile's warhead met less resistance than anticipated. The high-speed missile passed all the way through the diesel space before nosing right on through the bottom of the ship. Then it detonated well below the vessel. The massive blast from the three-hundred kilograms of high explosives shattered all four of the US ship's waterjets and gouged out a significant hole in *Canberra*'s narrow center hull.

The ship quickly slid to a lurching stop. The small crew was already working to put out the fires the PLAN missile set off when it plunged all the way through the ship. They also needed to stop the flooding in the engine spaces. Others reported on the damage to the captain.

Mercifully, the radar showed no more incoming missiles. When Gadliano glanced at the Link, she saw why. *Canberra*'s eight strike missiles, along with six more that had been launched from Joe Glass's NEMIS launchers on Barque Canada Reef, were all converging on the Chinese battle group. Those four destroyers would have their hands full for the next little while trying to defend themselves.

Meanwhile, Gadliano knew they needed to get the ship underway if at all possible. And right now, there was only one way.

"Rig out the Azi Thruster," Gadliano commanded. The little outboard azimuthal thruster was housed in the bow and normally only employed when they needed to maneuver alongside a pier. Not much, but it was the only propulsion they had left. It might be capable of pushing them along at an ambling two knots or so. And that was assuming the winds and seas cooperated. "Energize it and head for Barque Canada Reef."

The *Canberra* was not built to withstand battle damage. With flooding in the engine room and fires burning belowdecks, Gadliano knew she needed to get her little ship into protected, shallow water. There, it would be easier to rescue crewmembers if it came to that. And, if worse came to worst, the ship would be much more easily salvaged.

"*Canberra*, this is *Swift Rescue*. Docking DSAR-6 with survivors now. What assistance do you need?"

Gadliano keyed the radio. "Samuel, we're okay. You just get those survivors safely onboard and then run for Borneo. Your nearest medical facility is the *Chesty Puller,* and she's there. We'll cover you as far as we can but we're not going anywhere fast, I'll tell you."

"What are your plans?" Samuel Leong asked.

"Until we get this flooding under control, I'm going to drive into the shallow water by the reef. We'll try to find a nice shallow, sandy bottom to anchor in. And hope nobody else comes along that wants to barbecue us."

Ψ

Samuel Leong watched nervously as the DSAR-6 was yanked up out of the water and safely landed on its deck cradle. The deckhands were still securing the bindings when he spun the *Swift Rescue* around and opened the throttles as far as they would allow him to go. All the manuals said that the rescue ship was capable of only twelve knots at top speed. Leong had never felt moved to try it. But they were hitting better than fourteen knots by the time Barque Canada Reef was on their starboard beam and disappearing quickly astern.

It took the crew almost four hours to move the DSAR-6 to mate with the TUP unit and to transfer Captain Tranh Vu and the rest of his crew into the decompression unit. Mariveles Reef was on the starboard beam as the *Swift Rescue* swung around to put the setting sun dead astern.

During the night, the ship threaded the needle between the Ardasier Bank to the south and Investigator Shoal to the north. Then she came around to point directly at the center of the Balabac Strait, still one hundred and fifty miles ahead.

Leong had calculated that they would pass through the narrow strait that separated the Malaysian-owned Banggi Island from the Philippines sometime during the morning watch, assuming everything worked out according to plan.

That may well be too much to hope for, Leong thought.

So far on this project, they had attracted the wrath of the People's Liberation Army Navy by rescuing surviving crew from a submarine that PLAN had deliberately sent to the bottom. Then, probably to assure none of the rescued could tell the world about what had happened, they had come under attack by the Chinese from all directions. Thankfully, the *Canberra* had been there, and had come near to sacrificing herself to help save *Swift Rescue*. There had been other missiles from out of the blue, too. He had no idea whose they were or where they came from. Probably US Navy or an ally. It did not matter. Whoever it was had helped make it more likely that these poor, long-suffering survivors could soon return home.

But the Chinese still did not want *Swift Rescue* to succeed in this particular mission. They had already proven they would stop at nothing to make it so.

Leong could not shake the feeling that he and his rescue ship were not yet scot-free.

Ψ

PLAN submarine captain Qianting Laoda was gazing out the periscope, conducting surveillance of the Half Moon Shoal, a tiny uninhabited reef on the east side of the Spratly Islands. It was a good opportunity to train his crew on how to do covert surveillance at a time when there was very little chance of detection. Then they would be ready if they ever had to do it for real. Though he knew there were actions being taken, important military operations underway, his commanders had so far neglected to order him and his submarine to participate. So, he would train his inexperienced crew and continue to shake down his new boat.

The *Shizi Yu* was only a couple of kilometers off the reef's low surf. Qianting could clearly see a pair of small Philippine fishing boats working in the lagoon inside the reef, apparently making a good catch. But as far as his crew were concerned, they were observing and photographing an American Navy carrier at anchor.

The duty radioman startled Qianting when he tapped the captain on the shoulder.

"My commander, we have received new orders."

He handed Qianting a notebook computer with the orders displayed on the screen. The submarine captain read through the message once and, though the drill had not been completed, immediately lowered the periscope. He was still reading the orders for the second time when he looked up and ordered the *Shizi Yu* around to a course of one-eight-zero and to proceed to dive to a depth of one hundred meters. By the time he had read the contents of the laptop screen a third time and fully understood what he had been ordered to do, the submarine was at a full bell and heading directly for the Balabac Strait.

The crew labored to quickly load warshot YU-9 torpedoes in all six of the submarine's tubes even as Qianting and the navigator plotted a course to intercept and destroy their newly assigned target. It would take the submarine almost six hours to traverse the one hundred and thirty kilometers. They would have plenty of time to arrive ahead of the target's estimated passage. They could easily be in a position for the kill and there was no way anyone could know they were there.

Qianting could barely contain his excitement. To be assigned such an important mission on their very first patrol was a sign of the trust and high regard that Naval Headquarters had for him and the *Shizi Yu*. Sure, he was aware that he was the only submarine anywhere close by, and thus the only asset who could possibly do the job. Still, someone higher up had the confidence that he could, or they would not have received the orders.

Once in the area, *Shizi Yu* began a slow north-south patrol across the western entrance to the Balabac Strait. Qianting was enjoying a morning cup of tea when the officer of the deck called him to the periscope. Their target had arrived on the scene. At first, he could just barely see the white superstructure of a ship on the western horizon. It was exactly what he expected to see and pretty much when he assumed it would appear in the optics of his periscope.

The crew were quickly ordered to battle stations. The *Shizi Yu* was ready to strike, just as they had been drilling to do.

With a broad smile, the captain swung the ship around to make a periscope approach on the unsuspecting target.

Ψ

"Hey, Doc," the young Marine called to Sam Smithski. "You may want to take a look at this." He pointed to a trace on the screen. "It looks just like those practice tapes we've been playing with. You know, the ones of those Chinese boats. But this is a real trace."

The pair were sitting in a tent just off the beach on Balambangan Island, north of Borneo. Sam Smithski had been teaching the young

Marines the intricacies of analyzing the acoustic tracks from his new bottom-mounted array system. So far, other than an occasional noisy fishing boat or tramp steamer, they had only used his tapes to study what to look for. There really had not been much to listen to and analyze from the actual array.

Smithski jumped up from his lounge chair and peered over the Marine's shoulder. He grunted as he tweaked the gain and the center frequency a little. Then he rubbed his chin as he pondered what he was hearing. There was no doubt in his mind. It sure seemed to be a Chinese submarine, but intel had not said anything about any potential visitors. It was also obvious to his practiced eye that the interloper was working up on what tracked like a surface ship coming through from the west. The sub was stalking the surface ship. No doubt about it.

He was still tracking their new friend when the phone chirped.

"Sam, this is Stanton Readly. I wanted to let you know to keep your eyes open on that fancy new array of yours. We have a submarine rescue vessel heading through the straits and we have good reason to believe that the Chinese will probably take violent exception to them getting out of the South China Sea afloat."

"Colonel, you aren't going to believe this. One of your Marines just detected a Chinese diesel boat out to the west of the straits. It sure looks like he's getting in position to bushwhack what I'd bet is your sub rescue ship."

"You sure about this?"

"Yes, sir. The tonals of the submarine all match an Improved *Yuan*. But I didn't know they had any of those horses out of the barn yet. That was the only thing that had me wondering."

"Yes, they do. At least one. And you're hearing him right now."

"Damn."

"Damn indeed."

"To be sure, before we set the ocean afire, what are *Swift Rescue*'s coordinates?" Smithski asked.

"Stand by." A seemingly long half minute passed before Readly came back with a set of coordinates. "And what you got for the location of the vessel that nice new sub's circling out there?"

"That's her. The bastard's lining up on *Swift Rescue*. They're acting like they're going to shoot an unarmed submarine rescue vessel."

"Sam, tell your Marine to input the track in the Link. I think we have all the evidence we need. We are about to give our Chinese friend a very bad headache."

Seconds later one of the HIMAR launchers that had been carefully hidden back in the island palms suddenly moved, elevating its launcher. A RUM-139 ASROC abruptly roared out of the launcher in a cloud of flame and smoke. A split second later, a second missile jumped out and followed the same fiery path as the first into the sky.

The pair climbed and very quickly disappeared in tandem to the northwest.

Ψ

Captain Qianting had carefully maneuvered the *Shizi Yu* into a perfect shooting position. No need to rush. They were almost ten kilometers to the north of the target and it would be steaming past them. The doomed vessel's bright orange hull would be at ninety degrees to his submarine when he shot. There would be no way that a single shot of the YU-9 torpedo could possibly miss. Still, he would shoot two, just to be certain.

Now, he decided, he would take just one more look. Then he would be ready to fire and efficiently complete this highly important mission. He did not question shooting at a rescue ship. One that was likely unarmed. He had been ordered to sink it and that was what he would do. The State would have a valid reason for issuing such an order.

But when Qianting raised the periscope and placed his eye to the eyepiece, he saw something totally unexpected. He knew immediately what it was. Two rapidly moving smoky traces tearing across the sky at an impossible speed, coming directly at him.

As if in a trance, he watched as the missiles both splashed down a few hundred meters from his submarine. Within seconds, he heard his sonar operator screaming that there were two torpedoes in the water and they were coming directly at them. Qianting was transfixed, though. Too surprised to be terrified. Too shocked to do anything. On some level, he understood it was certainly too late anyway.

Once in the sea, the two Mark-54 torpedoes immediately detected the *Shizi Yu*. They were not programmed to hesitate. Instantly alerted that the big metal object out there in front of them met the specifications burned into their brains, they raced toward the submarine at forty knots.

Both torpedoes ran beneath the Chinese sub and then circled back, using their complex logic to verify their target was really a submarine and not a decoy. Satisfied, the first torpedo took aim and smashed into the boat's engine room. It exploded with the equivalent force of more than two hundred pounds of TNT. The second one hit just below the sub's sail, ripping it apart.

The shattered remains of the *Shizi Yu* quickly sank into the blackness and down to the bottom of the Balabac Strait.

19

Li Minh Zhou was obviously worried. Jim Ward could tell from her deeply furrowed brow and the fact that she had forced a laugh at his last very dry joke. She never laughed at his dry jokes. That was enough to cause Ward to worry, too. In his experience, the Chinese spy across the table from him did not worry about much. She preferred addressing the problem head-on and immediately rather than stewing about it. But now, something was clearly concerning her. Something she could not easily fix. And it had to be big.

"Are you going to tell me what's going on," the young SEAL finally asked her. "Or are you going to continue with the 'inscrutable Asian' act while I slurp my soup over here?"

The two were sharing a late dinner at a very nice restaurant in downtown Taipei, Taiwan. The city and the country were slowly returning to normal. Electrical power had been restored in many areas, even if it was being delivered from emergency diesel generators in some spots. The grid was proving very difficult to restore. Wires, poles, generation equipment, and more had remained intact but the complicated computerized distribution software remained mostly inoperative. However, in Taipei and many of Taiwan's other cities, many restaurants had resorted to candlelit dining rooms and cooking amazing meals over open flames.

Ward admitted the enforced limitations added a certain ambiance to dining out. And the flickering candlelight made his dining partner even more beautiful and desirably exotic.

Li Minh Zhou appeared to have read his mind when she gave Ward a look that was halfway between a smile and a grimace. But her answer to his question confirmed she was having no romantic thoughts of her own at the moment.

"One of my sources at the National Security Commission reports renewed and almost frenetic activity around an operation that is called Zhìmìng yī jī. That roughly translates from Mandarin to 'Operation Kill Shot.' I have been aware of it for some time but I was convinced it was a diversionary thing, designed to lead off into the weeds. They do that a lot in Beijing. But now, we know it was a double-blind. A real thing made to look false but, in reality, very real."

She paused to take a sip of her wine, leaving her own soup untouched. "Obviously, what I am telling you must be kept from all but the highest levels of your intelligence service. If they even suspected we knew Kill Shot was real, they would flip the switch on whatever they are doing immediately to give us no chance to learn more and try to block it. From what little I can learn, the operation is of the very highest priority—from the president himself—and it is about to be activated. My source doesn't have any idea what it is other than it will be another cyber-attack of some kind, but far more destructive than here and with the commuter train in Washington. It is being planned and implemented out of Hangzhou at something called the Wǎngluò Zhōngxīn. That translates to the 'Cyber Center.'"

As a SEAL, Jim Ward knew plenty about underwater demolition and small-team attack procedures. But he also had become more up to speed on all aspects of terrorism lately. Especially cyber-terrorism.

"And you and your folks don't have a clue what this Operation Zhìmìng yī jī is all about?" Ward asked, knowing the answer already. He took a drink of his beer. He was developing a real taste for Taiwanese craft beers. This "Grain Rain" Tea Ale was excellent. The restaurant had used what precious electricity it had to keep it very cold, too. But it would have been much better had it not been for Li Minh Zhou's answer to his question.

"We know a frighteningly small amount. Nothing more than that it is something cyber-related," she answered. She took a sip of her wine. "That's what bothers me the most, Jim. The not knowing. If we only knew more, we could prepare. It is like fighting an enemy we cannot see. But if it's another cyber-attack, I'm not sure Taiwan can survive. It will be months, if not years, before we restore from the last one. And if it is as big and bad as the few rumblings indicate it could be, there will be retaliation from other nations. There would have to be. And many good people in China and other countries will be hurt."

Jim Ward took another draw on his Grain Rain and nodded slowly.

"Look, let's talk with Dad," he suggested. "What's the use of having the US Navy's top spook in the family if you can't ask for a little help every now and then."

For the first time in an hour, Li Minh Zhou smiled. For Jim Ward it was almost as if the lights had suddenly come on in the restaurant.

Ψ

Henrietta Foster had steered the *Boise* south-southeast for ten hours. She figured that since they were three hundred miles off the Chinese coast by then it would be safe to come up to periscope depth and contact Submarine Group Seven up in Yokosuka, Japan. Far enough away to not be detected and likely in a relatively untraveled portion of the sea. She needed to report the success of the mining mission, but more importantly, Foster wanted to get medical help for Chet Allison. The skipper had been in and out of consciousness ever since the first episode when he collapsed in control. His heart had gone into atrial fibrillation—an erratic heartbeat—a couple of times, and Doc Ballman had to resort to shocking him back into rhythm again. There was a danger of it simply stopping again or churning up a blood clot that could be fatal in itself. Allison needed real medical attention as quickly as possible. Doc was doing all he could but that was limited to what equipment and medicine they carried onboard.

Foster, too, knew that Allison's life hung on getting him to a hospital as soon as possible. It had been a blood clot-induced stroke that suddenly killed her otherwise healthy dad.

Henrietta Foster glanced at the ECDIS chart to see their current location. Then she ordered Jeremy Chastain, the current officer of the deck, to slow to ahead one-third and clear baffles in preparation to come to periscope depth. She then walked to Allison's stateroom. When she stuck her head in the door, Doc Ballman, who had not left the skipper's bedside for the ten hours they had been steaming away from the Chinese coast, was scowling as he checked Allison's vital signs.

"How's the patient, Doc?" she asked him.

"No real change," Ballman answered. "He was sort of awake and lucid a few minutes ago, just long enough to ask if everything was okay, but he slipped back just now. Heart rhythm seems to be stabilized for now. I sure as hell wish I could figure out what's going on, XO."

"We're going to pop up to PD in a couple of minutes to call home," Foster told him. "We need to have as detailed a message as possible ready to send to the Group Seven doctor."

Ballman nodded tiredly. "The message is sitting in radio, ready to go. I'm telling them that we need an emergency medivac right damn now. If not sooner."

The messenger of the watch stepped around the corner. "Excuse me, XO, the OOD requests you come to control right away."

Foster nodded to Ballman, then stepped back into the busy control room. There she found the sub's navigator, Jeremy Chastain, intently staring at the BQQ-10 broadband display. A quick glance showed the waterfall display littered with contacts. The surface way out here was full of vessels of some type.

"XO, there's a strong layer at three hundred feet," Chastain explained. "When we came above the layer, we were suddenly smack in the middle of a fleet of some kind." He pointed to all the traces on the screen. "There has to be several dozen contacts up there. I've come around to course one-three-one. That seems to have the ones on the left drawing left and the ones on the right drawing right. It's going to take us a while to generate tracking solutions on this many contacts."

"Jeremy, we don't have time to screw around getting solutions on all these," Foster grumbled. "We need to call home and get the skipper some medical help like right now. Let's use the big ocean/little submarine theory and get our asses up to periscope depth. Maybe we won't put a hole in somebody's bottom in the process."

Chastain grinned and shot back, “Yes, ma’am.” He stepped back onto the periscope stand and ordered, “Silence in control. Coming to periscope depth.”

The already subdued conversations ceased at once. Everyone knew that coming to periscope depth was the most dangerous operation any submarine routinely performed. With the number of ships up on the roof, this one would be even more hazardous than usual.

“Ahead one-third, make turns for seven knots. Dive, make your depth six-two feet. Raising number two scope.” Chastain shot the orders out in a well-practiced, machine-like cadence. He reached up into the overhead and snapped the periscope lifting ring a quarter turn clockwise and knelt down as the long silver tube slid upward. Then he snapped down the training handles and placed his right eye to the eyepiece as he slowly made a circle, surveying the sea above them as they approached the surface.

Jeanette Walters, the diving officer of the watch, acknowledged the order and then guided the helmsman and planesman in their jobs bringing the *Boise* up to periscope depth. The scope broke the surface and Chastain’s view shifted from pitch black to the dark gray of an overcast tropical night at sea. As he swung the scope around, Chastain quickly realized that his periscope had poked up in the middle of a vast armada of what appeared to be fishing boats. There seemed to be hundreds of them, all steaming to the southeast. Several were close enough that he could see their decks lined with men.

“XO, you need to see this.”

Foster took the scope and quickly zeroed in on the closest boat, only seven hundred yards off their port beam. In twenty-four-power, she could easily see men dressed in what appeared to be combat gear crowded onto every square inch of the boat. Some standing, some sitting on duffel bags. So many men that the fishing boat was riding dangerously low in the water.

Foster did some quick mental math, multiplying the two hundred men she estimated she was looking at on that boat by the hundreds of boats they were seeing out here on their display. What the hell did all this mean? Thirty thousand or more troops could only mean the Chinese, and the only targets worth that much power in this area were either the Philippines or

Borneo. If they maintained this rate of speed, both nations were only about two days' steaming for this fleet.

"Okay, looks like we need to get another message off to SUBGROUP SEVEN. They got more troops on those boats than they do fish bait. Then we best haul tail out of here," Foster said as she handed the scope back to Chastain.

Three minutes later, the *Boise* was back down at four hundred feet and heading due east. Within an hour, the Group Seven medical officer at the US base in Japan was reviewing Chet Allison's EKG scans along with all of Doc Ballman's detailed clinical notes.

And Rear Admiral Dan Jorgensson, Commander Submarine Group Seven, was munching on Rolaids as he initiated an urgent JWICS call with the Pentagon to share *Boise*'s accidental discovery.

Ψ

The JWICS video feed was clear, but the audio was a little tinny, an artifact of the encryption layers that protected the security of the trans-oceanic transmission. Admiral Jon Ward was sitting in his office SCIF—a Sensitive Compartmented Information Facility—at the Pentagon. Ward called the small, protected room his "coffin" but knew it was practically impenetrable for anyone trying to hear or see what was being perused or discussed in there. Li Minh Zhou and Jim Ward were in a similar SCIF inside the American Institute of Taiwan, the de facto American Embassy in the country. As soon as their images flickered on his screen, Jon Ward was quick to note that his son and the Chinese spy were probably sitting a little closer together than necessary to be framed by their video camera.

He avoided doing any "dad jokes," though. This was clearly a serious call.

Li quickly reviewed what she had learned about Operation Kill Shot.

"Have you told any other intelligence agencies about your suspicions, including ours," Ward asked.

"Admiral, you know I prefer dealing only with you," she shot back. "And why I pretend to tolerate your son here. We, better than most, know some of the operatives in the various alphabet intelligence agencies in your government have been compromised, politically and financially, by other governments, ever since World War II. I trust you to only talk with those you can trust. And that you will protect me and my network over here."

The admiral nodded grimly. First things first, they agreed to use the American name for the operation since neither of the Wards was comfortable speaking Mandarin. Then she revealed the same information she had shared with Jim, including that the operation was being run out of a place called the Cyber Center in Hangzhou.

As she talked, Jon Ward grabbed a sheet of paper from one of files lying on his table. He studied it carefully.

"Li, we're not aware of a facility in Hangzhou named the Cyber Center, but they do have a very secret Cyber Warfare Center there, down near the airport. We have learned that it is run out of the Ministry of Foreign Affairs, of all places. Real nasty bunch and very secretive. You won't find a sign on the door. They don't even try to pretend that it is defensive. They have just done all they can to keep the whole thing under wraps so no deflection of purpose necessary. NSA thinks that both the attack on our Metro and on your power grid could have come out of that shop. I don't know if it's good news or bad news but what you're telling me jibes perfectly with what little we already know about that entity."

Li looked directly at the elder Ward from 13,000 miles away. Despite the distance, her concern was obvious.

"So, Admiral, what do we do?" she asked. "I'm really worried that this Operation Kill Shot—or at least a major part of it—may be aimed at my country. A death blow so they can charge in and claim to be rescuing their island and its long-suffering people from the corrupt and illegal government that can't even keep the lights on. You know the line. The truth is, Taiwan cannot survive another hit like the power grid attack. Nor, in that crippled condition, could it defend itself from any invasion. And if the rest of the world is occupied fighting some kind of super-hack..."

There was only the slightest brittle crackle of static on the secure line as the three of them considered the situation for a moment. Jon Ward finally leaned forward and spoke.

"Let me talk to some people—people I trust—over at NSA. If they are really about ready to mount some major operation, there will be traces, footprints that they have left already as they set things up no matter how careful they have been. Your people have seen signs. That means there are more of them. Maybe the NSA weenies can find those footprints and we can smash some toes and make them cancel their plans."

Li looked hard at the screen.

"Weenies?" she asked.

Both Wards broke into broad grins.

"I forgot 'submariner' was the one language you don't speak fluently," Jim told her. "'Weenies' is submariner for 'nerds,' okay?"

She nodded and smiled beautifully. But then, the anxiety returned in her deep brown eyes.

Ψ

Jon Ward's immediate call to the National Security Agency set a lot of things into motion. Barely an hour after he had made his secure call to his contact at the mysterious black glass building in Fort Meade, Maryland, he received an invitation to attend an urgent and highly classified meeting there. Before he could wolf down all of his tuna fish sandwich—Ellen still insisted on packing him a sandwich, an apple, and a cookie every day, knowing he often forgot to eat lunch otherwise—he was racing down to the helipad for the ride out to Fort Meade.

When he got there, the secure conference room three floors below ground level was filled with brass from each of the services. An Air Force general, the Director of the NSA, had already claimed his spot at the head of the long conference table. An Army general, who ran the US Cyber Command, sat at the other end. An admiral, representing Fleet Cyber Command, sat to his right. Arrayed around the rest of the big table were flag officers from the labyrinth of commands that directed the US cyber defense system. It was a group that had been formed and then grown quickly over the last couple of years, both in number of members and oversight responsibility, as the threat to the world's computer network infrastructure had appeared and then become more and more sophisticated.

Jon Ward did not have time to be awed by all the stars in the room. He found his seat next to General TBD Gray, head of DISA, the Defense Information Systems Agency. Gray gave Ward a quick nod of greeting.

A Marine colonel from the Tenth Fleet stood before the large-screen monitor and cleared his throat to signal the hastily called meeting was starting.

"Good afternoon, gentlemen," he began his brief. "I am Colonel Chris Boyd from the Navy Cyber Defense Operation Command. I am here to brief you on what we know of the activities out of Wǎngluò zhàn zhōngxīn, the Chinese Cyber Warfare Center, in Hangzhou, China. As you are aware, the Center has only recently been determined to be the home of China's major offensive cyber operations. Even so, we have been unable to determine the scope of their work there."

A satellite image of Hangzhou appeared on the monitor, then quickly zoomed in on a walled compound adjacent to the city's bustling municipal airport. A large, nondescript building was set in the middle of the heavily guarded compound. There were guard towers at every corner and a strong point built around the only gate that allowed access through the wall.

"We've been trying to gain any insight we can on the activities there for quite some time now, but we have had little to go on," Col. Boyd continued.

"Quit wasting our time," the NSA head interrupted, "and tell us something that we don't know."

Col. Boyd hardly missed a beat.

"Let me introduce Mr. Jeff Rease, the Executive Assistant Director of the Cyber and Infrastructure Security Agency. As you also know but I will remind you anyway, CISA has responsibility for cyber security for Treasury and Commerce."

A rather unremarkable-looking, middle-aged man rose from his seat at the table and stepped up to the lectern.

"Thank you, Colonel. We are quite aware that you know a little about the facility in Hangzhou. However, the information that Admiral Ward provided today, and the reason for this briefing, provides us a key piece of the puzzle that we have been trying to put together for some time. With help from the NSA team, we have been watching the Wǎngluò zhàn zhōngxīn as closely as we can. At first, we believed the whole operation to be diversionary, even when they began to show a great deal of interest in the Society for Worldwide Interbank Financial Telecommunication system—or the acronym SWIFT—for some reason. SWIFT is a cooperative system that banks worldwide now use to conduct international financial transactions. To say that it is the backbone of the international banking system would not be an overstatement. But we believed that their cybersecurity measures were so strong they could never attract the attention of any nefarious group, even the Chinese. That their interest was only to throw us off and discount their threat. Today, Admiral Ward provided us both the actual name and location of the outfit and also their internal code name for what they are up to. Operation Kill Shot. That allowed a fuzzy picture to be brought into much sharper focus."

The little man in the three-piece suit paused to let the information sink in. Before he could go on, though, the NSA general spoke up.

"So Admiral Ward, what is the source of this important bit of intelligence?" he asked.

"With all due respect, General, I am unable to share that at this point," Ward shot back.

"Unable or unwilling?"

"Both."

"Then how can we possibly take it seriously?"

Ward was about to respond when Col. Boyd interrupted.

"General, if you will, we were able to confirm the accuracy of the admiral's information within minutes. It was there all the time. We just had no idea where to look or how to connect the dots or whatever metaphor you might prefer for being, unfortunately, woefully ignorant."

The Air Force general still gave Ward a hard look. He had a reputation for being quite jealous of other agencies that found out things before his own did. Boyd tapped the wall with his pointer to get the eyes of the powerful men in the room back in his direction.

"Now, about SWIFT. If someone were to compromise their security and bring down that system, they could instantly throw international finances into catastrophic chaos. There is no hyperbole in that estimation, gentlemen. They would not even have to bring SWIFT down to do irreparable harm to the world's economic system. Even a hint that the system was under threat would be cataclysmic. The world's markets would crash."

The room had grown quiet. These men, accustomed to crises and threats, now clearly understood the magnitude of what Boyd was telling them. The colonel surveyed the room, then continued.

"This Operation Kill Shot that Admiral Ward has uncovered would be aptly named. It could kill the world economy. Except, of course, any who knew it was coming and had taken precautions. We now know that we have been observing such preparations within China's banking systems and in its financial interests around the globe. But it would be more than sufficient to draw the world's full attention while those who perpetrated the cyber-attack proceeded with whatever their primary goal was. Bad as it might be, bringing down the planet's banking system is likely not the end game. China, or at least someone near the top in its government, has a more drastic intention. Which means we were correct all along. Kill Shot is diversionary. And whatever the actual goal is, we must be ready to defend against both the cyber-attack and whatever it is designed to divert the world's attention away from."

The room grew very quiet as the men considered the implications of what they had just heard. Meanwhile, an aide stepped into the room, walked over to Jon Ward, and whispered something in his ear.

"Gentlemen, I need to get back to the Pentagon," Ward announced. "The CNO has called a meeting with Seventh Fleet and COMSUBGROUP SEVEN and I've got a non-cancellable invitation. I'll keep you updated on anything else we learn from our well-placed sources, but I believe General Gray and Colonel Boyd and their teams now have a better handle on Kill Shot, and with your help, maybe we can defuse that." Ward paused. "At least, let's pray we can."

Ψ

Deng Jiang stalked into the room, a man on a mission. As the Ministry of Foreign Affairs representative on the National Security Commission and Tan Yong's strong right hand for all things cyber, he was top dog at this facility. For all practicable purposes, he had lived at the Cyber Warfare Center in Hangzhou for the last couple of months, carefully nursing Operation Kill Shot toward its birth as a destructive cyber weapon.

Xiǎo Jīntiān, Operation Kill Shot's lead programmer, was the one person in the room to rush to meet his boss. Protocol required it. Otherwise, Xiǎo would have preferred to hide in the ones and zeroes that dominated his existence in this place. Deng Jiang would expect answers to whatever questions he decided to ask. Xiǎo knew full well that those answers had best be prompt. And they would absolutely need to be good news. Others who had preceded Xiǎo in this position had suddenly disappeared from the face of the planet when they were not forthcoming with the desired responses.

"Xiǎo, please report your progress," Deng ordered with no pretense of greeting.

The little man smiled and bobbed a quick but respectful bow.

"Honorable elder brother, the SWIFT system's cyber security was most difficult to penetrate," Xiǎo responded with an affected smile. "Their programmers seemed to have anticipated our every ploy, no matter how subtle or disguised. And they are also very quick to make security changes if they even catch a sniff of a penetration attempt, which could put us back to square one."

Deng's face grew a deeper and deeper red as the programmer spoke. Xiǎo instinctively stepped back as he sensed that he was on the verge of becoming the focus of Deng's notoriously short temper.

Eyes narrowed, Deng snapped, "Are you implying that, with all the resources we have provided you, you have failed in this vital project?"

Xiǎo was quick to answer, holding his hands up as if to deflect anything that might be hurled his way.

"Not at all. I merely wanted to explain how difficult the task was so that you could more fully appreciate the magnitude of the success that your team here, so well managed by you, has achieved." He pointed to a very complex flow chart on a large-screen monitor above one of the workstations. "Developers in practically any kind of system, including a security system like SWIFT, tend to program in a back door, a way for them to easily gain access to create patches or correct bugs without having to endure the usual entry procedures or in case the entry system crashes. Those back doors are almost always very well hidden to avoid being noticed and the developer being reprimanded for providing a potential security leak merely for his own convenience."

Deng waved his hand impatiently. "I understand. Go on."

"In this case, our task was to find any existing back door and then slip in without being detected. Then we could create our own secret and undetectable entryway to avoid being noticed from that point onward."

"Yes, yes."

Despite his leader's restlessness, Xiǎo wore a fawning smile as he moved the cursor to point at a bit of logic code on the monitor. "We found it here. We simply followed the mouse clicks from a Swiss contract developer who was in the system correcting a security problem. One, by the way, that my team and I implemented as a ruse. As you see, he was so kind as to lead us straight to the back door."

The flow chart was so much Greek to Deng Jiang, totally incomprehensible despite his supposed expertise in such things, but he was not going to admit that to the toady little developer. Instead, he finally relaxed and nodded approvingly.

"So, may I assume that Operation Kill Shot is ready for launch?"

The developer paused only long enough to nod and bow.

"Upon your order."

20

The transaction day for international bankers never really starts or stops. Or even slows down. Money is always moving somewhere, all day every day, whether it is moving a billion riyals from Geneva to Hong Kong to pay for a Saudi prince's new yacht or arranging for the quetzals necessary for financing a new hydro-electric plant in Guatemala, the SWIFT system is always in use.

Jon Ward and General Samuel "TBD" Gray were once again in the DISA Command Center watching as colorful graphics flashed across a wall of flat-screens. Ward was dazzled by all the information displayed but he was also struggling to interpret what he was looking at. Gray sensed his puzzlement.

"Jon, what you are seeing is the real-time traffic over the entire SWIFT network," he explained. "And yes, there is plenty of it. NSA is pulling it down from a whole bunch of sources, some that the banking networks know about and some that are, shall we say, a whole lot more subtle."

Ward nodded. "Conceptually, I can see that, but there is so much water coming from this firehose, how could you ever hope to see if anything is happening?"

Gray grinned. "Well, to start with, us Air Force guys are a lot faster than you swabbies, right? But I will admit that, in reality, we rely on AI. Artificial intelligence that is well trained to recognize any kind of anomalies. That is the only thing fast enough to find a hack on a system this complex. The AI system that we unleashed on SWIFT a while back is always finding and fixing hacks and hack attempts and doing it in real time." He pointed to a map display of the SWIFT network. As they watched, a node flashed red, blinked for a moment, and then flashed back to green. A counter was rolling up the numbers for attacks successfully countered.

"Each of these generates a report that gets studied by an analyst," the general said. "Most are the same bad actors we encounter all the time and we just want to be sure they're not getting any smarter. A few stand out for their sophistication or some other unique stamp. Those get top and immediate priority. Knowing what we're looking for and where it originates from will help tremendously in spotting a breach before it can do damage. At least we hope so."

Ward watched the mesmerizing displays for a few more seconds.

"Okay, how will we know when and if we win this round?" he asked.

Gray gave a half smile.

"The 'if" is easy, Jon. If the system doesn't crash and bring the world economy down with it, we know we won." He paused for a second for effect. "The 'when' is a whole hell of a lot harder. Other than dropping a tactical nuke on the Cyber Warfare Center, we have no way of knowing if they have given up until the hacks stop. But even then, there is every possibility that they've just developed a different approach and only shifted to attacking us using that. We can only hope it's not something so new and cute that we are unable to catch it in our nice net."

Ward nodded. The problem of staying ahead of a smart enemy with near unlimited money and resources was a common one across all the military. A race with no finish line.

"I guess that's why you're a cyber warrior and I'm not," Ward admitted. "Sometimes I just want to be able to blow somebody up. What you are describing is a cyber arms race. And it sounds as if there's no way to win it."

Gray looked at Ward, nodding affirmatively.

"Jon, you are absolutely right. No way to win it, but a thousand ways to lose it. And we can't afford to lose even one match."

Ψ

Henrietta Foster waited for six hours before going back to periscope depth for communications. She figured that was enough time for SUBGROUP SEVEN to figure out what needed to be done for her skipper and offer guidance—if any—on their report about the "fishing boats." The boss may or may not want them to get involved. But she had considered it prudent to get the *Boise* well clear of the Chinese armada. If it was an invasion force, there was likely plenty of cover, on, above, and below the surface of the sea. She had now put the submarine almost precisely halfway between the Vietnamese coast and Subic Bay, Philippines. She was poised to go either way. Or somewhere else.

It was zero-two-thirty local time when *Boise*'s SHF mast pierced the surface of the South China Sea. It was zero-three-thirty in Japan. Even so, the head cardiologist at the US Naval Hospital Yokosuka was up on chat with Doc Ballman even as Henrietta Foster was receiving orders to race at best speed to a point twenty miles from the entrance to Subic Bay, Philippines. There they would rendezvous with a US Navy helicopter and transfer Chet Allison to a hospital ashore.

There were no orders concerning the Chinese flotilla.

Foster hummed tunelessly as she quickly checked the ECDIS chart. They were twelve hours away from the rendezvous, even at a flank bell. It would seem like an eternity before they could get Allison the medical help that he so desperately needed.

No other options, though. She gave the orders to get them headed that way.

Ψ

Tan Yong listened as Sun Yang personally updated him on what Sun had warned would be matters of considerable importance. The two men were sitting in the Southern Theater Command's operation center. The room was filled with people, some scurrying around while others worked diligently at computer stations. This was their typical demeanor. They were not working extra hard to try to impress their president, who had never visited this place before.

The walls of the massive room were filled with flat-panel displays showing colorful maps and charts. However, all the noise generated by so much frenzied activity was filtered out by the glass-paneled walls that separated Sun Yang's raised conference room from all the action of the center's main floor.

"Honorable First Secretary," Sun Yang said, beginning his brief. "Our navy forces protecting Cuarteron Reef in the Spratly Islands have been attacked and I regret to inform you that they have suffered severe damage."

Most people delivering bad news to the Chinese president made every effort to cast it in the best possible light. Tan Yong had built a significant and well-earned reputation for—as the Americans so often say— "shooting the messenger." But Sun Yang, in addition to his duties on the National Security Commission, also headed the Guoanbu, the dreaded secret police. Delivering bad news was nothing new to him.

"Who? Who dared attack us?"

"It seems the Americans were trying to conduct some sort of underwater evolution near the Barque Canada Shoals. That, of course, is well inside our territorial waters. They were duly and adequately warned to immediately leave the area. When they failed to comply, an exchange of missiles occurred."

"And what was the ultimate result?" Tan Yong asked, uncharacteristically calm.

"Despite the courageous actions of our PLAN, we unfortunately have significant losses. We had two of our Type Fifty-Two destroyers and two of our Type Fifty-Five stealth destroyers stationed there. They bravely engaged the target ships with anti-ship cruise missiles and were attacked by American anti-ship missiles. All four of our ships suffered hits. The Type Fifty-Five *Dalian* is heavily damaged and remains in danger of sinking. The Type Fifty-Two *Jinan* suffered three hits and was lost. There are a significant number of casualties to the crews."

"And the American damage?" Tan Yong quickly asked.

"Honorable First Secretary, the American LCS vessel *Canberra* was heavily damaged and is now run aground on Barque Canada Reef."

Tan exploded. Even though there was no way any of them could have heard him when he pounded the table several times with a closed fist, several people inadvertently looked that way and saw their leader's detonation.

"The *Canberra*! It was reported sunk last week by our PLAN Air Force! Last week! How is this possible? Does this ship rise from the ashes like a phoenix? Are we being stalked now by ghosts?"

Sun Yang held up a hand. "I fear that I am not yet finished with my report, sir. We, of course, deployed a submarine to intercept and sink the retreating American ships. I regretfully must tell you that the submarine has now missed two communications cycles. As is our policy, it has been designated missing and possibly sunk. Though we have, of course, kept this highly classified until..."

This was more than Tan Yong could bear. His chin jutted out as he poked the air between them with his index finger.

"The first steps of Operation Southern Sweep have already begun, as you well know. We cannot risk any interference at this point. You will inform your forces that any warships encountered in the South China Sea are to be treated as hostile. They are to be attacked and sunk without any warning whatsoever."

"Even American ships?" Sun Yang questioned, his usual forceful voice now tentative.

The president glared at him and again slammed his fist down hard on the table.

"Especially American warships!"

Ψ

Brian Edwards had steered his submarine, the USS *George Mason,* to a position twenty miles south of Scarborough Shoals, some one-hundred-twenty miles west of the Philippines and five-hundred-sixty miles southeast of the nearest coast of China. Like most of the islands, reefs, shoals, and barren rocks in the South China Sea, both the Philippines and China claimed Scarborough as its own territory. Few of the fly specks of land or coral around here had only one claimant. But lately, China had been enforcing its contention at the point of a gun. Lots of guns. Commander Edwards and the *George Mason* were there to monitor that far more threatening action and maybe help determine what it all meant.

However, at the moment, it was lunch time.

The skipper looked up from his meal as Ashton Jennings entered the wardroom. Arriving at a meal late was normally a breach of etiquette. The offending officer would be expected to wait for the second sitting. Mealtime in the submarine wardroom was one of the few activities in which a modicum of formality among officers remained from the old, more formal ways of the surface Navy. But some allowances could necessarily be made when the boat was out there on the pointy end of the spear.

"Sorry to be late," the Weps apologized. "Permission to join the mess?"

"Repairs on tube nine complete?" Edwards inquired, as if Jennings's response might determine whether or not he would be allowed to join them. But then the captain nodded and waved Jennings to an empty seat.

"Yes, sir. We just retested the umbilical and buttoned up the tube. We're good to go." Jennings grabbed a thick, juicy pork chop off the platter as it passed by. "I'll be the happiest man on this ship when we kick that last UUV out of the nest."

Jackson Biddle, the *George Mason*'s XO, grinned. "You and me both, Weps. I think it's high time we went from being delivery boys and back to steely-eyed killers of the deep."

"Agreed, XO," Edwards said. "Right after lunch would be a good time. Now, please pass the green beans to the Weps. Hard-workin' boy needs his veggies."

The meal continued with the typical noontime banter. Until dessert, that is. Edwards looked down at the wiggly square of fruit Jell-O for a long moment and then glared at the supply officer sitting at the far end of the table. "Chop, what the hell is this?" he growled. "The menu clearly says ice cream for dessert."

The young ensign withered under the skipper's glare and swallowed hard before replying. "Skipper, we may be out of ice cream mix. Inventory says we should have three more boxes, but we couldn't find them. I'm going to empty number-two dry stores and re-inventory everything right after lunch. Hopefully, we'll find the missing boxes. They're somewhere."

XO Biddle looked hard at the clearly nervous young officer. "Fit your inventory around the launch evolution. I don't want the damage control parties stumbling over a bunch of number-ten cans while they do their jobs. And I sure as hell don't want them rattling around and making a bunch of noise right about then. Last thing we need is to be detected because you were looking for your lost ice cream." Biddle carefully rolled his napkin as he talked and then stuck it in the heavy silver ring in front of him on the tabletop. As he rose, he turned to Edwards. "Excuse me, Skipper. I need to get things rolling to make sure we're ready to launch the UUV."

Edwards nodded and was rolling his own napkin when his phone buzzed. He shoved away the dish of Jell-O and grabbed the handset from under the wardroom table.

"Captain."

"Captain, Officer of the Deck." It was Jim Shupert, the on-watch OOD. "We're picking up a bunch of sonar contacts to the west. Sonar is classifying them as probable fishing boats, but there are a whole lot of them. Range from the wide aperture array is in excess of fifty-thousand yards, but the bearings stretch over ten degrees, two-nine-zero to three-zero-four."

Edwards whistled. "That's got to be a whole bunch of fishing boats." He glanced at the wardroom clock and did some quick mental math. It would take an hour to run over and find out what was happening to the west and then an hour to get back to where they could launch the UUV. "We should be able to go take a look and get back. Come around to course two-nine-five and come up to a full bell. Close to twenty thousand yards. We'll see what's going on with all those fishing boats, then get back to finish the UUV launch."

Edwards took one last disappointed look at the jiggling blob of green Jell-O, then stood and quickly left the wardroom.

Ψ

Henrietta Foster sat on the little flip-down stool behind number two periscope. She was exhausted. In the last twelve hours, the *Boise* had charged across the South China Sea to finally arrive at the predetermined medivac rendezvous point. She had spent most of that time bouncing between checking the preparations for the upcoming medivac of her captain and checking on his condition. Thank goodness for that extra-large coffee mug. And the XO's head only a few steps from control.

Jeremy Chastain, the navigator and on-watch OOD, stepped forward from the ECDIS table. "XO, we are at the rendezvous, fourteen-point-five-oh north, 120 east. I'm slowing to ahead one-third and clearing baffles in preparation for surfacing."

Foster nodded. "Roger. Thanks. In the meantime, get the COB and the helo transfer party standing by at the forward escape trunk. And get someone standing by to rig the bridge. We got to make it snappy. We do not need to show off to the world for long at all. We'd prefer some folks don't even know we're in this hemisphere, right?"

The control room briefly bustled with activity as the boat slowed and came up to one-hundred and fifty feet. By the time they had completed clearing baffles—checking for possible ships on the surface in their sonar's blind spots—ETR-1 Hanson was standing at the base of the bridge ladder ready to man the bridge. The COB reported the helo transfer party was mustered and ready at the forward escape trunk. Sonar announced there were three contacts, all distant, classified as merchants, past CPA—closed point of approach—and opening, increasing the distance away from *Boise*. All good. The meet-up with the medivac aircraft would be in an empty part of the sea. In these waters, that was sometimes difficult to find.

Foster stood and made one final check of the sonar display, just to suit herself they would be unobserved by any nearby surface vessels. Satisfied, she ordered, "Officer of the Deck, proceed to periscope depth."

The *Boise* rose smoothly from the depths until Jeremy Chastain, staring out of the periscope, was treated to the sight of a bright tropical afternoon. Sure enough, the view of the deep-blue sea was unsullied by any other vessel in any direction.

"Surface the ship," Chastain ordered.

"Ahead two-thirds, full rise on the fairwater planes," Jeanette Walters, the diving officer of the watch, ordered. "Full rise on the stern planes."

The big submarine emerged majestically from the depths, pushed up by the planes and her forward speed.

The chief of the watch grabbed the 1MC microphone and announced, "Surface! Surface! Surface!" He then flipped the normal main ballast tank blow switches in order to port forty-five-hundred-pound high-pressure air into the ballast tanks. That forced the sea water in those big tanks out the grates in their bottoms. After fifteen seconds, he flipped the switches back down, securing the blow. With the ballast tanks filled with air and emptied of water, the boat's natural buoyancy kept them on the surface. Though far more sophisticated nowadays, that was pretty much the way submarines had surfaced since the US War Between the States. Diving, too, by flooding sea water back into those tanks. But an intricate system of valves and pumps had to work well together or either operation could be disastrous.

Walters checked the depth. "Three-five feet and holding."

In quick succession Chastain ordered, "Send personnel to the bridge and rig the bridge. To the COB, open the lower escape trunk. Send men into the trunk."

Foster grabbed a bridge-to-bridge radio and pulled on her ballcap. "Officer of the Deck, I'm going to the bridge with Petty Officer Hanson as my phone talker. Get the COB and helo transfer party topside. When Doc is ready, move the skipper topside."

She turned and had just started the long climb up the ladder when she heard the voice on the 21MC speaker. "Conn, Radio. In communications with the helo inbound. They report that they are ten minutes out." He gave her the radio frequency they would use topside.

Foster followed Hanson up the ladder and finally stepped onto the sub's bridge platform. The tropical sun and warm ocean breeze felt good.

"I see the helo. Except it ain't a helicopter. Looks like an Osprey," Hanson called out, pointing to a smudge on the eastern horizon. The bird was down low, near the wavetops, and coming fast. "Best guess it's about five miles or so out."

A voice broke the squelch on Foster's handheld radio. "Navy unit, this is Flight Nine-seven-four. I hold you visually. Request you lower all masts and antennas. Request you come into the wind. Will this be a main deck transfer?"

Foster turned to Hanson before she answered. "Tell control to lower all masts and antennas. Ahead one-third, steer course one-six-zero."

She engaged the push-to-talk button on the radio. "Flight Nine-seven-four, Navy unit. Coming to course one-six-zero, speed four. This will be a main deck transfer. One pax, not conscious, requires a litter. Masts and antennas lowered."

The CMV-22 Osprey slowed as it flew around astern of the sub and the pilot swung the engine nacelles up to bring the bird into a hover. Foster watched as the craft slowly slid sideways up the sub's stern. As it came up over the turtleback, a basket was lowered from the Osprey's side-hatch winch. The COB neatly caught the winch cable with the grounding hook—the difference in electrical potential between the sub in the water and the aircraft above could create a lethal voltage on a cable—and pulled the litter to the deck. It took only a couple of minutes to lower Allison onto the litter and strap him in. Then the COB signaled the men in the Osprey's open doorway to lift the basket and patient. Everyone on the submarine's deck and bridge saluted their skipper.

The Osprey pulled up and away even as the litter was still being raised. As Foster watched it transfer to horizontal flight, the radio in her hand crackled. "Navy unit, Flight Nine-seven-four. Transfer complete. Medical officer checking your patient. We'll take good care of him. Seven-four out."

"Seven-four, Navy unit. Smooth flight. Thanks."

Ten minutes later, nothing in this part of the South China Sea would offer even a clue that anything had ever happened there.

21

The *George Mason* ran toward the Chinese fishing fleet for an hour. Sonar was showing the range to the closest tracks at twelve thousand yards when Brian Edwards decided that it was time to go up to periscope depth and take a look. He figured at that range he should just be able to see the tops of their masts. But there was very little chance of anyone detecting him and his submarine. When the low-profile photonics mast broke the surface, Edwards could immediately see that a wide swath of the western horizon was littered with a stunning number of fishing boats. They were tightly packed together, like a school of fish swimming in formation, all heading due east. And *George Mason* was directly in front of the approaching horde.

"Weps, get a Blackwing loaded in the number one signal ejector," Edwards ordered over his shoulder to Aston Jennings. "I want to see what this bunch is up to and I'm guessing it ain't tuna fishing."

The fleet filled more and more of the horizon as the convoy steamed closer and closer. By the time Jennings reported the little unmanned aerial vehicle was ready to launch, the nearest fishing boat was at eight thousand yards and clearly visible. When Edwards zoomed in to maximum power, the large-screen display showed him that the vessel's deck was filled with troops, many at the rail. Some smoking. A few obviously seasick.

"Blackwing loaded in number one signal ejector, ready for launch,"

Aston Jennings reported. The Blackwing drone would give those on the sub a far better view of what was going on up there from altitude. And its images could also be routed on to other viewing spots around the world for instant, real-time analysis.

"Launch the Blackwing," Edwards ordered. As he did so, he swung the photonics camera around just in time to see the tiny UAV jump from the surface. Its wings scissored out as it quickly gained altitude. Within seconds it was invisible.

"Good downlink," Jackson Biddle reported, confirming the UAV was already relaying down to them exactly what it was seeing. The XO stood beside the panel operator as they both watched the video screen image build.

The UAV was barely nineteen inches long and had a wingspan of only twenty-seven inches. At five thousand feet, the thing was invisible from sea level. But its electro-optical/infrared "eyeball" could see amazing detail. It was now painting an improbable but unmistakable picture of blue-hulled fishing boats that covered the sea surface from horizon to horizon.

Edwards shook his head as he looked at Biddle. "XO, I don't know what the hell this means, but it is not good. Link this video feed to SUBGROUP SEVEN. We'll let SEVENTH FLEET figure out what this is all about."

Biddle replied, "Already linked to Yokosuka. Meantime, I suggest we skedaddle out of here before we get run over. That nearest boat is now at four thousand yards."

Edwards lowered the photonics mast.

"Weps, get us down to four hundred feet and headed back to Scarborough Shoal."

Ψ

Li Minh Zhou and Navy SEAL Jim Ward again sat together in the SCIF at the American Institute of Taiwan. And they were once more conferencing with Chief of Naval Intelligence Admiral Jon Ward at his own SCIF back in the Pentagon in Washington, DC. Jon Ward was trying to explain to them something that he was not at all sure he understood. He was hoping one of them—especially Li—might have ideas for some kind of plan to implement what he was describing.

He had found she oftentimes did. He prayed this was one of those times.

"The weenies over at DISA think they have come up with a solution to stopping this Operation Kill Shot before it's too late," Jon was saying. Jim and Li Minh Zhou both leaned in closer to the monitor. "They developed what they are calling a 'white virus' that they are certain will attack and destroy the 'Kill Shot' virus. And it can do it, they think, before it has a chance to spread through the financial markets. Before anybody, including the media, is even aware there is a problem. They think this is our only chance to beat it early enough to matter. The next best alternative would be to minimize the impairment, and that is not going to work. The damage will have been done by then. Real and psychological."

"Dad, I hear a 'but' in your voice." Jim sounded worried. Li Minh Zhou looked concerned, too.

"You jumped right to the heart of this call," the elder Ward answered. "There is one big stinking 'gotcha.' The only way for the white virus to do its job is for it to be planted and attack on the same server inside Cyber Warfare Center in Hangzhou on which the executable for 'Kill Shot' is installed. The geeks at DISA say it's a very clever way for the bastards to make the thing near unstoppable."

Jim Ward shook his head, frowned, and idly scratched his five-day stubble. His father almost smiled. Sometimes it was like looking in the mirror when he conversed over video with his boy.

"So, you are saying that someone will need to physically penetrate that place and manually load the virus on the server," Jim said. "I assume the center is a fortress, physically as much as digitally. No way possible to get in there, much less get out."

Li Minh Zhou laid her hand on Jim's. There was an odd smile on her face.

"Not so fast, young warrior. Did you ever watch *Mission Impossible*? If Tom Cruise can get into places like that, no reason we can't."

Jon Ward chuckled, but Jim just stared at her.

"I'm a little behind on my movie-going, I'm afraid. Slogging through jungles with a bunch of sweaty SEALs..."

"Let us just say that the facility in question has been on our radar for a while. We assumed most of the Middle Kingdom's cyber warfare originated from there. And we also assumed we'd either have to blow it the hell up or, even better, penetrate it and do something such as we are discussing. We may have a way." She paused just long enough for the meaning of her words to sink in. "Admiral, get the code for the virus to us. We will see that it is installed on that server."

The Chinese spy's words were emphatic. Jim Ward looked at her wide-eyed. She never ceased to amaze him.

"You'll have a memory stick with it loaded before you leave the Institute," Jon promised. "I understand it is an auto-executable file, so all you need to do is copy it to anywhere on the server and let it load up. But this is important. You will need to access the server with admin privileges. Right?"

"I understand."

"If you want to tell me how you intend on breaking into that joint, feel free."

The admiral knew she likely would not. And she didn't. He just had to assume she really did have a way. And one that would work.

"I'll brief you, Admiral, when Kill Shot is a dead duck."

As Li Minh Zhou and Jim Ward walked out of the Institute and onto the sidewalk next to busy Jinhu Road, the small memory stick was burning a hole in Jim's pocket. Then, as the light changed and they crossed the street to where their car and driver waited, Ward finally asked the question that had been bothering him ever since Zhou had so confidently taken on this mission impossible.

"Okay, Miss Bond...James Bond...just how do you think you will pull this off?"

Zhou looked at him with an enigmatic smile.

"I thought you didn't have time for movies."

"I saw one once. And I still say Sean Connery was the best Bond ever. But how are you going to do it?"

"Not me, boy wonder. Us."

Ward stopped cold and looked hard at her.

"Wait. What do you mean 'us?'" He pointed at himself, then her. "I don't exactly look like your run-of-the-mill Asian person. And I certainly don't sound like one. Even if I did, how in hell do you figure we'd pull this thing off? Charge in with guns blazing? Hold off half the PLA while we screw around on a keyboard? Then march out through a hail of gunfire to a waiting Osprey double-parked across the street?"

She laughed one of her rare, beautiful, bell-ringing kind of laughs, then walked on.

"Jim, just trust me," she told him over her shoulder. "And leave the planning to me."

Ψ

Jim Ward, the US Navy SEAL-team leader, was nothing more than an American businessman as he stared out the window of the Air China Airbus A330. His flight was now on final approach to Hangzhou's Xiaoshan International Airport. Thirteen million people inhabited this Chinese metropolis—half again as many as in New York City—and many of them worked in the area's computer technology industries. Quite a few of them had done very well. Ward had read that Hangzhou ranked eleventh in the world in the number of resident billionaires. With so many available gear-heads, it was little wonder the Chinese government had placed their most notorious cyber-mischief shop there.

As Ward knew, the flight path would take him almost directly over the top of the Cyber Warfare Center. Despite the thick smog, he could easily make out the large cement building surrounded by a high concrete wall. It looked impregnable, like a high-security prison.

Ward still had no idea how Zhou planned to get in there or what role she expected him to play. He was a team guy, good at digging in, then shooting, stabbing, choking, and blowing up bad guys. Surely there would be none of that going on here. But as the wheels of the big airplane touched down, he knew one thing. He would soon find out what the plan was.

He and Zhou had flown into Hangzhou on different flights and by different routes. Ward's manifest showed that he was coming in originally from San Francisco with a layover at Narita. He was there as a contractor to negotiate the purchase of electronic components for a company in Silicon Valley. Should anyone get curious and inquire, there was an elaborate backstory that could be confirmed by several people in the company's personnel office.

Zhou's flight had arrived a couple of hours earlier. She was flying from Inchon on a trip that originated in Vancouver, British Columbia, where she was a student at Simon Fraser University. Anyone requesting confirmation of her enrollment would be told she was a sophomore there, studying computer technology, with a GPA of 3.8. The reason for her trip to Hangzhou was to visit relatives who lived further upcountry.

Ward easily cleared customs and immigration control without incident. No one questioned his heavily-stamped tourist passport. Just another American businessman ready to spend plentiful dollars in exchange for Chinese goods and services. Thousands of others just like him—right down to the Brooks Brothers suit and Rolex watch—passed through these checkpoints each week.

But this "businessman" carried a very important commodity. A nondescript memory stick lay in the bottom of his laptop bag along with the usual electronic paraphernalia, earbuds, charger cord, spare battery. Should someone get hold of the thumb drive and look at its contents, he would see several gigabytes of obscure technical documents, all ensconced in folders and sub-folders multiple layers deep. One file, hidden deep down in the tree, was named "KIDS PIX." It was one of many that were protected by passwords. All different passwords.

Ward stepped out of the airport into the bright afternoon sunshine. It was warm, pleasant, and he was now totally lost. There had been no instructions beyond being at this particular portal from baggage claim twenty minutes after wheels-down.

He had just set his bag down between both feet and glanced around to get the lay of the land—and, as always, look for potential threats and an escape route—when a Hongqi H-7 limousine, very similar to many, many others zipping about, pulled to a stop at the curb three feet from him. The driver's side window was rolled down.

"Amelican saila-boy wanty good time Hangzhou?" Le Min Zhou mimicked a truly awful Chinese accent. Ward could barely contain his laughter as he opened the door and climbed into the passenger seat next to her.

It took his eyes a moment to adjust from the brilliant sunshine to the car's darkened interior. Even then, he kept his eyes on Zhou. He had not realized how much he had missed her the last few days. But then he noticed that someone else was in the limo with them. The man slumped down in the back seat appeared to be young, probably in his late twenties, reasonably fit, and well dressed in suit and tie. He also wore eyeglasses and, like so many other people on the street, had on a surgical mask. He was also very obviously nervous.

As she pulled away from the curb and melded into all the traffic, Zhou nodded in the direction of their passenger. "This is Nán Péngyǒu. He will help us."

Ward looked again at the man. Nán nodded.

"I am willing to do anything to destroy those devils." His statement was flat, devoid of emotion, but filled with iron-hard resolve. "They murdered my love, my Mie Ping. She had loyally done her job. But they killed her just to hide the evidence of what her work was."

"Nán works at the Center. Social media specialist. If you've ever been on Facebook, TikTok, LinkedIn, Instagram...most any of them...you've seen his work without knowing it."

"I may still have a Facebook account, but I've been kind of busy and..."

"He can get us inside."

The car was quiet for a while. Then the limo swung left onto Hezhuang Road and the Cyber Warfare compound came into view. The foreboding cement walls were easily twenty feet tall and the watch towers at the corners had a clear line of sight over the open ground that separated the razor-wire-topped chain link fence from the solid wall. There was no signage or identification.

Jim Ward did a quick assault analysis. If he had to storm that joint with his SEAL team and blow up something, how would he do it? It did not take him long to determine the answer: No freakin' way!

The traffic light changed, the mob of pedestrians finally cleared, and Zhou swung the limo to the west on Hongshiwu Line Road and then south onto Hongheng Line Road, following a route around the Center's perimeter. It appeared to be just as impregnable from all angles. The fence and the wall were only broken by the fortified gate house on the south side and a narrow, glass-enclosed walkway to what appeared to be the structure's main entrance.

Ward grunted. A direct frontal assault would take a battalion. And softening up before. If there was any back door, it was not readily visible.

"Well, friend, I hope you have a really good idea," Ward told their backseat passenger. The man did not react. He only slid down farther in the seat, as if someone might recognize him behind the mask and glasses.

Li Minh Zhou steered the limo away from the compound and on toward the Xiaoshan District, instinctively keeping an eye on her mirrors for anyone following them. Ward did the same in the right-side mirror. Neither saw anything of interest.

The densely populated old-town area would be the perfect place for keeping a low profile for a few hours. They chose the Abo Restaurant, a dimly-lit local place, to kill a few hours while the sun took its sweet time setting. Shift change at the Center this day was at twenty hundred. It varied each day to prevent anyone from getting a fix on the Center's routine despite the hardship it placed on those who worked there.

Twenty hundred hours. That was go time. By the time the three of them had finished a nice meal and many cups of tea, Ward and Nán were both finally aware of what was expected of them. Ward left the restaurant first, while Li and Nán settled up the bill.

Jim drove the Hongqi down Jinchang Road in the general direction of the Binjiang District. He had papers in the glovebox confirming he was licensed to drive in China, that the limo was a rental from China Auto Rental. He hoped he would not have to show them.

The waterfront down along the Qiantang River was much like that of any river running through any major city anywhere in the world. Warehouses and truck parks vied with seedy bars and rundown hotels. River-going barges and corroded-hull tramp steamers lined up along the dimly lit piers. Though it was still early in the evening, few people ventured out, although the bars seemed to be doing quite a brisk business.

Even with GPS helping, it took Ward almost half an hour to find the specific building that Li Min Zhou was sending him to. A particularly rusty tramp steamer rode easily nearby, tied up adjacent to the rundown pier.

Ward shook his head. If this was Zhou's idea of an emergency extract should things go severely south at the Cyber Warfare Center, then they had better get on their knees and pray for success. This rust bucket would be lucky to get underway, let alone evade the Chinese Coast Guard.

The ship's master, an almost toothless old man who identified himself as Chuán Zhăng, nervously guided Ward out the back door of the building and aboard the vessel. It bore the hard-to-read name *Shēng Xiùde*. He spoke broken English as he handed Ward a wad of documents, new identities for him and Li to use when leaving China. And he made it clear he would only be able to wait until dawn before he set sail. Otherwise, there would be much suspicion as daylight would display other discrepancies. And a favoring tide. This meant that if Ward and Li had to alter their plans and make a desperate run for it, and if they could make it to the pier in time, the *Shēng Xiùde* would be waiting and ready to steam away to its next port of call, just as it did on this day every week.

But—and the old man said it three times for emphasis—if they missed the morning tide, they would find this pier empty. And he would disavow any knowledge of the two or their reasons for being in Hangzhou should anyone inquire. And the considerable fee he had been paid would be his to keep, regardless.

Ward could still see the old sea captain standing on the ship's deck, watching him as he pulled away from the curb and headed back toward his pre-designated waiting lot a block from the night's objective. He had carefully noted landmarks along the way in case he would need to go back this route but at a much quicker pace.

Once he was parked, he checked the digital clock on the car's dash. Zhou and her accomplice would just be entering the Cyber Center about now.

He tapped the steering wheel with his fingers. Watched all the people moving about on the streets and sidewalks nearby. Unsuccessfully attempted to find some decent music on the limo's radio.

And tried to ignore the growing lump in his throat.

22

As soon as the streetlights began to blink on, Li Minh Zhou and Nán Péngyǒu left the Abo Restaurant, walked three blocks to a stop, and boarded a bus that took them and scores of others to another busy stop a mile or so from the Center's gate. The pair had kept their distance at the first bus stop. She knew Jim Ward could handle his assignment, but she also knew a thousand things could go wrong.

When they boarded the bus, she and Nán ignored each other and took separate seats, just another couple of government workers on their way to dull jobs. As they rode along, Zhou fingered the plastic ID card on the chain around her neck. The one that Nán Péngyǒu had "borrowed" from a friend and given to her at the restaurant. The picture on the card looked vaguely like Zhou, particularly since she had bobbed her long black hair and donned a frumpy pants suit with significant extra padding before beginning the day's mission.

Thankfully, the weather was nice. And the walk from the second bus stop to the Center was an easy one. Nán and Zhou kept their distance the whole way. Two strangers, coincidentally going the same direction on a nice evening in Hangzhou.

They also stepped up to the gate separately with several other workers between them. The guard at the gate barely glanced at her card—or those of the many other workers passing through for the night shift—before he waved her through. Once they were inside the gate, the long line slowed as they went through another security check—even less attention from the bored guard to her borrowed ID—and then to one of the steps of the plan that she most dreaded.

A metal scanner. Nán had assured her it was only to catch weapons or other metal objects. Explosives, too. Another one, at the exit, was far more sensitive. He was correct. The memory stick, hidden in the toe of her too-large shoe, did not attract the scanner's attention.

Zhou and Nán walked closer as they joined the big crowd in the brightly-lit corridor inside the building. He was relatively new with the Center and had few friends yet. His team typically worked the early morning shift. He saw no one he knew.

Nán led the way down the corridor with Zhou still ten or fifteen feet behind him, not obviously following him. Then they turned down another long, straight hallway with cryptically-marked closed doors on each side. Then another right turn down another hallway.

The number of workers had dwindled considerably. Soon, there was only the two of them. Nán stopped at a locked door.

"This is the central server room," he said quietly. "I do not have the code to open this door, of course."

"We will wait here. We will chat. How is the weather? Who is your favorite football team?"

Within a half-minute, the door swung open and a group of tired workers emerged, talking loudly, happy to have concluded a long day of monotonous work. They did not notice the bespectacled and masked man and the frumpy woman standing there next to the door talking. The group headed back down the hallway, chatting merrily.

Zhou had placed a foot in a strategic spot, blocking the door before it could swing shut. Nán looked at her questioningly.

"How did I know it would be this easy?" she asked quietly. "You are not my only assistant."

Then the two of them stepped into a large room filled with rows of floor-to-ceiling equipment racks that held many, many computer servers. The room was cold. The rumble and hum of air conditioning and cooling fans was constant. It was also empty of any personnel. Exactly as she had been told. Server room personnel were quick to go after their workday was finished, seeking warmth and quiet and respite from the incessant "inspirational" music the supervisor played on the loudspeakers overhead. And those just beginning their shift had a compulsory fifteen-minute "patriotic meeting" each day, held in a conference room down the hall. All to assure they knew the value of their work to the State and to the Party, and that they would perform at their best for both.

At the head of the room sat a desk that held only a single keyboard, a mouse, a workstation, and a couple of monitors. That and a huge stack of Party literature and brochures.

Zhou watched for a bit as meaningless gibberish danced across the monitor screens. Then she reached inside one of the desk drawers. It took her a few minutes, but she found it. Again, just as she had been advised.

One of the SysAdmins had helpfully written down the password for administrative access to the entire server farm on the back of a brochure, just in case he or one of his counterparts forgot it. Easy to do. It was changed often, without warning.

Zhou hoped it had not changed already and the SysAdmin had not had time to write down the new one. She quickly typed in the password, hit "Enter," and waited. It was only two seconds but seemed like an hour. But the message indicated she was in.

She quickly inserted the memory stick into the USB port on the workstation. She worked as briskly as she could without fumble-fingering the keystrokes to navigate to "KIDS PIX" and type in the password for that folder. She sucked in a deep breath and double-clicked the mouse with the pointer aimed at the only thing in the folder, an executable file named "kill_kill_shot.exe."

A blank rectangular bar appeared on the monitor. After a second's hesitation, it slowly started to fill in, from left to right, in green. The green bar seemed to build at an imperceptible rate. Zhou checked her watch. Hopefully nobody would jump out of the meeting early. Or some security guy would idly step in to check on things. The room was so cold, she had been told, that most people, including security, avoided coming in unless they had to work there.

But if someone did catch them before the program had loaded, Zhou knew that their mission would end in failure. And, of course, a rather painful and violent interrogation and death for both her and Nán Péngyǒu.

At least Jim might escape, she thought. If he was very good and very lucky. It could require generous amounts of both commodities, though.

Finally, the green bar filled the blank one across the screen. It flashed off and a drop-down box popped up. "Download complete. Initiating install." That was quickly followed by the message, "Installation complete. Executing program."

Could it have installed that quickly, she thought. Had something gone wrong?

But then, the screen shifted back to the gibberish displays.

Zhou realized she had not breathed since clicking on the executable file. She grabbed the memory stick from the USB port and headed for the door, waving for Nán to follow. She had not spoken to him since entering the room, either. She assumed he knew what was going on at the workstation, but he had only stood there, peering at the closed door that led out into the hallway. And he had not breathed either.

The door had just swung shut behind them and they were walking nonchalantly down the corridor when they met the group of server room workers heading back to start their shift after being filled with nationalistic pride. No one seemed to pay Zhou and Nán any attention at all.

As they passed down the last hallway before the exit scanner, Zhou casually tossed the memory stick into a trash can. With a place like this, the security to leave was even more thorough than the security to get in. Discovery of the memory stick was one risk they did not need to take.

Once again, the two of them walked at some distance from each other. They blended into still more workers leaving the place. Zhou even struck up a conversation with a guy who wanted to talk about some video game he planned to play all night once he got home. Whether that chat helped her remain anonymous or not, no guard—and there were quite a few, all along the walkway out—paid her any attention at all.

Ten minutes later, the pair were outside, breathing in the fragrant night air as they strolled down Hongye Road. They stopped and sat on a bench under a larch tree, a couple of friends waiting for a bus. But just then, Jim

Ward drove up in the limo, rolled down the driver's side window, and said, not too loudly, "Hey, pletty lady. You want good time with saila boy?"

Li Minh Zhou laughed as hard as she dared. Tension fled from her taut body. Nán Péngyǒu went ahead and opened the front passenger door of the Hongqi H-7.

She thanked him as she slid in, then looked up at him.

"Thank you, Nán. I hope this helps you. But be assured, what you did today has saved uncountable lives and prevented more suffering than you can imagine. And, whether you think so or not, you have done a good thing for your country."

He nodded. In the light from a streetlamp, she could see a tear on his cheek. He smiled, turned, and trotted off toward a bus stop several streets away.

"Are you okay?" Jim asked her.

"Let me start breathing again and I'll tell you." She turned toward him, then took his face in both hands and kissed him long and hard. She was now even more out of breath and her voice had gone husky. "Now, what kind of good time did you have in mind, saila boy?"

Ward smiled as he swung on to the G92 freeway heading east. They had more than 150 miles to drive to get to Shanghai's Pudong International Airport. But they had plenty of time. Their flight out to Tokyo's Narita Airport would not be until ten hundred the next morning.

They were certainly resourceful enough to find a way to kill some time on the way.

Ψ

Ward and Li sat quietly, deep in their own thoughts as the miles reeled out behind them. Some of what they were considering was likely the same. They would arrive at their destination with time to spare. Both had mentioned the need to freshen up before the flight to Japan. Maybe a few hours at one of the many hotels that ringed the massive airport. To "freshen up."

Even this late at night, the traffic on the Chinese throughway was thick. Heavy trucks vied with tiny compact cars and the occasional limousine for advantage in the roadway's multiple lanes. Still, even though they were both spent, as much from tension as exertion, they relaxed and watched what little scenery they could make out as it flowed past their windows. And, for the most part, even though the traffic was surprisingly substantial, the pace was brisk and their car blended in anonymously.

Ward had just swung smoothly onto the S32 for the final leg to Shanghai's sprawling airport when Li Min Zhou's phone buzzed, breaking the easy mood in the vehicle. They shot a quick glance at each other. While inside China, this was supposed to be an "emergency only" device. An incoming call could only be bad news.

"Nǐ hǎo," she spoke into the mouthpiece as she clicked the speaker option. He noticed she was gripping the cell so hard her knuckles were white. Even though the phone was encrypted and accessible to a very select few people, there was every possibility that this signal was being intercepted and the conversation overheard. After all, they were in the most closely monitored society in the world. Best to keep chats as short, succinct, and veiled as possible.

"Twitter has been taken." The voice was familiar. It was one of her agents in Shanghai. "Twitter" was the code name for Nán Péngyǒu, the social media operative who had helped them plant the white virus. "The airport will not be welcoming."

The line went dead.

Li Min Zhou looked at Jim Ward and shook her head. Without warning, Ward shot across five lanes of traffic. As he left the blaring horns and screeching brakes behind them, he accelerated down an exit ramp and onto the Puxing Highway. Time to activate the emergency extraction plan. A quick glance at the dashboard clock showed that they had about two hours to cover the one-hundred-thirty miles back to the Qiantang River docks and the old rust-bucket *Shēng Xiùde* before Chuán Zhǎng made good on his threat to be underway with the morning tide.

Once they were headed back toward Hangzhou, Li reminded Ward that the freighter captain had no particular loyalties. He only owed allegiance to the last person or entity to pay him the biggest fee. He would leave when he said he would. They damn well better get there before then.

Puxing Highway was a lesser used road and traffic was considerably lighter. But it was not a throughway. Frequent intersecting streets and traffic lights slowed their progress. Though both had studied highway maps of the area, neither could think of a better route. Speeding or running the traffic lights was not an option. An accident, or even just drawing the attention of the traffic police, would almost certainly lead to disaster.

Ward hit the wheel with the heel of his hand. "There is no way we can get to the *Shēng Xiùde* before she sails. Not unless you can teleport us there."

"Just get us on the G-15 westbound coming up at the next intersection," Li told him. "That's about the only road I really know around here. But I think it's more direct and maybe less busy this time of night."

The G-15 throughway did prove to be a lot faster. Ward pressed on the accelerator and sped along as fast as he dared. They discussed the possibilities that Nán Péngyǒu had also revealed to his interrogators the rest of the day's activities, including the planting of the white virus on the server. Even if he had, they could only hope the digital worm had enough time to infiltrate the code and do its damage before the Chinese learned it was there, tracked it down, and somehow neutralized it. The word from the geeks who developed it had been that once the file was executed, the thing did its job immediately. As they raced along, with the countryside whizzing past, they admitted to each other that they could only hope the wonks knew what they were talking about.

The sun was a mere glimmer on the eastern horizon as they shot across the Qiantang River on the Jiubao Bridge. Ward screeched into the rough parking area at the head of the pier with a spray of gravel. The right-side fender slammed into a thick post neither of them had noticed, stopping the limo with a crunching jolt.

"China Auto Rental is going to be royally pissed with you," Ward quipped as they both jumped from the car.

"I bought their rip-off collision insurance. They have no complaints. But about your driving, Lieutenant Commander..."

The *Shēng Xiùde* was just backing away as they ran down the pier, calling out to Chuán Zhǎng, who finally turned and saw them coming. He frowned and shrugged, but still ordered a deckhand to drop the brow just long enough for them to charge up onto the deck and collapse in a heap.

By the time they had caught their breath and stood, the tramp steamer was already out in the middle of the broad Qiantang River, finding the channel and heading northeastward toward the open sea.

Ψ

Henrietta Foster sat in the back of the *Boise*'s control room and sipped coffee as she watched her team operate. And for the time being, it really was her team.

The sub had been heading south-southwest as ordered, skirting Palawan, staying just outside the twelve-mile limit for the westernmost of the Philippine Islands. They had been running at a full bell, making over twenty-five knots, since CDR Chet Allison had been lifted off the boat, now more than twelve hours ago.

Foster glanced up at the digital clock. It would be morning in a couple of hours. She knew she really needed to get some sleep. They had just over a day's steaming before they would be pulling alongside the *Chesty Puller* in Palau Maiga off the northeast coast of Borneo. She would need to be rested before she guided the sub through the myriad reefs and rocks that protected the *Puller*'s anchorage. But she could not seem to force herself to leave the control room. There simply was too much to do. To supervise. To double-check. And now it was all her responsibility. And would be until they reached their destination. There was no one else to turn to. Not out here, submerged and separated from the world.

She shook herself, took another draw on her big coffee mug, and wondered if every sub captain had felt that way the first time he was underway without "adult supervision" looking over his shoulder. Probably so. She also reminded herself she was hardly on her own, either. She had a fine wardroom and a great bunch of well-trained sailors to back her up.

But she was also aware of another heavy load of responsibility she now carried on her shoulders. So far as she knew, she had just become the first female to command a US submarine, interim or not. Lots of female officers would be depending on her to do a good job.

"Best you represent in a proper and professional manner, Hen," she told herself. She had not realized she had spoken the bit of self-advice out loud until she looked up and saw Bob Bland, the officer of the deck, standing there with a quizzical look. He had just stepped back to where Foster sat between the ECDIS tables.

"Say again, XO? Or should I call you 'Skipper' now?" he asked.

"Bob," she said softly. "I'm still just the exec. The skipper will be back, fit as a fiddle, before we know it. Hell, he'll probably be waiting on the pier when we get in, complete with a critique of our landing."

"Reckon so," Bland answered, but his tone said otherwise. "Anyway, it's time for the twenty-hundred-zulu comms pass. On course two-one-zero, depth one-five-zero feet, speed ahead two-thirds. I've cleared baffles to the right. All sonar contacts are beyond twenty thousand yards, all past CPA and opening. Request permission to come to periscope depth."

Foster rose and stepped over to the BQQ-10 sonar display and quickly confirmed for herself what Bland had reported.

"Proceed to periscope depth, copy comms, and then get back down to proceed on the transit," she ordered.

Bland nodded, turned to go, then stopped.

"XO, every crewmember on this boat is with you," he said over his shoulder. "You know that, right? And they'd all be fine if you get..."

She held up her hand and smiled. "I appreciate it. Now get up there and let 'em know back home that we're still afloat."

Ten minutes later, *Boise* was back down at four hundred feet and once again on course and at a full bell. ETR-1 Luke Hanson, the boat's leading radioman, delivered the message boards to Foster where she once again sat in the after part of control. He had a big grin on his face when he handed the aluminum clipboards to her.

"I think you need to read the top message first, Skipper," he said. "Then you might want to look at the second one."

Foster quickly read the top message, then grabbed the 1MC microphone. Her voice rang out on speakers throughout *Boise*.

"Attention all hands, this is the XO. We just received a message from the US Embassy in Manila. The skipper is in the Philippine Heart Center. He is doing okay. He has regained consciousness and vitals are stable. The docs there are giving him a bunch of tests to find out what happened and to determine if it is safe for him to travel back stateside. I'm sure he appreciates your thoughts and prayers."

She replaced the mike, flipped the page, and read the second message. This one was from SUBGROUP SEVEN. The first paragraph came as a surprise to her. She was directed to immediately assume command of the USS *Boise* until such time as a replacement commanding officer could be designated. It was official. For the moment, she was CO of the submarine. She did not have the time or the inclination to reflect on how hard she had worked to be able to reach this pinnacle, the discrimination and cuts she had quietly endured, all to make herself ready should she ever have the chance. Or to consider it was only temporary and the Navy really had few other options until the submarine was back in port.

She still had a job to do, one that required her full attention.

The second paragraph of the message was equally as surprising as the first. The *Boise* was re-directed to intercept and surveil an abnormally large and suspicious fleet of fishing boats last observed heading in the general direction of northern Borneo.

Foster shook her head as she looked at the ECDIS chart. The new track had the *Boise* heading right into the center of the Spratly Islands. Dangerous territory. And she was not at all sure what they would be able to do with an almost empty torpedo room should they need to shoot at something or somebody. And even if she had a full load of torpedoes, a bunch of fishing boats did not sound like worthwhile or legitimate targets. Well, anyway, they would do whatever the boss told them to. And they would do it to the very best of their ability.

Over her shoulder, she ordered, "Officer of the Deck, come right and steer course two-six-zero."

"Skipper, coming right," Bob Bland answered.

Foster was so intensely occupied in getting the ship on its new course, she did not even notice or appreciate being correctly called "Skipper" for the first time.

23

By the time the *Shēng Xiùde* passed beneath the southern cable-stayed section of the Hangzhou Bay Bridge, the rusty ship had melded with all the other local maritime traffic. Fishing boats, barges, ferries, and even the occasional junk plied the protected waters of the Hangzhou Bay and the Yangtze Delta. Before the world's longest ocean bridge was opened, allowing other means of transportation to easily reach the area, these boats delivered the lifeblood for this section of the Chinese coast. Even now, they remained a vibrant part of the local economy.

Chuán Zhǎng swung the *Shēng Xiùde* south, hugging the coast as he threaded through the hundreds of tiny islands there. He and Jim Ward were standing in the ship's wheelhouse, both watching the colorful traffic plying the mud-colored waters. Chuán noted the questioning expression on the SEAL's face and headed off his inquiry about the abrupt course change.

"It is best that we take the Jintanggang down to the Loutou Channel," the ship's captain explained. "It is the shortest route to Taizhou."

"And why, exactly, are we going to Taizhou?" Ward asked. "My friend and I really do need to get out of China. Like now."

"I have a load of refrigerators to deliver in Taizhou and then we pick up a cargo of dried fruit bound for Fuzhou," the grizzled sea captain grunted.

"I have a ship to maintain and a crew to compensate. Your mistress does not pay me enough to cover all my bills. I have to make an honest living as well."

Before Ward could question him further, Li Min Zhou stepped into the wheelhouse.

"Jim, Chuán's way makes sense. We have to assume the Guoanbu are looking for us to try to escape by sea and by the quickest way, now that we did not show up at the airport. Out in the open ocean, we are an easy target for the Haiijing, the Chinese Coast Guard. Here we are lost amongst all the coastal traffic. Better for the fox to hide at the forest's edge than to run across the open meadow."

Chuán grinned smugly, as if he had just won some competition.

"One of your ancient Chinese philosophers?" Ward asked.

"No, English fox hunting. From my days at Cambridge," she answered, employing an affected English accent. Li's matriculation in a long list of prestigious universities was a running joke between the two. Ward only claimed to have graduated from some little military school in southeastern Maryland.

By nightfall, the *Shēng Xiùde* had passed Fodu Island to port and swung around to the southeast. From this point and on down to Taizhou, they really had no choice but to head across open waters. There would be no convenient barrier of islands to hide behind. But at least it would be a night passage. And with the thousands of fishing boats lighting up the night, the Haiijing would have a very difficult time picking out a lone steamer, even if they knew for certain that was what they were looking for.

There was no real reason why the Chinese and their coast guard would know how Li and Ward might now attempt to get away. Nán Péngyǒu would not have known anything about the *Shēng Xiùde*. Li trusted everyone else in her network who might have some knowledge of the contingency escape plan. Even so, there were only a limited number of ways to escape. The Guoanbu had more than enough resources to cover them all. Easiest to just assume Chinese intelligence did somehow know how they were running and aboard which freighter and then act accordingly.

It was almost midnight, with the lights of Shatoujiao Island abeam to starboard, when a Haiijing cutter finally singled them out for attention.

Chuán Zhăng had been watching the cutter as it approached from the seaward on the *Shēng Xiùde*'s ancient radar and gave the heads-up to his two passengers, who were catching catnaps on the wheelhouse deck.

While the cutter was still a mile away, its searchlight suddenly snapped on. The powerful beam cut a swath of light across the water, shining like the sun onto the *Shēng Xiùde*'s bridge wing. At the same instant, the freighter's marine radio crackled with, "This is the Haiijing cutter *Shaoxing*. Come to 'All Stop' and stand by for boarding. We intend to search your vessel."

Chuán Zhăng grabbed the radio microphone and pled, "*Shaoxing,* this is *Shēng Xiùde.* We are peaceful and loyal sailors. You have no need to bother innocent peasants like us. If I do not deliver my load of refrigerators by tomorrow, they will be rejected and I will lose everything."

The searchlight did not dim. There was no more radio traffic. The coast guard cutter drew closer. They offered no sympathy for the poor seafarer.

Chuán did as he was told. He stopped the engines and swung the rudder over so that the *Shēng Xiùde* was broad to the Haiijing cutter. Turning to Li Min Zhou, he said, "Quick, there is scuba gear in the locker at the base of the portside ladder."

Li and Ward scurried down the ladder on the opposite side of the bridge from the approaching vessel. Meanwhile, the *Shaoxing* eased to a full stop five hundred meters from where the steamer bobbed in the current. Even in the darkness, the gleaming white warship towered over the old rust bucket. A boat with a boarding party aboard was lowered and began the quick trip over to the old ship.

Shielded from view by the ship's bulk, Li and Ward quickly strapped on their tanks, checked each other's gear—only a mask, tank, and regulator for each—and headed to the rail. As Ward was tying a line to a deck stanchion, they heard the motor launch come alongside on the other side of the deck. They would keep their clothes on. A shoe on the deck or clothing floating in the water next to the ship would be a giveaway.

The pair walked the line down the steamer's side and lowered themselves into the pitch-black sea. The one sure place where they would not be seen was directly under the *Shēng Xiùde*. They submerged and eased their way beneath the vessel, holding the line to keep from being swept away in the current.

There they waited in the darkness for a long, long time. Occasional flashes of light on the surface indicated something was going on up there. What if the old freighter and its captain were hauling some other contraband? What if this search lasted into the next day? What if the captain gave them up for a bounty?

Hell, they were not even armed. Worse came to worst, they could not even shoot their way out of it. Enough to make even a Navy SEAL a tad bit perturbed as he clung to the bottom of a rusty steamer like a barnacle.

No way to discuss his worries with his partner, either. No way for her to assure him that she had covered all contingencies. In his experience, she always managed to do just that. But this operation had been hurried and hinky from the get-go. He could not even see those remarkable eyes of hers through her mask in the blackness beneath the old rust bucket. Much less get a pep talk and affirmation that all was going to work out.

Then they heard the unmistakable sound of the freighter's engines starting up. They felt the line go slack as it fell into the water.

Ward grabbed Li's hand tightly and they both kicked hard, quickly diving as deep as they could manage. There was only one reason that Chuán Zhǎng would start *Shēng Xiùde*'s engines. He was saving his own skin and abandoning them there in the East China Sea.

And if they could not dive down far enough quick enough, the ship's screw would turn them into so much shark chum.

Ψ

Brian Edwards whistled softly as he read the just-received message on his computer tablet. SUBGROUP SEVEN was ordering the *George Mason* to cancel launching the UUVs at Scarborough Shoals. Instead, they were to head back to the fishing fleet that the submarine had reported twelve hours before.

"I'm starting to feel like a ping-pong ball, bouncing back and forth across the South China Sea," he said to no one in particular. But all eyes in control not on screens or instrumentation were on the skipper. They knew they were about to get commands from him.

Launching the sensor packages into the Scarborough Shoals anchorage in order to monitor what the Chinese were doing there made perfect sense. Sending a nuclear sub out to watch a bunch of fishing boats made no sense to him at all. But Edwards knew there would be no debate about it. They had their orders.

"Nav," Edwards called out over his shoulder to Jim Shupert, "come around to course two-seven-zero and head back to where our fishing buddies are."

"Come to two-seven-zero, aye," Shupert acknowledged. He was the on-watch OOD. "Skipper, sonar still holds them about forty miles west of our position. They don't seem to be going anywhere. Just circling on-station. We can be over there in a couple of hours."

Edwards looked intently at the ECDIS display. Nothing seemed to be going on there that would warrant the interest of a fleet of fishing boats. Especially not boats filled to the gunnels with armed troops. He decided to approach cautiously, particularly since he had no idea what those guys were doing.

Or who else might show up in a bad mood and a hell of a hurry to help them do it.

Ψ

Jim Ward felt the swirling water as the old steamer's screw passed just a few feet above his back. He fully expected it to rip into his skin at any instant but he kept paddling and kicking deeper.

Then the ship passed on, its bulk and noise soon disappearing into the darkness. As nearly as he could tell, the *Shēng Xiùde* was steaming away to the south, toward her original destination, while the *Shaoxing* was heading off to the east, hopefully searching for another steamer that might be harboring dastardly cyber-saboteurs.

They waited a while. After the sea above them had been dark and quiet for a good ten minutes or so, he reached out and touched Zhou's shoulder. He had just been able to determine through the murkiness that she was still there, moving, kicking easily to remain floating next to him at what he estimated was a depth of about twenty feet.

They kicked hard, swimming to the surface, simultaneously breaking into cool, fresh night air, gasping, sucking in as much of the precious stuff as they could manage. There were no ships in sight. No moon. Just darkness. And they were treading water far from shore.

"I never did like that guy," Li Minh Zhou said once she got her breath back. "Never trusted the SOB."

"I thought you never worked with anybody you couldn't trust," Ward told her as he treaded water.

"Sometimes they're the most valuable. Remind me to tell you about double-, triple-, and quadruple-twist scenarios."

"Yeah, I'll be sure to do that." He splashed a big handful of water at her. She deftly dodged it. And flashed him that gorgeous smile he saw far too little.

"I just wish I had not mentioned to Nán Péngyǒu that we would be flying out of Shanghai," she said. She had turned over and was now floating easily on her back to preserve her strength. "Either he was not nearly as broken-hearted over the murder of his girlfriend as he let on or the bad guys used their typical methods to get all they could from him before they fed what was left of him to the crows."

It was the first time Ward had seen her make any kind of mistake in judgment. Somehow, it made her even more endearing.

"Probably both. Water under the bridge," he assured her.

"Yes," she said. "Water under the bridge."

They both floated quietly for a long moment.

"Well, now what, Wonder Woman?" Ward finally asked.

"I suggest we start swimming," Li shot back. She pointed to the west. If Ward squinted hard enough, he could just make out something that might be specks of light on the far horizon. "Those lights should be Shatoujiao Island. Couple of miles, maybe. A piece of cake for a frog boy like you, right?"

"You learn to swim at Cambridge or MIT or...?"

"If you must know, second-team All-Ivy League swimming at MIT."

She sent a big splash of sea water back in his direction, then flipped over and headed off, using long, smooth strokes, in the direction of those distant specks of light.

Ward grinned, shook his head, then followed after her, but working really hard to keep up.

Ψ

President Tan Yong and his financial advisor, Qián Dài, sat across from each other, sharing a small lunch of cha siu bao and jiaozi. The fragrant aroma from the steamed barbeque pork buns filled the office. The two of them had spent a large portion of the morning discussing the finer points of international finance. At the moment, and between bites, Qián Dài was extending his ideas of business as an instrument of warfare and how to exploit the international banks as ammunition for that weapon.

He was simultaneously munching on a vegetable dumpling and reaching a key point in his lecture. "Even the Americans, or at least some of them, recognize these facts," he said, waving his chopsticks for emphasis. "One of their scholars, Professor Lin, who is of Chinese descent, of course, has written, 'Finance may be the most powerful weapon of war.' If their politicians ever ..."

But just then, Min Tau, Tan Yong's obsequious aide, slid into the office, interrupting the lesson. He bowed toward Tan and then Qián. "Please excuse me, elder brother, revered teacher, but Minister Deng Jiang is calling. He says it is a matter of most urgency."

Tan Yong swallowed, then punched a button on his desk phone. Deng Jiang's voice blared from the speaker. "Please excuse the interruption," he began, his words rushed, his voice betraying tension. "I regret to report that we have suffered a penetration at the Cyber Warfare Center. The culprits managed to reach the servers. However, our security forces were successful in capturing one of them after he had exited the premises. He is a technician in the facility and fell under suspicion when he entered and exited within less than an hour and outside his assigned work time. The Guoanbu conducted one of their normal interviews and were ultimately able to get the information about the breach from him. Unfortunately..."

Tan Yong interrupted the report with the most important question of all. "What about Kill Shot? Were they successful in compromising the...what's the right term...program?"

There was a moment's pause.

"I am pleased to report there is no indication that they were able to penetrate the server security," Deng finally shot back. "Our cyber experts are continuing their analysis, of course, but to this point, they have seen no traces of any successful penetration through our most effective defenses. Honorable First Secretary, please remember that our cyber warriors are the best in the world. It is not surprising that whoever these people are, they would never have been able to get inside our systems. Not even with the traitorous assistance of one of our own people. We will continue the analysis, but our launch timetable remains unchanged."

Qián Dài joined the conversation. "You keep saying 'they' and 'these people,' but you have only reported capturing one person. Where are the others?"

"This Nán Péngyǒu, the traitor, gave up two accomplices, a Chinese woman and an American man," Deng answered. "They eluded our people, but the Guoanbu are certain they have not managed to escape the country. We will find them at any moment."

"Then I assume the Guoanbu will continue to interview this...this Nán Péngyǒu...and learn more about our unacceptably lax security," Tan said.

Again, there was the briefest of pauses as Deng carefully framed his response.

"As I was about to report, the traitor unfortunately expired during his interrogation. Apparently an existing misdiagnosed embolism of some kind."

Tan nodded as he listened, understanding Deng's shorthand perfectly. He plucked a cha siu bao with his chopsticks.

"Then there are still factors regarding this attempt that we do not know. That means it is even more important that we proceed not only with capturing and dealing with the perpetrators but with executing the operation as planned. Kill Shot will launch in twenty-four hours. Then Southern Sweep twenty-four hours after that."

The president hit the disconnect button on the phone and calmly bit into the savory bun.

24

"Nav, close to fifteen thousand yards and then circle the bunch around to the north." Commander Brian Edwards rubbed his chin and considered *George Mason*'s situation. "Maybe we can get some idea what's going on." He paused for a few seconds, lost in thought. Then he had an epiphany. "And get the Weps up here. I have an idea."

He and his submarine had carefully approached the huge fleet of blue hull fishing boats and were about to commence with the task of determining what might be going on with them. The skipper thought he had a way to put into service an asset they had initially thought was no longer of value to them.

Ten minutes later, Aston Jennings, the *George Mason*'s weapons officer, walked into the control room, nursing a cup of black coffee, eyes heavy from sleep.

"You wanted to talk to me, Skipper?"

"Sorry to interrupt your beauty sleep, Weps," Edwards started. "That UUV in tube nine. Is it all checked out and ready to go?"

Jennings nodded. "Yes, sir. Batteries all topped off, nav systems and sensors aligned and checked. Payload checks 'sat.' All other systems check normal. Everything was ready for it to make the run up to Scarborough before we got redirected. But aren't we heading away from there now?"

"I have another mission that I'm thinking of for your little friend," Edwards answered. "If his optics and EM sensors are working, is there any reason we can't use him to help corral all these fishing boats?"

Jackson Biddle, the XO, stood nearby, munching on a sticky bun. He had been listening to the conversation as he chewed. Now he turned and looked at the tactical display on the ECDIS table. He licked the gooey icing from his fingers and then said, "I think I get your drift, Skipper. These fishing boats are taking up a lot of real estate. You figure our little friend could circle them one way while we go the other?"

"That's pretty much what I had in mind," Edwards responded. "We use the UUV as another sheep dog to keep track of this flock."

Jennings grinned. "Okay, it'll take about an hour to reprogram the mission. I'll get Chief Schmidt and the team right on it."

"I figure these guys aren't much of an ASW threat," Biddle chimed in. "Maybe we can use this to our advantage. What if we keep the UUV shallow with his mast up and on the link with all his data. We may be able to herd the flock pretty much where we want to and we'd have continuous intel for the entertainment of the guys back in Yokosuka."

Edwards listened and thought about the plan for a moment. Then he replied, "I like it. But set the programming up so that he goes deep if he picks up a threat emitter of any type. No sense in him committing suicide unnecessarily. Lord knows what the sticker price is on one of those models."

Right on schedule, an hour later, UUV Mission Nine lifted off vertically from the *George Mason*'s aftermost mission module tube. Once it had successfully cleared the submarine, the UUV maneuvered to a horizontal position and then, following its revised orders, headed off to the southwest. Once the unmanned submersible was a few thousand yards away from the *George Mason*, it eased its sensor mast upward until it was in the open air, just above the sea surface. Mission Nine checked in on Link 16 and began slowly circling in a clockwise rotation around the horde of Chinese fishing boats. The sensor mast swept the air of all the electronic signals emanating from the fishing fleet and faithfully reported every one of them. Meanwhile, analysts sitting safe and dry in Yokosuka, Japan, sorted through the mountain of data, analyzed and evaluated it, turning it into hopefully useful intelligence to report back out on Link 16 for everyone to use.

Mission Nine closed the fleet until the blue boats were just visible on its optics sensor. At that range, the reed-thin sensor mast remained invisible to anyone on one of the blue-hulled boats, but the analysts in Yokosuka were treated to a high-definition picture of the threat.

Meanwhile, Brian Edwards steered the *George Mason* to the northwest and began a slow counterclockwise circle at periscope depth. Just like the sensor mast on Mission Nine, the number-two photonics mast was up and sucking down the electronic spectrum. But, unlike the little UUV, the submarine was on the link in passive-only mode. The sub had a team onboard to analyze the intercepts. No reason to risk being detected by also sending an outgoing data stream.

Edwards and Biddle stood together, watching the big screen above the command console. The picture was quickly developing that there were far more contacts than they were capable of tracking, even with two vessels now doing the work. The visual, sonar, and ESM contacts were already well above a hundred and growing what seemed like exponentially.

"I think we need to get a Blackwing up so we can get a better handle on what's going on," Biddle recommended, unknowingly coming to the same conclusion as his counterpart on *Boise*. The little UAV, flying at better than five thousand feet, would allow them to see out to one hundred miles in all directions.

"Good idea, XO," Edwards answered. He turned toward Jim Shupert. "Officer of the Deck, launch a Blackwing." He pointed toward where they thought the center of the fleet was. "Have it initially circle here until we see just how big this armada is."

The forty-inch-long cannister was ejected out of the three-inch signal ejector and catapulted upward. When a sensor detected the surface of the sea, high-pressure air shoved the little airplane out of the cannister. Scissor wings unfolded and the electric motor started the pusher propellor spinning. The bird quickly rose high into the air. As it reached its assigned altitude just below a thick cloud deck and leveled off, its tiny transmitter started sending a data link back to the *George Mason* just as its EO and IR sensors came online. The picture on the large-screen display was of an ocean impossibly crowded with ships, all the way to the horizon and beyond.

"Wow!" Edwards gasped. "There has to be at least a thousand ships out there. Our Chinese friends are up to something big, and I'm guessing it ain't going fishing."

"I guess they counted on the cloud cover not allowing any sats to see how big a fleet they have out here," Biddle speculated. "Or see just enough of it to make us think it was really a fishing fleet. Dang Chinese are trying to catch every fish in the ocean to feed their folks, you know." Then he noticed something else on the screen. It immediately caught his attention. "Skipper, look over there, toward the east. Those sure as hell don't look like fishing boats to me." He pointed to a cluster of much larger ships just coming into view in the distance. "Way too big and the lines are all wrong. Chief, steer the Blackwing over that way."

Chief Schmidt keyed in the course change on the uplink to the drone. The camera panned as the bird changed course and then steadied up with the newly discovered ships now in the center of the screen. As the UAV flew closer, the ships came into much better focus.

"Those are RoRo ferries," Biddle exclaimed. "Roll on/roll off" vessels designed to carry wheeled cargo, like automobiles and trucks. But also like tanks and troop assault landing vehicles. "They'll each carry an armored battalion. I count a dozen ships. That's a damned assault force up there!" He turned to Edwards, who was also studying the images. "Captain, I think it's time we phone home."

Just as Biddle was delivering his assessment, the video screen broke into a maze of jagged pixels. Chief Schmidt called out, "Loss of link to the Blackwing!"

The 21MC speaker blared, "Conn, ESM, heavy jamming. We are being jammed on all frequencies. They've detected the data link. And somebody has a real big jammer, real close."

"Guys, I think we may have overstayed our welcome," Edwards said. "Let's go deep and open out a bit and see if we can get outside this jamming so we can report home. Too bad about the Blackwing, but maybe we can try to sneak back in again before its battery dies or that jammer takes it out.

Officer of the Deck, make your depth four hundred feet and steer course zero-six-zero."

The *George Mason* had just passed through one-hundred and fifty feet on the way down when ST1 Hannon suddenly yelled out, "Active sonar! Detecting SQZ-262 Rice Ball active sonar. Bearing zero-seven-six. Signal strength plus fifty. Probability of detection eighty percent."

Somebody very close was pinging the submarine. Edwards took a quick glance at the sonar display. Whoever and whatever it was, he was just off the starboard bow. They needed to turn and get out of there. Stealth was no longer a primary concern. They had been found already.

"All ahead flank!" Edwards shouted emphatically, then issued a string of commands. "Make your depth one thousand feet, max down angle. Launch two evasion devices. Left full rudder, steer course three-one-zero."

The big submarine shot forward and heeled over as the pump jet bit into the ocean and the rudder shoved them around dramatically. Everyone aboard not wearing headphones heard two bangs as an evasion device was launched from each dihedral.

"Man battle stations," Edwards commanded. Best get the entire crew ready for a fight, just in case it should come to that.

"Up-shift in frequency. Rice Ball shifted to targeting mode," Hanson reported. Then the sonarman added a disturbing deduction. "Rice Ball carried on Upgraded-*Yuan* class submarines."

That only increased the problem they now faced. A Chinese submarine had drawn a bead on *George Mason*.

"Damn," Biddle groaned. "He's going to be hard to lose."

"Best plan is to put a lot of confusion in the water," Edwards said. "Launch two more evasion devices." Just as he felt the devices being ejected into the sea, he ordered, "Right full rudder. Steady course two-three-five."

"Skipper, don't you mean left rudder?" Stan Dewlap, the co-pilot, questioned. "We're on course three-one-zero now."

"No! Right full rudder," Edwards replied. "I want to loop back through the noisemakers and then head directly toward their fleet. We'll see just how smart this guy is."

"Launch transients!" Hannon yelled. "Second launch transients. Torpedoes in the water. Detecting two torpedoes! Best bearing zero-nine-zero on both weapons."

They were not just found. They were now a target under attack.

"Snap-shot, tube one, on the *Yuan*!" Edwards ordered. Whether they survived to see it or not, they would at least shoot back at their ambusher. And that ADCAP would make one hell of a big, deadly evasion device.

Biddle jumped over to the fire control panel and started setting in a TMA solution for the Chinese sub. The torpedo needed at least a rough solution to shoot. Aston Jennings jumped onto the launcher panel to get tube one and the weapon inside it ready to go.

"Incoming torpedoes bearing zero-eight-nine and zero-nine-one. Both closing." The sonar operator's voice had gone up an octave. "Rice Ball still in targeting mode."

"Launch the port CRAW at the torpedo bearing zero-nine-one," Edwards ordered. With only two degrees of separation between the two weapons, it really did not matter which torpedo he shot at. They only needed to pray that the little lightweight counter-weapon hit one of them.

Stan Dewlap tapped a couple of buttons. They could feel the bang as the six-inch-diameter mini-torpedo blasted out of the port dihedral and went searching for the incoming torpedoes.

Jackson Biddle called out, "Solution ready!" just as Ashton Jennings yelled, "Weapon ready!"

"Skipper, ship not ready," Jim Shupert advised. They were pointed in the wrong direction. "That guy is dead astern of us. We're going to need to come around to shoot him and stay out of the ACR limits." The anti-circular-run limits were built into every torpedo to prevent the submarine from accidentally shooting itself. That was what happened to Dick O'Kane and the *Tang* back in World War II. Now ACR prevented the target-seeking torpedo from accidentally coming back at the sub that launched it, but also from shooting anyone behind the boat.

"Steer course south," Edwards ordered.

Seconds later, Shupert called out, "Ship ready."

"Shoot on generated bearings," Edwards ordered. They felt the lurch and whoosh as the two-ton ADCAP torpedo was flushed out of the tube and sent on its way toward their attacker.

"Normal launch," Jim Shupert called out. "Torpedo running normally."

"Normal launch from sonar," Hannon called out. "Incoming torpedoes bear zero-nine-one and zero-nine-three. Own-ship unit bears one-zero-one. On-ship CRAW bears zero-eight-nine."

"Cut the wire tube one," Edwards ordered. The umbilical wire to the launched torpedo was severed. The weapon was on its own to hopefully hunt down and hit the target. "Launch two more evasion devices."

Jim Shupert called out, "Wire cut."

Edwards ordered, "Right full rudder. Steer course two-four-five."

"Incoming torpedoes bearing zero-nine-one and zero-nine-three, still closing."

They were still very much under the gun. Their time to evade, confuse, or dodge was growing short.

"Launch the CRAW from the starboard dihedral," Edwards ordered.

"Own-ship weapon bears zero-eight-nine. Incoming torpedoes bear zero-nine-one and zero-nine-four. Loss of active Rice Ball," Hannon reported. "He shut down."

The Chinese sub skipper now knew he was under counter-attack and was about to do his own feinting and ducking. Edwards wiped the sweat from his brow with his shirt sleeve. He could feel it trickle down the back of his neck. This was getting hairy. Way too hairy.

"Incoming torpedoes both ran past the first CRAW!" Hannon yelled. Damn. Now they had to hope that either the second CRAW got them both or that they could successfully evade the onrushing death.

Jackson Biddle stood by the ECDIS tactical display. "Skipper, why don't we try to get in among their fleet. They'd make good evasion devices."

"That's where I'm heading," Edwards shot back.

"No, Skipper," the XO responded. "I mean get our ass up on the roof. Make their torpedoes have to figure out which one among the hundreds is us."

The discussion was interrupted by a loud explosion that shook the boat hard.

"CRAW got the starboard torpedo," Hannon called out. A three-second pause. Then he yelled, "Port side torpedo survived. It's range gating! Shifted to high speed. I think he's got us!"

"Emergency blow all groups!" Edwards ordered. "Get us on the surface, forty up-angle."

Forty-five-hundred-pound high-pressure air rumbled into the ballast tanks, pushing the water out of the submarine through the bottom grates. The stern planes and bow planes bit into the ocean and directed the sub's nose up at a sharp angle, toward the open air. The *George Mason* shot for the surface.

Edwards grabbed a stanchion to keep from being thrown into the after bulkhead. Jackson Biddle was a half-second slow and ended up in a heap on the bulkhead between the ECDIS tables.

The sub bolted high out of the water, like a sounding whale. Then it seemed to pause, its bow high in the air, before it splashed back down below the surface, sliding to two hundred feet before bobbing to the surface again.

Edwards ordered, "All stop, raise number two photonics mast."

The big-screen display blinked on just in time to see the *George Mason* pass a scant fifty feet astern of one of the big RoRo ships. Men aligned along the deck watched wide-eyed. Thankfully, the sub had not come up directly beneath the massive ship and its heavy load. Likely neither would have survived that fender-bender.

Edwards ordered, "Right full rudder, steady course three-five-zero."

The aim was to slide the sub in on a course parallel to the towering surface vessel. A torpedo was still out there looking for them and it already knew just about where they were.

"Torpedo bears zero-nine-zero, still range gating!" Hannon yelled, the fear heavy in his voice. "Best range, two hundred yards!"

They would know their fate within seconds. Everyone braced for the explosion. Some prayed silently. Some out loud.

The stunning blast shoved the submarine hard. It slid impossibly sideways and then bounced upward, as if yanked from the sea by a huge hand. Again, men in all compartments grabbed to hold on to something solid. Some of them tumbled.

But then the boat settled, quit bouncing. Amazingly, they were still afloat.

The big display allowed those few in the right place to watch what had happened. Edwards, clinging to the stanchion, had observed from much closer than he wanted to be as the Chinese YU-9 torpedo detonated beneath one of the RoRos. The sodium hydride warhead immediately boiled the sea water to better than two thousand degrees. The resulting steam bubble engulfed the ship, breaking its back and venting the high-pressure steam into the hull. Just as rapidly as it formed, the bubble collapsed, dropping the two halves of the ship into a void in the ocean. Men, tanks, equipment all dropped away and disappeared into the roiling water.

Edwards shook his head. That quick exhibition of death and destruction could just as easily have been him and the *George Mason*. He shook his head again to clear it of the awful scene he had just witnessed.

Time to play submarine again.

"Co-pilot, open all ballast tank vents. Pilot, dive and make your depth three hundred feet. Ahead two-thirds." Then he remembered a very important point. "Sonar, where is our weapon?"

Hannon was already busily searching through a plethora of noise and reverbs from the sinking ship, breaking up even more as it plunged toward the bottom. Then he reported, "There it is. Own ship weapon bears zero-six-three. Sounds like it's in close-in re-attack."

The weapon had not yet given up on its target, despite all the confusing noise and turbulence. And appeared to have found it. A couple of seconds later, they heard a loud, rumbling explosion to the northeast. A huge boiling bubble and debris rose from the surface. The *Yuan* was no more.

Brian Edwards had the same thoughts as before. That could have been him and his submarine instead of the Chinese boat.

He closed his eyes for a moment and held onto the stanchion, riding his submarine back down toward where she belonged, in the depths of the sea.

Ψ

Min Toa, Tan Yong's assistant, opened the heavy oak door and slipped into the First Secretary's expansive office. The PRC president looked up from his reading—he spent two hours each day after lunch perusing a compendium of the world news—as the aide made a perfunctory bow.

"Honorable elder brother," Min told him. "Deng Jiang is calling, as is Sun Yang. With which would you prefer to speak?"

"Both. Tie them together in a conference call," Tan directed. "I expect they are both looking for final approval to commence their respective operations."

Min pressed a couple of buttons on the control that he clutched. The video monitor on the president's priceless Song Dynasty writing table blinked on. Sun Yang, the director of the Guoanbu—but currently supervising Operation Southern Sweep from the Southern Theatre Command Center in Guangzhou—appeared on the left side of the screen. Deng Jiang, sitting in the Cyber Warfare Center in Hangzhou, filled the right side.

"First Secretary," Sun Yang began, his voice betraying his anger. "The Americans have launched a submarine attack against our Luzon force. They have sunk one of our ferries with the loss of the First Artillery Battalion and the Regimental Headquarters Unit for the Sixth Tank Division's Artillery Regiment. They even had the audacity to surface their submarine to watch as the ship sank."

Tan Yong seemed unmoved. He asked, "Does this affect our Luzon operation to any great degree?"

Yang answered, "We have ten battalions of armor and artillery in that force. Any effect will be minor, but now that they have discovered our assault force, I urge immediate attack before the Americans have time to respond in force."

The Chinese leader showed no emotion whatsoever. "We will stay with the planned schedule. It is time to first launch Operation Kill Shot. The world will hardly notice this skirmish in our territorial waters. Not when the economy of the entire planet is falling down around them."

Deng Jiang had been listening quietly. He nodded.

"It is as you ordered." He signaled to someone off-screen. "Operation Kill Shot has now been launched."

25

Secretary of Defense Harold Osterman descended deep into the bowels of the Pentagon, into the National Military Command Center, a spot he rarely visited. His job was to remain visible, to appear vigilant, to campaign for his boss the president, and to try to squeeze even more money from Congress.

This day, the NMCC was an even bigger bustle of activity than usual. The theater-sized room was never quiet, as intelligence and reports filtered in from all over the world and orders were sent out directing fleets and entire armies. But today, an element of anxiety hung heavily in the air.

There was a very real possibility that the personnel in this room could be directing an all-out war with China before the day was finished.

Secretary Osterman plopped down in the chair at the head of a long conference table positioned in a glass alcove that looked out over the command floor. It provided a clear view of the massive video displays that completely covered the room's walls. The members of the Joint Chiefs of Staff and a couple of service secretaries occupied the rest of the seats.

Upon Osterman's arrival, a brigadier general, the current floor watch officer, launched into a briefing on the situation in the South China Sea.

"We have reports from several sources of at least two very large assemblies of Chinese fishing boats: one currently two hundred and fifty miles off the Luzon coast and the other about two hundred miles off the Malaysian

Borneo coast. We have very reliable intel that the boats are loaded with Chinese combat troops. The best estimate is there are over ten divisions in each group."

The chairman whistled. "That's over one-hundred-twenty-thousand troops for each. This ain't good. What's their escort look like?"

"That's the mystery," the briefer answered. "There is no surface escort. The PLA Navy is in port, although we are seeing that they are at a high state of readiness. That's why this fishing fleet—the so-called 'blue hulls'—escaped our notice until now. The blue hulls appear to have some submarine protection, though. One of our boats, the *George Mason*, reports that it was attacked by a Chinese submarine that apparently accidentally sank one of its own 'roll-on/roll off' ships when it attempted to torpedo the *George Mason*. Our sub reports that it sank the Chinese sub in self-defense."

Osterman looked over at the Chief of Naval Operations. "Where are our damn aircraft carriers?"

"Mr. Secretary, you will recall that the president ordered all our available carriers north, to protect Taiwan, Okinawa, and Japan," the CNO quickly answered. "It was on all the TV cable channels. We've assumed all along that any attack would occur against Taiwan. The nearest carrier strike force is now over two thousand miles away from the South China Sea."

"Admiral, command enable those EMP mines you planted in those harbors," Osterman ordered. "That's our only hope to bottle up their fleet if they really mean to push this to war. Maybe once we give him the heads-up, that will convince Tan Yong that invading his neighbors would be a very bad idea."

"There is one other item," the briefer tossed out. "It appears that the Chinese have launched their Operation Kill Shot cyber-attack."

"And?" Osterman shot back, sitting up in his chair. "I haven't noticed any screams of pain from the world's banking establishments. They wouldn't be so stoic if somebody was squeezing their gonads."

"So far, the white virus has stopped Kill Shot in its tracks. The only way we even know it was launched was because we were cyber monitoring our counter-virus," the general answered. "Our little program is quite proud of itself, apparently, and happy to let us know how well it's working."

Osterman nodded. "Now, while we are holding a winning hand, it's probably time for diplomacy to bring it all home. Please get me the president on the secure phone. I'm sure he's ready to have a chat with Tan Yong."

The secretary reached for the red phone with one hand and waved at everyone with the other. "Please clear the room. Thank you."

Ψ

The SLMM-I submarine-launched mobile mine received its command enable signal. The sensor logic system came alive as the electromagnetic pulse warhead arming circuits energized. The logic circuit went through its pre-programmed list and recognized that all the requirements to detonate had been met.

The warhead section broke free and floated gently to the surface. When the broach sensor saw that the device was in air, not water, the EMP warhead detonated. The blast caused the mine's explosively pumped flux compression generator to develop a millisecond-long, extremely-high-energy electromagnetic pulse. The brief pulse sent a very short wave of millions of amperes of electricity and hundreds of terawatts of electromagnetic energy into the atmosphere. The same kind of radio-frequency blast that would have been caused by the detonation of a nuclear bomb. But without the nuclear detonation. In fact, the blast energy was rather unimpressive.

Because the mine was located inside the submarine cave at the Yulin Naval Base, and because the cave had been designed to prevent an outside EMP pulse from penetrating it or doing damage, the interior pulse instead was reflected and amplified by the cave's structure. It worked exactly opposite of how it had been intended to. The high-energy thud destroyed all the electronics for the Chinese submarines unfortunate enough to be tied up there.

The EMP blast happened a couple of feet aft of the nuclear submarine *Liǎng Wàn*. The boat's reactor was critical, it was fully armed, and it was ready to go to sea. The warhead's pulse instantaneously destroyed all the electronic systems on the submarine, including the critical reactor safety systems. The temperature and pressure in the sub's nuclear reactor began an inexorable rise until the mechanical relief valves lifted, relieving the pressure. But the temperature continued to climb until the fuel cells began to liquify. The melted fuel dripped to the bottom of the pressure vessel and the reactor lost critical mass. It essentially quit generating nuclear heat and energy. The crew had maybe an hour to vent the reactor and flood it with potassium tetraborate to keep the reactor shut down and to prevent a steam-hydrogen explosion from ripping it apart. Such a major nuclear accident would keep the cave and everything in it inaccessible for many decades into the future.

Outside the cave, EMP mines popped to the surface and detonated all around the Yulin Naval Base. Up and down the South China coast, the same story was repeated in or very near various other navy bases.

In the port city of Zhanjiang, the dock landing ship *Hainan* was just getting underway when an EMP mine detonated alongside. The mammoth ship lost power and drifted, helplessly driven by the current, and piled into the Zhanjiang Bay Bridge. The collision toppled one of the bridge support columns, with a section of roadway and a dozen automobiles following it into the bay water below. The debris fell across the *Hainan*'s broad flight deck, entangling its inert mass in the wreckage.

That was the only outward indication that much of one of the world's largest and most powerful navies had just been reduced to little more than floating junk.

Ψ

Tan Yong and Qián Dài sat alongside Deng Jiang in the central hall at the Cyber Warfare Command, waiting expectantly for the mayhem to begin. Operation Kill Shot had been launched for twenty-four hours. It was now time to watch the world financial markets' reaction to the highly sophisticated assault. The day would begin with the Tokyo banks and then spread west to Singapore and Mumbai before extending to the Middle East and then Europe. It would be obvious by then that the chaos had been unleashed, but the virus would be at its most virulent by the time the American banks were attempting to conduct their first transactions of the business day.

This realization would coincide very nicely with the news of Operation Southern Sweep as a one-two punch to the West. China would have boldly liberated the oppressed people who occupied some of the colonial territories that bordered on the South China Sea. And greedy capitalists worldwide would see their banking system crumble under its own weight, finally collapsing due to corner-cutting and unwillingness to invest in infrastructure.

Both events—though unrelated, as far as the world knew—finally provided a powerful response to what China always referred to as the Century of Humiliation.

"The major banks in Tokyo and Singapore will start the snowball," Qián Dài lectured. "The event will be triggered by the first significantly large transactions of the day. The SWIFT system is tightly coupled but has distributed independent control mechanisms. The virus will spread like a forest fire. And just like a forest fire, it will incinerate all in its way, building intensity as it goes, and, once supposedly controlled, will flare up again and do still more damage."

The three men waited expectantly, quietly, the First Secretary idly tapping his fingertips on the table in a monotonous rhythm. The other two had smiles frozen on their faces. But nothing happened.

Deng finally picked up a phone and dialed a number. The cyber experts all verified that the virus appeared to be functioning exactly according to specifications, though they were yet unable to see any of the damage it had caused. But for some reason, there still had been no reaction from any of the world financial markets. No squeal of pain. No cries for help. Nothing.

Just then, Min Toa slipped in and whispered something in Tan Yong's ear. The president sat upright for an instant and then said, "Excuse me, gentlemen. There seems to be some sort of minor problems with a few of our warships." Turning to Deng Jiang—who noticed that much of the color had disappeared from the leader's face—he said, "I need a secure communications line with the Southern Command Center."

Deng Jiang jumped up, relieved Tan would be otherwise occupied and distracted until he and Qián could determine what was happening. Or not happening.

"Of course. Please come with me to my office," he suggested. "You will be most comfortable using the secure landline from there." He led Tan Yong toward his office and waited while his technicians set up the circuit, then went back to the observation room in the central hall.

The First Secretary had just begun speaking with Sun Yang when Min Toa again entered the room. He held up both hands. Someone even more important than the Southern Commander wanted to speak to Tan.

"A thousand pardons, elder brother," Tan told Sun. "President Smitherman is calling me from the USA. He assures that the purpose of his call is of the utmost urgency. Unlike his most recent calls, I must say."

Tan Yong smiled as he asked the commander to wait. The fact that much of his country's navy had been mysteriously disabled was suddenly less of an issue. The assault force was still enroute. Kill Shot would surely have done its work by this time. And now, the American sheep of a president was already calling to beg for mercy. The war had not even started yet, and the coward was checking his polling numbers and already surrendering. The weak sister should have at least held out for long enough to barter for some more under-the-table election support.

Sun Yang had just begun to describe the issue with the naval vessels when Tan Yong had stopped him.

"I ask that you please give me a moment," the First Secretary said, then waited until Sun had sputtered to a halt. "I have the American president on the other line. I suspect what he is going to tell me will soften the blow you feel we have suffered. But be assured, we will receive recompense for the damage done. Whoever may be responsible. From this historic day forward, China will dictate the terms, and the world will stumble over each other to be first to capitulate."

Ψ

President Stan Smitherman had the speakerphone on so that Defense Secretary Harold Osterman could listen to his conversation with the president of China. Other than the secretary, the president had banished everyone from the Oval Office and strictly ordered that no one else listen in on the call between him and Tan Yong. Typically, when the president spoke with another head of state, a horde of interpreters, cultural experts, diplomats, lawyers, and various highly compensated hangers-on would be gathered in various offices around the White House, listening, trying to tickle the most minute or veiled inference from every word spoken. That even included a real-time psychological analysis of tone of voice. And, of course to make certain their boss did not stray off into territory from which they may not be able to draw him back.

Such a listening gallery would particularly be present when a war hung in the balance. But President Smitherman insisted that this conversation would be strictly private, assuring it was what he called "mano-a-mano."

On the other end of the line, Tan Yong had also eschewed having an interpreter or anyone else on the line. But he did activate the recording device. When sparring with a political snake as slippery as Smitherman, it was best to have a permanent record of every word spoken. It might one day make for useful leverage.

Tan Yong began the conversation on a cheerful, almost playful note. "Good evening, President Smitherman. Or should I say 'good morning?' It is...what?...one o'clock in the morning there in Washington? Should you not be in bed by now, Mr. President? Surely someone of your age—and particularly someone who finds himself weighted down with the worries of the office—requires adequate rest. And especially with your election cycle about to begin."

Smitherman, on the other hand, came across as gruff. It had been a hard day and he, in fact, was tired and needed sleep. Whatever diplomacy he had thought of using went out the window with Tan Yong's smug words and condescending attitude. The double bourbon had not helped the chief executive's mood at all.

"Tan, my health should be the least of your worries. You would be better served being concerned about the acts of war that you seem more than willing to authorize and commit."

The Chinese president was quiet for a moment, clearly taken aback by Smitherman's bluntness. But more so by his uncharacteristically aggressive attitude. The man was not known for his suaveness. But the political animal should be dancing, trying to conceal that he was coming from a position of weakness and seeking mercy. No, if he thought bluster and threats were the ways to strike back at a superior enemy, the American president was taking the wrong approach.

Tan Yong quickly decided to change his own tack, to meet aggression with aggression.

"But Mr. President, I am offended that you believe we have initiated any act of war. The Chinese people are a proud but peace-loving people. We have merely responded with force after having been faced with extreme provocations and hostile acts on the part of the United States and others. One of your pirate submarines attacked and sank a defenseless ferry that steamed well within Chinese territorial waters. We have begun our appeal before the world's nations that the submarine and crew be immediately surrendered to the Chinese People's Liberation Army Navy to be put on trial for war crimes and other transgressions against humanity."

He paused, expecting Smitherman to launch into his usual incoherent emotional reply. There was only quiet on the other end of the line. "Further, it is our demand that the United States immediately cease all military activities within the First Island chain and remove all units from the area within twenty-four hours. It is well past the time for the United States to recognize that all seas within the First Island chain are rightful and historic territorial seas of the People's Republic of China and we expect you to do so within..."

Now there was a sound on the phone line. An unmistakable sound. That of President Stan Smitherman chuckling, as if Tan Yong had just told a mildly amusing joke.

"Now why would I want to do any of that?" Smitherman finally asked.

"Because if you do not, the West's financial institutions will dramatically fail and much of the world's economies—including yours—will immediately collapse. And we are at this point fully prepared to exert our right to defend our sovereignty and territorial claims with armed force, if necessary. That will come with great loss of life for your forces, I fear, as well as..."

That sound once more. Smitherman chuckling, as if these threats were actually proving to be enjoyable to the president.

"Now, Yong, old boy, if y'all are referring to that silly 'Operation Kill

Shot' thingamajig, I reckon you might oughta ask some of your joystick-ridin' gearheads about just how that's working out for y'all by now."

Tan was aghast. Yes, the Americans had tried to throw a wrench into the gears of the virus, but that had failed. Miserably. But how could they possibly know the actual name of the top-secret plan, Operation Kill Shot?

"I...I do not know anything about such a thing," Tan responded unconvincingly. For the first time, he was wishing some of his top generals were on the call with him. He was losing leverage quickly.

"Well, play it however you want to, Tan, but y'all need to be a tad more careful if you plan on such bullshit," Smitherman drawled. He was well aware that his exaggerated Texas accent—the one that played so well on the campaign trail—would grate heavily on Tan Yong's Oxford-educated sensibilities. "Now looky here. That nasty virus of yours seems to have caught an even nastier one. You need to remember that letting loose one of them virus things like y'all done constitutes an act of war. By all rights, we could be shootin' at your boys right now, but we're Americans, and we're a peace-lovin' bunch if there ever was one." Smitherman was on a roll. After a couple of decades of chairing various Senate committees, he could spar with the best of them. "So, listen to me, Yong. In the name of peace, let me recommend that you don't try to send any more of your PLAN warships to sea. Word I'm hearin' is that a whole passel of them are havin' some kind of electrical problems. I'd hate to hear the rest of them had the same kind of screw-ups and left y'all mostly defenseless. Lots of mean bastards out there in the world nowadays, you know."

"Passel? I do not..." Tan sputtered. What could the damnable Americans have done to disable his navy?

Smitherman had paused to take a sip of bourbon. He had not had this much late-night fun in a very long time. He had one more gig he would use to prod the uptight Chinese leader.

"And that innocent little ferry that sank, the one that just happened to be full of tanks and what sure as hell looked like part of an invasion force? Maybe you should check the torpedo inventory on your diesel submarine that was out there close to it. The one that took a damned pot-shot at our sub and missed it. That would be a good place to start your all-fired investigation into the ferryboat sinking. That is, if that submarine of yours ever makes it back to port, which I think is about as likely as finding tits on a boar hog."

"I am...Mr. President...what you are saying? I do not understand..."

By this time, Smitherman was regretting he had not set up this call as a video link. He was only able to imagine the color of Tan Yong's face.

"Now, President Tan," Smitherman interrupted, emphasizing "President." "I think it's about time we discussed a future that could mutually benefit us—you, me, our nations—one that keeps you in power, allows us to help you move toward a free enterprise economy that will make you and anybody else you want filthy rich, assures you got enough rice and wheat to feed all them damn mouths you got over there, and—by the way—makes damn sure I win my second term in a landslide over here in the good old USA."

"But how...what?" Tan switched off the recording device. Best that no records of this conversation remain.

"Well, since you're asking, I'm thinking that we decide not to go before the world and give them the details of what y'all have already done and what y'all were trying to do, with names, pictures, documents, and more than enough evidence to leave no doubt. And we just don't throw that switch again and avoid making hulks out of all your remaining warships. Or flip another switch and unleash the rest of our little blocking computer virus back on *your* financial institutions. In exchange, you agree that them geeks over there at your Cyber Warfare Center can quietly develop some products that may be useful for my party to get some right-minded folks elected to Congress. And get me that second term, too. And, Yong, I could sure use a dollar or two under the table for some legitimate needs of my campaign, too. What you think...Pardner?"

Harold Osterman's mouth had been open in consternation since just after the beginning of the call. But at least now he understood why Smitherman insisted that no one else be a part of the exchange with the leader of China.

Tan Yong, of course, recognized that he was beaten. And that if word of this disaster somehow reached the Party Congress, he would be lucky to only find himself locked away for the rest of his days in a cell at one of the Guoanbu's many hidden prisons.

He had no choice. He would have to agree to the American president's terms. Then he brightened. He was still president. Still First Secretary.

At some point, he would figure a way to regain the upper hand, to make the haughty Americans regret the day they underestimated him and his ability not only to survive but to conquer.

But first, he would have to develop an explanation for why the long-planned assaults were being suddenly canceled. Why the invasion fleet was being recalled. A reason why the sabotage of the world financial system was never initiated. How it was possible for such a closely-guarded operation to become known to the Americans and who was responsible for such a breach.

But most importantly, he would have to concoct a story about how he and the nation had been betrayed by his most trusted staff—Lei Miayang, General Shao Jing, Deng Jiang, Qián Dài, and Sun Yang—traitors whose treachery had been exceeded only by their incompetence.

It would be a difficult case to make, but he was confident he could do so. Especially with the help of some of the others who were so anxious to take their own place at the big table in the small conference room in Qinzheng Hall. And he would also be able to ensure the five accused men would not be around long enough to mount any reasonable defense.

A wise and prudent leader, after all, emerged with credit for success but had in place others on whom to blame failure.

EPILOGUE

The sun was high in the sky, just past its zenith, as the USS *Boise* slid into position on the northern edge of the vast fishing armada they were tasked to monitor. The submarine's fire control system was tracking hundreds of sonar, visual, and ESM contacts. Henrietta Foster continued to watch the impressive parade through the boat's periscope. This was, she was thinking, clearly one of those situations that if you were not dutifully watching the constantly maneuvering mass of ships, you could easily lose the mental picture of what was going on. The only way to regain it without the risk of running into one of those blue hulls was to go deep, open out several miles, and start the approach all over again. That was why legendary World War II submarine skipper Mush Morton usually put his XO, Dick O'Kane, on the periscope during attacks. Morton knew he could better keep mental track of all the lines and angles, speeds and bearings, threats and traffic if he was not distracted by what little he could actually see through the 'scope.

In this case, Henrietta Foster was the skipper and the XO, too. She would just have to keep it all straight visually and mentally.

"I just don't get this," Foster finally muttered. "They act like a bunch of runners at the start of the New York City Marathon. Or, maybe better, all the Sooners at the start of the Oklahoma land rush, all toed up and spilling over the line waiting for a starter's gun."

Bob Bland, sitting on one of the bench lockers in front of the fire control panel, was busily trying to bring order to the chaos of contact tracks that cluttered his screen. "I hear you, Skipper. Looks like rush hour traffic on the I-5 waiting for a fender-bender to clear. All jumbled up and going nowhere fast."

"We're well blessed with the metaphors, aren't we?" she responded. "Okay, let's work in closer. I wanted to get some pictures of those blue hulls, up close and personal like, and we best do it before they bolt for wherever they're going to do their mischief. I want to see if this bunch is loaded down with troops like *George Mason* reported on the others." She turned to the ship control party and ordered, "Helm, come left and steer two-three-two. Make turns for five knots."

As the *Boise* slowly approached the milling gaggle of ships, the armed troops at the rails came into better focus. And there were plenty of them, lining the rails, covering all decks. She could even see one seasick soldier vomiting over the side.

"Thanks," she murmured. "Thanks for messing up my nice, clean ocean. We gotta swim here..."

"Conn, Sonar. Picking up a weak twenty-two-hertz line on the towed array, best bearing either two-one-two or two-five-two. Tonal equates to a *Yuan*-class diesel submarine."

"Sonar, Conn, aye," Foster acknowledged, shaking her head. Picking up a *Yuan*, even on a low frequency tonal, usually meant he was pretty damn close. And based on *George Mason*'s recent experience with another one of them, they were hair-triggered and feisty these days.

Foster did not hesitate. Best to get the gun cocked, just in case this one was not in a friendly mood either.

"Snap shot, tube one on the *Yuan*."

Foster glanced over for a second and observed her watch team jump into action, making the ADCAP torpedo ready for self-defense. Now to find out for sure where this guy was and try to determine if he was going to get all aggressive-like.

"Sonar, line up to go active, sector search on the *Yuan*. He obviously knows we're over here. Let's get a solution on this guy and let him know that we mean business. Maybe that'll be enough to convince him to keep his gun in his holster."

"Lined up to go active," Paul Warsky, the sonar supervisor, reported.

"Go active, single ping," Foster ordered.

A second later, the active sonar display on the conn blossomed with the outgoing ping. Then a blip appeared at sixty-five hundred yards.

"Positive return, range six-five-hundred yards, bearing two-five-seven," Warsky called out. "Transients on the bearing of the *Yuan*. Sounds like he is opening outer doors."

The Chinese submarine was getting its torpedo tubes ready to fire.

"Not exactly the reaction I was hoping for," Foster said.

"Possible contact zig!" Bob Bland yelled. "Confirm zig away. Hold it. Hey, looks like the whole herd up top is moving now, too. And they're turning."

"You sure? All of them?"

"Definite zig away, Skipper. And right now, they're steadying up, heading west. All of 'em! I don't see a single stray."

For a moment, Foster had gotten so wrapped up in the very real threat from the *Yuan* that she had neglected looking out the periscope. She gave herself a solid mental kick. A right-thinking, experienced CO would have dropped down deep to give more flexibility in dealing with the submerged threat, the Chinese sub acting all ill-tempered. But since they were still at periscope depth, she looked out to see the blue hulls turning westward. Large plumes of black smoke emanated from the stacks of several of them, as if someone had suggested they hurry on back home. They were moving all right. Moving in the direction of the barn.

"Firing point procedures, on the *Yuan*, tube one," Foster ordered. He was still there, still loaded and cocked. If the guy was thinking about shooting, it was best for *Boise* to be the first shot.

"Conn, Sonar, receiving twelve-point-two-kilohertz active sonar. Equates to Chinese Red Gill underwater communications."

Something was happening and Foster was baffled by what it could be. The PLAN sub was chatting it up with somebody on the surface. Was the *Yuan* going to shoot at them or not? Should she still be considering shooting him first? Where were all the blue hulls going in such a hurry and what were the underwater comms all about?

"Conn, Sonar, loud transients on the bearing to the *Yuan*." The Chinese boat was not even trying to keep quiet.

"Shooting?" she asked.

"No, ma'am. Sounds like he is blowing ballast tanks." Then, a long, significant lull. "I think he's surfacing."

"Uh-uh. Can't be." This was getting more and more strange.

Foster swung the periscope around just in time to see the Chinese submarine pop to the surface. Without even pausing, it lit off its diesel engines with a large cloud of gray-black smoke, then swung around and, with what appeared to be top surface speed, headed away, directly into the late afternoon sun.

Ψ

Chief of Naval Intelligence Admiral Jon Ward carefully read the message traffic several times. Only then did he slowly put the pieces together. The *Boise* and the *George Mason* had vacated the suddenly lonely South China Sea and were both now tied up alongside the *Chesty Puller.* There they would get needed voyage repairs and some crew R&R before they headed off toward home port.

He also had stacks of analyses of satellite imagery and maritime tracking that were following what the Chinese still insisted were merely peaceful fishing fleets heading back to the Chinese mainland, their holds filled with the bounty of the sea. Jon Ward and a few others knew better. And that the fishing fleet was oddly being escorted by several surfaced *Yuan*-class submarines.

There were also confirmed reports out of Vietnam that the PLA armored units that had crossed into that country were now in reverse, heading back up the National Highway toward the Chinese border. And they were doing so remarkably quickly. Almost as quickly as they had attacked in the first place.

There was another stack of documents, deep-level espionage reports, vaguely referencing what appeared to have been a major shakeup in leadership at the highest levels of the government and military of the People's Republic of China. Several of the First Secretary's top men had simply disappeared. Tan Yong remained in power, apparently as solidly as ever. High-level US intelligence analysts had determined that those missing officials had apparently dared to overstep their bounds, had instigated a series of poorly executed cyber-attacks and were planning potential armed assaults on countries ringing the South China Sea, starting with Vietnam. None of this had been approved by the First Secretary and Tan Yong had been quick to punish them when their activities came to light.

But the best news of all for Admiral Ward had come in the form of a very brief telephone call from his son. He and Li Min Zhou had managed to elude capture, following a leisurely swim. They had slipped back into Taiwan, but the details of their adventures would have to wait for another time and place. At the moment, Jim was asking his dad to speak with the SEAL's squadron commander, pull rank, and arrange approval for a few weeks of leave. He and Zhou were thinking of taking some R&R of their own at a resort they knew somewhere in the South Pacific.

Ward grinned and shook his head. But then something caught his eye on the Fox News feed on his office television. He quickly unmuted it.

President Stan Smitherman was holding a press conference, touting the wonderful new and peaceful relationship with China, the "Cooperation in Asia" initiative, that he and his administration team had negotiated and would soon sign. A deal that included massive amounts of trade and financial cooperation, a crackdown on intellectual property theft in that country, and a mutual partnership to lead the world in the fight against cyber-terrorism. Tragic events like the Independence Day commuter train disaster in the nation's capital, which the Chinese now reported had originated with a new terrorist cell they had discovered in Eastern Europe.

Jon Ward leaned back in his chair and put his feet up on the big oak desk. Then he removed his new glasses, partly so he could rub his tired eyes, but also so he could no longer see the president bask in all that glory for which he rightfully deserved little to no credit. It was Jon Ward's team, as well as those of Li Minh Zhou, Taiwan, and other nations, and so many other US Navy men and women who had faced death and danger to head off an unimaginable threat. One most of the world would never believe should they ever hear about it.

But that story, like so many others, would certainly remain forever buried. Ward decided that it was probably for the better, but it still grated. It just wasn't fair, but then again, life rarely was.

No, it would be Stan Smitherman and his political party that would take all the credit, accept the glory, and leverage the victory to ensure his re-election and that his party would continue to maintain control of both houses of Congress.

A tap on his office door interrupted Ward's reverie. His aide, Lieutenant Jimmy Wilson, opened it a crack. Ward muted the TV.

"You awake, boss?"

"You know I am, Jim. The Navy pays me to never sleep."

"Well, two things." Wilson opened the door and stepped inside. He carried a thick file folder in his hand. "This one's a doozie and you'll want to take a look at it immediately." He gingerly placed the folder on top of the stack of similar ones piled up on the desk in front of Ward.

"Can't wait to see it," Ward growled. "Some bad guy somewhere threatening to disrupt the peace and tranquility of the planet and launch World War III?"

"You've seen the report already?"

"You said you had two things."

"We're ordering in from that pizza place in the food court. You want the usual on your pie?"

The admiral grinned.

"Yeah. Yeah, I do. And I feel like celebrating, so throw on some extra anchovies and onions."

"Aye, aye, Skipper." Wilson turned and left the office.

Jon Ward caught a glimpse of the president on the TV screen, still explaining how he had changed the course of history with his China deal.

Then the admiral shook his head, opened the cover of the new file, took a deep breath, and began reading.

SNAPSHOT

When an international crisis erupts in eastern Russia, the US Navy must race to avoid a nuclear apocalypse.

The Sea of Okhotsk north of the Japanese Home Islands is a cold and unforgiving place. Its icy, dark waters can change from a glass-smooth calm into a raging maelstrom in a heartbeat. The shores surrounding the sea, home to Siberian tigers and prowling wolf packs, are equally forbidding. Far from Mother Russia, beyond Siberia, it is a mostly forgotten land—even though it is the home of the Russian Navy's Pacific Fleet.

It is here that the Children of the Gulags, descendants of Stalin's infamous prison camps and long-time inhabitants of this harsh land, have slowly maneuvered into position. Their leaders are convinced they can now carve out and lay claim to a homeland of their own. But they must fan the flames of international tension among the Chinese, North Koreans, the Russians, NATO, and the Americans. Pitting them all against each other as the Children attempt to wrest away their new nation from Russia.

Thrust into a simmering conflict that threatens to spill over into nuclear Armageddon, head of US Naval Intelligence Admiral Jon Ward is faced with the impossible task of keeping the peace between nations. Forced into a game of intrigue and sinister political maneuvering, he must utilize the stealthy US submarines, SEALs, and other US assets to extinguish a conflict at the edge of the world—all while trying to give hope to a historically oppressed people in their own dreams of freedom.

Admiral Ward is about to face the toughest mission of his career..and one wrong move could ignite a nuclear war.

ACKNOWLEDGMENTS

No book writes itself, much as we wish it would. And there are people that we need to thank for their efforts in helping us write this one.

Our medical expert, who was invaluable in diagnosing and treating Chet Allison's problems, is Dr. Dennis Vidmar, CAPT MC USN (ret). Denny is a classmate of mine (George) at Ohio State and a former submarine medical officer. He brings a new meaning to concierge medicine; I tell him the symptoms I need and he gives me the problem and the treatments. The medically cognizant reader will find symptoms of CDR Allison's Graves' disease salted away throughout the story, although you never hear the term "Graves' disease" as that diagnosis wouldn't occur until Allison was in a hospital.

Another old friend and shipmate, Ron Aiello, helped with the decompression concerns during the submarine rescue. Ron is a diving buddy from our days on the *Woodrow Wilson* and is now a diving instructor of some renown.

We would be remiss if we didn't thank our agent, John Talbot. Without John, the *Hunter Killer Series* would not have happened.

And, of course, we need to thank our wives whose love and support really make everything possible. Charlene (Don) and Penny (George) are the light of our lives and our inspiration in all that we do. There is nothing quite so comforting when you find yourself mulling over a particularly sticky plot point, working a thousand different possibilities in your mind, than to have your loving wife lean over and whisper softly in your ear, "The syntax in that sentence is all wrong."

ABOUT GEORGE WALLACE

Commander George Wallace retired to the civilian business world in 1995, after twenty-two years of service on nuclear submarines. He served on two of Admiral Rickover's famous "Forty One for Freedom", the USS John Adams SSBN 620 and the USS Woodrow Wilson SSBN 624, during which time he made nine one-hundred-day deterrent patrols through the height of the Cold War.

Commander Wallace served as Executive Officer on the Sturgeon class nuclear attack submarine USS Spadefish, SSN 668. Spadefish and all her sisters were decommissioned during the downsizings that occurred in the 1990's. The passing of that great ship served as the inspiration for "Final Bearing."

Commander Wallace commanded the Los Angeles class nuclear attack submarine USS Houston, SSN 713 from February 1990 to August 1992. During this tour of duty that he worked extensively with the SEAL community developing SEAL/submarine tactics. Under Commander Wallace, the Houston was awarded the CIA Meritorious Unit Citation.

Commander Wallace lives with his wife, Penny, in Alexandria, Virginia.

Sign up for Wallace and Keith's newsletter at
severnriverbooks.com

ABOUT DON KEITH

Don Keith is a native Alabamian and attended the University of Alabama in Tuscaloosa where he received his degree in broadcast and film with a double major in literature. He has won numerous awards from the Associated Press and United Press International for news writing and reporting. He is also the only person to be named *Billboard Magazine* "Radio Personality of the Year" in two formats, country and contemporary. Keith was a broadcast personality for over twenty years and also owned his own consultancy, co-owned a Mobile, Alabama, radio station, and hosted and produced several nationally syndicated radio shows.

His first novel, "The Forever Season." was published in fall 1995 to commercial and critical success. It won the Alabama Library Association's "Fiction of the Year" award in 1997. His second novel, "Wizard of the Wind," was based on Keith's years in radio. Keith next released a series of young adult/men's adventure novels co-written with Kent Wright set in stock car racing, titled "The Rolling Thunder Stock Car Racing Series." Keith has most recently published several non-fiction historical works about World War II submarine history and co-authored "The Ice Diaries" with Captain William Anderson, the second skipper of USS *Nautilus*, the world's first nuclear submarine. Captain Anderson took the submarine on her historic trip across the top of the world and through the North Pole in August 1958. Mr. Keith lives with his wife, Charlene, in Indian Springs Village, Alabama.

Sign up for Wallace and Keith's newsletter at
severnriverbooks.com

Printed in the United States
by Baker & Taylor Publisher Services